The Last Deer Hunt
A Yooper Mystery

Jerry Sarasin

Outskirts Press, Inc.
Denver, Colorado

This is a work of fiction. The events and characters described herein are imaginary and are not intended to refer to specific places or living persons. The opinions expressed in this manuscript are solely the opinions of the author and do not represent the opinions or thoughts of the publisher.

The Last Deer Hunt
A Yooper Mystery
All Rights Reserved.
Copyright © 2008 Jerry Sarasin
v 4. 0

This book may not be reproduced, transmitted, or stored in whole or in part by any means, including graphic, electronic, or mechanical without the express written consent of the publisher except in the case of brief quotations embodied in critical articles and reviews.

Outskirts Press, Inc.
http://www.outskirtspress.com

ISBN: 978-1-4327-1741-4

Outskirts Press and the "OP" logo are trademarks belonging to Outskirts Press, Inc.

PRINTED IN THE UNITED STATES OF AMERICA

This book is for my beautiful wife Carol who Survived the writing of this novel.

Cora Anderson is a real person and was indeed the first woman in the Michigan Legislature in 1925, as well as being an Ojibwa Indian. In all other respects, this novel is a work of fiction. Fairhaven, Michigan does not exist. Fairhaven, and all names, characters, places and incidents either are a product of the author's imagination or used fictitiously, and any resemblance to actual persons, living or dead, events or locales are entirely coincidental.

ACKNOWLEDGEMENTS

Many thanks to all the people who helped me finish this book, my family, my extended family, and friends for their patience and support.

A grateful thank you to Gail Backus, Patti Maguire, John Litchfield, Tom Meyer, and Karen Sarasin. Without their efforts, this book would never have evolved. Thanks to Liz Blake, French teacher at Applewild School for double-checking my rusty French. I would like to thank Paul Marin and Gene Rauhala for their advice on the justice system.

Thanks to my family, My daughters Suzan Sarasin and Sue Ballard for their support and a special thanks to my daughter Cheryl for all those weekly meetings, editing, proof reading and cheerleading.

Also, a special thanks to my editor, Georgess McHargue for her excellent editing and encouragement.

And thanks especially to my wife Carol, whose patience and confidence in me inspired me to keep going.

A special thanks to Jackie Boyson, my Production Supervisor at Outskirts Press, for helping me through a very tough time, and all the time and effort she put into making this book a reality.

ONE

It was autumn in the Upper Peninsula of Michigan, and on the southern shore of the great lake the Ojibway Indians called Kitchi-Gami, the fog rolled in on cooling evening breezes and slowly enveloped the majestic white pines and tall pointed balsam firs. It settled in river valleys, low meadows and swamps as it drifted up the sides of the Huron Mountains until even Mount Arvon, the highest point in the state, would remain shrouded in mist until burned off by the warmth of the next day's sun.

Near the bottom of Huron Bay where the Slate River flows out into Lake Superior, the little town of Fairhaven struggled to life under a wet, cold blanket of dense morning fog. The headlights of an old Ford pickup bored two holes through the gloomy mist as it moved slowly down Main Street, past deserted brownstones and empty storefronts, and pulled to a stop in the glare of a sign in the shape of the Eiffel Tower flashing red, white, and blue neon; loudly announcing the location of Frenchy's Diner.

Hank Duval parked in the first vacant space in the line of cars and trucks along the street and turned off the lights and engine. As he sat in the silence, a sudden shiver moved through his body as the face from last night's dream flashed through his mind. It was the same recurring dream and it always frightened him. It was always the same face in the dream. He thought, *What the heck does it mean?* taking a minute to shake off the feeling and clear his mind. *It's just a dream, it doesn't have to mean anything.*

Outside, he stopped, rubbing the soreness from his shoulders, "Damn, it sure was a heck of a lot of work putting all that wood into the truck." Shaking his head, he thought, *You wouldn't think I just turned thirty-one.* A quick check in the truck door mirror reflected a three-day growth of whiskers covering his boyish face. "Yeah sure," he said, rubbing his chin, "today, I look more like I'm fifty."

Taking a copy of yesterday's newpaper, the Mining Gazette, dated Tuesday, October 11th, 1983, Hank Walked back towards the diner, passing the long line of vehicles, mostly pickups, and mostly rusted out premature victims of the chemicals used on the road surfaces during the long harsh winters. *Looks like the whole town is here this morning,* He took a deep breath of the cool morning air, feeling it fill his lungs. Then exhaling slowly, the anticipation of the solitude of the river and the strike of the fish erased all vestiges of last night's dream. *Yeah, I have the feeling that today will be my lucky day.*

Inside the bright, warm diner, the blended aromas of coffee brewing and breakfast cooking intermingled with cigarette smoke and noisy conversation. Hank pushed his way through the standing-room only crowd and finding a just-vacated stool at the counter, removed his cap and stuck it in the pocket of his black-and-red-checkered mackinaw. Just as he sat down, a cup of coffee slid in front of him from behind the counter, followed by, "Good morning Hank."

"Morning Frenchy," Hank replied, holding the cup up. "The diner's really packed today, you offering free breakfast or something?"

Frenchy LeRoche's head appeared from behind the

counter. "Maybe everybody's finally heard about my great French cooking." A quick smile curved across his slender face.

"Yeah, that's gotta be it, Frenchy," Hank said, wrinkling his nose, "Except you don't do any French cooking here."

"Sure do Hank, French fries and French toast." Frenchy's grin faded quickly with Hank's lack of response. "What, no sense of humor today?"

"Sorry Frenchy," Hank replied, trying to wipe the sleep from his large brown eyes, "Just kinda slow getting going this morning."

Frenchy peered across the counter. "Where you been hiding all week? I thought we were gonna get together at millpond rock yesterday."

"Yeah, I know, I'm really sorry about that. I went up to Copper Country to pick up some lumber I bought from an old Finlander. Pretty good wood, mostly oak and maple and I really need it for my cabinetmaking business." Feeling the soreness in his shoulders, he added, "And there sure was a lot of it."

"You were gone nearly a week. Where'd you find a place to stay up there?" Frenchy said, moving quickly between the grill and delivering plates of food to customers. "I woulda thought every place on the Keweenaw Peninsula would have been filled with leaf-peepers looking at foliage this time of the year."

Hank hesitated, then said very quietly, "I ran into Harvey Turcotte in Copper Harbor and stayed over at his place."

Frenchy put the busing container full of dirty dishes he was carrying down hard on the counter, looking directly at Hank, "Did I hear you right? Did you say Harvey Turcotte?"

Hank nodded.

Frenchy wiped his hands on an old rag, worry lines deepening on his forehead. "Wasn't Turcotte one of your drinking buddies at the tavern back when—"

"Hell Frenchy, that was a long time ago." The implication in Frenchy's question annoyed him. "Harvey's married, got a little baby now and raises llamas on his farm. He's got ten acres overlooking the lake."

"Just thought I'd ask. You look kinda beat. You okay?"

"Yeah, I could use a shave—"

"No, Henry Duval, what I meant is you look like shit this morning."

"Yeah, so what. I just had a rough night, okay?" Hank said, waving Frenchy off. "I'm stiff and sore and I didn't get much sleep. I didn't get home till after midnight and then something woke me about three and I couldn't get back to sleep."

Big blond Toivo Niemi, sitting on the stool at Hank's left put his newspaper down and with his heavy accent, said, "Probably heard dah gunshots. A bear got into Crabby Mary's screen porch over on Skanee Road and raised hell with her pantry." Toivo shook his head, "Dat Sheriff McCarthy and dat stupid Barney Fife of a deputy, dey went and killed it, shot it six times..."

Hank stopped listening, *Yeah sure, it had to be the gunshots that woke me up. Just like when...*His memory failed him and he could not bring the rest of the thoughts into his conciousness.

Toivo put his big hand on Hank's shoulder as he stood, his large round face softened with sadness. "Yeah, but he was only a little cub looking for something to eat, dey didn't need to kill it. Folks gotta quit feeding da bears down at da dump at night, it's gotten to where dey ain't afraid of people anymore." Toivo buttoned his coat, and moved through the crowd towards the door.

Frenchy leaned across the counter, "Hank, I hope I didn't offend you by asking about Turcotte. You know I was just —"

"It's all right buddy, no offense taken." *This guy just never lets up.* Hank stared at his coffee. *And I'm glad he doesn't.* Memories filling him; memories of a friendship born of hard times, of when he was determined to self-destruct and Frenchy was even more determined to keep him from sinking further. *Yeah, Frenchy can be a pain in the butt—* Memories of last summer spent together building the diner warmed him, and Hank managed a small grin. *But then again, Frenchy sure knows how to cut through the shit and get right to the point.* Without looking up, Hank asked, "Are we still on for fishing today?"

No answer, Frenchy was already back at the grill behind the counter and Hank looked up and watched his friend flipping pancakes, scrambling eggs, frying bacon, and delivering them to customers.

The strong coffee was having an effect and as the sleepiness faded, Hank opened the newspaper. As he started to read, he was interrupted by the words "renaissance," and "mill," repeatedly rising above the cacophony of indistinguishable noise that ebbed and flowed around the diner. Another drink of coffee and Hank wondered aloud. "What the heck's going on out at the mill?"

"Excuse me?" From Hank's left. "But were you talking about that old wood products mill?"

Hank turned and faced a middle-aged man who had taken the stool that Toivo had just vacated. He had a swarthy complexion and black hair pulled back and tied in a pony-tail. "I'm sorry to bother you my friend," the man spoke with an slight accent. "That wouldn't be that old run down mill over by the river by any chance, would it?"

"Yeah, that's right. They were doing some renovations to it, but it sounds like something else is going on over there. Have you heard anything?"

"No, I'm sorry I haven't; but I am interested in it. My name is Ben Epstein. I am from the University of Michigan in Ann Arbor and I just got into town when I saw the light from this diner and stopped in for a cup of coffee. I'm up here to meet with Sarah Hoffman to talk about consulting work on the renovation of the Renaissance wood products mill into an arts and music center."

Frenchy appeared, put a coffee cup on the counter in

front of Ben and filled it from a pot. "Anything else today?"

To Frenchy, Ben said, "Thanks, nothing else for now." Then to Hank, "This is my first trip up here and I am fascinated with the natural beauty here in the Upper Peninsula...I guess you folks up here call it the U.P. right?"

Hank nodded in reply.

"And you people up here call yourselves Yoopers, right?" Ben managed a small chuckle, his dark eyes dancing in the light. "I saw that on a sign down around Ishpeming on my way up here."

Hank looked directly at Ben. "And we call you folks who live downstate below the Mackinaw Bridge; trolls."

"Hadn't heard that one." Ben laughed, offering his hand and a soft smile. "I know very little about the history of this area, I wonder if you could share a little with me."

Hank took the offered hand and returned the smile. "There isn't too much to tell. The area was settled mostly by immigrants from Sweden, Finland, Italy and French Canada. The economy up here was mostly lumber, copper mining up on the Keweenaw Peninsula, and iron mining down around Ishpeming and Negaunee. The copper mining and lumbering petered out a while ago and has been replaced by tourism.

About 1892, the Iron Range and Huron Bay Railroad Company, built this town of Fairhaven, the lumber mill, a railroad grade and large wooden ore docks out into Huron Bay. They had planned to haul iron ore up through the Huron Mountains from the mines at Champion and load it on ore-carrying ships from the docks. On the trains initial test run, the railroad bed gave way and the train engine ended up in a ravine. They never used those tracks again. They tore down the docks for the lumber, packed up the train engine and shipped everything down state somewhere. The only thing left is the town and the old mill."

"Fascinating. Tell me about the mill." Ben finished his coffee and held up the empty cup.

Hank reached across the counter, picked up the

coffeepot from its warming plate, filled his cup and offering the pot to Ben said, "The mill supplied all the timber during the building of the ore docks, over three million board feet of white pine."

Ben took the pot and filled his cup and motioned for Hank to continue.

"In the twenties, the mill was converted to make wood products for automobiles such as the paneling on the woody station wagons. It shut down in the late fifties but was re-opened again a few years later by the Canadian Michigan Paper Products Corp. For about five years, this was the toilet paper capital of the world. Then CMPP shut the mill down, shipped everything south and the mill's been closed ever since."

They were interrupted by a noisy commotion erupting from the diner, another of the loud frequent arguments between two of the diner's old regulars, Kurt Hurla and Homer Perrin.

"You're wrong as usual Homer, they found it at the old mill power house."

"Hell Kurt," Homer's voice came back, "as usual, you don't know what you're talking about. Will Saari and Mutty Mufti been down to the mill and they say it was at the maintenance building, and that's the truth."

Hank was about to ask what 'it' was all about, but Homer and Kurt had melted back into the noisy haze.

Ben took a drink of coffee and made a 'this coffee's cold face.' "You know, this area and that old mill is going to be an ideal place to have an art and music camp like we have at Interlochen Center for the Arts or the Blue Lake Fine Arts Camps down in the Lower Peninsula."

"Some folks thought this would never happen." Hank laughed. "It's kinda hard to get any interest in something like art and music when the big happenings around here are deer season, the annual fishing derby and feeding the bears down at the dump on Saturday nights."

"Hank, don't sell this area short. There are a lot of

sophisticated people up here and you are within seventy miles of three colleges. I think this area will support it." Ben was standing, buttoning his long black coat. "I have taken too much of your time and I must be going." Ben offered his hand and a business card. "Thank you again my friend, you have been very informative and hopefully we will meet again soon."

Hank took the business card and accepted the hand. "Glad you could come up, Sarah needs all the help she can get. And oh, if you want more information about the area, I suggest you go over to the Witz Marina just on the other side of Skanee. Also, the library in L'anse has information, or give a call over at the Baraga County Historical Museum in Baraga. They might be able to help you out."

"I'll do that." Ben said, putting money on the counter, then with a wave, turned towards the door. "Thanks again for everything."

Hank looked around the diner hoping to find someone who might invite him to join in the discussions, but everyone was divided up into small groups and the voices of these groups joined the voices of other groups until the room was filled with one anonymous drone. Hank opened the copy of the *Daily Mining Gazette*, and leafed through it.

The front page showed a report by the Federation of American Scientists that at the present time, there were over thirty wars and conflicts currently being waged in the world, especially in the Middle East, and President Reagan was demanding retaliation for the bombing of the Marine's barracks in Lebanon. *Seems like the more things change, the more they stay the same.* Hank looked around the diner through the smoky haze at the gathering of men in caps and hunting clothes or jackets embroidered with 'Detroit Tigers.' *Yeah, especially here in beautiful downtown Fairhaven. This town is still stuck back in the sixties. Maybe I should have got out of here right after graduation, just like all my buddies.*

The sports section reported an exceptionally good year

for the Detroit Tigers, ending up second to the Baltimore Orioles. The usual rumors of trades or the closing of Tiger Stadium would supply more than enough controversy and discussion to keep the diner regulars arguing, analyzing, and replaying every game throughout the winter.

The financial pages carried an article on the Renaissance wood products mill. The citizens of Arvon Township had voted to turn down a proposal by ReVenture Corporation to use the old mill as a waste disposal and collection center. This proposal could have possibly resulted in many new jobs, giving the area economy a desperately needed boost. The whole Upper Peninsula was teetering on the brink of economic disaster with little, or no expectation of aid forthcoming from the state capital located in Lansing on Michigan's lower peninsula. It was felt that they knew little, and cared less about the U.P. and its people.

The editorial page contained a letter stating that the defeat of the trash project and the decision to use the old mill as an art and music center was the work of Project S.T.O.R.M., Save The Old Renaissance Mill; a misguided group of yuppies who have no vested interest in the area. This small group of liberals and outsiders were able to influence some gullible locals to vote against the trash proposal thereby losing the opportunity to create the jobs and economic growth that people in this area needed.

Hank gulped, knowing that the letter referred to him and his friends. The debate over the use of the mill had split the town and he was in the middle, caught between the two sides.

Frenchy came around the counter struggling under a large load of plates. "You know Frenchy, you could really use some help around here."

"Oh yeah, that's right, you've been out of town and wouldn't have known." Frenchy grunted under the load, "I did hire a girl and she was supposed to start this week." He dumped the dishes into a bus bin, "She moved out here a couple of weeks ago from the east and needed a job." His face brightened into a broad grin and he added quickly, "You got to meet her. Her name is Lucy and she's something special. She's kinda funky, far out, but she also has a degree in accounting and she says she can straighten up my lousy bookeeping."

"Funky? Far out? Lucy?" Hank asked, watching his friends beaming face. "How come you been keeping her a secret? What's she doing around these parts? And where is she today?"

"She came out here to live with her grandmother who is pretty sick. She couldn't make it in to work today, had to go down to L'anse for something—"

"Hey Frenchy, can we get some service around here?" Called out from the back of the diner.

"Yeah, yeah, coming." Frenchy was off in the direction of the request. "Keep your shirt on."

When he returned, Frenchy poured some pancake batter on the griddle and while it cooked he turned to Hank and asked, "What you gonna have for breakfast, the usual?"

"Thanks, but I think I'll pass for now." Hank patted his stomach. He regretted stopping at the Hilltop Restaurant in L'anse on the way home from the Kewenaw and picking up a half dozen of their world famous very large cinnamon buns. The one he ate this morning lay heavy in his belly and on his conscience. "I'm still trying to lose some weight."

Frenchy nodded, flipping the pancakes. "How much you lost?"

"About fifteen pounds."

"Well, there you go now. Maggie's diet must be agreeing with you, eh?" Frenchy spatula'ed the pancakes onto a dish and added bacon and left to deliver it somewhere in the diner.

The mention of Maggie brought her into sharp focus and her large soft brown eyes and head full of dark red curls filled his mind. Their on-again, off-again relationship was currently running towards the off-again. When they were apart, he missed her and wanted to be with her, but when they were together, it always seemed more like two porcupines dancing.

Maggie Reed had come to Fairhaven three and a half years ago from Los Angeles to do an article on a family of lynx for a nature magazine and into Hank's life through her friendship with his wife, Sandy. The thought of Sandy caused the heaviness in the pit of his stomach to spread as a dark weight but he pushed it back. *Not now, not here.*

Frenchy's voice brought him back into the present. "Hello, Henry, you okay?"

Hank stammered back, "Yeah, all Maggie talks about are fruit and veggies and exercise and the need to make life style changes. Life style changes? Yeah sure, all that means is a lifetime of bean sprouts, tofu and celery sticks." Outwardly, he complained about her frequent comments, but down inside, he knew she was right.

Frenchy leaned over the counter towards Hank. "Don't you just hate it when they're right?"

"How the heck did you know what I was...Ah, never mind." Hank reached inside his coat to check the suspenders that Maggie had given him for his birthday. She had suggested he needed them; not because he had gained weight, but because, "Your heavy woolen hunting pants needed help being held up." *Yeah sure*, Hank thought, *very tactful of her.*

Frenchy had returned from delivering another round of breakfast. "But what's this I hear, Sarah mentioned that Maggie might be thinking about going back to California?"

"I didn't hear that." Hank felt the anxiety in his voice. "Maggie is moving back to California?"

"No, I didn't say that. What I said was I had heard she was thinking about it, that's all."

"Hell, if Maggie wants to move back to California, that's her business, eh? Anyway, why would she even want to stay around this place?"

"Hey good buddy, you don't have to tear my head off.

Sarah thinks Maggie might just have her reasons for staying." Frenchy's smile spread across his face, his gestures indicating Hank.

"Oh give me a break, Frenchy. Maggie, an intelligent girl from L.A. would have the hots for an uneducated northwoods hick like me? Talk about culture shock!"

"My good friend Henry, your entire relationship with Maggie is a continuous culture shock loosely held together by the fascination with your mutual differences."

"Frenchy, I don't know what the hell you just said, but you know as well as I do that she has her own reasons to stay around here. She stayed up here because the magazine she is working for keeps giving her new assignments. After the article on the lynx, she did that article on reintroducing moose in the U.P., and now she's doing the article on the wolves."

"Yeah, sure Hank, think about it, this woman could work anywhere in the world. I think she's here cause she likes you—and don't tell me you don't have any feelings about her. I mean after all you two have been through together."

"Come on, Frenchy, you know our relationship isn't like that...she is...I mean she was Sandy's best friend and we're both having a difficult time dealing with Sandy's..."

"Hank, it's been three years since your wife passed away." Frenchy reached over, his face softened, and he put a hand on Hank's shoulder. "Don't you think it's time to—"

"Let's drop the subject, okay?" It didn't seem possible that it had been that long since Sandy died...*Why was it so difficult to let go?* Again, the dark heaviness started in the pit of his stomach, and again he pushed it back. A deep breath, exhaling slowly, letting it clear his mind. And now Maggie...the thought of Maggie both excited him and frightened him. *Yeah, that is a good question. Why does she stay around here?*

A flurry of noisy commotion broke into his thoughts and he swirled his stool around to investigate. The rusted stool

THE LAST DEER HUNT

screamed in protest and Hank found himself facing the diner full of people, silent and staring at him. Among many newcomers, he could pick out the faces of the old regulars who he saw every morning in the diner.

"Morning folks," he said, managing an embarrassed smile.

"Morning," came back in unison, followed by a series of remarks through the smoky haze of the diner.

"Hey Hank, when'd you get here?"

"Watcha been up to, eh?"

"You all ready for deer season?" The subject of deer season was almost inevitable this time of the year.

"Heard what the weather's gonna be?"

"Nope," Hank answered. The subject of weather in the U.P. was inevitable.

"Heard there might be frost on the pumpkins tonight, eh?" This time Hank recognized Bill Roberstson's thick Swedish accent.

"You got that right." Stan Lubiwitz offered quickly. "Gonna be a tough winter this year. Them squirrels are sure gathering lots of acorns."

"Yeah, sure, you bet," Bill Robertson agreed, "And I see lots of them big woolly-bear caterpillars too."

"I hear it might snow by the end of the month." Homer Perrin rasped, "Too early for snow, it'll drive all the deer into the swamp by the start of deer season."

Pete Peterson spoke very loudly, as he did when he didn't have his hearing aid turned on. "They say Lake Superior might freeze over completely this year, first time in about thirty years. We could be in for our worst winter yet." Voices of agreement filled the diner with predictions of the coldest winter ever and a good chance to break the record snowfall of 320 inches.

Kurt Hurla grumbled. "You old farts have been predicting the worst winter ever, every year since I can remember; and you know, sooner or later, you're gonna be right.. But you're wrong about the lake. If it freezes over, we gonna get less snow."

Hank couldn't remember a time when old Kurt didn't disagree about everything, and this argument could go on for a long time. Just then, Stan Lubiwitz pushed his way to the center of the diner, his gravelly voice filling the small room. "Hey Hank, what do you think about the goings on over at the old mill?"

Hank cringed, waiting to hear how he was responsible for losing the opportunity to create jobs. "I believe the art and music school was the best choice—"

A voice cut through the the din like a knife. "Yeah sure Duval, but what about all the jobs we're going to lose?"

Another voice from the back of the diner. "You bet, eh? Them STORM people, they don't give a darn about us folks up here."

Frenchy snapped back. "If you'd bother to look at the facts, you'll see that the ReVenture company has never lived up to its promises about jobs and their record on the enviornment has been terrible. You need to understand—"

"No, no, Stan weren't talking about that." Homer Perrin was in the center of the diner, and looking directly at Hank and Frenchy. Then speaking very slowly, drawing out every word, "Ain't you heard?" He hesitated, assuring he had the attention of everyone in the diner. "While they was doing some work over there at the mill yesterday," Homer paused again, "they dug up a body." He stuck out his chin and nodded, accentuating his point, and every head in the diner nodded in agreement. Hank sat back on his stool and felt the color drain from his face as an icy cold feeling passed through him. Looking up and seeing Frenchy watching him closely, Hank said quickly, "Probably just a rumor — right?"

"Right." Frenchy echoed, "Probably just a rumor."

"No sir, this ain't no rumor." Pete Peterson talked very loudly, "Them construction workers was talking out at the Bayside Tavern last night, and they was saying they saw it, the body that is. Looked like a big bag of bones all wrapped up in a rug, they said."

The diner fell into a heavy silence, all eyes focused on Pete Peterson, hanging on his every word, waiting to hear more.

For an instant, Hank sensed a vague image reaching up from a grave, and as the fog of the past lifted, it revealed a vision of six young boys standing in a circle staring down at the face from his recurring dream. In the total silence of the diner, Hank heard his own quiet words. "Somehow, we're involved?"

Pete Peterson's loud voice boomed through Hank's thoughts. "That's all we know right now."

But that did not stop the speculation. The voices in the diner erupted into loud babble as questions with no answers and answers to no questions were tossed around and discarded. While the debates and arguments ebbed and flowed, Frenchy drew his face close to Hank's to talk over the noise. "Are you all right, my good friend? And who did you mean when you said you were involved?"

"I don't know, I'm not sure." Hank said, standing, "Excuse me a minute."

Inside the very small toilet, made smaller by boxes and clutter, Hank stood looking at himself in the old mirror. "Okay, slow down Duval, take it easy." As he tried to mentally sweep away the cobwebs of time, spectral figures floated in and out of the edges of his consciousness. As they came into sharper focus, the figures took on the faces of his school buddies. First Gino, then Tom, Eddie, Ollie and Bob slowly circled around him, faces of young fourteen year old boys. They moved around him, looking at him and talking in hushed tones that Hank could not make out. As Hank pushed closer to hear, he fell back onto a pile of boxes and the vision faded. Hank stood in silence trying to bring it back and trying to understand the connection with the body, but it was gone.

Back in the diner, Hank watched as Frenchy was busy waiting on customers, hoping to catch his eye. *Don't look like he'll get out of here this morning to go fishing.* He sat tracing the graffiti carved in the counter top; initials, promises of undying love co-mingled with carvings of lust, who to call for a good time and statements pro and con about the Vietnam War. The counter, along with the stools, as well as other diner items were from Harvey's Malt Shop and were headed for the Fairhaven dump when Frenchy rescued them. Harvey's was where Hank and his pals and everybody else who went to Fairhaven High School spent many afternoons after school and many nights before and after basketball games in various bonding and mating rituals. It closed in 1970.

"Lot of memories, eh?" Frenchy said, standing behind the counter. "I decided to just leave the counter the way it was, with all the writings."

"Yeah, for sure. I was just thinking about the old gang back in school. We were always hanging out together, doing things." Hank rubbed his chin in reflection.

"Including, I might add, getting into a lot of mischief." Frenchy laughed.

Hank nodded, "Yeah, I can remember lots of fun things we did." A smile crossed his face, but the vision of the friends together with the face in the dream moved into his mind, and the smile faded. *And some things I can't remember.* "Frenchy, I got a really dumb question. I know you had training in psychology, and do you think it's possible for someone to forget something that happened in his life, even if it is really important?"

"Hell yes, especially if it is something bad, people can block things out, kind of bury them in their sub-concious."

"Do they ever come back again? I mean the memories?"

"Oh yes. It's called PTSD or Post Tramatic Stress Syndrome. Sometimes it could take years and years, but then, something could trigger it and what's been suppressed comes out."

"What kind of trigger?"

THE LAST DEER HUNT

"Could be most anything. A face, someone talking, a smell, a sound, anything that could connect you back to that other time or event. Sometimes, reliving it can help bring it back. Why do you ask?"

"Ah, no special reason. I was just wondering." The memories of his young friends flashed through Hank's mind. How many times they had come to his rescue, how many times they had bailed him out of trouble. *I bet if they were back here, they would trigger something, something that would help me remember.* "You know Frenchy, I was just thinking, my old friends used to come back here for deer season. I think it would be nice if they would come back one more time, you know, even if was just for one last deer hunt."

Standing across from Hank, Frenchy slowly smoothed his trim mustache. "When did you think of that? Just now in the toilet?" He moved his face close to Hank's, looking directly into his eyes. "This wouldn't have anything to do with them finding a body at the mill, would it?"

Hank backed up with a look of surprise. "The body at the mill?" Fidgeting, he grasped for words. "Maybe, I mean, no...why the hell would it have to do with an old body that's been buried at the mill for eighteen years?"

"Eighteen years?" Frenchy's eyes narrowed.

"Yeah, remember? Pete Peterson say he heard it was just a bag of bones, right? I just kinda figured it had to have been there a heck of a long time and—"

"Yes, but why eighteen?" He peered intently at Hank.

"Hell, I don't know, it just popped into my head. It could have been seventeen, or twenty-five...or anything. Hell, I don't know."

"Yeah, that's the point, it could be anything." Frenchy's face softened as he leaned back. "Heck, remember that old Italian fellow, Louie-what's-his-name? He wandered away from the nursing home a couple of years ago in that big storm. He was never found, was he?" Frenchy wrinkled his nose. "I'd think he'd be nothing but bones by now."

"Yeah sure, that might be it." Hank's words brightened a little. "You're right, it could be anything."

"Sure Hank," Frenchy said, hanging up pots and pans on hooks over the grill, "It could be anything. I wouldn't worry about it."

Hank put on his cap and catching Frenchy's attention, made a motion of casting his fishing rod. "You gonna be able to go fishing today?"

Frenchy made a sweeping gesture around the diner and stopped at the door where the constant jingling of the bell above the door announced a steady stream of people still coming in. "Sorry buddy, but I can't go today. I thought Art Haakala would fill in for me, but he called and can't make it, said something about real bad stomach pains. I wouldn't be able to get away until I closed at two. But hang around a little while, when I get a break, we can talk, okay?"

Hank sat back on the stool, disappointment written across his face and in his voice. He looked up at the old Bosch Beer clock on the wall. "Nah, I'll get going now, don't think the fish are gonna wait." Then quietly, softer, "How about getting together on Sunday over on the millrock? I really have to talk to you."

"Great. You pick up something to eat and I'll meet you there about two-thirty. Oh, by the way, where you going fishing today?"

"Don't know yet, might try the Slate River, right at the lake. I hear they been catching some big ones there. Or maybe I'll go up the Huron River and see if I can catch that old lunker."

"You know Henry, it's a good idea to let people know where you're going, especially this time of the year when there's not many people out fishing. You never know what might happen."

"Frenchy, sometimes you worry too much." As soon as he said it, he knew that in the past, he had given Frenchy reason to worry. Frenchy had come to Fairhaven from Sault Ste. Marie to help a buddy who was sick. *Night after night, when he would come into the Bayside Tavern to get something to eat he would find me hanging onto the bar like I held on to the ghost of Sandy. There were times when I just let go and fell, and there were times I couldn't pick myself up.* Bad memories, bad times. *Frenchy took a big chance on me when he hired me to re-do the diner and for that whole year, he kept me on a short leash while we worked side by side, day and night so I didn't get a chance to stray. Saved my life. Thank you Frenchy.*

The diner broke into loud animated conversation, a large knot of people were all trying to talk to a man who had just entered the diner. Pete Peterson moved to Hank's side, and with excitement in his loud voice said, "That guy is from the state police crime investigation lab. He said that from the clothes and stuff on the body, they figured the person was a male and had been there from about 1965."

Frenchy leaned over the counter, and in a soft voice, said, "That would make it about eighteen years ago, wouldn't it?"

Hank shrugged. "Lucky guess."

Frenchy looked directly at Hank. "So, is the deer hunt with the gang still on?"

Hank felt the pressure building in the back of his neck. "I don't see what one has to do with the other—"

"I didn't say they did, did I?" Frenchy said, continuing to look directly at Hank. "Why are you so defensive?"

"I'm not." The pressure on his neck grew more intense. "It's just that it would be good to see the guys again, besides, what's the big deal anyway?"

"What did you guys call yourselves then, the hunt club? Should have been called the drink club, cause that's all you did was sit out at that old hunting camp and drink."

"Oh, so that's what this is all about. You know I'm getting a little tired of it, if I wanted a drink, I sure as hell don't need to have all those guys come back here to get one, do I?"

The two men sat quietly in a tacit agreement of mutual understanding. Finally Hank broke the spell, "Not to worry my friend, I'll be okay. You'll just have to trust me on this one."

Frenchy took a cigarette, tapped it on the pack, lit it and took a long deep puff. "Different subject, good buddy, you've been taking a lot of heat from the locals over your decision to back the use of the old mill as an art and music center. That must be uncomfortable."

Hank waved his arm over the diner full of men. "Yeah, I kinda feel like I might have let these guys down. They need jobs, and they need to have their pride and self-respect back. And maybe now they won't be able to have that."

Hank had known these men since he was a boy and he still referred to them as "Mister" with their last name. He could remember them walking the half-mile from town through all kinds of weather with their hard hats and black metal lunch buckets to work at the Renaissance Mill. Every lunch bucket contained a Cornish pasty, a dry meat pie introduced into the Upper Peninsula by Cornish miners. It was adopted and adapted by every ethnic group and became a staple throughout the Upper Peninsula.

He could recognize most of the regulars of the diner by their raspy voices. Too many cigarettes and too many years in the harsh environment of the mill. Homer Perrin, Stan Lubiwitz, Pete Peterson, Bill Robertson, and Kurt Hurla were among a dozen men who could be found in Frenchy's diner finding a shared identity in the misfortunes of their lives or the fortunes of the Detroit Tigers baseball team. Over coffee, they debated the idiosyncrasies of Upper Peninsula weather, when the big lake froze over last, how good the deer season would be, or who had the best pasty in town. They would spend hours at the diner discussing these imponderables until they could no longer find a reason to keep from going home.

Hank slowly shook his head. "This trash site could have been the last chance for these guys. They have no skills, they are too old for re-training and they need the kind of jobs this proposal can give them."

"Don't be so hard on yourself. You know that trash

THE LAST DEER HUNT

project was fraught with problems." Frenchy reached over and refilled Hank's cup. Chances are we will realize a lot more jobs with this art and music center. And you know Sarah and Patti Culpepper are going to make this work." Frenchy was up again, clearing tables and taking checks.

Hank hoisted his coffee cup up towards the large dusty deer head that seemed to follow every customer in the diner with its slightly crossed eyes and broad grin. "I don't have any good answers;how about you, John Deer?"

Frenchy had found the deer head up in a back room somewhere and at first they debated putting it up in the diner. The mouth had been deformed into a permanent smile by a bad job of taxidermy, but it had an impressive rack of over twenty-seven points and they finally decided that for the diner and for Fairhaven, it would be appropriate. They named it John and in jest, started to ask it for advice and consent.

"Just as I thought," Hank said, standing. "John has no answers for us, never does."

"Maybe you didn't ask the right question, or maybe you didn't ask the question the right way." Frenchy laughed.

"Enough with your psycho-babble LeRoche," Hank said, heading for the door. "John never has any answers to anything. All he ever does is grin. We'd have better luck with a Ouija board." Hank waved as he moved through the door.

"Not true my friend, John always has the right answer. The trick is that I only ask John questions I already know the answers to." The warm smile grew across his face as Frenchy watched the door to the diner close behind his friend and looked up at the old deer head staring down on him. "What do you think, Mr. Deer? Do you think I worry too much sometimes?" His hands parted in the form of a question. "Who's body did they find at the mill? And what is the connection between the body and Hank wanting his old hunting buddies to come back for deer season?"

John Deer looked back at Frenchy and smiled.

Two

Hank walked slowly back to his truck, stopping to button up his coat against the damp chill of the morning air...or was it the specter of a body found at the mill? He took a step back towards the bright windows of the diner where Frenchy was still sitting at the counter, *I gotta be more up-front with him.* One more step, he paused, and then turned towards his truck. *I'll talk to him when I get back, right now, I need time to think.*

Hank slid onto the driver's seat, gray from layers of duct tape, and worked the door closed on its rusted hinges. Being careful where he placed his feet on the rusted out floorboards, he crossed his fingers and turned the ignition key. The starter motor turned over slowly, then even slower, until just as it drained the last ampere of power from the battery, the engine burst into life in a clattering of valve lifters and tappets.

"I really gotta do something about this truck, and I better do it pretty darn quick. Winter's just around the corner." Hank shook his head and moved the long floor shift into first gear. The old truck groaned, made a U-turn, and headed back down the four blocks of Main Street and crossed the

THE LAST DEER HUNT

Slate River Bridge. On the east side of the bridge, he passed an old weather-beaten sign riddled with bullet holes.

FAIRHAVEN
MI
POPULATION 765
A NICE PLACE TO LIVE

Next to the sign was a locked gate, the entrance to Lumberjack Park, once the home of the six-foot tall wooden statue of Paul Bunyan and Babe, his blue ox, honoring the lumber business of the area.

Somewhere beyond the locked gate, beyond the rusted swing set and an old slide, the charred wooden arm and hand rose from the ground; all that remained of Paul Bunyan. Hank did not look for it, he knew it was there, a continuing reminder to him of something he would rather forget.

But the park was also a reminder of other times, a time of families, a time of youth, and later, a time of dating—and Sandy. This time he let the memories back into his thoughts and once they entered, bittersweet emotions flooded over him. Sometimes it seems it was just yesterday, sitting on the swings holding hands, listening to Sandy's laughter. Sometimes, it seems like it was so long ago—like it was just all a dream.

No, it was real, all of it. The good times, and the bad. The good times—The times she was happiest, her smile, her laughter when she was in the back yard with her little dog, in the garden she loved so much. Or the time she spent at her loom, weaving carpets from discarded scraps of cloth, a craft she had learned from her mother and over time, perfected it into a technique for creating colorful and appealing rugs. Maggie Reed had been quick to see the rugs would sell well in more affluent markets around the country, and the two women worked together to create a flourishing business grounded in friendship, energy, enthusiasm and laughter. *It should have been a time for us to dream of the future, of starting our family. It should have been the best of times, but...*

The world fell apart. It was the worst of times. "Twenty-six is too young to die, it was too soon, we never got to start that family we were waiting for..." After the funeral, He watched his dreams slip away in the bottom of a beer bottle, determined to push himself down into a place so deep he would not have to face the pain of reality. The further his life spiraled downward, the more difficult it became to stop—and the less he cared.

Other thoughts, thoughts about the weaknesses he always feared he had, and thoughts of strengths he never knew he had. Memories of the summer building Frenchy's diner, and of Maggie's winter two years ago, only three months after Sandy's death...*Those two months up in the Huron Mountains studying a family of Lynx. It was a time when Maggie studied and I sketched. While she wrote, I healed. And then we were trapped in the hiking shelter for two nights during that blizzard...Sandy's husband and her best friend and one sleeping bag...*

"Maggie and me?" Hank shook his head, "No way, and yet, the feelings that we felt while in that shelter..." The growing light to the east created a surreal landscape of wispy fog and shadows among the tall trees as Hank drove north along the river, his mind filled with the image of Maggie, her magnetic smile, warm brown eyes, and face framed by her auburn curls cascading down. "Nah, no way, forget about it Duval, it'll never happen..."

Just past the park, Hank turned into a large overgrown parking lot and stopped under a weathered, bullet hole riddled sign dangling crookedly from a single chain, the letters CMPC barely legible. Sitting in the truck, peering off into the mist, he could make out the large dark shape of the water tank sitting on wooden stilts. He could not see the

THE LAST DEER HUNT

graffiti, but he knew it was there with many, many coats of history painted on that tank.

Thoughts of Sandy and Maggie were pushed aside, replaced by the distant voices of another time. Hank was just finishing his freshman year in high school; it was an unusually warm May evening, peepers were blasting out their calls, and a bright moon played peek-a-boo with the Clouds.

Hank watched the light play off the faces of the five boys seated quietly in a circle around flickering candles. He was invited here by the others to become a member of the Omega Gang, an invitation that was received with excitement, curiosity and fear.

Eddie Mahoney was the first to speak. "Anybody saw Vic?"

"No," Ollie Bjornson spoke softly, "Not since we left him back at Harvey's Malt Shop."

"Yah," Bob Lindstrom added, "He said he was coming right over."

The moon moved out from behind a cloud, turning the darkness into near daylight and Hank could see the other boys, each looking at each other, then at Hank and back to each other.

"The shit's gonna hit the fan when he gets here." Gino Grappone said, lighting up a cigarette, "When he sees we brought Duval with us."

Again, the moon disappeared and the only light came from the dozen candles dancing in the slight breeze.

"Come on Gino," Tom Peters' soft voice was barely a whisper, "We all agreed Hank deserves to be here, that he should be a member of the gang, after all, he was with us when—"

"Stuff a sock in it, would yah," Gino spoke up quickly, "We all know it, we just don't need to talk about it."

Bob laughed, "Duval will fit right in, after all, remember, he incinerated old Paul Bunyan."

"Yeah," Tom threw his hands up in the air, "A thirty foot high geyser of fire. That was really neat."

"It sure was," Ollie added, "Then it came down all over poor Paul Bunyan. Geez, he was gone in less than five minutes, totally burned down."

"Then the sheriff came just as you were pulling that stupid blue ox out of the way. You got to be a hero." Tom laughed, "If only they knew who started it."

"Wait a minute, that was an accident," Hank stood, hands outstretched, "You all know that. You were there. Heck, you guys told me to shoot at that can with my .22. I didn't know the can was full of gas or that it would explode like it did." He was watching the other boy's faces, looking for support.

"Christ, don't worry about it Duval." Gino spread his hands to encompass all the other boys. "Nobody ain't gonna say nothing, right?"

The boys sat watching the candles.

"I said ain't that right?" Gino repeated loudly. This time heads nodded enthusiastically, with comments, "Yeah sure, you bet." "You can count on us buddy," and Eddie's squeaky voice, "Yeah Hank, it's all for one, and one for all." Gino motioned towards Hank, "Then we all agree, Hank can be part of our gang."

More nods of approval from around the fire. Ollie stood, looked around nervously, "Yeah, we all agree, all we need now is for Vic to agree. What do you think Gino? You know him better than anyone."

Gino stood, lit another cigarette and looked around the circle. "Yeah, we agree, but that ain't gonna cut no ice with Vic."

"What ain't gonna cut no ice with Vic?" The voice came from off in the darkness, from behind the glow of a lit cigarette.

Hank peered hard, but could not see who had spoken. From the looks on the other boy's faces, he knew that Vic Pollo had arrived.

THE LAST DEER HUNT

The slender figure of a boy, black hair greased back, appeared at the edge of the small circle, and in the play of light from the candles, his face took on a menacing countenance.

Gino spoke first. "We brought Henry Duval with us tonight, we think that —"

"Who gave you shitheads the right to think?" Vic snarled, moving back into the darkness. "That's the trouble with you turds, you think you can think." Vic Pollo laughed at his own attempt at a joke and a few other chuckles arose from the boys sitting around the candles. Vic blended back into the darkness and Hank followed the glowing cigarette as it moved back and forth just beyond the candlelight.

The lit cigarette bobbed, "My name is Vic Pollo and I do all the thinking around here and don't you forget it."

Eddie's shrill voice chuckled in the semi-darkness. "Hey, Pollo means chicken, right?"

Hank could hear gasps go up around the circle. He had heard people call Vic Pollo chicken behind his back, but never directly to his face.

The glowing cigarette made a quick arc, landing on the ground. Vic walked into the light and grabbed Eddie by the collar, lifting him off his feet. "You call me that?" Vic shook Eddie violently, "You skinny little turd, you piece of shit, I ought to tear your head off and shove it up your ass."

"Christ Vic, Eddie didn't mean anything by that." Gino moved next to Vic, "It was just a joke, right Mahoney?"

Eddie didn't answer as much as he whimpered, "Yah, right Vic, I didn't mean anything by that. I don't know what I was thinking."

"Yah, okay, you keep it that way, you pathetic little worm. And don't you ever say that chicken word to me again, it makes me crazy." Vic let go of Eddie, who fell to the ground, then turned and looked at each of the other boys, slowly, one at a time. "Anybody else think that was funny?"

No sound came from the circle of boys.

Vic stepped over and put his hand on Hank's head. "So why is this little kid here with us tonight? Did we sign up for baby-sitting or something? Someone bring his diapers?"

Someone in the dark snickered, then silence. Vic grabbed Hank's shirt and pulled him to his feet. "Christ, look at that, he's only a widdle itty-bitty freshmen."

"Yeah," Gino laughed, lighting up the two cigarettes dangling off his lip, "And Vic, you're only a sophmore like the rest of us cause you stayed back twice."

Vic and Gino stood facing each other, inches apart, Gino was heavier, Vic, thinner but taller. The circle became quiet, waiting for Vic to explode in a rage of anger as he pushed up against Gino. "Damn Piasano," Vic sneered, taking one of the cigarettes from Gino and sticking it in his mouth, "Anybody said that but you, they'd be dead now." Then a husky laugh started in Vic's throat, working its way out into the night, soon joined by Gino, and then Eddie's shrill laugh.

Vic's stopped laughing as he faced Eddie. "What are you laughing at, you shit for brains? Nobody told you to laugh. That was a private joke between my buddy Gino and me."

Eddie moved back to the edge of the circle, Vic took a long drag on the cigarette and tossed it in a glowing arc in the direction of Eddie. "So, help me to understand how this mere kid will help our gang?"

Tom answered, "Hank's Uncle Andre owns a hunting camp two miles up the river and we could use it as a hangout. It's really cool, it has a stove and everything. "

"Yeah Vic, you know, like for deer season, or just hanging out." Eddie added.

Vic walked, more like swaggered over, his face inches from Hank's.

Hank could feel his hands shaking as he stood looking up at the taller Pollo. He could smell the cigarette smoke on Vic's breath and the garlic oozing from his pores.

"Okay, so this little pussy has something to offer us." Vic

said, his face inches from Hank's. "You are a little pussy aren't you Duval?"

Hank pulled back, the tone of Vic's words sent a tight knot of fear growing inside.

"Then there ain't no objections to this pussy joining the Omega Gang?" Vic's head turned slowly, watching the other boys.

"No, no objections," came back in unison.

"So what you think we should do for an initiation for this little pussy?" The words hung heavy on Vic's tongue.

Hank stood tensed, torn between fear of staying and the consequences of running away, listening to his heart beating, hoping no one else could hear.

"We ain't got time for that tonight Vic," Gino said, blowing out the candles, "We gotta go over to the mill, remember?"

"Well, we'll just have to postpone the initiation for this pussy till another time." Vic said slowly, his voice a cross between disappointment and anticipation, "Duval, because all these other shitheads here think you will make a good member of the Omega Gang, you are now a lifetime member. That means there ain't no leaving it for no reason." Vic's hand came up, carrying a long object that with a click, revealed a six-inch long switchblade knife. Holding the blade inches from Hank's face, Vic said very slowly, very deliberately, "No reason, you understand, pussy?"

"Yeah, sure Vic," Hank felt the panic in his voice, "you bet Vic, I understand Vic, I really do, I under—"

"Put a lid on it Duval." Vic said, closing the blade on the knife. "Yeah, that's kinda cool being able to use that camp as our gang headquarters. You are okay Duval." Vic delivered a hard slap to Hank's shoulder.

Hank could feel tears coming, *Dammit, I'm not going to let him know that hurt.*

Vic lit up a cigarette and handed it to Hank. "You are coming with us tonight. We will do the initiation right after we are done with our other project.

Hank took a long drag, then was too busy coughing to answer.

Vic gave Hank a hard poke to the arm. "How'd you like that butt, kid? That's a KOOL, got menthol in it, really mellow, eh?"

 Hank was too busy coughing.

Vic lit another cigarette, "Let us get going, we are going to have a fricken blast tonight."

After a quick walk, the boys stood, surrounded by cans of paint and brushes looking up at the water tower, Vic gave Hank a hard poke in the other arm, and said, "You can stay down here and be our lookout."

Before Hank could object, Eddie's shrill voice rang out, "One for all, and all for one." The older boys scrambled up the tower ladder with cans of paint and crudely painted letters became crudely painted words.

Hank could not see the boys on the tower, the catwalk blocked the views, but he could hear the laughter and felt the paint drops as they splattered everywhere.

"Watchit, you idiot, you got paint all over me." Ollie yelled at someone, and Gino called out, "Hey Eddie, where'd you learn to spell?"

"Why don't you all shut up," Vic sneered, quickly calling out F, U, C as he painted, "And let's get some good words up here."

"Hey, you can't paint that word up here," Bob called out, "We can get into really bad trouble."

"Maybe we should get out of here," Tom said, his voice shaking. "I thought I saw car lights coming up the road."

"Don't be such a wimp," Gino answered. "God, you guys are such sissies."

"Yeah, we are a bunch of sissies." Eddie echoed.

Hank stood below listening to the boys working on the tower. A cloud moved in front of the moon, and standing in the blackness, a stab of apprehension moved quickly through him...there was something moving on the edge of

THE LAST DEER HUNT

the darkness and he froze with all his senses on high alert. Silence...Then, the snap of a twig, someone moving close by. He heard his voice yell out, "Somebody's coming, let's get out of here!" His heart was pounding in his chest, the rising excitement overcame his fear and he was running.

As he ran, he was passed by a large figure moving towards the water tower, and heard a loud voice call out, "This is Sheriff McCarthy, you boys stop in the name of the law!"

Hank turned and looked back to see Vic jump from the water tower's ladder, kicking the sheriff directly in the face.

The moon stayed behind the clouds as Hank moved swiftly through the thick underbrush, his feet tripping on unseen roots and his face being whipped by branches. Just as he emerged from the brush and headed for the road, he ran into something very solid. His head was jolted back and his feet came up from under him and he hit ground gasping for air. Hank looked up in time to see old Gus Lundgren, wild hair and beard, moving away silently into the undergrowth. *Jesus, where the heck did he come from?* Panic started to take over as he lay on the ground, trying to regain his breath. As suddenly as old Gus had appeared, he was gone. All Hank could hear was his own hoarse breathing and when it seemed Gus wasn't coming back, he scrambled to his feet, crossed the road and headed home, looking over his shoulder every step of the way expecting to see old Gus coming after him. *What the hell was old man Lundgren doing at the mill in the middle of the night? Would he tell anybody about this?*

The next morning, School Principal Phil Richardson stood on the stage next to the school's mascot, the four-foot high wood replica of Babe, the Blue Ox. A large 'GO LUMBERJACKS 68' banner spread across the back of the stage. The student body was assembled on the floor of the school auditorium, beneath black and orange crepe-paper streamers, dangling ghosts, goblins and witches that decorated the assembly hall for the upcoming Halloween dance. A steady hum of noisy chatter punctuated by giggles and laughter filled the large room.

Gino, Tom, Eddie, Bob, Ollie and Vic sat by themselves off to the side. Andrew McCarthy, the Baraga County sheriff, his right eye swollen and closed, the right side of his face a collage of reds and purple, hovered over them, arms folded around his lean supple body, trying to evoke an air of authority.

The school principal motioned for quiet and after several attempts, the noise abated to a low murmur. "The incident at the mill water tower last night stands as a black day for Fairhaven, for our high school, and our faculty."

Richardson paused and the snickering and comments from the students grew louder. His face grew red, his voice became high-pitched. "This is the worst humiliation the school has suffered since Paul Bunyan, the beloved symbol of our school and our livelihood was burned down by vicious vandals."

Hank sat looking at the floor and trying to be invisible, feeling every eye in the auditorium was focused on him. Looking up, he saw the sheriff and principal watching him closely.

Principal Richardson motioned towards Hank, "Henry Duval, you are a hero. We were just so lucky that Henry happened to be in that area that day, and it was his quick thinking and bravery that saved our mascot Babe."

Hank could hear the rustle and scratching of chairs and a series of snickers from across the room where the other members of the Omega Gang sat against the wall, watched closely by Sheriff McCarthy.

Richardson shook his finger in the direction of the six members of the Omega Gang. "You boys could learn a lot from someone like Hank Duval who was willing to put his own life at risk to save a wooden blue cow."

"Ox, Mr. Richardson. Babe was a blue ox." Mrs. Merke, the Senior High English teacher called out across the room.

"Yes, of course Mrs. Merke, as I meant to say, Babe the

THE LAST DEER HUNT

Blue Ox." Then turning to the Omega Gang, added. "It was only through the good work of Sheriff McCarthy and Deputy Jankyzyzewski that the delinquents who defaced the water tower were apprehended and you can be assured the perpetrators will be dealt with harshly." The principal gazed slowly over each of the members of the Omega Gang, but he saved his longest and most intense glare for Vic, and their eyes locked on each other in a combat of wills. The Principal's face tightened into a mask of determination while Vic stared back with his twisted grin, a cigarette tucked in behind his left ear in open defiance of school policy. Finally, Vic broke the impasse by slowly and deliberately giving the finger and silently mouthing "screw you."

Hank pulled himself back into the present as the memories faded. The water tower had been painted over many times since that night and the incident was lost in time. No one ever revealed that Hank was involved and the rest of the Omega Gang members all received a fifteen-day suspension with the exception of Vic, who was placed in reform school for three months.

Vic threatened Hank with terrible things for failing to warn them in time about the sheriff at the watertower, but the other boys stepped in and defended him, reminding Hank that this was not the first time they had to come to his rescue.

Hank drove slowly down the length of the long parking lot and as the fog continued to lift, it revealed old brick buildings, and behind them, tall mill smokestacks appeared out of the wispy haze like giant specters.

"What the..." Something unfamiliar was standing high in the air where the maintenance building was located. Hank pulled to a stop, and staring through the mist, he could make out a large crane hanging its long neck over the gutted maintenance building. Peering harder into the fog, his heart beating quickly, he could see a large pile of bricks and debris that had been smashed out of the west side of the building exposing the interior of the shop.

"What the hell is that?" He looked again to make sure of what he was seeing. *Jesus, they are tearing up the floor, they really are...* A cold chill passed through him. *That's where the body was!* Now his recurring dream seemed just a little more real.

Hank sat back in the truck and took a deep breath, a technique Maggie had shown him. "Yeah, okay, that's it, then. That's what I need to do." Another deep breath, one more slow exhale. "I need those guys back here one more time so we can deal with this once and for all. Once more for one last deer hunt!"

Three

Hank listened to the silence but no answers came to him. He hadn't realized he had nodded off until the light dancing across his face wakened him. One small ray of sunlight had managed to find its way through the pines surrounding the parking lot and glistened off the small silver cross hanging off the rear view mirror. It was the cross that Mom had given him just before she died of a broken heart in the spring of 1977, six months after her husband Paul passed away.

Hank reached up, touched the cross, setting it into motion, and as it slowly rotated, the reflected light moved across Hank's face in a hypnotic, soothing rhythm and he slowly leaned back against the truck seat.

"Didn't I tell you, Henry Duval?" Mom's voice startled him and he quickly looked around expecting to see her, sitting in the truck in the same flowered housedress and white apron she always wore on her slender frame. Without seeing her, he sensed her presence; her long black hair straight on her shoulders, her face, the beautiful face from her wedding pictures, her dark eyes looking at him, dark eyes that expressed her feelings more than her words ever could.

"When you were a kid Henry, didn't I always tell you to behave or it will come back to haunt you?"

"Mama?" Hank answered, filled with surprise, "When you said it would come back to haunt me, I didn't think that you personally would come back, unless…" Hank took a quick glance towards the large crane looming over the maintenance building, "Am I in some sort of trouble?"

"Henry, you know the answer to that. Vos amis étaient ennui." As she did often when excited or angry, Mom slipped easily into the French she knew from when she lived with Grand-Mère in a home filled with her French-Canadian relatives.

I can't believe this, I am having a dream that I'm talking to my dead mother, and she's scolding me in French! "Speak In English, Mama …"

"I just said, your friends were nothing but trouble. How many times did we tell you how much we worried about that gang you hung around with? Especially after I watched the newsreels about those gangs in Los Angeles and Detroit."

"Mama, this isn't Detroit or L.A., this is Fairhaven and we were just a bunch of kids hanging around together."

"Ne discutez pas, Henry. You even had a name for your gang, the Omega Gang, the Greek word for last. It should have been called the last straw, for all the trouble it got you into." There was a hint of anger in her voice and Hank was sure it was dancing in her eyes. Mama continued. "We could tell all those boys would be trouble, you only had to look at the families to figure that one out. Take that Eddie Mahoney's parents. Every night they were down at the Bayside Tavern drinking. That's all the Irish do, you know."

"Yeah sure Mama, how about Papa and Uncle Andre sitting in the garage every night drinking beer and playing cribbage. They must have been Irish?"

A long quiet followed, an indication that Hank must have been getting the dark silent stare that said very loudly, "You better watch your tongue, young man."

THE LAST DEER HUNT

Mama sighed, then spoke quietly, "Every Sunday, Tom Peters' parents sat like two tall beanpoles in the first pew in church like they had no sins. Sidney Peters dressed in his expensive suits, Dorothy Peters in one of her very large hats, and that son of theirs, Tom, the alter boy, Mon Dieu! To think that, when Sidney was president of The First Superior Bank, he made all his money off the backs of the mill workers by foreclosing on their homes after the mill closed from the strike." Real anger in Mama's voice now. "And your Papa said the Peters never gave one red-cent to the church."

"Mama, how would Papa know that? He never stepped inside that church in twenty years. And oh by the way, did they let Papa in up there? Or did they send him down below?"

Her dark eyes must be flashing and dancing now. "Henri Duval, vous regardez comment vous parlez de votre père …"

"Yeah sure," *That I understood, I heard it enough times,* "I'll watch how I talk about Papa, I wouldn't want him coming back down here."

Mom had more. "How many times did we have to tell you not to hang around with that Gino Grappone. His mother was divorced and you know how your father felt about that."

"Mama, Gino's mom was a nice lady, she always had cookies and milk and help with our homework when—"

Mom would not hear that, she would just echo Papa. "Henry Duval, you know how those Italians are. You know what your father thinks about Italians. Bunch of Mafiosos."

Mama didn't forget Bobby Lindstrom and Ollie Bjornson, they were Lutherans that lived on the other side of town with the Finns and the Swedes and nothing more needed to be said about them.

But Mom saved her most scathing anger for Victor Pollo. "Something was not right about that boy. I think he was soft in the head, living out on Proctor Road in that tarpaper shack with his Uncle Pasquale. That place should have been condemned, goats and chickens and pigs running all over, even in the house." Mama did have one opinion of her own, "Italiens dégoûtants."

Mama was probably right about Vic being soft in the head, but she was wrong about Vic's house. In July of 1967, I found Vic's cigarette lighter and went over to his house to return it. His uncle Pasquale told me that Vic was out of town working during June and July, but he let me in. Yes, the house was messy on the outside, but inside, it was immaculate. And there were more religious statues, pictures and crucifixes around that house than in the catholic church.

Her voice softened, "Henry, I could never understand what you saw in that Pollo or why you hung out with him? He was too old for you and you weren't like him at all."

"Mama, back then, I thought he was cool. I thought he knew just about everything, and he taught us all about life, love and sex — even though he got most of it wrong most of the time. Hanging around together made us feel special, like we belonged to something, and we cared about each other, even if no one else did."

"Henry Duval, your father and I always cared about you and took an interest in what you were doing. Sometimes we worried that you would spend so much time in your room drawing pictures."

Hank could feel the frustration and anger starting to rise as it did every time he thought about it. "Mama, you were never interested in what I did in school. You and Papa never talked to me about what I did in school, about getting an education, or giving me any encouragement with my art or to go to college. I can't remember one time that you came to see me in the school plays or when I was on the baseball, basketball, or track teams."

"You know I wasn't feeling well—"

It seemed Mama never did feel well, at least while I was in High School. I don't remember a time when she wasn't sick. Many trips to health clinics could never supply any answers, and when she died, it seemed it was due to everything and due to nothing, I suggested her epitaph should have read, 'I told you so.'

"Yeah Mama, no matter what I did, how well I did it, it wasn't good enough. All I ever heard from you was, 'Why can't you be more like your sister.'"

"That's because your sister Diane never caused us any problems, she always got good grades, worked to help us with bills, and worked around the house helping me."

"Then how come, if she was such a goody-goody, she went to live with Aunt Helen in Ohio as soon as she graduated?"

"That was a misunderstanding between Diane and your father. We, I mean, your father thought it was best for her."

"Yeah, for sure. She wanted to go to college and he thought that was a waste of good money."

"And look what happened to her, she went to that Kent State and got into that anti-war stuff and almost got killed. Your father was so ashamed of her getting her picture in the paper demonstrating against those young soldiers."

"Mama, those guardsmen shot at unarmed students."

"Well, she didn't even need to go college, Papa told her that she had a good job at the school as a secretary. What she should have done was stayed here and married that boy she was dating, what's his name, Melvin? That's what she should have done...he was always so nice to Diane—"

"Yeah sure Mama, all he ever did was beat her up."

"Your Pa said she probably deserved it."

"Mama, You can't believe that. Didn't you ever have opinions of your own? How come all you ever say is how Papa felt or what he thought. Why did you always go along with everything he said?"

"Because he was my husband, that's why. And he was your father, and you should respect that. He always tried to do the right thing for you kids. I remember when you got into trouble for breaking into that car behind Twill's service station and the sheriff caught you. Your father saved you, and it was a good thing he did too. You had received some nasty head wounds and you would have surely ended up in jail."

Now Hank could hear the anger and frustration in his voice, "Yeah Mama, I remember too, but that's not quite the way it happened. Here's the way it really happened that night. It was a hot summer night in August and Angie Grappone and I were walking when it started to rain. We ducked into the back of Percy Twill's old Oldsmobile that was sitting behind his shop. We didn't break in, it was never locked, Heck, it didn't even have a motor. All of a sudden, Pa and the sheriff show up and drag us out of the car. Pa pushed me against the car and hit me upside the head with the flashlight. He'd been drinking and he would've hit me again, except the sheriff stopped him and told Pa to just take me home because I was only fifteen."

Mama spoke, her voice sounding tired and strained from having to defend Papa too often.

"Henry, there were times when it was difficult to understand why your father would do things, but he was after all, your father. He was a good provider and in his own way he did love you and always tried to do the best for you. I hope some day that you come to understand that."

Her presence now felt like that of a frail and prematurely old woman in a nursing home waiting out her final days.

"But Mama, I don't think Papa—"

"Henry, you can't change what was, you can only learn from it and move on. You just have to believe in yourself and trust that you will do the right thing…"

The sun had moved in the sky and no longer reflected off the necklace. Hank, sitting up in the empty cab of the truck at the mill on this cold September morning, could no longer sense the presence of his mother and he felt a sadness of not being sure he ever really knew her. He softly rubbed the cross as he looked back over the mill and the crane at the maintenance building.

Four

The sun had moved up higher in the eastern sky painting the tall pines in a red glow. Hank sat in the truck recalling the conversation he just had with Mom. "Yep, Mama was sure right about Vic Pollo. He was a certified nut case and belonged at the nut house over in Newberry." *Yeah, and I probably belonged there too, just for hanging around with him.* "But did I learn my lesson? Oh no, not stubborn little Henry Duval. I kept hanging out with the gang and in summer of 1968, in the heat of the dog days of August, I came to the realization that Vic was absolutely, without a doubt, totally insane. We hadn't seen him since he got out of reform school. It didn't do any good, he sure wasn't reformed.

God, it was hot and we were just a bunch of young kids hanging out, no worries in the world and not looking forward to starting school in less than a month."

Hank met Bobby and Vic at Harvey's. Vic was excited on the telephone when he called earlier in the day with something that they "had to see."

"What's up Vic?" Hank asked. He hadn't seen Vic this

excited about anything before.

Bobby looked on with apprehension, never sure what Vic was up to. "Yeah Vic, what's happening?"

"You guys gotta see what I got." Vic, jogging at a good pace, pointed at his shirt. "This is really cool."

Hank and Bobby followed Vic around the corner of Harvey's Malt Shop and down the alley behind Main Street.

"Slow down!" Bobby shouted, but Vic ran faster and faster.

"Jesus," Hank added, gasping for breath, "where the heck are you going?"

They followed Vic around the corner onto Pine Street, only to find him sprinting ahead, turning onto Glory Drive heading for the cemetery.

Leaning forward and grasping his knees, Hank wheezed, "No use running anymore. Whatever it is, Vic'll have to wait for us."

Walking quickly, the two boys reached the cemetery, still out of breath. Vic was nowhere in sight.

"Where's Ollie and Tom? I haven't seen them today." Hank asked, through labored breathing.

"They couldn't make it." Bobby panted back.

"You seen Gino or Eddie?"

"Vic said they'd meet us."

"Where?"

"Dunno."

Walking through the Catholic section of the cemetery, the two boys met up with Gino. Dressed in jeans and a white T-shirt with a pack of cigarettes rolled up in the left sleeve, his trademark smile flashed across his dark, handsome face and slightly crooked mouth. "What's up, guys?"

"Don't know, hoped you would." Bobby answered.

"Gino," Hank avoided eye contact, "What's with Angie? Did she move away, or what?"

Gino pulled a Pall Mall from a crumpled pack and put it on his lower lip. "Went to live with our aunt down in

THE LAST DEER HUNT

Escanaba. Our Ma thought she would be better off down there." The cigarette jiggled on his lip as he talked.

"Geez, I heard she was knocked up," Bobby put out his hand to Gino for a cigarette, "Vic's been telling everyone he did it. That ain't true, is it?"

Hank stopped, his mouth fell open, *No, that ain't true, Angie wouldn't have done it with Vic. Hell we were going steady...* "That isn't true is it Gino? *Please say it isn't so...*"

Gino handed the crumpled pack of cigarettes to Bobby, turned to Hank with his crooked little smile and shrugged.

God I hate Pollo, and I hate Angie, lying little slut. Pa was right about Italians—

"Hey, you assholes." Vic was waving at them from the top of the hill that separated the old Swedish cemetery from the newer sections. The three boys moved towards him slowly, then, in anticipation of what Vic was up to, broke into a full gallup up the hill. Vic never disappointed them when it came to something exciting.

"What the hell took you so long?" Vic said as the three boys stopped in front of him, his dark eyes flashing with irritation.

I really do hate him. Hank debated his chances of surviving in a fight with Vic. *Geez, he'd tear me apart.* Still upset, but curious of what Vic was up to, Hank decided to go along with the others.

Vic motioned Hank, Bobby and Gino down the hill towards the old Swedish headstones. Sitting in the shadow of the large crypt with "ERICKSON" chiseled over the door, surrounded by headstones bearing names like Buckstrom, Swenson and Dahlstrom, Bobby and Gino stared at Vic, curiosity making them want to ask, but remaining silent, fearing anything they said would break the magic of the moment.

Hank sat staring at Vic and thinking of Angie and debating the wisdom of confronting Vic. He decided he would think about this some more, a lot more.

"Hey Vic," Bobby stood, hands jammed in his pockets,

"Where you been the last couple of months? We ain't seen you around."

Gino stood next to Bobby. "Yeah, we heard they threw you back into reform school again, that right?"

"Nah, I been down at Marquette working. I had me a job doing road construction." Vic continously flicked his Zippo cigarette lighter, waiting for someone to ask him why he had wanted them to meet him here. When he felt that he had reached the maximum suspense, he put away the lighter, reached under his shirt and pulled out a handgun. Slowly he alternated between fondling the gun and passing it from one hand to the other.

"Look what I just got." He said, his dark eyes darted from one boy to the other. "Ain't this the greatest?"

"Holy shit!" Bobby whispered, falling backwards. "What the hell are you doing?"

"That's really cool," Gino said, his crooked smile spreading into a wide grin. "but you shouldn't be showing it around."

Vic laughed. "Hell man, you guys ain't gonna say nothing."

"Where the heck did you get that?" Hank finally managed to speak, looking at the gun with wide unbelieving eyes. "Did you steal that thing?"

"No frickin way," Vic said, pulling a handfull of bullets from his pocket. "Uncle Pasquale brought it with him when he came to live with us. He said he took it off some frickin Nazi in the war." He looked slowly from one boy to the next, who sat in silence looking down at their feet.

Hank just stared at the gun.. "Is that a German Luger?"

"7mm German Luger." Vic replied, pulling the clip from the handle of the gun and sliding shells into it one by one. "Pre-war model. None of that war shit built by Jew slave labor. They woulda put sand in the molds to sabatoge the guns, Uncle Pasquale told me that."

As he watched Vic shove the clip back into the gun, Hank said, "I don't like this. We could get into real big trouble with this."

Vic pulled the action back on the gun, putting a shell into the chamber.

Hank shook his head. *This ain't good. I think I want to get out of here.* "Why'd Pasquale let you have the gun anyway? That old man don't even know his own name anymore."

"That old shithead don't need it." Vic was aiming the gun at different targets of opportunity, mostly tombstones. "Kapow, kapow," Vic shouted in mock firing, complete with a realistic fake recoil.

Gino and Bobby stared at the weapon, then at each other.

"Christ, ain't this a thing of beauty." Vic was running his hand slowly and sensuously over its barrel. "And now it's mine, it's all mine."

"Can I hold it?" Hank asked, staring at the gun.

Vic sneered at him. "Hell no! It's loaded and you gotta know how to handle guns." He aimed the gun at a small bird sitting in a low branch of a maple tree, just over Bobby's head. "Kapow!" Vic yelled again, and before he could fake the recoil, the gun belched fire and kicked back, sending him sprawling backwards, the Luger pointing straight at Hanks' face.

"Holy shit," screamed Hank, diving behind the Erickson head-stone. Feathers and bird parts floated down as Bobby and Gino back-peddled against the Sven Swenson stone as far as they could go.

"Shit! At least I know where the safety is on a gun, you dumb ass." Bobby screamed, as he flailed at falling feathers.

Gino, giggled nervously, "Wow, nailed that birdie, blew the shit right out of him."

Vic stood up in a trance-like state watching the smoke slowly wafting from the barrel of the Luger, the gun still pointing at the Erickson headstone. Hank crouched down, pressing himself hard against the back of the gravestone,

"You got the freakin safety on that thing yet?" He shouted, the anger and fear strong in his voice.

"I'm outta here." Bobby was on his feet backing away from the others. "I don't want any part of this crap!" His eyes danced from one boy to the other. "We should have never let you..."

"Shut up," Gino snarled.

"Vic, I'm coming out, please put that damn gun away." Hank's voice was still quivering as he looked around the side of the Erickson family marker.

Vic still focused on the gun, slowly lowered the muzzle towards the ground. Hank followed Bobby as they backed up, constantly watching Vic until they reached the entrance to the cemetery. Just as they turned to head away, Vic brought the gun up, pointed it in their direction, and shouted "bang," at the top of his voice.

Hank and Bobby were instantly on the ground, pressing themselves into the soft earth, and screaming at Vic not to shoot.

Vic stood, and putting the weapon into his belt laughed and pointed at Hank and Bobby. "What a couple of shitheads."

Gino joined in his laughter as they both lit cigarettes and walked towards the back of the cemetery.

Hank brushed the dirt from his face and stood, finding himself shaking violently in the warm summer air. "Christ, Vic is one sick puppy."

"He sure is, and I ain't gonna say anything to anyone about this," Bobby looked back towards the cemetery, "Now that whacko prick has a gun."

They turned onto Glory Street, headed towards town, looking back over their shoulders. Bobby shook his head. "Yep, we're going to be very sorry that someone let him have that gun."

Hank wiped a few feathers from his hair. "Yeah, someday, that gun will end up killing somebody."

Five

The hell with Vic Pollo, the hell with that body at the mill, and the hell with everything else – I'm going fishing. It'll give me a chance to think things through and maybe I'll come up with some answers. Maybe, just maybe, when I'm done fishing, this may all have gone away.

Hank turned the key, the engine turned over begrudgingly, then wheezed and coughed its way to life. "Yeah, like hell it will!"

Hank concentrated on thinking about the river and fishing, pushing out other thoughts from his mind as he drove north on River Road. The morning light was breaking in the eastern sky and the dark forest along the road gradually grew lighter. Water dripping from the pines moved partridge into the openings along the side of the road to be startled into flight as the old truck drove by. He turned right on Turners Road and drove carefully, the deer would be moving now and many had been struck by cars along this stretch of road.

In four miles, Hank reached the Huron River, drove over the old bridge and parked. He carefully put the truck key on top of the right front tire. It never bothered him that everyone in the county knew where he hid his car keys when he was fishing. It's something he always did, and it was something his father always did. He got the old telescopic fishing pole that had been his father's and his grandfather's before that. With the rest of his fishing gear out of the back of the pickup, he took a few moments to change out of his shoes and into the hip boots.

With the fishing bag over his shoulder, his net on his hip and his pole extended out to full length, he walked on the overgrown trail along the water, coming out just below Huron Falls at the wide opening of the river.

Hank drank in the mystical beauty of the river glistening in the reflection of the morning light. The sun was breaking through the mist and moving down the maples on the bluffs along the western shore. Much of the foliage had left the trees but the woods were still a blaze of color that reflected off the fast flowing water creating a glow that only comes with the mid-autumn in this north country.

Hank had never been a deeply religious person, but when he was alone on the river, he felt closer to God than he did anywhere else. The cool morning air filled his lungs as Hank breathed in the familiar sights and smells.

Checking his tackle, he added another sinker to the line. When he was satisfied, he wiggled a nightcrawler on the hook, and stepped into the river.

He could read the water, the way it moved swiftly around rocks and other obstacles which the smaller rainbow and brook trout always seemed to prefer, or the deep pools where there would be food for fish, and hopefully, with any luck, a very hungry, large trout.

Overhead, an osprey was flying quickly up the river carrying a large fish in its talons. "Hey bird, that ain't the big German Brown from my fishing hole, is it?"

The osprey answered with a series of quick squeals as it continued on its journey upstream. Hank watched until the bird was out of sight and the only sounds were those of the water moving through the rapids.

Hank made his first cast of the day, putting the worms above a small eddy and just below a large rock near the other bank. The line floated down a foot when Hank felt the first strike. He pulled sharply on the rod, but felt the line go slack. *Lost him!*

A moment later he felt the second strike. Instinctively, he pulled up on the rod and knew he had the fish hooked. Nothing existed now but himself, the fish, and the river. The fish fought hard, leaping a foot into the air trying to shake the hook from its mouth. *This couldn't be the lunker. Large German Browns hardly ever broke water when hooked. No, this had to be a rainbow.*

Hank played the line, keeping it taut at all times so the hook would not come free, until finally, the fish, exhausted, could fight no more. Hank slowly reeled it in and when it was close, moved the net under it and scooped it up. Back on the bank, Hank carefully removed the fish from the net and held up a flapping sixteen-inch Rainbow Trout. He held the fish by its gills, felt it struggling for life, and paused, fascinated by the intricate camouflage markings, bright spots, and glistening red stripes along the sides of the fish.

A moment of doubt, it was always a difficult choice. But the roots of his hunting and fishing culture were very strong and the fish was, after all, food. Quickly, he placed the fish in his creel along with a couple handfuls of grass to keep it from drying out and, sitting down, poured a cup of coffee from a small thermos.

Standing on the tall bank above the deep hole, Hank could see something very large swirling under the surface. *That's him, that's the lunker I been trying to catch for so darn long and I'm finally going to get him.* Normally, Hank would fish this deep hole from the other side of the river, but in the excitement, he wouldn't waste the ten minutes needed to go back to the bridge, cross over, and walk down the other side. Instead, he scrambled down the steep bank and into the water. Putting new worms on the hook, he flipped the line out through two elders into the slow moving water. Hank leaned out further, trying to get past the brush, trying to guide the line farther out into the middle of the hole. Not enough, he needed another six inches, and he slowly worked his right boot out in front, testing his footing, but the bottom dropped quickly and the water came over the top and trickled down inside his boot, *Far enough!* Frenchy's suggestion to be sure to tell someone where he was fishing flashed into his mind, but was gone. The strike was huge, the line was running out at high speed, the drag on the reel screamed against the tension of the whirling outgoing line. The big fish was taking the bait and heading upstream, leaving a wake on the water surface. Needing just a little more distance to keep the line from tangling in the brush, Hank reached out with his arm.

"Holy God." His right boot had slid further into the river and the current caught it, ripping it into the river, taking Hank with it. The hip boot quickly filled with water, pulling him under and dragging him out into the deeper water.

His body was rolling over the rocky bottom, stabbing his arms and head with flashes of pain while the intense cold of the water was rapidly sapping his body strength. He kept his lips held tightly together, trying to keep more water from filling his mouth. He tried to remember the river at this point, and where he was being dragged, tried to remember where the shallows were.

Fear was tearing at him. For an instant he could see himself near this spot fishing with his father. He remembered falling into the river just below this same place, floating down through the big hole and reaching shallows about fifty feet downstream where his father was waiting for him and pulled him out. He recalled the only thing his father said to him. "Bet you won't forget this lesson, son."

The river was becoming shallower as he rolled along the bottom, grabbing at everything and anything, but it was difficult to function in the icy waters and he was still holding tightly to the fishing pole. His left hand felt the tangled branches of a tree as he swept by and a large branch snagged his arm, swinging him around

As Hank fought to hang on to the branch, the cold numbed his senses and a vision of the face from his dream, distorted by the swirling waters, motioned him downward into the tangled branches at the bottom of the river. He was carried further downstream to another deep hole where the river made a sharp turn to the left. As he sank deeper, wispy reflections of light reached down from the surface towards him. These reflections swirled together into the face from his dreams and the faces of his boyhood friends, and in an instant, the memories of something that he had held suppressed in his brain for so many years leapt into his consciousness. As the memories flooded back, the realization of the horror that had been hidden in his mind for so long shocked him and he flailed at the visions, trying to make them go away. The effort drained what little strength he had left, and he was tiring, his will to survive draining away, other arms were grabbing at him, and more indistinct faces swirled around, beckoning to him.

A quiet calm came over him, he quit struggling and he slowly released the branch. As he floated downward into the darkness of the deep water he rolled over and Sandy was reaching down for him, her head encircled in a halo of light from the surface.

With all the strength he could muster, he pulled himself towards her when suddenly, the upper half of his body was violently rotated upward as he hit the trunk of a submerged tree and his head broke out of the water. Gasping for air, he screamed and Sandy's face disappeared, leaving him alone with the current pinning him tightly against the log.

Fighting the cold, his lungs filled with precious air every time he inhaled and coughed out water when exhaling. With great effort he was able to slowly pull himself up the tree trunk to the bank.

After what seemed to be an eternity, Hank managed to work his way onto the shore and crawled onto the grass above the riverbank. The autumn sunlight played on the surface of the river, and reflected upwards as broken shafts of light that reminded Hank of the stained glass windows in the church where he attended mass as a young boy. From behind this curtain of dancing sunlight, a calming voice said, "What did you do, Henry Duval, jump in and try to beat the poor fish to death?"

Shocked at hearing his name, Hank said weakly, "Is that you God?" Wiping water from his face he looked up and could barely make out the figure of Gus Lundgren, standing on the hill above the river looking down at him. *Why does this guy keep showing up when I'm lying on my back?* It was only then that Hank realized the fishing creel had been torn off and he was still gripping his fishing pole, now broken into four or five parts held together by the fishing line. Instinctively he slowly pulled in the line only to find an empty hook. "Got away, I guess." His body was shaking violently from hypothermia and with his strength gone, he lay back on the ground exhausted.

SIX

Both men were silent as Gus' truck moved south on the county road that followed along the west bank of the Huron River. Hank was thankful the heater fan was so loud, it masked the noise of his teeth chattering as he sat wrapped in an old army blanket. His cold, wet clothes were still heavy with the smell of the river, and his mind filled with the watery vision of he and his friends and the closeness of death. *God yes, it did happen, what am I going t do? What should I do?*

After an eternity of a few minutes, Gus turned left and the truck bounced down two worn tire ruts for a quarter-mile through the trees. Passing two large hand-painted "KEEP OUT" signs, Gus drove through a gate of sorts, constructed of old logs, various boxes and other pieces of lumber and stopped in front of the house.

"Welcome to the old family homestead," Gus said, stepping out of the truck.

Following Gus, Hank tried to remember what he had heard about the houses along the river in this area. Rumor had it they were originally built in the mid-twenties by the Chicago Mafia as a place to come and hide out if things got too hot back home.

Up close, the house itself was well constructed from Lake Superior Sandstone, and even with badly peeling paint, Hank could tell the house had been well-built and was still in good condition.

Gus waited by the door. "Originally there were five of these homes built, but this is the only one still standing. I admit, it doesn't look like much from the outside, but that's the way I like it. It keeps people from coming around." Gesturing Hank in, he said, "Please come in, be my guest."

"Wow." Hank let out a low whistle as he quickly scanned the interior. One complete wall was covered with built-in shelves filled with books. *More books than the Fairhaven library*, Hank mused. Other walls were painted off-white and covered with numerous antique prints, paintings, and maps. *More stuff than the Arvon Township Historical Museum.*

Hank stopped, staring in amazement at a large map of the world mounted on the back wall of the room behind a bank of telephone and electronic equipment. Then turning to Gus, he asked, "What is it?"

Gus smiled at Hank's perplexed look. "Impressive isn't it," and with a sweep of his hand, Gus continued, "floral business, wholesale. I connect sellers all over the world with buyers, mostly in the States and Canada. All the very latest and greatest stuff, and the beauty of this is, I don't even need to leave my house. I can take an order for ten thousand mums from a florist in Chicago," Gus sat down at an electronic console and as he typed, lights on the map flashed different colors as they tracked across the continents of the world, "and I will have this order shipped from Thailand within the hour." He quickly typed again. "Done, the florist will have her flowers by tomorrow morning."

Hank watched him, thinking, *This is not the grizzled dirty old man I remember.* Gus' lean body looked hard and muscled under his shirt and belied his seventy plus years. His green chamois shirt and Levi jeans fit as if tailored for him. His face was handsomely chiseled and weathered, his gray beard was cut short, neatly trimmed, and his gray hair pulled back and tied into a ponytail. *What ever happened to the town drunk that–*

In anticipation of Hank's thought, Gus interrupted. "I guess you've heard all the stories about me. Gus the drunk, the bootlegger, the gangster, and oh, yes, Gus the hermit."

"Yeah . . .I guess I did, but..."

"It's okay Henry." Gus interrupted Hank's awkwardness. "They were all true—at one time or another, but we can talk about that later. Right now, we need to get you out of those wet clothes." Disappearing into a back room, he returned with a set of Calvin Klein pajamas, then pointing, "The bathroom is through that door."

Hank went through the door, changed quickly into the warm dry pajamas, and back into the main room, handing his wet clothes to Gus. "I'll just stay long enough to warm up, then I'll be on my way."

"Don't worry Henry, you can stay here as long as you need." Gus disappeared with the wet clothes.

The one wall was covered with pictures, mementos, and certificates. An under-graduate degree in science from Kings College in London, Ontario, a law degree from Carleton University in Ottawa and various certificates and commendations. A set of pictures featured young RAF airmen next to British fighter planes as well as framed medals and more commendations. A row of paintings, watercolors, oils as well as sketches filled out the wall.

"See anything interesting?" Gus asked, gesturing across the wall.

"Well, yes, with all this great stuff on your wall, why do you have this one really bad sketch?"

"Ah, the family of whitetails. I think it's extremely well done. A local artist, I believe, not widely known yet, that's why I got it so reasonably. It's a good investment though, I expect the artist to do very well some day as I suspect the value of the sketch will also."

Hank shook his head, "Sorry but that artist is over the hill, haven't you heard? He retired."

"Well, I for one have not given up on you Henry, you are very talented, you just need to pursue it." Gus moved towards the kitchen area. "Would you like to have something to drink? I'm going to have coffee myself, but I have beer, wine and some very good Kentucky bourbon."

"Coffee's fine," Hank said, without thinking, "and I'd really like to thank you, Mr. Lundgren, for being at the river today. If you wouldn't have shown up, I, I, I'm not sure what would have happened, I could have—"

"First of all, please call me Gus, and I really didn't do anything, I just happened to be there, and I was glad to help." Taking two cups from the sink and rinsing them, he continued, "But, I do believe this isn't the first time we've run into each other, is it?"

"No it isn't Mr. Lundgren, I mean Gus. But that was such a long time ago, and it was so dark, and it happened so fast, I didn't think you even knew who I was that night. I guess I always wondered why you never said anything to anybody."

"Somebody wants to decorate the water tower, that's their business, not mine."

Gus carried the coffeepot to the table. "I generally don't get mixed up in other people's affairs." Gus poured coffee into the cups, gave one to Hank and sat down at the table. "What do you think about the rumor?"

"Rumor? What rumor?"

Surprise spread on Gus' face. "The one about the body at the mill? I thought everybody had heard."

Weariness was pressing down on him. *Damn, I forgot all about the body. Yeah, It came back to me in the river, what the guys and I did up at that house that night. That has to be the same body, the body from my dreams.* As Hank played that night over in his mind, he realized that there were large gaps missing. He tried desperately to lift the last veil of fog from the memory of that night long ago but the details lay hidden somewhere back in the recesses of his mind. He looked up to see Gus watching him intently. "Yeah, I did hear about it. I stopped at Frenchy's this morning." The fatigue was making him feel vulnerable, "The diner was full, and everybody was talking about the murder—"

"Somebody said it was murder?" Gus asked, peering intently at Hank, "Did you hear something new?"

"No, I just thought that since it was found under the concrete floor in the maintenance building..." *I better just shut up.*

Gus went back to check on Hank's clothes and when he returned, reported them just about dry. He sat down at the table across from Hank, folding his hands in front of his face, his eyes narrowed, "I ran into Toivo Niemi today, and he told me about the body they just found at the mill. We got to talking and figured out we both were working at the mill one night just before they sealed the floor in the maintenance building. Toivo was working as a security guard at the mill at the time and I was working as a legal consultant. I was working late and Toivo came into my office and said he had seen something odd. I followed him and he pointed out some kids running from the maintenance building pushing a wheelbarrow and carrying shovels.

"You know Henry, I can't swear on it, but as I recall, those boys looked like that gang you hung around with back then."

Hank studied his coffee cup. "I wouldn't know. I wasn't there that night." *Damn, I answered that too fast.* "I mean I don't remember that particular incident."

"Well, Toivo and I thought those boys were just hanging out and Toivo was going to ignore it, kids were always hanging around the mill, but he thought he better go check anyway, stuff was being stolen from the mill and he remembered that he thought he had seen that Vic Pollo kid hanging around earlier that evening. Toivo wanted to keep an eye on him."

"Vic was there that night?" Hank asked, suddenly awake.

"Toivo said Pollo had been sleeping behind the power station and had a large bag with him. He said he woke Pollo up, said he stunk of moonshine, and told him to get the hell off the property and stay off. Toivo couldn't remember much about that, his mind isn't that good anymore." Gus' face became tense, "I wished Toivo would have been able to find some way to lock up that asshole and throw away the key."

The sudden sharpness in Gus' voice startled Hank and he shook his head trying to loosen the tired cobwebs from his mind, "Why — I mean, I don't understand? What did Vic do?"

"Let's just say, I have a score to settle with Mr. Pollo." Gus' blue eyes closed into slits. He looked as if he had bitten into something bitter. "One night in October of 1968, I was walking out near the cemetery with Alex, my Irish Setter. Alex had run ahead out of sight over a hill, when I heard a shot. I ran to the top of the hill and saw the dog laying on the ground with Vic standing over him with his gun. Without thinking, I ran over, grabbed the gun from him, and told him that if I ever saw him around here with a gun again, I would use it on him. I must have scared the hell out of him because he ran away without a word and without the gun."

"Vic never told any of us about that, at least I never heard about it. He told us he threw the gun into Luther's swamp." Hank held back a laugh, "You must have scared the hell out of him. He quit school and left town and nobody knew where he went."

"I never saw him around after that, and he never came and asked for the gun back." Gus took an inlaid wooden box out of a desk drawer, removed the gun from the box, and held it out to Hank. "It's a beautiful gun, 7mm, German pre-war issue. Turns out it belonged to one of Hitler's aides and it's worth a fortune today."

"Yeah," Hank said, backing away from the weapon. *Damn, it's the same gun from the cemetery.* "Vic's Uncle Pasquale came to live with him in 1968 and brought the gun and all kinds of war souvenirs with him. In August of that year, Vic had that gun out in the cemetery, shooting at everything."

Gus removed the clip from the pistol and counted out the shells. "Oh by the way, Alex never made it, he died two days after being shot. I went looking for Pollo, but he had disappeared. It was just as well, I don't know what I would have done if I had caught up with him."

"Yeah, Vic left town in a hurry, just before he would have started school as a senior. We...I mean, I never talked to him after that."

Gus refilled his coffee cup and gestured to Hank. "More?"

Hank shook his head, his eyes getting heavy, the fatigue moving over him in waves.

"Pretty tired, eh?" Gus said. "Well, you've had a busy day." Gus' face grew serious. "Hank, besides my floral business, I still practice law in Michigan. I'm not a trial or criminal lawyer, my practice is in import law and Canadian-American relations, but if you ever need legal counsel, let me know, I know other people who can help. You will remember that, won't you?"

Why would he want to help me? Hell, he doesn't even know me. "Thanks Gus, I really appreciate the offer, I mean, it's nice of you, but I don't think that would be necessary."

Gus smiled at him. "I would like to help out if I could. It has to do with a debt I owe to your father."

"My father?" Hank tried to fight the fatigue, push it aside. "How do you know my father?" *What is he talking about? What does he mean, debt?*

"Paul Duval was a good man. It's too bad that life treated him so harshly, especially after all he went through."

Hank was speechless, struggling with what he was hearing. *What the heck did Pa ever go through, besides a lot of beer?*

It was Gus' turn to register surprise. "Are you telling me you don't know about what your father did? I owe him a debt of gratitude. "

Hank looked at Gus trying to understand, but the weariness became heavy. "My Pa? A debt of gratitude?"

Gus looked at Hank. "Yes, your Pa, he was a hero. You must have been about five years old at the time it happened."

Hank sat trying to shake the fog of sleep from his mind. Except for Ma, Uncle Andre and the priest at Dad's funeral who had to say nice things, he hardly heard anyone say a good word about his father. Now the words bounced around inside His mind. *My Father? A Hero?* There were other words as Gus talked, a fire, children burned, Pa running into the fire...

Hank tried to hold on to them, make some sense of them, but they blurred into a dreamy semi-consciousness. He was back in the cold dark water of the river, gasping for air as he was carried swiftly downstream. As he was swept down the river, he passed the spector of his young friends pointing to him and laughing, then the face from his dreams reaching up to him, trying to pull him down. Then a vision of Sandy, her light brown hair blowing in the wind, moving from the other bank into the river and reaching out for him, but when he tried to hold on to her, he found no substance to her arms. She blew a kiss and waved goodbye as he swept past her on his way to much needed sleep.

Seven

Shaking the sleep from his head, it took Hank a minute to realize where he was. Evening shadows had started to move up the walls of Gus' home and slowly through the fog of sleepiness, the events of the day came back to him. The aroma of coffee led him to a brewed pot, his clothes neatly folded and a note. 'Help yourself to whatever you need, I have to go out for a while, Gus.'

The coffee was good as Hank changed into his own clothes, and with a pair of boots that Gus had left for him, went outside. His body was stiff, a few aches and pains, a few bruises, but no broken bones. The pickup was still parked back at the dam, about a mile and quarter walk. *Maybe I should just stay here tonight and get some rest? Maggie would be worried, I think I better get back home tonight.*

The evening air was crisp with the feel and smells of fall when the silence was broken by the cacophony of honking as a flock of Canada Geese flew low over the marshes behind Gus' house. Hank stood admiring the large birds against a sky streaked with pinks and purples until the noisy sounds of the geese landing in the marsh had quieted to an occasional honking. He walked out of the rutted driveway, turned south onto Wind Hill Road and followed along the river.

From the left of the road, ancient white pines towering eighty feet high gave way to balsam and hemlock, which then gave way to the spruce and cedars of Luther's Swamp until the undergrowth became so thick that most of the swamp floor never saw sunlight. From here, the swamp followed the river north and south for eight miles and in places ran five to six miles deep.

Luther's Swamp derived its name from Luther Dolittle who homesteaded the area in the late eighteen hundreds. The current patriarch of the Dolittle clan, Moses Dolittle and his family of twelve children still live in their old house on the south side of the swamp where they seem to spend most of their time hunting and trapping.

Stories of the swamp, monsters and lost hunters abound in legends that started with the ancient Indians. Most of the local people respected the treachery of the big swamp and never ventured very far into it. Hunters from the city however, were willing to gamble their life to penetrate deep into the tangle of the swamp by the lure of a big buck. Just last fall, a downstate hunter was the latest who entered the swamp and lost his way tracking a wounded deer during a big snowstorm. The search party followed a trail of cast-off clothing and accessories and found him the next morning with a smile frozen on his face, half-naked, covered with hoarfrost and still hanging onto his rifle. Poor guy was only fifty feet from the edge of the swamp.

Even now for Hank at thirty-one, those monsters in the swamp still brought back feelings of the past. *It was what? Nineteen-sixty-three, I was eleven years old and things weren't going well for the family. There was a strike at the mill, money was tight, and there was a great deal of tension between Mama and Papa. It was late in November of that year, Thanksgiving had come and gon. Deer season was*

THE LAST DEER HUNT

down to its last days and Papa still did not have his buck and without the buck, there would be no venison on the table for the winter.

Paul Duval, then thirty-six, was already worn down by the harshness that life had handed him and he had refined it into a cheerless person going through life without enthusiasm. But on this night twenty years ago, something had rekindled the spirit of youth in Papa and he sat at the supper table, alive and excited.

Talking with his mouth full, Paul Duval mumbled, "I tell you Marie, somebody else spotted that large buck along the old railroad grade near the edge of the swamp. It's that damn swamp buck that I been tracking for five years, just gotta be."

"Slow down Paul and chew your food." Mom was not enthusiastic. Her husband had talked about this deer for every deer season since she could remember. "That old deer's got to be old as the hills by now."

"Papa, what's a swamp buck?" Hank had heard the term, but never knew what it meant.

"It's a buck that never comes out into the hardwoods like the other deer. He stays in the swamp all year eating cedar and getting fatter and his rack of antlers just keeps getting bigger and bigger." Excitement danced in Dad's words.

Mom said, "What that means is, the meat gets tougher and since all it eats is cedar, it gets more bitter. That's what it gets."

Diane, Hank's older sister, sat looking at her father. "Dad, why is it important to kill this animal?" She said. "I just cannot understand why men need to hunt."

Mom looked at Diane and said, "For food dear. We need to eat."

"We shouldn't even be eating meat." Diane said sharply.

Dad shook his fork in the direction of Diane, "That buck will break the 'Boone and Crockett' record for the biggest set of antlers in Michigan, probably the whole country."

Diane could only look at her father. "Dad, you would kill this beautiful animal just for its horns?" Throwing her napkin across the table, she stood, "Just so you could be important? That is so stupid!" And as usual, Diane got up from the table and left the room.

Mama could only shake her head. "You better not bring home no big swamp buck, Paul. The last time you brought home that stupid buck that was supposed to be a trophy head, it be so damn tough that it had to be cooked in the pressure cooker for a week before you could eat it." The tone of her voice had become sharp. "What a waste."

Hank felt uncomfortable, looking between his parents. Mama never lectured Papa like this before.

"Well now Marie," Papa patted her hand softly, "maybe I could sell the carcass to one of those city hunters and make a few dollars off it." Paul Duval looked at his wife, waiting for her approval. "Then maybe you could get that pretty dress you been looking at in the Sears and Roebuck catalogue."

Mom's eyes narrowed and her gaze reached across the table to Dad. "Don't you go soft-talking me Paul Duval. And don't you go bringing home any swamp buck." Her fingers beat a loud tattoo on the table. "We don't need no big ol' swamp buck, we need something we can eat. We need meat on the table this winter."

Normally, Mom's glaring look caused Dad to shrink away and stop whatever he was doing, but now, she was being met with a look from Dad that equaled hers in intensity and defiance.

Dad was finished eating, the conversation was over. Looking right at Hank, he said, "I think we should at least go and see if we can find that big old buck." Putting his hand on Hank's shoulder, he said, "You ready to go deer hunting son?"

Hank nearly choked on his food in surprise. Papa had never taken him deer hunting before. Never even mentioned it. Slowly the impact of it filtered into his brain.

THE LAST DEER HUNT

Yes! I'm going deer hunting with my father! Hank could not help himself and broke into a wide grin. Finally going deer hunting. It was the defining rite of passage into manhood. It was crossing the imaginary line that allowed acceptance into that inner circle that only men could belong.

For the next two days, Hank walked two feet off the ground. He had called Bob and Ollie that same evening to tell them and got their congratulations. Both had been hunting for two seasons already and now he was one of them, a deer hunter!

Nights were filled with fantasies of walking down the old Western Lake railroad grade with his father's 30-40 Kreig nestled in his arm. Visions of a large buck leaping over the grade as the gun was raised and fired. In his dreams he could not kill the deer, no matter how many times he fired, then his dream ended and he woke up. Fears and doubts tried to creep into his thoughts, but this time there was no room for failure. Hank would do well and impress his father.

Two days later, Paul Duval woke his son before sunrise. They were going into Luther's Swamp to look for the buck! Hank gulped down his breakfast and raced around getting ready in anticipation of the hunt and the realization of his dream.

Hank hurried through the ritual of dressing against the minus 20° weather, a layer of cotton long underwear, a layer of cotton, then wool to shed the snow and block the cold. After what seemed an eternity, they had left the house, drove to the parking area near old man Paget's homestead and were out of the car and walking towards the swamp.

The idyllic illusion of the hunt was quickly shattered. His first deer hunt was turning out to be a lot of hard work. The trail through the swamp was difficult, the double barrel Ithaca shotgun was heavy and the snowshoes tangled in the thick underbrush. It wasn't long before his body ached and was wet from sweat. So much for fantasies. Hank struggled to keep up with his father who, even with a very noticeable limp, moved at a very quick pace, his snowshoes skipping in an easy practiced rhythm.

"The old Johnson logging camp." Dad announced as they reached a large clearing in the swamp. He propped his gun and snowshoes against a tree, took a can of beer from his pack, opened it and lit a cigarette.

"Papa, why is this buck so important?" Hank managed to get out between deep breaths.

"Cause it would make me be somebody." Paul Duval, thirty-six years old, sat with his back against a tree stump in the middle of Luther's Swamp looking at his son. His face still had the same features as Hank's with the same large dark eyes, but bore the deep marks of a hard life. "I guess I just got to do something that would let me be..." His voice trailed off in thought.

"You mean like a hero, Pa?"

"Yeah sure, I guess I always wanted to be a hero. When I was your age, I can remember playing war games and I would always die young doing something brave, you know, like winning a Medal of Honor or something." He drew heavily on his cigarette, exhaled the smoke and threw the butt into the heavy snow. "Hell, I never got to be a soldier, I missed the big war and was too old for Korea. Besides, they wouldn't take me cause of my injuries ..."

Hank watched his father drift off into thoughts of what might have been. Father and son sat in the silence of the snow-covered woods surrounding the clearance.

Without talking, Paul Duval walked over to Hank, unwrapped the waxed paper from one sandwich and handed it to Hank, then opened another for himself. Hank opened a can of Hires root beer and both father and son sat and ate in silence.

Gathering up his courage, Hank asked, "Papa, how did you get hurt?"

Paul Duval opened his eyes and stared off at some distant memory. "I was stupid and blew my chance to be a hero and die young." Another can of beer and another cigarette appeared.

"How'd you do that?"

"That don't matter none," Paul stood, "it was a long time ago. I just screwed up, that's all. Problem is that it also screwed up my legs and I haven't been able to do much ever since. I been thinking of quitting the mill and opening up my own carpentry shop, you know, cabinet making and things. Then I'd be able to make decent money and I get your Ma everything she wants."

"Yeah Pa, you're a really good carpenter and your shop is going to be great and you'll be able to get Mama all those things, you'll see. And when you open your carpentry shop, I can help you do all kinda things, you know, keep it clean, pick up stuff, run errands, anything at all you need done."

A smile crossed Dad's face, but his eyes remained closed. "Yeah, thanks son, that will be good. I'm gonna need all the help I can get, I ain't as young as I used to be."

Paul walked over and picked up the shotgun. "Soon you'll be getting your own rifle. I got Uncle Andre restoring that old Winchester model 68 that I had down the cellar for so long. It'll be a beauty when he finishes with it. It takes a 210-grain slug. No distance, but good for hunting in thick brush and anything you hit within 150 yards is dead. Until then, that shotgun will be good enough.

"Grand-père shot his first buck with it and I got my first buck with it. It's the first hammerless model Ithaca came out with, got a 42 inch barrel and full choke, good for long range, heavy as hell, but that cuts down on the recoil."

Hank finished his peanut butter and jelly sandwich. He shivered and his hands shook from the excitement of finally being on a deer hunt with Dad, or was it the cold? He looked at his father as if to say "What now?"

Paul Duval opened another beer. "We're not going to give up now boy; we're too close. I want to get that buck."

Hank had never seen his father so determined. "Pa, even if we get that buck, it might be too far to drag him out of the swamp tonight." As soon as he said this, Hank knew he should have stayed quiet.

Dad glared at Hank. "Drag him? Hell, all I want is that head and horns. I can come back with Andre in the morning and we'll get the rest. Won't be much work dragging him out with all this snow."

Geez, now he knows I'm a sissy. "Yeah Pa, that's what I meant, we can come back tomorrow and get the buck."

"Boy, you stay here in this clearing. I'm going to circle around for about a half mile to the south. Could be I'll drive the buck right through this opening. You get a chance, you shoot. You got a slug in one of them barrels, shoot that first, then if you need to, use the buckshot in the other barrel, it'll scatter and give you a better chance to hit something moving very fast."

"Sounds good Papa."

"You stay alert now." With that, Paul Duval disappeared into the deep underbrush of the swamp.

Sitting on a stump at the edge of the opening, not moving, the cold started to penetrate through his clothes. First the fingers started to freeze and he wiggled them to try to keep the blood circulating. *Wish I had worn the warm mittens, but can't shoot a gun with mittens.* Then the toes were getting colder and he wondered what hunters who froze to death were thinking while they froze.

Time moved very slowly. He wasn't wearing a watch, but Hank knew it was early afternoon and low dark clouds were building up threatening snow. The woods had always been a place to hide and be safe but the stories of the swamp played on his mind as unnamed shadows leapt from behind trees and disappeared into the dark tangle of the swamp. Hank pushed these thoughts into the back of his mind. *I've never been able to please Papa no matter what I did, and now I finally got this chance to prove that I can and I gotta do this right!*

A sudden movement caught his eye. Something was on the edge of the clearing. Slowly, he moved the butt of the

THE LAST DEER HUNT

gun into his shoulder and waited. All thoughts of being cold were gone and Hank was left with the anticipation and excitement of being there, having a gun and really hunting.

Something moved on the perimeter of the opening, knocking snow from a tree. He tightened the shotgun against his shoulder and pointed it in the direction of the movement. *Gotta be calm, too many stories of people having buck fever and in the excitement shot a doe by mistake, or even worse, another person.*

Then suddenly, a burst of flying snow erupted at the edge of the clearing, his finger tightening on the trigger, a flash of something dark. "What the —"

A large black raven, flitting from one tree to the next was sending snow falling from the branches. Quickly taking his finger off the trigger, Hank could feel his heart pounding and his hands were physically shaking. *Wow, that was too close, almost shot that darn bird!* Quiet returned to the clearing and his adrenaline slowly subsided and the cold settled back in. Two muted thumps came from somewhere in the swamp and the adrenaline was back. *Gunshots, a rifle! Could be Papa?*

More waiting, getting colder. Shivering and teeth chattering, wait-ing. *Really cold and I gotta pee, but can't move cause as soon as I do, a buck will come through the opening.*

Seconds turned into minutes. The swamp was bathed in silence, sounds muted by heavy snow on trees. The end of the shotgun barrel shook from trembling hands as Hank held it aimed at the center of the opening. *Buck fever? Or just cold?*

A small movement to the right caught his eye and the barrel of the gun moved slowly in that direction. Another movement, his breathing stopped and he moved his finger to the trigger.

"Hello boy, it's your Pa." Dad moved out into the opening, his gun nestled in the crook of his arm.

In one move Hank turned, letting out the air in his lungs at the same time he unzipped his pants and relieved himself in the snow. Done, he turned back to his father. "Any luck Papa?"

"Yep. Twenty-eight point rack on that beauty. Good chance he'll break the record." Dad was grinning ear to ear. "Come on, let's go."

Hank stood looking at his father. "Go where?" The questions must have shown on his face.

"Gotta clean him out boy. I didn't have too good a shot at him in this thick brush and he was shot in the gut. Gonna be messy."

The buck lay on its side surrounded by an ever-widening circle of red snow. *Dad was right, it was a beauty.*

It twitched. Hank backed away from the buck. "It's not dead!"

"It's dead." Dad stood with the cleaning knife, handing it to Hank. "Those are just nerves twitching."

"Me!" Hank yelped, backing away from the knife. "I don't know how to clean a deer."

"Gotta learn sometime son if you're ever going to hunt. Better get to it, it'll be dark soon." Dad took out a small Kodak Brownie camera, snapped a couple pictures of the buck, leaned back against a tree and opened his last can of beer.

With his father's instructions, his coat off and his sleeves rolled up, Hank pushed the large buck onto its back. The long cut along the stomach opened up the deer and the steam and smell hit Hank in the face. As the entrails fell out of the cavity, the vomit came up from Hank's stomach and filled his mouth and nose, then spewed out.

"I can't...I can't do this."

"You can't do this?" Paul Duval's voice was filled with anger and disappointment, "What the hell you mean you can't do this? Either you do this or you won't ever hunt deer again."

"I'm sorry Papa, I just can't do this." Hank grabbed his coat and ran into the darkening swamp in the direction of

THE LAST DEER HUNT

his footprints in the snow. Rage at himself drove Hank on, tears of shame blurring the branches and bushes that whipped his face as he ran.

Wet with sweat, teeth chattering and fingers frozen, Hank reached up and took the car key down from the top of the right front tire. Afraid to start the car engine for heat, he fell asleep. The night was a blur but Hank could vaguely remember his father carrying him from the car to his bed. He thought he heard his father say, "It's okay son, we'll go back and get the deer tomorrow."

The next day, Papa and Uncle Andre went back to drag the buck out of Luther's Swamp. When they returned, Paul Duval's seething anger deterred Hank from asking.

"Well, Paul," Mom said, wiping her hands on her apron as she moved between her husband and Hank, "what happened? You look like you're ready to blow your top."

"It was gone, the Goddammed deer head was gone, we didn't tag it last night and somebody come and took the Goddammed deer head!"

Back at his Ford pickup at the dam parking lot, Hank thought back to that day long ago, he had disappointed his father and lost his trophy buck. That was one hell of a lot for one young boy to accomplish in one day!

Standing in the cool evening air filled with the complex smells of cedar and spruce mixing in with the rich loam and peat from the swamp floor, he was lost in deep thought. *Papa was right about one thing, I never hunted deer with him after that. Papa never asked again if I wanted to, and I was too ashamed to ask.*

Somewhere, a loon's haunting wail floated up from the river and the first stars of the night started to show themselves. He retrieved the key from on top of the tire and worked it into the ignition and cranked the engine, which burst to life on the sixth try.

Around here, people measure how good a year was by how many quarts of blueberries were picked, how the

Detroit Tigers baseball team did, how close to the first day of deer season they got their buck, and if their truck or car was still running in the spring.

This year, the way things are going, this year might just turn out to be the worst winter on record.

Eight

Heading west towards Fairhaven, the eastern sky behind him was turning from cerulean blue to a deeper shade of ultramarine. In front of him, over Huron Bay, the cloudless sky danced slowly in shades of purples and pinks, then into bright reds and oranges and funneled into the spot where the sun slowly dropped below the horizon.

The deep woods on both sides of the road became shrouded in darkness and cooled quickly without the warm rays of the sun. Hank pushed the heat selector to warmest and turned on the fan to its highest speed and was immediately greeted by cold air. Beating on the dash with his fist did nothing more than cause the glove compartment door to open, dumping tools and papers on the floor. "What the hell else can go wrong with this stupid truck."

At Grover's Corner, Hank turned west and drove past side roads marked by trees and posts covered with small arrow shaped signs indicating the location of various hunting and fishing camps along the river. One small red sign, 'Antlers Hunt Club' pointed down a rut road towards Uncle Andre's camp that Hank and his friends used as their clubhouse and where they got together for their annual deer hunt. After the incident with the gun in the cemetery and Vic Pollo moving away, the old gang started to drift apart and after the older boys graduated, Bob and Ollie were drafted and the others left the area in search of work. Before they left, they made a pact to return every year during the first week of deer season. Hank, remaining in the area, was chosen to assure that the appropriate arrangements were made and the camp was available and ready for the annual get-together. Over the years the men continued to come back for the first week of deer season to enjoy the camaraderie and catch up on each other's lives. Surely not for the hunting since over the years, with the exception of Hank, none of the other men ever had the fortune of bagging a deer. After a while, the excuses came back instead of the men. Life was getting in the way and participation dropped off one by one until by tacit agreement, the annual event ceased The last get-together was four years ago.

The shared intimacies that had held the group together were the same shared intimacies that kept the group at a distance and these bonds, fragile at best back then, were about to be tested again if it were agreed that they come back for this one last deer hunt. "It's time we faced this after all these years of tiptoeing around it." Hank thought out loud, "I'm still not sure what happened that night, the guys, the gun, the dead guy. Nothing seems to make sense, it's like a jigsaw with some of the pieces missing."

A large field opened up on Hank's left where the foundations of the old Conservation Corps buildings had stood. Called the CCC camps by local people, it was here that Hank learned his hunting skills back when the fields and woods were alive with partridge, sharptails and prairie chickens. Hunting birds with his bird dog Daisy brought back warm memories of walking through the autumn hardwoods, the excitement of the birds being flushed and bittersweet feelings of shooting and killing them.

THE LAST DEER HUNT

Wished Daisy was here now; God I loved that dog! Papa shot and killed Daisy. Dad's reason was simple enough, "Because once a dog chases a deer, it's no good for hunting anymore."

The glow ahead signaled the junction of Skanee Road and Arvon Road. Neon signs flashing brands of beer lit up the windows of the old sway-backed building on the southwest corner of the intersection. The Bayside Tavern and Grill leaned heavily to one side and stood as a testimony to how long a structure could stand up without maintenance.

Hank looked at his watch but the dial was still filled with water from the river. *Better call Maggie and tell her I'm going to be late.* He pulled into the half filled parking lot on the side of the building, turned off the engine and waited while it continued to cough and run for several more seconds.

It had been a long time since he had been in the tavern and every step was measured in hesitation and uneasiness. Opening the door to the bar, he was greeted by the usual lilting sad country and western song, the stench of stale beer, and clouds of blue smoke. The name of the bar had been shortened to the Bayside Tavern, or just the Bayside. In actuality, it was nothing more than a smoke filled bar and the grill part of it had turned into a microwave for heating sandwiches from a cooler of shrink-wrapped foods. The tavern was a dingy place with a long wooden bar, booths around the outer walls, a pool table, and a dance floor that also held a dozen plastic top tables each with four plastic chairs.

The walls of the bar were hung with banners of sports teams and mounted deer heads with antlers, and antlers mounted without deer heads. In the correct light, large cobwebs could be seen floating from one deer head to another.

The pride and joy of the tavern was a decrepit full sized stuffed moose located at the left end of the bar. This moose, with full rack of horns adorned with small twinkling Christmas tree lights, stood with head held up, grazing on artificial tree limbs hanging from the ceiling. Large pieces of fur hung off its stained body and it was missing one glass eye.

Nothing ever changed much at the Bayside Tavern. The same clientele were always there at the same hours, sitting in their same spot and in the foggy haze of smoke and beer, they could share memories and opinions without judging or being judged.

Harry, the bartender waved. "Hey Hank, where the hell you been, haven't seen you in a coons age. We sure miss you around here."

Yeah sure, wouldn't bet on that. Miss my beer money is all. "How you been Harry? Do you mind if I use the phone?"

Harry nodded and motioned towards a phone at the end of the bar. "Getcha a drink buddy, for old times sake?"

Hank shook his head and moved along the bar towards the phone.

Harry followed along with Hank. "What you think of the body being found at the old Renaissance Mill? You know, I think they paved the floor on that maintenance building back in sixty-five. Imagine that body lying there for eighteen years."

"I don't know anything about the body. Hell, I was only thirteen at the time." He picked up the phone, dialed and reached Maggie's answering machine and left a message.

Harry was still standing watching Hank. "How do you think he died? Who would have killed him and buried him in that maintenance building?"

"I couldn't tell you," Hank shrugged. "I don't think the cops know who it is yet."

Harry poured a pitcher of draft beer. "What you think? Maybe it was those Sloan twins that killed him?"

Running his hand through his hair, Hank said, "Peter and Paul Sloan had nothing to do with this. They're just retarded, not killers. Their only crime is being different and that makes people uncomfortable."

Fuzzy Walstrom scraped the spots off one more instant game card and threw it on a large pile of used scratch tickets on the floor. "You got that right Duval, they are different and they do make me feel uncomfortable. Give me the creeps, they do." Look-ing directly at Hank. "How would you like them to be alone with your wife and kids?"

Coming from you Fuzzy, that's a real laugh. Back in high school, Fuzzy was one of the jocks and in the infathomable mind of an adolescent, picked Hank as a target for intimidation and threats. That was until Vic and Gino took Fuzzy behind the school and educated him on the consequences that would befall him if he continued. He stopped.

The sounds, smells and familiar sights flooded into Hank's thoughts and old memories welled up inside him. The years faded away and he was a young man again who found the bar a place to meet his friends after work or after hunting, have a beer or two, and discuss the latest news around Fairhaven.

Then Sandy's funeral. After the funeral, every memory, every discovery of something of Sandy's drove him back to the bar, not to socialize, but to bury himself in a bottle. He became a regular. He had his own stool right at the bar and others knew it. They would be sure that it was available for Hank whenever he arrived, and if not, they would politely move. Harry would have his beer ready before Hank could sit down.

On the two stools to his left, Fuzzy and his wife Mary spent their evenings drinking beer and munching on snack foods. While Fuzzy read the sports page of the newspaper or sat scraping spots off instant game tickets, Mary would sit and watch the soundless television in the corner. She was always ready to repeat her sad soliloquy about life to anyone who would listen, usually in whispers to Hank who was too polite to ask her about the large bruises that kept re-appearing over her face, until one night, he said to her, "He ain't going to change Mary, the only way you're going to stop it, is to leave."

On the other side of 'Hank's stool,' Bert Nappi spent night after night in deep conversation with the other stool denizens, Wally Kotaanen, Carl Martin, and Helen Hauser, discussing the local obituaries, who was sick, and who moved into a nursing home. When that was exhausted, they would talk gossip about everyone in town. When that became uninteresting, they would make up new rumors.

Hank shook his head. *Just about anything to keep from going home and enough beer to help make it through the night.*

"Been doing any sketching lately?" Harry asked, uncapping bottles of beer.

"Haven't had a chance. I been too busy with the cabinets for the Huron Mountain Club. Pretty big job."

"Yeah sure, guess it would be. That must be something, working up at that club with all those snooty people. I guess the place is pretty exclusive, eh?"

"I couldn't tell you, I just go in, do my work and leave. The members don't seem to be stuck up."

"Well, ain't it true that it was so exclusive that Henry Ford was black-balled and not allowed to join?"

"No," Hank said, "Henry Ford got in and built a small 40 room cabin for himself and his wife. Cost about $100,000 back in 1929, and the heck of it was, that when it was finished, Ford didn't like it."

"Phew, must be nice to be rich. But if you do some more sketches, you can bring them in, we can sell all you have. Especially during deer season."

"I'll see what I can do, but can't promise anything." Hank had thought of his drawings and paintings as nothing more than doodling, but Sandy had convinced him to bring some of his work to the bar and to his surprise, people bought it. When Sandy became sick, Hank put the art supplies away. Then, when Maggie used his sketches for her article in the national nature magazine, he had to think that maybe there was something to his talent. He made a mental note to see what art materials he had and find some time for getting back to it.

A quick look around the bar, and except for Fuzzy Walstrom, all the people at the bar were new faces who Hank didn't recognize, members of a younger generation who thought they found the way to cope with the harshness of life.

A young man was sitting on Hank's old stool with a number of beer bottles on the bar in front of him. *Scary how much the young man looks like me when I was there.* The face already blotched from the beer and a glazed look blocked out the reality of living a life that was going nowhere. It frightened Hank to think of how close he came to oblivion on that stool.

Harry opened two beer bottles and put them on the bar in front of the young man. Then motioned to Hank. "Can I get you a cup of coffee or anything?"

Hank shook his head, he wanted the coffee, but now he needed to get out of the bar, the memories were becoming too heavy.

Harry had the look of someone who wanted to make a point, and with a thin smile, asked Hank. "What you think of the decision to kill the trash project at the old wood products mill? People in town sure could have used the jobs at the Trash Company."

Every head in the bar turned towards Hank, but before Hank could answer, Harry continued, "Them environmentalists sure blew it, ruined our chances to get some jobs up here." There was a good deal of malice in his voice.

The young man sitting on Hank's stool played with his beer bottle. "Them out-of-towners screwed things up. They just waltzed in here and started to tell us how to live our lives." The young man did not need to say it; everybody in the bar knew these out-of-towners were Hank's friends.

Another voice spoke up from the end of the bar. "Yeah,

that don't put food on the table."

Fuzzy was off his bar stool and standing right in front of Hank. "I betcha you made sure you're gonna get some sweetheart deal out this." Then looking around at the other men, "Duval here, sold us out for his buddies over at that STORM project so he'd get all the work at that art place. Just you watch and see, he's gonna come up smelling like roses."

Hank had to turn away from the smell of beer on Fuzzy's breath and ignoring the urge to argue and feeling the need to leave, Hank headed for the door. "See you around Harry."

"Good to see you Hank, come back soon." Harry called after Hank, knowing that Hank probably would not.

Hank opened the door letting out a large blue cloud of cigarette smoke and walked out into the clear cold evening air.

The truck turned over slowly, but didn't start. Hank sat in the truck taking deep breaths, the muscles in his body hurt as they constricted against the cold. The vision of the frozen hunter came back into his brain. *Who ever said that freezing to death was a nice way to go.* Reaching behind the seat, Hank took out a can of starter fluid. With the hood up, he was unscrewing the air cleaner when Fuzzy Walstrom staggered his way across the parking lot, a beer in hand, towards a brand new pick-up truck.

"Whatsa matter Duval? That piece of shit won't start?" His face turned into a nasty grin. "That thing was a piece of shit when your old man had it." Fuzzy stood watching Hank remove the air cleaner. "That's about the only thing your old man was able to hang on to, never could hold down a job."

Hank felt the anger taking over. "You should talk Walstrom, you couldn't hang onto your wife and kids."

The grin was gone, Fuzzy's face had transformed into a snarl. "Yeah, and I'll betcha I know who put that bug in her ear." His head cocked to one side, Fuzzy was trying hard to focus.

THE LAST DEER HUNT

It burst out of Hank. "Fuzzy, did you ever think that maybe the reason she left is that you're always drunk and you kept beating the crap out of her?"

Fuzzy's mouth dropped open, then mouthed, "Fricken asshole. You're still an asshole." He took a step forward and stood within a foot of Hank, holding his keys in Hank's face. "You'd better be careful Duval, you don't have your buddies with you tonight to protect you."

Hank reached out, grabbed the keys and tossed them into the woods beyond the parking lot. "And you shouldn't be driving tonight. Drunken asshole."

Fuzzy came around with a right hook that missed Hank's head by a foot, his momentum carried him around into nearly a full circle where he weaved back and forth before falling back on his buttocks.

Nine

Hank sprayed the starter fluid into the carburetor, got back into the truck and pleaded with it to start as he turned the key. The engine turned over slowly, finally responded. Hank replaced the air cleaner and closed the hood.

As the old pickup moved out of the parking lot at the tavern, Hank checked his rear-view mirror. Fuzzy had fallen back on his rear-end and was sitting in the middle of the parking lot looking towards the spot where his keys were last seen.

As he drove along towards Fairhaven, the talk back in the bar about the body and the Sloan brothers bothered him. The word murder made him shudder, as if he touched or tasted something very repugnant. A sudden movement caught the corner of his eye, and he instinctively slammed on the brakes. The brake pedal hesitated for an instant and went all the way to the floorboards. The truck continued forward without slowing, straight towards the large doe crossing the road. In one bound, she was across the road and was gone.

Pumping the brakes had no effect and Hank's body

THE LAST DEER HUNT

tightened as the large buck emerged at the side of the road unsure if it should follow the doe. Hank stepped down hard on the emergency brake and turned the steering wheel hard to the right; the truck swerved onto the shoulder, grudgingly slowed down and came to a stop. Hank sat bathed in cold sweat, his whole body aching from stress.

Taking deep breaths to relieve the tension, he watched as the buck with its large rack of horns slowly sauntered across the road stopping long enough to paw the ground and snort at Hank before disappearing into the trees at the far side. Slowly he got out of the truck and stood looking at it. *What the hell else can go wrong with this thing?*

Standing in the cold dark night, headlights of another car approached and he found himself being drawn back to this same place in an earlier time and thoughts filled his mind, memories that he had not allowed himself to think for a long time.

Hank let his mind travel backward in time to April 2nd, 1979, the night of the 'Second Annual Hawaiian Luau' at the Bayside Bar and Grill. Back to that night when his whole world came crashing down.

The restored '57 Chevy was in perfect condition and Sandy and Hank had just moved into his parent's house which had been vacant since Mom died. Sandy loved working in her flower garden and she was in high spirits. Her rug weaving business was up and running full time. Woven rugs filled the house and UPS and FEDEX trucks were constantly coming and going.

It should have been the best of times, but Sandy was too busy with all her work and new friends and I was angry and upset that she didn't have time for me. So angry that I couldn't see the changes happening in her.

Sandy suggested, well, insisted, that they should go to the Luau at the Bayside. She always liked everything Hawaiian and her room was decorated with all types of trinkets from the islands. Her favorite was a small charm bracelet with little gold figurines of hula dancers.

That night, everybody had come to the Bayside to dance to Bobby Dingleburt and his Wildwood Trio, but mostly they came to have a chance to win the lottery, an all expense paid trip to Hawaii! The Pelletier's had won it the year before and when they came home they held a show complete with slides and keepsakes from the islands. It always had been Sandy's dream that one day she would go to Hawaii.

Sandy had dressed in the red dress that she only wore for very special occasions. *Cut a little too low*, Hank thought, *but God she was beautiful in it.*

They sat in the booth talking about movies, politics, weather and Sandy's rug weaving business. Hank knew Sandy had something on her mind, but she would only talk about it when she was ready.

The tavern was decorated with paper Hawaiian flowers and birds. Large cardboard cutout figures of Hula girls complete with grass skirts taped on were scattered throughout the barroom. A giant poster of Elvis from 'Blue Hawaii' had been set up near the dance floor and crepe paper banners and balloons covered the ceiling.

Harry banged on the gong at the bar and announced that the raffle tickets for the vacation in Hawaii were not available and were being replaced with four tickets to see the Calumet Players performance of Verdi's 'Falstaff.' His announcement was greeted with howls and boos from the patrons, accented by bottles and glasses banging on tables, signaling the mood that would prevail through the evening.

When the announcement was made about the raffle change, Sandy became withdrawn, quietly sitting in the booth drinking her Mai Tais. The sounds of the Bobby Dingleburt and his Wildwood Trio filled the barroom overdriving the speakers to distortion.

After shouts of "Too loud," "Turn it down," and "Shoot the bum."

THE LAST DEER HUNT

Harry responded with, "yeah, yeah," and turned down the volume until the distortion and music were almost unnoticeable.

"Hank, why'd they cancel the tickets to Hawaii?" Sandy asked, heavy sadness in her voice. "I was hoping we would win. I wanna go to Hawaii. Would you please take me to Hawaii?"

"You got to be kidding, right?" Hank responded sharply. After a moment he added, "You know how much it costs to go to Hawaii?"

Sandy was glaring at him. "Yeah, about the price of another used pickup truck or another damn hunting rifle." She said, swallowing the rest of her Mai Tai in one gulp and slamming the glass down.

Hank was about to argue with her, tell her that a hunting rifle did not cost as much as a trip to Hawaii, but something in the way she was looking at him told him not to. Sandy was angry and getting angrier.

"Hank," there was a noticeable slur in her voice, "There's something we need to talk about."

The band broke into an almost unrecognizable version of 'Unchained Melody.' Hank stood and took Sandy by the hand, "Come on honey, our favorite song. Let's dance."

As they danced slowly in the dim light, Hank could feel the tensness of her body against his and he moved away from her so as to see her face. Even in the dim light of the dance floor, he could make out the tears on her face, "What is it Hon?"

Sandy stood, biting her lip, then shook her head and turned away, just as the the dance floor lit up and a gong sounded announcing the Luau had started.

As the music started to the strains of Don Ho singing 'Tiny Bubbles,' people in plastic grass skirts and leis moved onto the dance floor, attempting to perform a hula, moving back and forth to the music without rhythm or reason.

Hank took Sandy's hand to lead her off the floor, but she pulled him back, "Come on Hank, Let's do it." They slipped into plastic grass skirts and leis that someone handed to them and Sandy started dancing.

She flowed to the music, looking at Hank, imploring him to dance. When Sandy swayed to, Hank swayed fro, and as hard as he tried, his hips would not move to the music. Although he could see nothing through the smoky haze and glare of the spotlights, but he knew every eye out there was watching him. Touching Sandy's hand, he motioned towards their booth. Sandy stopped dancing and glared at him. Just as she started to speak, the record stuck, repeating 'bubbles' over and over. The crowd was now loud and drunk, throwing popcorn and other snacks onto the dance floor. 'Bubbles, Bubbles, Bubbles,' now the people were chanting it. 'Bubbles, Bubbles, Bubbles.'

The dancers were milling around the dance floor, 'Bubbles, Bubbles, Bubbles,' Hank took Sandy's hand, "Come on, let's get the hell out of here." 'Bubbles, Bubbles, Bubbles.'

Harry was on the floor, checking the sound system, and a large mass of wires. "Hold it justa damn minute, I think I found the problem!" A sudden flash of sparks emitted from the wires and the bar plunged into total darkness.

Hank pulled Sandy along as he went to their booth to get their things. "Come on, we're out of here." Grabbing her coat and purse, he led her out the back door and into the night.

Shoving the Chevy into drive, they roared out of the parking lot just as the tavern came alive with light and noise. *Shit, I hope she doesn't puke in the car.* As the car hit the pavement of the road with a loud squealing of tires, his anger turned to Sandy and he looked over and saw she was slumped against the passenger's side window sobbing convulsively, tears flowing down her cheeks.

"I'm sorry Hank, I'm so very sorry. I just thought it would be so nice to go to Hawaii, just the two of us, somewhere beautiful..."

Watching her, he couldn't hold on to the anger.

THE LAST DEER HUNT

"Honey, we can't just do that. You know we can't afford to go to Hawaii, not right now, maybe some other time."

"There is no other time, Hank." She was looking at him, mascara and tears running down her face. "I was hoping that maybe tonight we could win the trip to Hawaii, but they screwed that all up for us."

The Chevy was going very fast when the headlights picked up the large doe standing in the middle of the road, frozen in the glare of the lights. The tires screamed and left large black stripes on the road surface as the car came to a stop on the right side of the road. In two leaps the deer hit the crest of a hill at the side of the road and was gone.

"I gotta get out of the car." Sandy said, opening the door before Hank could stop her. Looking back at him, she screamed. "It's too late Hank, there is no other time. Don't you know? It's too fricken late!" She slammed the door and ran down the road in her red dress, high heels, hula skirt, and leis, tripping and falling as Hank followed her progress in the glow of the headlights.

Out of the car, he ran after her, panic filling him as he went. *What in hell was going on? What the hell did I do?*

Ahead, Sandy fell and was lying in the grass and mud at the side of the road. Hank knelt beside her, slowly and gently turning her over and cradling her head in his arms as she lay crying. "Why me? Why Hank, why me?"

The headlights of another car cut through the night, pulled over and stopped in front of Hank and Sandy. Hank heard the car door open and a voice from the other car calling through the darkness.

"Everything all right here?" Hank recognized the voice of Sheriff McCarthy coming around the front of the car, a large flashlight shining in his face.

"Yeah, no problem sheriff," Hank called back, "Just got sick."

The sheriff disappeared back into the darkness and the car door closed behind him. The other car hesitated as if the sheriff was trying to figure out if it was really okay to leave, then finally pulled away.

Hank just sat holding Sandy. "Hon, do you know how silly we look in these dumb Hawaiian grass skirts? It was lucky the sheriff didn't haul us in." He said, hoping that he sounded funny enough to cheer her up.

Sandy spoke softly, the words were so quiet that Hank could hardly hear her in the softly falling rain. "I'm dying Hank, I'm dying."

"Yeah, me too. It's really cold out here, I'll get you home, I promise."

"No Hank, I'm dying, I really am dying...Cancer."

"Come on, quit kidding, that's not funny." Looking at her face in the glare of the car lights, mascara mixed with mud, tears and rain, it seeped into his brain. *Christ, she's not kidding!* "Cancer?" *My god no. No, no, this can't happen!* Waves of every emotion washed over him and he could not make his body move. He could only sit there holding Sandy tightly. The tension in his body was building and his breath came out in large gasps and he was on the verge of exploding.

"Please dear God, no."

Ten

With those words still echoing through time, Hank was jerked back into the present by the glare of the car lights that had pulled up behind his truck. A car door slammed and Sheriff McCarthy appeared at his window with a large flashlight. "Got a problem Mr. Duval?"

"Brakes."

"You really should do something about that old truck." Sheriff McCarthy turned the flashlight off. "Can I give you a lift back to town?"

Hank got his fishing gear out of the back of the truck and sat in the sheriff's car, feeling the warm air blowing, taking away the cold that had settled throughout his body.

"Thanks, sheriff." Hank got his gear and walked towards his house.

"What the—" The small white dog surprised him. "Orphan! What the heck are you doing here?" He quickly looked up and saw the flicker of color on the porch. "Maggie? What are you doing here?"

"Are you all right Hank? I was really worried when I saw the sheriff's car pull up." Maggie had her usual sneakers and a long orange dress on, but she had worn a dark sweater to ward off the evening chill. "Frenchy called and mentioned you were fishing."

"Frenchy should stick to his cooking." Hank said feeling irritated.

They met on the stairs of the porch. "I didn't expect you to be this late." Then seeing the broken fishing rod, "What'd you do, try to kill the fish with your pole? It's all broken."

He held out the pole and looked at it. This had been his father's pole and his grandfather's before that. He was tired and his frustration level was rising. "It's only an old fishing pole. Who the heck cares anyway?"

Maggie moved close to him and looked him in the eyes. "Could be other people care." Then backing up, she wrinkled her nose, "You reek of cigarettes and beer. Where have you been?"

Hank shot an angry glance at her and snapped. "I just stopped at the Bayside Tavern to call you."

"Whoa mister, no need to bite my head off!" Hands on hips, Maggie returned his gaze. Then softly she added, "And I do care about you."

Her response caused him to hesitate. "Sorry about that Maggie, it's been that kind of a day. First, I fell into the river, now I'll have to get the truck in and the brakes fixed." Hank rubbed the stiffness out of the back of his neck, adding, "And I thought this was going to be my lucky day."

She was quick to smile. "It still might be. I have dinner on the stove and I will expect you in half an hour." She gave Hank a quick kiss on the cheek as she walked past him down the porch steps. "Hank, why don't you keep Orphan here with you and bring him when you come over?"

Hank reached up and touched his cheek where she had kissed him as he watched her slowly walk down the street towards her apartment. Orphan was running around him pulling at his leg, backing off into a stretched out stance and then attacking again. Hank stooped over and petted the small dog.

In the kitchen, he stripped off his clothes and threw them

in the washer. *Maggie was right, they did stink.* After a steaming shower, he made his way back to the kitchen and automatically started a pot of coffee. Sitting at the table in his shorts and T-shirt, he reflected on the day. So much had happened. The memories of the mill, the body, Gus, and Vic and the new revelations about Pa all kept running through his mind.

Orphan lay on the floor, ears back, and big eyes watching Hank. It had been a long time since Orphan and Hank were together in the house and the memories of Sandy flooded up from inside him pushing aside the other thoughts. Inside the small house, the memories were intense and sadness moved over him, his body heavy with grief.

Opening a cabinet door over the range, he pulled down a bottle of Jack Daniel's Sour Mash whiskey that had been in there for over a year unopened. The urge to open it was strong. He wiped his mouth, could almost taste the whiskey, and knew that it would give him peace, if only for a very short while.

"Damn Sandy! Why didn't she didn't tell me she was sick? How come she waited so long?" His hand tightened on the bottle cap and started to turn it. His anger shifted from Sandy to himself. "And where was I when she needed me?" The anger in his voice sent the little dog scurrying into the bedroom, toenails scratching against the linoleum. At that moment, the coffeepot blew out a great sigh and the smell of coffee filled the kitchen. The aroma seeped into the innermost crevices of his brain and brought Him back under control.

Opening the cabinet under the sink, Hank tossed the bottle in the trash container, then taking a cup out of the sink, filled it with coffee and sat at the kitchen table. "It's okay Orphan, come on out, it will be all right." As the dog warily returned, Hank stroked its ears and he let the thoughts of Sandy sweep into his mind, back to late May 1980.

Eleven

Sandy was sitting in her old blue denim dress with her legs under her, carefully planting multicolored pansies around a large maple tree. She was wearing the yellow and purple knit hat that Maggie had given her to cover the few tufts of hair that were left after her weekly chemotherapy treatments.

Sitting on the back porch, Hank put down the carburetor that he had been going through the motions of cleaning, but his mind was on Sandy.

Wiping his hands with a rag, he stood up, "How you doing? Anything I can do to help, or get for you?"

"Just fine." Sandy called back. Her little white Yorkshire terrier was at Hank's feet circling him and jumping up on Hank's legs. "Stay down Orphan, good doggie." Orphan had been part of her life ever since she found him nearly starved to death behind Maude's convenience store last winter.

"Good Orphan." Hank threw an imaginary stick that would have gone nearly over the old barn and into the woods, and Orphan was after it like a bullet. "Really smart dog you got here," he said, smiling at Sandy.

THE LAST DEER HUNT

She smiled back and took his hand as he came up next to her and their eyes met. *Those beautiful eyes, always so full of life and fun, where had the brightness gone?*

He closed his eyes and waves of feelings flowed over him. *This cannot be happening. When I open my eyes again, this will all be just a bad dream, and everything will be all right.*

"Watcha thinking?" Sandy broke through his thoughts.

When his eyes opened, nothing had changed, and Sandy was still sitting in front of him, holding his hand. Emotions forced their way up from deep inside his soul and he turned away, not being able to stand seeing her like this.

Hank watched a pair of Cardinals weave in and out of each other as they passed through space and time. "Sandy, are they really sure?"

"Yes," she was looking at his back, hoping he would turn around, "I been to the best, had every test done and get the same answer. It's already spread to the Lymph nodes. That's why they are doing the Chemo, hoping they can get it under control."

Hank shaded his eyes against the bright sunlight. "How about Mayo's over at Rochester, Minnesota? They're supposed to be very good."

"That's a really long ride Hank, I don't know if I could make that trip now."

"But we need to do anything...everything we can possibly do, we can't just give up." Needing to break the tension inside of him, Hank picked up another imaginary stick, this time he threw it completely over the house, and watched as Orphan flew around the side of the house, feet digging up grass and dirt. "You know yourself how lousy medical care is up around here. There's gotta be something else they can do."

Sandy looked at him, the resigned look on her face giving him his answer. "Hank, I love you."

He felt he would burst from feelings of powerlessness and frustration. This time he could not solve Sandy's problem.

Seeing the anguish on Hank's face, Sandy said, "Hon, I know you want to do something, to fix this for me because that's what you have always done, but this time Hank, maybe you just got to accept it."

She coughed a husky deep cough. "I can see how hard this is for you Hank, but right now, what I really need from you, is for you to be here with me."

"Something to drink?" He asked, hoping she would say yes, so he could leave, if only for a minute, to break the tension he was feeling.

"Yeah Hon, I think I'd like some lemonade."

Hank walked back to the house overcome by resignation and weariness. His feet were two dead weights that required all of his energy to move, and a large coat of lead was draped over his shoulders and was squeezing his chest. Somehow, he managed to pour the lemonade and bring it back outside.

"Please sit by me Hon." Sandy slowly rubbed Orphan's back. "How was your day?"

He slipped down beside her, wanting to tell her how he had messed up everything he tried to do today, but seeing her sitting in her funny little hat, hands dirty from planting the flowers, his day did not seem so important. "It was a good day Hon."

Standing, Sandy stretched her back, her hands on hips. "I hope so Hank, you deserve it after all you've done for me." With that, she opened the screen door and slowly walked into the house.

Hank stood looking at the door as the evening closed in around him and streetlights blinked on up and down the street. Finally, the tension lessened and he followed her into the house.

She was sitting in the dining room and had changed into the long flowing dress with white lacy trim that she only wore to special occasions. In the flicker of candlelight, on that night, she was the most beautiful person Hank had ever seen. He had to fight for his breath at the sight of her.

THE LAST DEER HUNT

She looked at Hank with sadness. "Hon, I'm going to let Maggie have Orphan."

"No Sandy, I—"

She silenced him with a hand gesture. "Maggie and I have talked about this many times."

Over his protests she continued, "Maggie loves Orphan, her cat loves Orphan and he likes them and Maggie likes to walk him, she's already started. I don't want him to be a burden to you, you don't have the time, and this will give you the chance to get that big hunting dog you always wanted."

Before he could speak, Sandy reached across the table and put her fingers to his lips. "Hank, that's what I would like."

Hank held back, not wanting to be argumentive. Then, gesturing around the house, "Let's fix this place up, you know, get some new wallpaper and stuff."

"Didn't I tell you this wallpaper is ugly?" She carried out the word ugly until she was sure he had gotten the message.

"Yes you did, but I guess I was too dense." But we can put in new appliances, maybe even a dishwasher." Hank stood looking around the house; it *would take at least a year to get this place fixed up.*

No response. Sandy and Orphan were sleeping. Hank lifted Orphan and put him into his small bed kept in the corner of the kitchen. Then he gently lifted Sandy and carried her into the bedroom.

He sat by the bed watching Sandy sleep, her breath labored. He knew he did not have a year. Within two months, the cancer had consumed Sandy, and she had died.

Twelve

The phone was ringing. Hank reached over, picked it up, and mumbled, "Sorry Maggie, I'll be right over."

Hank quickly dressed, grabbed his jacket, and opened the door. Orphan was outside, Hank right behind him. Shutting the door, he added, "Orph, I guess I'll never know if there was something else I could have done for Sandy, Did I push hard enough, should I have insisted on going to Chicago or Mayo's?"

The cool night air felt good on his face and he took a shortcut across the old Town Park as he walked to Maggie's apartment. In the dim lights from the street lamps, Orphan ran ahead and circled back around the large gazebo in the center of the park where the weekly music concerts were held when Hank was a young boy.

On the north side of the park, they walked past the ashes and debris that was once the old Union Meeting Hall. Gutted by fire, it stood vacant for years. Hank never liked the old hall, an ornate structure with ugly gargoyles in the front corners. It brought back memories of his father's long and bitter union strike. It had been a harsh winter and supplies of food and fuel were desperately low. That Christmas, the union reached out to the men and invited their families to come to the union hall where every family received a tiny chicken, oranges, and vegetables. Each child received a box of Cracker Jacks from old man McNamara, dressed up as Santa Clause and reeking of whiskey.

Hank welcomed the warm light from the second story bay window of Maggie's apartment. The window protruded out over Saari's Finnish Bakery and a small gift shop carrying crafts by local artisans. The Butler Block that housed the apartment and bakery had been renovated only four years ago, but time and lack of maintenance had allowed the paint on the trim to start the process of peeling and it was slowly catching up to the shabby buildings around it. Maggie's fifteen-year-old blue Volvo sat under the apartment window, still with California license plates. *Amazing it still runs, I don't think she ever changes the oil.*

The silhouette of Hemingway, Maggie's large Maine Coon cat sat motionless in the window watching Hank's approach. That was all Hemingway ever seemed to do.

Orphan stood by the door of the apartment; tail wagging furiously as Hank knocked. The door opened and Orphan disappeared inside as Maggie ushered Hank in.

She wore a pair of blue jeans, a man's old white dress shirt pulled out at the waist, and sandals. Following her into the apartment, the room smelled of garlic, herbs, and other aromas emanating from the kitchen. A Beach Boy's tape was playing on Maggie's very old stereo player.

"It'll just be a minute." She tossed her dark red curls out of her eyes as she headed back into the kitchen area.

Orphan jumped up on the cushion of the old stuffed chair that dominated the room where he greeted Hemingway with a lick of the tongue. Hemingway backed away in disgust at this sloppy intrusion. Happy to be home, Orphan danced around Hank alternating with his paws stretched out in front of him and dancing in circles with his wagging tail straight up in the air.

Hemingway sat on the back of the chair watching Orphan's antics with a look that indicated this was beneath his dignity. As Hank moved around the room with Orphan, the cat followed his every move. Hank put on his best mock glare and stared back at the cat. As Hank moved near him, Hemingway's eyes narrowed to slits, the cat moved backwards and fell off the chair into an undignified heap. Hank broke out into a loud series of laughs.

"Sounds good to hear you laugh, you should do it more often."

Surprised, he did not realize he had laughed; he took his coat off and put it on the chair.

"You can change the music if you like." From Maggie in the kitchen, "And get the dishes from the hutch, please."

The dishes on the table, Hank flipped through the large collection of tapes. "You really need some new music around here, you know."

"Change it to whatever you like." Maggie called from the kitchen. "What would you like to drink?"

"Water's fine." Hank replied, replacing the Beach Boys tape with a Bee Gees cassette. "What we having tonight? Tofu and bean sprouts?"

Maggie returned with a butter dish, a bowl of grated cheese, and a small loaf of French bread. "Pasta Primavera, but no meat."

Maggie put two napkins on the table, and poured herself a small glass of wine. Then, uncovering the steaming bowl with a sweeping gesture she said, "Dig in."

Hank took a second to survey the room. Candle light, music, good food set out nicely, and Maggie sitting across from him, her hair, and eyes catching the flicker of the candle, and wearing the silver blue heron pendent he had given her for her birthday last year. *Looks like a setup,* he thought, taking in the ambiance. A short feeling of skepticism moved through him but he decided he would just try to enjoy it. Maybe tonight they would not let something come between them. He looked at Maggie and smiled warmly. *It is going to be a very nice evening.*

THE LAST DEER HUNT

With cheese on the Primavera and bread buttered, Hank slowly savored his first bite when Maggie casually remarked, "Wasn't it something about the body they found in the maintenance building at the old mill, and can you believe they've already identified it?"

Hank nearly choked on the food in his mouth. "Damn, it's him, I know it is."

Startled, Maggie asked quickly, "Who? Do you know who it is?"

Hank swallowed quickly, "No...I mean I'm not sure...did they say who it was?"

"No, I didn't hear. Sarah said that the coroner was over from the county morgue and they identified the body. It's been there for a long time and they only said it was skeletal remains of a middle-aged man."

Frowning deeply, Hank asked. "But they didn't say who it was?"

"They said they won't release the name until relatives have been notified." Maggie said between bites. "Hank, you seem to be really anxious. Why are you so concerned about this?"

Hank felt the frustration. He looked at the room, the soft candlelight, the music, and Maggie sitting across the table. He knew the mood had vanished. It seemed it always did.

"Do you mind if I take Orphan for a walk?" He needed to be alone for a little while. "I could use some fresh air."

Maggie surveyed the half-finished dinner, stood, and in a gesture of frustration, said, "Yes, of course, why not?"

"Come on Orphan, let's get out of here." He grabbed for his jacket off the chair, found it was not there, took it out of the closet, and headed outside, the dog following along eagerly.

The cool night air felt good. Orphan was happy to be out, running in circles in front of Hank who kicked at an old beer can lying in the street.

Hank mimicked picking up an invisible stick and threw it across the empty lot towards what was left of the union hall.

Orphan was after it in a flash. Hank stood breathing in the cool night air replaying the evening in his mind. *Seems to be a pattern here. It begins with a nice evening; we start to feel close, then pushing away, finally separation. Damn!*

Orphan had returned with the invisible stick and put it at Hank's feet. Hank tossed the invisible stick and with orphan chasing after it, the two walked around town, going nowhere in particular and ending up back at Maggie's apartment. Feeling better, he put his coat on the back of the chair.

Orphan was back on his bed and Maggie came out with coffee for Hank and tea for herself. She had cleaned up all the supper dishes and a new Beach Boy's tape was playing. Hemingway watched Hank from his perch in the window.

"Feel better?" Maggie asked, "Are you still upset over falling in the river? Or is it about the decision to use the old mill as an art and music center?"

"Oh, the hell with that, everybody in this town thinks I'm a traitor, and you know, they're probably right. I wish the whole mill would fall into the river and the whole town could go in right after it."

Maggie turned and with hands on hips stared at him. "Brother, aren't we ever negative tonight. What's biting you?" Her look caused Hank to reconsider responding. Wiping down the counters, she continued, "It would do you some good to get more involved with this town. You have lived here your whole life and everything you have ever done is in this town. Don't you feel some sense of obligation to Fairhaven?"

Hank felt hemmed in emotionally. "To tell the truth, there isn't a heck of a lot about this town I would like to remember."

"Hank, if that's the way you feel, maybe you should just move somewhere else."

"Believe me, I've thought about it..." He was tired; the long day had caught up with him.

Maggie sensing it, asked quietly. "Want to tell me what

happened today? Did the lunker pull you under?" She leaned back, giving Hank room.

"Just fell in below the falls. I got caught on some branches and pulled myself out. I feel really bad about Dad's fishing rod, I don't think it can be fixed." His body was aching from the day, he was really tired, and he wanted to tell her about almost giving up.

Maggie moved over to him and put her left hand on his arm. "God Hank, that had to be scary, and that water is so cold! You were really lucky today."

It came out of him in a torrent. "Maggie, this is hard for me to say, but today, while I was in the water, I let go."

Maggie looked at him, unsure of his meaning. She held back pursuing the issue, allowing him the time to continue. She sat with her hand on his arm and waited.

Only occasional noises from Orphan, dreaming of chasing sticks broke the silence. Hank spoke, the words came out with heavy effort. "I just gave up. I gave up, let go, and was just floating down the stream. If I hadn't been hung up on that tree, I would have just stayed under."

Maggie took a blanket off the back of a chair and put it over his shoulders. She could feel him trembling. She sat next to him and put her arms around his shoulders, hugging him. "It's O.K. Hank, you were cold and wet. You know what that does to your body. All your body functions stop working."

"No Maggie, you don't understand, my body didn't quit, my brain did. I just watched my body float away and I just let it go. That was what was so scary." He started to tell her about Sandy in the river but the words trailed off.

Maggie held him. His body was shaking and he felt the cold of the river flood through his memory. What was scary now was that he had told Maggie, he had let himself be vulnerable, and he had taken a chance. He had opened up his soul and let her in.

In the warmth of Maggie's body against his and in the comfort in her arms, the coldness of the river slipped away and the feeling of vulnerability slipped away. Slowly he sat up, looked at Maggie, and said, "Maggie, I know who the body is that they found at the old mill."

Maggie moved around to where she could see Hank's face, but said nothing, just watched him, waiting.

Hank cleared his throat. "I have a story to tell. It's a long story that I must have blocked out of my mind for many years, in fact, it just started to come back to me after I heard they found the body at the mill, and while I was in the river, I guess what I had was what Frenchy called a flashback. I have never told this to anyone till now." He sat back, took a deep breath, and told his story.

It was back in 1965. A Saturday, August 22^{nd,} I think. With the exception of a few maintenance buildings and some offices in use in the main building, the old mill was closed and boarded up. It was a great place for kids to play around all the old buildings and all the old equipment.

I was thirteen, kind of a loner, hanging out at the mill by myself when I ran into the guys; you know; Gino, Bob, Ollie, Tom and Eddie. They were always hanging out together and called themselves the Omega Gang. I always thought they were really cool, but they didn't have too much to do with me. I was a year back of them in school and they thought I was too young for them, but because I could get them cigarettes that I could swipe from my Uncle, they would sometimes let me bum around with them.

It was a hot and sticky night and I had a couple of packs of Lucky Strikes, so they let me hang out with them. We were playing a game of cork ball when this Mr. Pettiford, Ronald J. Pettiford that is, came up to us and asked us if we would like to go up to his house for some burgers and use his swimming pool.

We had heard stories that some boys had accused Pettiford of trying to do something, you know, something inappropriate, but the sheriff looked into it and nothing was ever done about it.

THE LAST DEER HUNT

Anyway, we figured that with all of us, Pettiford wouldn't try anything, and besides, rumor had it that he would let us have beer up at his place. So we decided to go, well, the gang decided to go, but Gino said I shouldn't 'because I was too young. Anyway, after I pleaded with them, they finally let me go with them.

So we went up to the Pettiford house up on Mansion Hill, and boy, was it ever a mansion! It had more rooms than we could count, and a huge back yard with an Olympic sized swimming pool and a sauna.

It all started out innocent enough; we sat at tables with umbrellas and chairs out on the patio while Pettiford cooks burgers and hot dogs. He tells us to help ourselves to drinks in a big cooler. Sure enough, with all the cokes and sodas, there were cans of beer. Needless to say, the cokes and sodas were left in the cooler and it wasn't long until the guys started to act really silly and started roughhousing. Pettiford didn't say anything, even when Gino and Eddie pushed Ollie into the pool.

After we ate, Pettiford suggested we play a game of hide and seek before we went swimming to let the food settle. No, he said, we needn't worry, we wouldn't need swimsuits, and nobody would see us. Thinking back, we should have known better, a big red flag should have gone up, but the beer had definitely had an effect on our brains.

The guys scattered into the house and Pettiford sat with his head in his hands, counting aloud. I start to feel nauseous so I went to use the bathroom by the swimming pool. In the bathroom, I got sick, I mean really sick, like I had never been this sick in my life and I puked until I thought I was going to die. Finally, I went outside into the fresh air and I fell down by the pool and hit my head. Everything starts spinning around and I began to feel sick again, but this time, I think I must have passed out.

I heard a shot and woke up. I don't remember how, but I found myself standing in a room holding a rifle. In the dim light of the room, I could make out Eddie in a corner, curled into a ball, crying. There at my feet, Pettiford was lying on his back on a thick rug, a large red spot was forming on the front of his shirt, and his small beady eyes were open, staring out at nothingness from his fat piggy face.

I was trying to think, but my head was pounding; I felt the fear and panic race through me. I held the rifle out, looking at it, when Gino ran into the room followed by Ollie, each carrying a beer. "Holy shit, what happened here?" They both said as one.

"Shit." Ollie said, as he knelt down next to Pettiford and put his fingers on Pettiford's neck. "No pulse. Dead as a doornail."

"What the hell happened? Did you kill him?" Bob yelled as he burst into the room from a side door.

Before I could answer, Tom was in the room shouting. "I thought I heard a gunshot," then seeing the body, "Holy shit, I did hear a gun shot!

All four boys stood staring at me, "I didn't do anything, I just came into—"

"Help me, somebody help me." Eddie had pulled himself up into a sitting position. "That bastard tried to—" Then, seeing the body on the floor, whimpered, "Oh, God, what the hell happened?" Then Eddie, Looking around at the others, squealed, "Who did that? Who killed that bastard?"

"We ran into the room and Hank was standing with the gun in his hand." Ollie pointed to me, "Your face is all bloody, what happened to you?"

"I don't know, and I don't know how I got the gun." I yelled back confused, my head was splitting. I threw the gun to the floor and stepped back, staring at it.

"Come on guys," Tom stepped into the middle of the room, looking down at the rifle, "We need to think through this, we need to figure out what to do."

"Yeah, you're right," Bob said, moving next to Tom, "We got to figure out what to do."

"Well, we know who killed him." Ollie said, and all four boys looked in my direction.

"Oh no you don't," the seriousness of what was happening was quickly cutting through the confusion, "No way in hell are you going to blame me! Pettiford was already dead when I came into the room, and Eddie was over in the corner crying . . ."

"After what that that fat bastard tried to do to me..." Eddie's voice trailed off.

"Did you kill him?" Gino asked, staring at Eddie.

"Hell no," Eddie shot back, "I was trying to fight that big pig off when he suddenly stood up and yelled, 'What the hell do you kids think you are doing?' and then the gunshot.. I had my eyes closed and didn't see anything...That fat pig got what he deserved, but I didn't do it."

"Well, I know Tom and I didn't do it." Bob nodded at Tom.

Tom nodded back. "Yeah, we were together, hiding behind some suit of armor."

"And Gino and I were together," Ollie said, "and I know we didn't do it."

"Yeah, that's right." Gino said, walking over to Pettiford and giving the body a small kick.

Everyone jumped away, afraid Pettiford would sit up, but hoping he would, hoping none of this was real and Pettiford was not really dead.

Eddie had picked up the rifle and as we watched, put the gun to his shoulder, pointed it at Pettiford, and pulled the trigger. Nothing happened. Eddie took off the safety, aimed and fired right into the red stain on the chest of Mr. Ronnie Pettiford. The concussion from the exploding gunpowder hurt my ears and the smell of cordite filled the room. The boys stood with their hands covering their ears, their faces contorted by the shock of the violence caused by the discharge of a gun in a small, enclosed room.

"He won't do that to anybody again." Eddie dropped the gun. "Now you don't need to argue about who shot him."

"Jesus," Ollie dropped his beer bottle, "what the hell do

we do now?"

Gino took a long drink of beer, put the bottle down, picked up the gun, and ejected the fired shell casing. The others, realizing his intent backed away. Gino put the rifle to his shoulder, pointed it at Pettiford's chest, called out, "One for all, and all for one," and fired. The boys jumped again, but this time, from the revulsion of what Gino did.

"Now it's your turn." Gino ejected the shell and passed the gun to Ollie.

Ollie stared at the rifle, holding it cautiously, as if it were evil.

"Come on asshole, all for one and one for all, remember?" Gino took another drink of beer.

Staring at Gino, Ollie put the gun to his shoulder and said quietly, "One for all and all for one," aimed at Pettiford's chest and fired. The body jumped as the bullet ripped through the chest cavity.

I could not believe this was happening. I could only watch as Ollie passed the rifle to Tom who ejected the spent cartridge, pointed the muzzle at Pettiford's chest, and said quietly, "One for all, and all for one." He fired and the large body twitched again.

Bob walked over, took the gun from Tom, ejected the shell, said quickly, "All for one and one for all," and fired. Tom worked the bolt, ejecting the shell and stood holding the rifle towards me.

I was torn between the fear of joining them, and the fear of not going along with them. I grabbed the gun away from Bob and started to point it towards the body on the floor. Everyone was staring at me and the barrel was moving all over the place from me shaking so badly.

"Christ Hank, be careful," Ollie squeaked, "You'll kill somebody."

"That's a laugh," Tom said, looking down at the body on the floor.

Come on, we've waited long enough." Gino moved quickly and grabbed the rifle from me. "We got to get going, someone could have heard that shot and that fat bastard is going to bleed over everything." Gino gave me one last look. "Besides that, Hank already had his shot before we got here."

I was so angry I could hardly see. "No way in hell did I kill him."

Bobby shook his head. "Come on Hank, you were standing over the body with the gun."

"But, but, I know—"

"It's okay good buddy." Tom reached out towards me. "You know we would never let anything happen to you."

Before I could protest, the boys had moved into a circle around the body staring down at it

"What are we going to do with it?" Tom asked.

"We'll wrap him in that big yellow rug." Gino was now in take-charge mode. "Someone find something we can use to tie up the rug."

Everyone was moving, doing something. Gino had let go of the rifle, I took it and moved out of the way. The other boys moved towards Pettiford, and quickly wrapped him in the yellow rug, and tied him with cords from the drapes in the study. "Okay, we'll take care of the body," Bobby put his arm around me, "and you can take the gun and bury it in the bog behind the camp. Nobody would find it there in a million years."

I frantically crawled all around that room, found five empty shell casings, and put them in my pocket. Then with the gun, I left the house through the back door and ran non-stop the two miles to the bog. I dug down through the wet soil with a shovel from the camp. I buried the rifle and the spent shells and covered them up, and then I moved brush around so it wouldn't look like someone had just dug there. I did not ask, and it was two months before Tom finally told me that the body had been buried under the floor at the maintenance building at the old mill the day before the floor was covered with a thick layer of concrete.

Done with his story, Hank stretched trying to relieve the tenseness in his muscles. "The only thing that I can't remember, and it bothers me, is how I got to be in that room with the rifle and not knowing how I got there, or what happened. Until I know that, I won't know if I shot that fat bastard or not."

"Is there anything else you can remember?"

"You know, I do remember that rifle. It was a 1918 Mauser, a German military rifle. I recognized it because when I stayed with my Uncle Andre, he was a gunsmith and he would convert these military guns into sporting rifles.

"The only other thing was a small newspaper article that mentioned Pettiford was missing and foul play was suspected."

Hank and Maggie stayed locked in each other's arms, unaware of time, unaware of everything except their own breathing and closeness.

Hank could feel the warmth of her closeness and smell the fragrance of her body and he moved to face her. "Maggie, those nights when we were trapped in that shelter up in the mountains—"

"Hank, we been through this, nothing happened up there. We were just—"

"But Maggie, I would have let it happen, I wanted it to happen, if it wasn't for you...and it would have happened while Sandy was...I mean she had only just—"

"Hank, you have to quit being so hard on yourself. You weren't the only one tempted that night; I came very close to letting it happen."

They sat, locked in each other's arms, neither daring to move or wanting to break the mood. He was not sure when Maggie left the room or when Orphan jumped up on his chest and licked his face, but in the darkened room, he drifted off into a deep untroubled sleep.

Thirteen

Thursday, October 13th broke damp and gloomy with the high temperature for the day expected to be 45° and rainy. The gray flat light filtered through the big bay window of Maggie's apartment rousing Hemingway from his deep sleep. The big cat stood up, stretched to his full length, leapt from the window to the floor and up onto Hank's chest. One glaring look from Hemingway, and Orphan scrambled off Hank and onto his bed in the corner, head buried in his paws. The two animals had worked out who was boss.

Hank did not like cats. Well, not disliked, as much as did not really understand them. *They're too independent, kind of like Maggie in a way.* But Hemingway adored Maggie and Hank felt he should try to make friends with this big hairy cat with the tufted ears. Tentatively, he ran his hand down the cats back and was rewarded with a purr that sounded like a chainsaw. "So, does this mean we're friends?" Hank asked warily, putting out his hand towards Hemingway's paw.

Whack! In one move, the cat had swatted Hank's hand, glared at Hank as if to say, "Not on your life," and leapt to the floor and onto his windowsill.

"Guess you told me." Hank scratched his head, "Never will understand cats...or women."

The smell of coffee moved Hank to the kitchen where he found the coffeepot plugged in, a coffee cup, and a note: 'Gone to civic center to meet with Sarah, will meet you at Frenchy's around two. Love, Maggie. P.S., If you have a chance, please take Orphan for a walk."

The coffee cut through the fog in his mind and slowly he remembered the conversation with Maggie the night before. *The mill, the body, yeah...I gotta find out what's going on.* The adrenaline kicked in as he finished his coffee.

Quickly dressed, a short whistle and "Come on Orphan," and Hank and the dog were out the door. During the walk to Frenchy's, Orphan ran in circles ahead of Hank as they moved through the crisp cold of the late autumn morning.

"Okay dog, we're going to take a shortcut through the Town Park." Hank said and hurled an invisible stick out in front of them.

Orphan was after the stick like a shot and was back quickly, head down on his front paws, rear end up in the air, and tail straight up wagging wildly. Stopping in front of Hank, the dog dropped a large stick, about a foot long and an inch in diameter.

Hank picked up the new stick and tossed it, end over end, then watched as the stick landed near the town bandstand in the middle of the park. It had been years since the park echoed with the sounds of the Fairhaven military band and children playing freely and loudly in and around the gazebo. Now, the bandstand was in disrepair and covered with graffiti.

Hank scratched Orphan behind the ears, and said, "Let's go over to Frenchy's Orph, maybe there's something new about the body."

Hank tied the dog to a lamppost outside of Frenchy's Diner and went in. The diner was full. The aromas of cooking and cigarette smoke still hung in the air and Frenchy was working feverishly behind the counter. Today, his hair was hidden under a red beret. He seemed to be everywhere at once.

Hank was about to ask Frenchy when the new girl, Lucy, would show up for work, when the jingling bell hanging from the door announced the arrival of two new customers.

The taller slender man in a black leather coat removed his dark glasses and sat down in a booth just vacated. As he sat, his coat opened and Hank could make out the butt of a handgun holstered on the man's belt.

With him was a shorter, heavier man dressed in a wrinkled corduroy sports coat with a wrinkled flowered tie who carried his weight like a person uncomfortable with the newness of extra pounds. His face was puffy and splotched with red and had a day's growth of beard. *He drinks too much!* Hank knew the signs from personal experience.

The thinner of the two had a sculptured face and his darting, piercing steel blue eyes scanned the diner not missing a thing and locked with Hank's. Hank moved his gaze to the other man, but the heavier man focused on the antiques that hung haphazardly around the Diner. He looked like he would rather be anywhere but here.

"Lucy, come out here, we got customers!" Frenchy yelled at the door going into the back of the diner.

"Good Grief!" Hank muttered with his mouth wide open, holding his gaze on the young woman in her early twenties who burst through the swinging doors in the back of the diner.

A mop of straight orange colored hair, a ring through her left eyebrow and several more up both ear lobes had caught Hank's eye. She had on a bright yellow shirt and a very short orange skirt covered by an apron decorated with a blue and red image of the Eiffel Tower and numerous greasy accidents.

Hank had seen young people dressed in all sorts of odd clothes and hardware sticking out of every part of their bodies. On television in New York, L.A, and even in

Marquette, up near the college. But, *never in Fairhaven!*

As Hank swung around to look at her, the stool protested loudly. Hoping she did not see him with his mouth wide open staring at her, he quickly turned back to his coffee and noticed Frenchy looking at him.

"Hard to get good help these days," said Frenchy without further explanation.

Lucy was standing in front of the two men with pad and pencil at the ready. Her young expressive eyes scanning their faces.

"Got a menu?" Asked the thinner man looking at Lucy with an exaggerated sense of urgency.

"Yep." Lucy said slowly with purpose and smiled directly back at the man while pointing to the large board over the counter containing the handwritten breakfast and lunch menu. Nothing ever changed on the menu board, not even the daily specials. Located over the counter opening, it was surrounded on both sides by rows of old beer cans lined up on shelves recalling many of the local brewers which dotted the area for many years before finally giving in to the economic pressures of corporate America.

Lucy wrote quickly on her pad as the men muttered their orders to her. Tearing a sheet off the pad, she walked with an exaggerated swagger and hung it on a wheel located on the counter. She dinged the little bell next to the wheel even though Frenchy was watching her every move, then without asking, she quickly poured two cups of coffee and placed them on the table in the booth between the two men.

"Impressive." Hank observed. Then to Frenchy, "You were right about her being funky, but she sure is efficient."

The man with the leather coat and his partner were definitely not deer hunters.

Why would they be carrying a gun? Must be state police up here about the body. Oh boy, this is getting out of control.

Frenchy scooped piles of food on two dishes, put them

on the counter, and tapped the small bell. Lucy appeared from somewhere, picked up the dishes, and put them down between the two men in the booth. The leaner man watched her every move, the other man looking down at the table.

Sheriff McCarthy entered the diner, moved to the counter and draped his large frame over the center counter stool; center stage, polishing his badge.

"A very, very large fish in a small pond." Hank said under his breath as he nodded to the sheriff.

Homer Perrin, sitting in the booth fidgeting with anticipation, said loudly to anyone who would listen, "You folks heard the new information about the body?" His exaggerated nod emphasized that he was first with the news. He continued, "Yep, they think that body has been under the floor of that maintenance building for eighteen years, ever since they poured that concrete floor. That's something, eh?"

Pete Peterson, in his loud voice, added. "Yeah, we knew that already, that ain't new."

Stan Lubiwitz, sitting next to Homer added, "Yep, and I heard that he had been shot a whole bunch of times. I think it had to be a Mafia killing."

"Yeah, shot six times in the heart." Hank muttered quietly to himself, sipping on his coffee. Then, holding his breath, he quickly looked around to see if any one had heard him. Both Frenchy and the sheriff were staring at him.

"You say something Hank?" The sheriff eyed Hank suspiciously for a minute, and then puffed up with the weight of his title and looking smug with his privileged knowledge, he continued. "The victim was shot with a 7mm. Can't tell yet what kind of gun it was, ballistics is complicated stuff, you know." The sheriff's large jowls quivered with importance. Then looking directly at Hank, "Nobody said many times he was shot."

The man in the leather coat stood and motioned to the sheriff to join him. Sheriff McCarthy got up and moved slowly until he was face to face with the thin man. The sheriff did not look happy with the conversation, his face lost its confidence, and he started to seem confused, and then appeared angry.

Back on his stool, Sheriff McCarthy attempted to regain his composure. "I think that's all I can say about this situation, I don't want to screw up the investigation." He was staring at the thin man.

Hank leaned towards the sheriff but before he could ask, Andy McCarthy, talking softly explained. "Those two guys over there," pointing to the thin man and his heavy-set friend, "Are detectives from the Michigan State Police." His face dropped, "And they ordered me to cool it, you know, not talk about the case to anyone."

Pete Peterson's loud voice rang out in the diner. "Well, can you release the name of the victim?"

A hush fell back over the diner. The heavy-set detective nodded to Sheriff McCarthy.

The Sheriff stood up, with a renewed sense of authority, adjusted his gun belt on his large girth, and hooked his hands in his belt. "It was Mr. Pettiford, that's who. Yeah, it was Mr. Ronald Pettiford. All these years, everybody thought his disappearance was due to foul play, but nobody could prove it." A hush returned to the diner, each person looking around at everyone else to see what his or her reaction was. Hank tried to look surprised as Mr. Pettiford's face filled his mind. That fat round face with the little piggy eyes. *God he was an ugly human being.*

He looked up to find the thin state police detective looking directly at him. As soon as they made eye contact, the man moved his gaze to the others in the diner. Hank thought he could make out a thin smile form on the man's face. The stout man was writing furiously in a small notebook.

With the name of the body disclosed, the conversations in the diner turned to debates about who could have done this to Mr. Pettiford. The intensity of the arguments increased, no one listening to the others and theories becoming more convoluted as they built on each other.

The diner became quiet as the two state police detectives moved from their booth, left money on the counter, stopped, looked at the sheriff, and walked out the door.

Sheriff McCarthy sat upright and rubbed his hands together. He had again assumed his role as the person in charge.

The debate over who could be responsible for this killing was heating up again as every possible suspect was analyzed, accepted, or discarded.

Pete Peterson spoke loudly, "It's those two brothers, the crazy ones, Paul and Peter Sloan."

From an anonymous voice in a back booth, "Yeah, for sure, it's got to be those crazy twin brothers."

Kurt Hurla jumped in, "I still think it's that Vic Pollo guy, probably him and those other crazy kids that bummed around with him in that gang. They was always in trouble."

Hank winced uncomfortably at the mention of Vic Pollo's name in connection with the dead body and his own association with him.

"Still think it was a gangland killing, Pettiford musta been doing something with the Mafia." Stan Lubiwitz shouted.

From a back booth, "Coulda been that secretary, didn't she disappear at the same time?"

"Nah, she showed up over in Ontonagon. It has got to be them, the crazy Sloan twins." Pete Peterson boomed.

The diner fell silent. Everyone looked towards the sheriff. "What do you think Andy? Do the state police have any suspects?" Stan asked.

Slowly patting his 38 police special in its holster, Sheriff Andy said, "Yeah, we got suspects." Then glancing quickly at the booth vacated by the two State Police troopers and finding his authority again unquestioned, he sneered, "Can't say who they are right now, but you can be sure we'll find out whoever did this and get them."

All eyes turned to the front of the diner as the little bell on the door dinged and Lyle Burke, the part time attorney for Arvon Township burst through the door. "They're coming; they're all coming to town!"

"Who the hell is coming?" Frenchy had come out from behind the counter.

His question was answered when everybody tried to leave the diner at once to see a large truck with antenna apparatus and a Channel Four television station logo roar past.

Frenchy put the closed sign on the diner's door, then came around the front of the counter with a cup of coffee and sat next to Hank. Taking off his red beret, he handed it to Hank and mumbled, "Lucy's idea. She pointed out that it's a state law that cooks need to be wearing something on their head."

Lucy, still bouncing with energy and carrying an armful of papers strode over and sat next to Frenchy.

"God I hate perky," Hank and Frenchy said in unison. Lucy smiled at the men and Hank studied her face trying not to be obvious. He had not looked closely at her before. Her turned up nose and dark eyes made her look like a sensual pixie, the orange hair adding to the effect. Sitting next to Frenchy, she was sorting various business receipts and checks. The way she looked at Frenchy was more than business and Hank decided to see what Lyle Burke was doing. He moved to the end of the counter, but watched Frenchy and Lucy out of the corner of his eye.

After Lucy had put all the papers in neat piles, she put her hand on Frenchy's thigh. "Wow, did we have a great week, or what? I've never like, seen so many people in here at one time."

"Great." Frenchy replied with a wide smile, making no effort to move his leg or her hand. "We're doing great because of a dead man they dug up out at the old mill, go figure."

"Yeah, go figure." Lucy said, giving Frenchy's thigh a squeeze and a light kiss on the cheek. Gathering all the papers from the counter, she said, "And when we capitalize all our assets and take a write-off on the depreciation for the freezer units, we'll be in really good shape." She gathered up the papers from the counter and stood, "I'll put these away and I need to run over to Gram's for a minute. I'll be right back for the meeting." She whirled around causing the stool to scream, and with her short skirt and long legs, moved quickly towards the door.

"Yeah, nice." Frenchy said as they followed her movements out the door, her colorful mini-skirt swinging as she walked. As they watched her through the front windows of the diner, Lucy swung her long legs and short skirt into a rusty old Buick and roared out of the parking lot followed by a thick cloud of blue oil smoke.

Frenchy leaned back, deep in thought, then said slowly, "You know, at first I didn't think she would last a week, but now I think she could run this place."

Walking back over to Frenchy and leaning on the counter, Hank said. "Looks like she already is."

Frenchy shrugged, "You going to stay for the meeting on the mill restoration?"

"I gotta pass. I got too much on my plate right now." Hank's thoughts had already drifted back to the policeman in the diner with the gun and to the body at the mill. He ran the night of the shooting repeatedly in his mind. *Except for that ugly dream, I guess I had shut this out of my mind for all those years. Those guys, my buddies, almost had me convinced I must have shot Pettiford first and I believed it because I was half drunk and couldn't remember what I did...If only I could remember what happened after I passed out until I was standing there with that rifle. If only I could remember.*

The bell on the door announced the arrival of Maggie and Sarah accompanied by Patti Culpepper. Besides being the town's self-appointed matriarch and only female Arvon Township board member, Patti was a real character. A very large woman, she usually dressed in bright colorful flowing dresses, sometimes accompanied by a large brimmed hat. She wore large color-coordinated horn-rimmed glasses on her round happy face. But, as Maggie had warned, "Don't let those looks deceive you, Patti is a brilliant and articulate woman and does not suffer fools gladly."

Hank headed for the door.

"Just where do you think you are going Henry Duval?" Maggie's voice cut through the diner like a knife.

"I got too much to do and I don't want to get any more involved with this STORM thing, it's already got the town divided, nobody around here wants this center."

"I think this area could use some culture."

Hank looked down the counter at Lyle Burke, the lawyer who worked for the township pro bono. A slightly plump young man in his disheveled navy pinstripe suit and red tie, Lyle was busy going through a large pile of papers. "Gosh Lyle, I didn't know you appreciated art?" Hank felt his words dripping with sarcasm.

"Frankly Duval, my minor was in fine arts when I attended college at Princeton University." Lyle rolled the college name around on his tongue, savoring it. Then looking directly at Maggie, he said, "and I have paintings hanging in the Albany Art Museum."

"Lyle, I am impressed." Maggie said.

Hank wrinkled his nose at her.

Frenchy quickly injected, "Yeah, well Hank has some of his sketches hanging in the township hall over in Skanee. Haven't you seen any of his sketches?"

"You mean those pencil drawings?" Lyle did not look up. "Yes, I have. They're quite...primitive."

"Well, I for one think Hank's artwork is beautiful." Sarah nodded.

"Whatever." Lyle said, returning his attention to the papers in front of him.

Hank leaned over to Maggie. "There is something about that guy I don't like. I just don't trust him."

"You're just jealous. You know you could do that too, if

you tried."

"Whatever," Hank answered, turning towards the door.

At the door, he turned and scanned the diner. "Look, if you folks want to work on the mill restoration, go for it. Just don't include me. Heck, everybody in this town thinks I'm a traitor for hanging out with you yuppie scum."

Everybody looked at Hank. "Yuppie scum?" They replied in unison.

Hank, seeing the people staring at him, started to laugh. "Yeah that's right, latte sucking, Cappuccino sniffing yuppie scum!" Then, more seriously, he added, "I don't think I could be much help, people around here think I've already sold out and that I don't care about them getting jobs. Heck, none of my old friends even talk to me any-more."

Patti was looking at Hank; the blue eyes blinked and grew softer. She put her glasses back up her nose and smiled at Hank. "We kind of put you in real conflict between helping us and siding with the folks from town. I think we need to let you figure out what you need to do without pressuring you."

The pent-up animosity in the room died away as Maggie nodded an understanding and the others followed. Sarah started the meeting with reports from various committees and the meeting turned into a steady drone of meaningless noise as Hank opened the door and walked outside.

Fourteen

A week had gone by with no new information on the body at the mill. Thursday, October 20th, and the morning's weather was pleasant, a large warm front continued to block the cold Canadian air from coming down. Today he would call his old buddies and make sure they would come up this year for deer season. *Hopefully, we could work through this and come to some resolution, and just maybe, I can find out one way or the other what really happened at Pettiford's house that night.*

Inside of Hank's cabinetmaker shop, it seemed colder than it did outside and he started a fire in the old wood stove that he used for heating with scraps leftover from his work. Hank started working at the cabinetmaking shop with his father after losing his own job at the mill when CMPC closed in 1971. Pa had struggled and the business had been neglected. With Hank's assistance, they managed to keep the shop open until they were able to win bids to refurbish the kitchens and bathrooms at the restoration of the Huron Mountain Club located up near Big Bay. Pa's health declined shortly after and when he passed away, Hank took over the whole business.

THE LAST DEER HUNT

Wood working machines and large sections of cabinets of all kinds filled the shop. Neat piles of walnut, oak, cherry and birch wood were stacked against the back wall. This was old forest, or virgin forest wood, prized for its very close grain, wood that was not found in second growth forests today. It was becoming increasingly more expensive and more difficult to find.

The room was warm, the coffee perked and poured, and Orphan was lying on his bed near the stove. "Well dog, I better get with it and start calling the guys. I got to make sure they get up here this year for deer season." He could feel the stress beginning to build, as it did whenever he had to do something he disliked.

Hank stretched, pushing the tightness out of his shoulders and neck, put on his reading glasses and dialed the first number on his list. While the phone made clicking noises, Hank thought about Ollie.

In high school, Ollie was the six-foot two-inch roly-poly Ollie, the happy go lucky Swede. Nothing ever seemed to bother him, everything rolled off his back. He probably had to learn how to cope by living with his seven sisters in that little house over on Thompson Street. Each sister blond, tall, and, God they were gorgeous. Hank sat back, trying to envision Ollie's sisters. *Britta, Ingrid, Johanna, Marta, Gerda, and...* He could not remember the other two. Every boy in school wanted to be best friends with Ollie just to be around the girls. For a quarter, Ollie would let his friends peek through a little hole in the sauna while his sisters took their baths. All of his sisters went on to college, three majored in music, two became doctors, and two became actresses.

Ollie hung around Fairhaven for six months after graduation when the draft caught up with him. After he got out of the army two years later, he moved to Detroit to find work in the auto industry. After knocking around for a couple of years, he finally earned a degree and went into social work and although he was no longer roly-poly, he still was one large boy.

Like everything else, Ollie did not take his hunting too seriously and had never shot at a deer since high school, seeming to be content to just come back, have a few beers, and share some time with the guys.

The phone clicked, "Hi, Ollie here."

"Hey Ollie; Hank Duval here. How's it going up in Duluth?"

"Hank, it's good to hear from you. We're having great weather right now, my vegetable garden is still flourishing, and it looks like a bumper crop of tomatoes this year if the frost holds off."

"And how's Katie?" Hank asked.

"We're still not married. She's getting nervous, thinks I'm just putting everything off, but I can't seem to find the time to even think about it. The Social Services Department keeps increasing my caseload and cutting our funding. I love the work, but it's starting to wear me down."

Hank could sense that life and time were taking their toll on Ollie. He was never the same after Vietnam. "Maybe it's time you slowed down a little."

"Yeah, I know, it's really been getting to me more and more. Seems I'm tired all the time, I'm putting on the pounds again, don't eat right, and I'm not getting exercise."

"Better start taking care of yourself, guy. Life's too short, you know."

"Yeah, I hear you Hank. But how are you doing? Are you still keeping up with your art?"

"Been really busy lately, but I've been thinking of getting back to it." Hank replied, "Been thinking of going over to the community college and take some courses after the holidays." *Yeah*, he thought, *I should do that.*

"Better start doing what you want Hank. Life's too short, you know."

"Touché Ollie. You are right. I'll look into it the first chance I get."

"That's good. You know you a have really great talent," Ollie said. "And how are Maggie and Frenchy doing?"

THE LAST DEER HUNT

"Maggie, Frenchy, and Sarah have formed a committee on the restoration of the old mill."

"That's good Hank, with all your knowledge of the mill and the area, you could really be a big help."

"Not you too, Ollie," Hank laughed, "You been talking to Frenchy or Maggie? Seems like everybody thinks I give a damn about what happens to that old mill." A moment of silence on the phone, then Hank said quietly, "I think you better make it back this year for deer season. They found the body at the mill..." Another pause, then added, "And identified it as Pettiford's."

A long silence, the only sound on the phone was air being slowly drawn into lungs. "You still there Ollie?"

"Yeah, Christ. When did all this happen?"

"They just found the body last week."

"Nobody knows anything do they?" Ollie said quietly on the phone.

"Not that I know of, but I think it' important that we get together and talk about talk about this."

On the phone, Ollie said. "Have you talked to any of the other guys yet? How do they feel about this?"

"No, you're the first." Hank heard another deep breath being taken into the other end of the line.

"Damn Hank, I was hoping this whole thing was dead and buried," another deep breath, "No pun intended."

"I did too." Hank said with a nervous laugh.

"I'll tell you what Hank, I'll drive over from Duluth, and be there a couple of days before deer season. I'll call you when I get there."

Hank would have liked to talk longer but Orphan was whimpering and scratching on the door to go out. "Got to go Ollie, it will be good to see you this year."

"Yeah, it will be good to see all of you guys. I'll get back to you when I'll be able to get there."

Hanging up the telephone, Ollie moved through his backyard garden filled with tomato plants. Even though he covered the garden every night to guard against frost, autumn had continued to be exceptionally mild and the climate around Duluth, moderated by the lake had resulted in the tomato vines hanging heavy with red fruit. The terraced garden, which covered half of the yard, teemed with large full plants of zucchini, squash, and eggplant. Pole beans climbed up and covered the entire length of the back fence. The garden was a place where Ollie could come after a difficult day working in the social services office. The difficult days were getting more frequent and it did not look like things would improve.

From his house, Ollie could look out over the dark blue of Lake Superior and Duluth Harbor. Two large ore ships were passing each other in the harbor, one coming in with a load of coal for the large Duluth power plant and the other leaving with iron ore from the Mesabi iron range.

Ollie had asked Katie to marry him with the hope they would live in this house, but Katie just finished her master's degree in advanced fiber optic design and there were no prospects for work in the Duluth area so she was looking elsewhere.

Autumn was the time of the year he loved, but too soon, the colorful fall season would give way to winter. Ollie could already feel the aching pain that signaled the onset of the crippling arthritis that would come with another harsh winter. But this was where his work was, and he loved his small home in the quiet suburbs of Duluth.

Ollie zipped up his jacket as a slight chill blew in from the lake, or was it the thought about Hank's phone call. "I guess this call from Hank had to come someday. It's almost be a relief after all these years.It's always there, on or just below the level of consciousness. Sometimes it comes back in the quiet of the night, sometimes as a flashback triggered by a word, a feeling, or a thought."

Ollie shook his head, thinking of all the conversations at the hunting camp in previous years. "Amazing, this whole thing hanging over our heads all these years and us guys couldn't talk about it."

THE LAST DEER HUNT

Katie's smooth voice broke through Ollie's thoughts. "Hey Honey, who you talking to out there? You really look worried, what's up?"

"Hank Duval just called to see if I'm going back to Fairhaven for deer season." Ollie leaned over and kissed Katie's cheek. "I told him I would be there." Noticing the envelope in Katie's hand, "What you got there?"

Katie held the letter towards Ollie. "It's from Sandia Corporation out in Albuquerque, New Mexico. I guess I did well on the interview and now they want me to go out to New Mexico to talk about a job." Katie said, watching Ollie for any reaction.

"That's great honey." Ollie shrugged as he propped up an overloaded tomato bush.

"Ollie, this is something I have to do. I need a life and a career too." Katie put the envelope back in her purse. "I will be flying out to New Mexico the week before Thanksgiving and then I'm going on to visit my mother in Denver. We had always promised each other we would take a trip to Australia and if we do that, we won't be back until the first week in January."

"Katie, I think you should do that. It sounds like it would be a great time."

"You know Ollie, with your job as a social worker, you can work anywhere, and you don't need to be in Duluth."

Yeah, I can work anywhere, but this is my home. "Katie, we'll talk about this when I get back from Fairhaven and you're back from your trip."

Ollie thought. *Yeah, we'll see what happens in Fairhaven, then for the first time I'll feel free to deal with my life back here.*

Hank's news came back into his head and the wind took on a sudden chill.

"We're expecting a killer frost tonight, Ollie, don't forget to cover the tomato plants."

Fifteen

Orphan was only one-step outside when he stopped and raised his leg. Back in the shop with the dog in his makeshift bed dreaming of chasing his new stick, Hank decided to call Eddie Mahoney next. Eddie always came back for deer season and a chance to see his buddies again, especially Gino, so convincing him to come back was not a problem. Dealing with Eddie's other issues could be a problem.

The phone was answered with a terse "Hello."

"That you Eddie...Hank Duval here. How are things up there in Toronto?"

"Hey Hank, what the hell's up, eh?" The Canadian accent was evident.

Hank thought he detected a slight slurring in Eddie's voice and checked his watch. 10:30 A.M. "Sorry to bother you Eddie, just called to let you know that we are planning to get together this year for deer season."

"Yeah sure Hank, I don't think that will be a problem. How's the hunting look this year?"

"Not too bad, seems like lots of deer. I went out to the camp and it looks in good shape. Everything will be ready."

THE LAST DEER HUNT

"Oh, by the way," Eddie said, "I don't think I have a gun this year. I think Trixy took it when we split."

"Tell you what, you can use the Remington 257 Roberts, and I'll use my Winchester model 68. I think I can still find bullets for it."

"Isn't a 257 caliber a little light for deer?" Eddie asked.

"No, not really, if you use a 150 grain bullet you have the same energy at 200 yards as the Winchester 308 and about twice that of a 30-30 Winchester and twice the velocity of either. Will that be okay?"

Hank waited and when there was no response from Eddie, said, "Eddie, listen to me, they found a body at the old mill today. They identified it as Ronnie Pettiford."

A crashing sound in the phone followed by a guttural "shit." More noises, then Eddie again. "Sorry about that Hank; I just dropped something...Geez, you sure about that Hank?"

"Yeah, they identified the body, found it under the maintenance building floor."

"Shit." A long pause, then in a low voice, "Yeah, I'll come back for one more deer season."

Hank decided not to ask Eddie if he was having a good day. "Have you been playing any gigs with your jazz trio? You sure could blow a mean saxophone."

Eddie paused as if to think about the question. "Nah, been too busy working, you know how that is, eh? Are you doing any more with your pictures? You sure could draw good."

"The same here Eddie, too busy." Hank decided against any more small talk. "So then I will see you on the 12th?"

"Yeah, sure. It'll be really good to see all you guys down there again, eh? It'll be good to be able to sit around and tell stories about all the great times we had when we were kids." Eddie takes a deep breath, his voice sad. "We were really tight, always ready to help each other, right?" Then more cheerfully, "We sure did some wild things, eh?"

"We sure did Eddie, we did some wild things." Hank

hung up. He was feeling depressed.

Eddie hung up the phone. "Bunch of assholes." The bottle had broken when it hit the floor. The room smelled like whiskey, he had cut his foot on the broken glass, and now it was bleeding.

Eddie was tired. He did not sleep well last night. The terrible nightmare had come back again, just as it did ever since that night. The specter had returned, slowly moving across the room towards the bed reaching for him as he slept. But he was not sleeping, he was awake, his arms and legs frozen to the bed in fear. Eddie wanted to scream, but the screams stuck in his throat. Only the daylight coming through the window broke the spell and allowed Eddie, soaked in sweat, to move away from the bed.

Slowly, yesterday returned to his mind. Eddie was the repairman at Olson's appliance shop, but old man Olson fired him when that bitch, Mrs. Butterrump complained that Eddie had shown up late to repair her clothes washer.

Or was it because I had left the hose off and the basement flooded ruining her precious antiques? No way! She was just pissed because she was coming on to me and I told that old hag to screw off. Damn women are all the same.

Eddie managed to get a small amount of whiskey from the broken bottle and strained it through his shirt to get rid of any glass.

"Jesus, now Duval calls to tell me about the body. Like, what the hell am I supposed to do about it? That asshole Pettiford got what he deserved. I better get back there so I don't end up being the one holding the bag." The anger was rising in Eddie's voice. "So much for this one for all and all for one shit. Where were they all when I needed them? I mean, I was the only one who...Shit; I don't want to think about that. They were all somewhere else and didn't even try to help me. It's like they abandoned me and they can all go to hell."

He sipped the last of the whiskey. "I'm glad they finally found the damn body. Now maybe the demons won't

THE LAST DEER HUNT

come at night. Now maybe I'll be able to get some sleep."

Eddie took his saxophone out of the case and slowly wiped it with a soft cloth. "We go back to Fairhaven this year and we figure out what we need to do to resolve this mess, and then we can all go on our separate ways. I'll tell you one thing, there's no way I'm going back to hunt after this year, it's going to be the last deer hunt for me!"

Eddie, his foot bandaged, found a half-full bottle of whiskey in the bottom of a kitchen cabinet and sat on the couch with his saxophone and between drinks from the bottle, Eddie blew sweet and sad. The blues wafted across the room and out the window. Somewhere out there, the demons waited for the music to end so they could return and resume their nightly reign of terror.

Sixteen

"Hey Guys." Maggie's voice and head appeared in the door and she entered the shop wearing a bright yellow rain coat and rain hat.

Orphan was in front of her in a second, proudly showing Maggie his prized stick. "Hank, how about lunch? I'm meeting Sarah down at Frenchy's to talk about the Arvon Township meeting."

"I've got a lot to do here; can I have a rain check?"

Maggie was looking at Hank, laughing.

"What's so funny?"

"You know, with your cute reading glasses and red suspenders, you look like Gepetto in his workshop. I would expect all the clocks to start bonging, and Pinocchio to come dancing out here at any minute."

"Yeah sure," He reached for his flannel shirt, "And you look like a giant rubber ducky!"

"O.K. Sweetie, I'll see you later. Are you sure I can't buy you lunch? One of Frenchy's greasy hamburgers maybe?" She made a disgusting face at the thought.

"I'll pass on that too. I think I'll just run home. I have

some left over chicken in the fridge. Would you take Orphan with you? I won't be able to walk him later."

"Bye, bye." Maggie said, following Orphan and his new stick out the door.

Hank watched her go and checked the clock. He sat looking at the phone and brushed his hair back. Taking a number from a small scrap of paper, he punched in Tom's new telephone number in San Francisco.

Tom had been Hank's favorite member of the gang, and had been the gang's conscience, always arguing with Vic and Gino about going too far. He could be funny but there was something different about him, sometimes he could be reserved and moody.

After five rings, the answering machine picked up and Hank left a message. "Hey Tom, this is Hank Duval calling from beautiful downtown Fairhaven. Hope you are well..."

Tom Peters stopped and looked for a moment down the street and took a deep breath. The recent rain glistened off the cable car tracks that ran down the hill into San Francisco Harbor. Each day he had to pause and reflect on how lucky he was to be able to live and work in this beautiful spot.

He unlocked the door and stepped inside the bookstore. The light on the phone answering machine was blinking, but Tom's attention was directed to the large basket on the floor below the cash register and the furry ball that transformed itself into a large yawn followed by a long drawn out MEOW!

"Good morning Tobias, I trust you slept well and the bookstore has been well guarded."

The large torti-shell colored cat stretched its full length, feeling that an answer to that question would be undignified.

Tom put the mail on the counter and pushed the playback button on the answering machine. Four messages played. Three were about the store and the fourth was from Hank Duval, Fairhaven, Michigan.

Apprehension filled him as he listened as Hank's voice

came through the speaker.

"Good Morning Tom, this is Hank Duval calling from beautiful downtown Fairhaven, Michigan. Give me a call when you get a chance. Something important has come up concerning a night back in 1965 and about the pact we made many years ago as a bunch of young kids. Something about 'All for one and one for all,' remember?"

The machine clicked off. Tom and Tobias looked at each other.

"Damn."

"Meow."

"This can only mean one other thing. Something that a stupid bunch of kids got mixed up in a long time ago, something I've tried to forget all these years."

Tobias looked at Tom with disdain, as if saying, "Boy, you humans sure can find more ways to complicate your lives."

"You got that right Mr. T. We go into debt to open this bookstore, we find out our partner Phil is dying of AIDS and we're struggling just to keep this place open. Now we have to deal with this thing from our past." Tom poured fresh water and new food into bowls. "You know Tobias, it was hell living in Fairhaven and being gay."

Tobias squinted, making his chirping sounds indicating his displeasure with something. "Yes, I know Tobias, that can't be as bad in comparison to you being fixed, but it seems all I ever did was deceive my family and friends."

"Meeeow." Tobias rubbed against Tom's leg. As if to say, "I accept you just the way you are."

"Thanks Tobias, you're never judgmental." Tom stooped down and picked up the big cat. "Yes, I think I need to go back this year. While I'm back there, I can see if Mom will talk to me now. She was so angry and hurt when I told her. She was so ashamed of me and I think she even blamed me for Dad's stroke and her having to live in the assisted living center."

"Meow." Tobias was rubbing his head against Tom

"You know cat, I've lived many years thinking there was

THE LAST DEER HUNT

something really wrong with me and I didn't understand what it was to be gay." Tom could feel tears well up in his eyes. "Phil taught me I'm okay, that I'm not a bad person, and now I'm going to lose him."

Tom sat back and took a deep breath. Hank's message evoked visions of the hunting camp, the worst characteristics of the male animal jammed into a small twenty by twenty foot smoke filled prehistoric cabin. A week dedicated to killing things and an excuse to get drunk, a week to tell bad jokes and all the arguing and bickering about issues that don't matter and never get resolved anyway. Damn depressing thought; *If Hank's message is about what I think it is, I will go back there this year, but we are sure as hell going to resolve this issue once and for all and God help me, this will be my last deer hunt.*

Tom's call back to Hank reached an answering machine. "Hello Hank, Tom Peters' answering machine here, talking to your machine. I got your call and I think I understand your message. I will be up there this year and you can fill me in when I get there. This year I will hunt using my Nikon 35mm with the 500-mm telephoto lens. It will be good to see you. Say hello to Maggie and Frenchy for me."

Tom hung up the phone, opened the door, stepped outside, and let the fresh cool San Francisco air flow through the shop.

Seventeen

Bobby Lindstrom's phone was busy so Hank dialed Gino Grappone's work number.

"Hello, you have reached Excello Electronics Corporation, the solution based company that keeps the customer first. We are sorry. All lines are currently busy, but please stay on the line, your call is very important to us." The robotic voice on the phone was followed by elevator music that sounded vaguely like 'As time goes by.'

After the third "Please stay on the line..." message, Hank put the phone back in the cradle.

Eleven O'clock. *Too late to start anything with the cabinets, too early to go over to the diner.* Hank sat back in the chair and pushed the coffee away. *Enough coffee, I'm starting to float.*

Thoughts of the last couple of days swirled through his brain at high speed but some of the answers seemed to hang just on the other side of the fog in his mind.

Gepetto! The thought of Maggie brightened the room. *Maggie thinks I look like Gepetto, I think I'll take that as a compliment.* Hank rummaged through old paint cans until he found a can of brown paint, went outside, grabbed a paintbrush, and stood in front of the graffiti covered bandstand on the town square.

The graffiti gone, Hank stood back. *Not too bad, the paint almost matches. The old place needs a lot of work, but it would be nice if they'd start having the Wednesday night band concerts again.* The cool air of autumn felt good on his face as he sat watching a typical Friday morning in Fairhaven, Michigan. "Yeah, with a little work, this could be a nice small town." Hank headed back towards his shop.

This time, Bob Lindstrom's phone answered on the second ring.

"Hi Bob, Hank Duval here, just called to ask if you plan to come back for deer season this year."

"Hadn't thought about it much lately Hank. We've got a lot to do around here with church and the kid's home schooling."

"Yeah, I hear you. How are Hannah and the kids?"

"They're all doing fine. Boys are getting big. Hannah and I are very active in the church; I might be in line for a ministry."

"Sounds great, and I'd like to hear more about it, but the reason I'm calling is to convince you to come back for deer season this year."

The tone in Hank's voice told Bob there was more than just a friendly request. Bob took a deep breath. "Sounds important. What does it have to do with?"

Hank was direct with his answer. "They found a body under the floor of the maintenance building at the mill, looks like it was Ronnie Pettiford."

The phone line was silent, then Bob said quietly, "Yeah, okay, I understand." Followed by more silence.

Hank did not wait for Bob's answer. "I can count on you then; you will be coming up, right? Oh, and just to let you know, it's going to be a media circus around here and there are some men from the state police up here investigating the body."

"I have faith we'll be okay, but I have to be honest Hank,

this is going to be the last deer hunt for me."

Hank listened to the dial tone, "Bobby, I think everyone agrees with you on that." He replaced the phone in its cradle.

Bob sat at a table holding the phone listening to the dial tone. He was trying to think of all the possibilities and outcomes. Putting the phone into the cradle, he thought, *I have spent many years preparing for the ministry. It is my whole life. I have put off accepting the ministry of the church because I have been living this lie.* Bob picked up a Bible from the table and holding it, said quietly, "Say to them that are of a fearful heart, be strong, fear not, behold, your God will come with vengeance..."

Hannah's voice pierced his thoughts. "*He will come and save you.* Isaiah 35:4-5." She was standing in the kitchen door watching him. "Who was on the phone, Bob?"

Bob put the Bible down on the table. "Hank, Hank Duval from Fairhaven."

Hannah looked at her husband with concern. She had not seen him look so worried in a long time. "Bob, do you want to talk about it?"

"Oh it's nothing, Hank just wanted to know if I would be up for deer hunting this year."

Hannah waited, and when he did not answer, she asked, "What did you say?"

Bob slowly stood up, walked around the table, and put his arms around his wife. "I said yes, but this is my last deer hunt."

"Why would you want to go? You don't hunt, you don't like to hunt, you don't drink, you don't even like to go to that camp, so why are you going?"

Bob stood holding his wife. "Hannah, this is something I need to do. I don't think you would understand."

"You know, when you say I wouldn't understand, I always feel like you are hiding something from me."

"It's a guy thing. It is about a bunch of guys who made a commitment to each other a long time ago. I know it sounds really silly, but we went through a lot together and I guess I feel obligated to be there."

Hannah backed up to arm length and looked at her husband again. It was time to stop asking the questions and to trust in her faith in her husband and in his faith. "It's O.K. Bob, Jesus will guide you," then smiling slightly, she continued, "Just make sure that Joshua's home schooling needs are taken care of before you go."

Bob managed a weak smile as Hannah left the kitchen. He felt relieved that Hannah had stopped asking him questions, but it bothered him that he had not been truthful with her. Softly he said to himself a quote from Numbers 32-23, "Behold, you have sinned against the Lord, and be sure your sin will find you out."

I cannot live with this lie on my conscience anymore. I must go back to Fairhaven and together we must work together to cleanse our souls and make peace with Jesus. I must do this and face whatever consequences arise. I just hope that through my faith in Jesus, I find the strength to go through with this.

Eighteen

Hank was going through the inventory of cabinet hardware for a third time and knew that he did not want to make this call. Gino was never his favorite person. "I never knew if Gino could be trusted," Hank thought aloud. "He was Vic's best friend and he was scary at times. But he had one hell of a sense of humor...and he was a good man to have on your side."

Hank emptied what was left in the coffeepot into his cup and dialed. It was already after lunch and he was hungry. But first, he needed to make this call.

He sipped on his coffee while the robot lady on the line kept repeating how important this call was and that somebody would be with him shortly. After eleven minutes, an automated operator came on directing Hank through a whole series of number sequences only to be given to another robotic lady's voice telling him that his call was important followed by nameless elevator music.

God, I hope I never buy anything from Excello Corporation and need to talk to anyone about it.

Gino stood up in his corner office and looked out over

THE LAST DEER HUNT

the sea of cubicles that covered the square block sixth floor of Excello Electronics Corporation.

The phone jangled and his nerves jangled with it. The voice of his manager, Harvey Wittier burst through the receiver. "Hey Gino good buddy, how you doing on the new budget figures? I'm going to need them by tomorrow at two at the latest."

Damn it. How the hell am I going to meet my new budget numbers? The stress made him ache. It made him tense and was building more and more as the office environment worsened. *How long would it be before they figure it out? Most of the time I don't even know what the hell I'm supposed to be doing. What did that shrink call it? Imposter's syndrome?* "I'll have them on your desk by the time you get in to work tomorrow. Have I ever let you down before, good buddy?" What Gino wanted to say to Harvey was that good old Harvey shouldn't have waited until now to ask for the budget. But no, he's been too busy sleeping with his secretary. *Did Harvey really think his wife believed that bullshit about a corporate meeting again?*

Harvey's voice broke into his thoughts. "I knew you wouldn't let me down Gino. Oh, by the way, that Chinese woman in your group, what's her name, Sally Liu? When you do your manpower budgets this year, you might keep in mind that she filed a sexual harassment charge against Razz. Just find a way to make sure the problem goes away. I know you can take care of it for us. See you on the golf course good buddy and we'll discuss this year's stock options." Harvey hung up without waiting for a response.

Gino just looked at the phone, his hand trembling, and slowly put it back on the cradle. "That lousy bastard. He's setting me up to fail. He knows I can't lay Sally off while she has the sexual harassment suit open against Razzaboni, and on top of all that, I have to let one of my two top people go. Damn, I lose both ways!"

Gino went over the list of engineers in his group again. He needed to downsize his department by two more people. He added Paul Simpson's name to the six others that he would let go. *Nothing personal, just business.* Paul wouldn't understand, he had worked here for six years and his wife just had an operation for breast cancer and they have two kids in college. "It'll be tough, but he can't take it personally." *What a laugh, of course he's going to take it personally, they all do.*

The stress in his back and neck was intense. The psychiatrist he'd been seeing wasn't helping, *She just sits there and asks how I feel about it.* Sitting back, his hands behind his head, the thought came to him and rolled it around in his head. The more it rolled around, the more he realized it was political suicide, and the more it appealed to him. "Screw this job, I've had it, and I don't care what happens." His face twisted into a weird grin and sitting forward, he rubbed his hands together and typed a note recommending that Sally Lui be promoted to the new opening in corporate marketing. In that position, she would work directly with Harvey, he would have to deal with her every day, and he will not be able to do a thing about it.

Gino giggled at the prospect. *Probably lose my job over this, but it'll be worth it. I just wish I could see that bastard's face when he figures it out.*

Marsha wanted a new Mercedes. All the other wives had new cars and God forbid, ours is two and a half years old. *Jesus, we can't even afford furniture for the new twelve-room house, we can't afford the new swimming pool for little Kristin who's only 2 months old and now, a car we can't afford.* "Screw it; I've had it with this job."

The phone jangled again and the papers flew out of Gino's hands in a convulsive spasm. He watched the phone suspiciously for several seconds before picking it up. "Hello," he said hesitantly.

"Hello Gino." Hank Duval's voice came through the receiver, "Hate to bother you at work, but I don't seem to have your home phone."

A great sigh of relief came from Gino. "Hey Hank, good

THE LAST DEER HUNT

buddy, I was just thinking about you. I was going to call you about deer hunting this year. I was up in Maine last week and stopped in a gun shop and you wouldn't believe what I found."

Probably not, Hank said to himself, *I thought there was no way to top that NATO assault rifle you brought last time.* "Christ Gino, I'm not sure I want to know."

"Come on Hank, take a guess."

"What is it this time Gino, an UZI machine pistol?"

"Nope, that's not a sporting weapon Hank, you know that. I found a real deal on a new Remington 7400 automatic. It's a 300 magnum caliber and I had a muzzle brake installed on a 24-inch barrel to tame the recoil."

Hank whistled, "I'm impressed Gino, but we have whitetail deer up here, not elephants or rhinos."

Gino was still talking. "Eight power telescopic sight too."

"Good work Gino, now all you have to do is see a buck at about ten miles with your telescope and you can knock him down with your artillery." Hank fought back the urge to argue with Gino. *Hell, he never shoots anything anyway.*

Gino did not indicate he heard the sarcasm. "Boy, am I psyched! Can't wait to get there."

"Got some news Gino, they found a body when they dug up the maintenance building at the old paper mill." Hank said, and waited.

A long silence, then a quiet, "Shit. Are you sure Hank?"

"Yeah, Ronnie Pettiford. They just identified the body." Hank waited in silence again.

Without thinking, pure reflex, Gino responded too loudly. "Christ, just what I need right now, up to my ass in alligators and you have to throw in another one."

Hank was surprised at Gino's strong response. "Sorry Gino, but this has come up and we need to deal with it."

"Yeah, okay Hank, I'll be there and we can fix this problem for you."

"My problem? Hell Gino, whatever happened to 'all for one and one for all?' I thought we were all in this together."

"Yeah, okay, but let's not do something stupid." *Hell, Duval was never able to do anything on his own and then he just fell apart when his wife died.*

"I don't plan to Gino. I think we'll need to figure this out together," Hank said bluntly.

"I will call you with my plans for coming out there."

Hank hung up the phone and looked at it. *Like, Gino's going to fix my problem?* He closed up the shop and walked across the park towards his house. He picked up the phone to call Maggie, thought about it and decided to spend a quiet evening alone. A quick lunch of chicken leftovers and he sat down to watch the news on television.

Hank had no idea how long he was sleeping in front of the television when the ringing phone woke him. "Hello." Hank said, trying to shake the sleep from his head.

"Hank? I'm so sorry to bother you. Beth Roberts here, I don't know if you remember me, I was a friend of Sandy's."

"Beth, yes," Hank said into the phone frantically trying to recall her face. "What's up Beth? What can I do for you?"

"You know my sister Christine, well, she's a nurse over at the clinic in Ironwood, and she called tonight to tell us that Vic Pollo was brought into the clinic today."

When it seemed that Beth was not going to continue, Hank asked. "What did Christine say?"

"Well, you know, she said Vic was killed."

Again, the long silence. *Killed?* It was Hank's turn to hold his breath and the only sounds were the droning of the television. Finally, when he could stand it no more, he asked. "How did Christine know it was our Vic? I mean Vic Pollo from Fairhaven?"

Beth surprised him with her quick response. "Gee Hank, doesn't everybody know Vic? Christine said she knew he was from Fairhaven. He lived in Ironwood for a couple of years and married a local girl. Seems his wife was in the clinic every week with some broken bones or a smashed something or other. I remember you used to hang out with him, so I thought I would call."

THE LAST DEER HUNT

"Thanks Beth. Do you know what happened?"

"Christine, she said she had heard that Vic went home one night completely smashed and I guess started to beat up his wife. She pulled out a gun and fired. One shot right in the head. She said that was the warning shot. Boy that's something, isn't it?"

"Yeah, that sure is. And thanks for letting me know."

"You bet. I hope that doesn't make you feel too bad."

Hank suppressed the urge to laugh at Vic's demise. "I'll check with the sheriff to see if Vic's Uncle Pasquale knows about this."

Hank still tried to remember Beth. Was she the very pretty petite blond with the beautiful smile who attended Sandy's funeral? He hadn't really known Sandy's friends very well. "How are you and your family doing?"

"Oh yeah, Butch and I have two kids now and Butch just got a new job over in Iron Mountain with that new electronics company, Excello Corporation. You ever heard of them? He does problem solving with customers over the phone and really likes it."

"I think I've heard of them." Hank thanked Beth again and hung up the phone. He turned off the television and sat in the quiet darkness with his thoughts.

Nineteen

Early Sunday morning, the 23rd of October and temperatures were expected to be in the high sixties. No one could remember it ever being this warm after Columbus Day. The week had flown by, and the work out at the Huron Mountain Club was starting to wind down and money was flowing in.

The bright sunlight streaming in the kitchen window warmed the room, but also accentuated the wear and age of the cabinets and appliances. Hank shook his head. *This place is really in bad shape.* In the living room, the wallpaper glared at him. *Ugly, this place is really ugly.* The furniture he kept from his parent's house stood around the room looking old and threadbare and clashed with itself and everything else in the room. The dark trim paint made the house feel oppressive. *Just can't seem to find the time.* Hank ran his hand through his hair. *Maybe it's time I do something about this.*

Back into the kitchen with his coffee, the only sounds were the ticking of a clock, the low hum of the refrigerator going on and the clanking sounds as the warm water ran through the radiators. As he sat listening to the quiet, the

THE LAST DEER HUNT

loneliness closed in around him. *Since Sandy died, nobody's really ever been inside the house.* He shook his head at the thought, opened the kitchen window over the sink, and let the freshness of the clean bright air waft through the room. Taking a deep breath, a feeling of new energy moved through him. "No, not later! Now! This week, I'm going to start this week. First, I'll see what I have for cabinets at the shop, I'll get over to Marquette and see about a new stove and fridge and look at some wallpaper. Maybe Maggie could help pick them out."

Outside, the sun felt good on his face as he stood looking back at the house. It had been his parent's house all their lives before he and Sandy moved in. Many lives, many memories lived in this house, but it was old and needed a great deal of work. The inside was just the way it was when Mom lived here. Sandy had done a great job in the yard and it had looked beautiful, but now had gone back to seed. *Next spring Sandy, I promise, I'll get to your garden.*

Inside, Hank found a sketchbook and his box of drawing pencils and after a quick detour through town to stop at Margaret's pasty shop, headed towards the river, and the millpond.

The red and gold leaves of the maples were gone, only a few of the russets and browns of the oaks remained on the trees. *Better enjoy this weather,* he thought. It was only a matter of time before the first Alberta clipper came roaring down from Canada bringing heavy snows and the frigid temperatures that marked this part of the United States as one of the coldest and snowiest areas in the country. Millpond Rock was actually a group of large boulders rising along Huron Bay just above the dam across the river from the Renaissance Mill. The county had put picnic tables around the area and it was a place where families would take their children during the day. In the evening young people would come for private moments of romance.

The large pond and mill across the river dominated the landscape. Looking south across the pond, the town of

Fairhaven with its tall clock tower, fire station and harbor lay quietly along the Slate River. Big willows with long flowing strands of yellow danced in the slight autumn breeze as families walked along the tree-lined riverbank heading for Sunday morning services.

Hank took out his sketchbook and pencils and as he drew, he sat out of the wind in a small niche between two boulders enjoying the warm sun, lost deep in thought. *Not a bad little town, it still has a lot of opportunity.*

"Want some company?" Frenchy was standing behind Hank with a pair of six packs of Budweiser. Dressed in his usual army style T-shirt and army style camouflage pants, he wore heavy-framed dark glasses that hid his eyes.

"Glad you came." Hank said and passed a brown paper bag to his friend, "I brought us some pasties and ketchup."

Frenchy sat down next to Hank, unwrapped a pasty, opened a can of beer, and put the remaining cans in a small pool of water.

Hank put his sketchpad and pencils away, unwrapped his pasty and took a bite, holding it in his hands, poured a good amount of ketchup on the end and took another bite. He poured a cup of coffee from a Thermos he had brought with him, took a sip, and made a face. "Not very hot." Shading his eyes from the sun so he could see Frenchy, he said, "How's it going?

"Can't complain. How about you?"

"Could be worse."

"You're doing some more sketching, I see."

"Yeah, I'm so out of practice. I've been thinking of looking at some art courses at one of the local colleges in January, but..." He let it trail off; the eagerness to keep up with his art was dampened by doubts about his own ability. It seemed that others were more enthusiastic about his sketches than he was. "I guess I'm my own worst critic."

"Everybody is. Very few artists are ever happy with their work. Maybe if they were, they would have nothing more to strive for. I think you should accept the fact that people think you are really good and go with it."

"Thanks Frenchy, I'll work on it. And what's new with you?" Hank finished with the pasty, crumpled up the bag, and put it in a trash container.

Frenchy started to say something, but changed his mind. "Women."

"Sarah?" Hank looked at Frenchy, looking for a reaction, but not being able to read anything behind Frenchy's sunglasses.

When Hank did not see any sign of reaction, he asked, "Lucy?" Still no reaction, he asked, "Both?"

"Something like that." Frenchy opened another can of beer.

"Something like burning the candle at both ends?" Hank offered.

"Something like that." Frenchy repeated.

"So what's with Lucy? I didn't think she was your type. Kinda young too, don't you think?"

"There's something about her that fascinates me. It's like she's in control of her life. She is like, so aware of herself and who she is. She's into Buddhism and she's like teaching me mediation and all kinds of new things. But, it's not like I'm in love with her."

"If it's not like you love her, then, what is it like, you know, like, like you like her?" Hank said, laughing at his own spoof. "Geez, you're even talking like her now."

"Give me a break." Frenchy laughed. "She's just great to be with."

"And what about Sarah?"

"She's kinda put out with me right now, but we're still talking and we want to be friends. I guess I wasn't ready for that deep of a relationship right now. There are some other things I've been looking at. Lately, I've been thinking about Vietnam quite a bit...it's been twenty years and...Nah, it's not important."

"You know, you never talk much about that, Vietnam, I

mean. What was it like to be over there, to be a Green Beret? Were you a hero?"

"I'd rather not talk about it. It's gone, it's past, and it's over, okay?"

"Okay, Mr. LaRue, okay. But what about Sarah...and Lucy?"

"When I was doing social work over in Sault Ste Marie. I remember in one of our group meetings, Cindy, a very bright, but troubled thirteen year old, said, "This ain't your practice life, this is it, the real thing and if you're not happy with it, you better change what you're doing, cause you're not going to get a second chance."

Frenchy continued, "It's not that I am totally unhappy with my life, but I feel there are still things I want to do and I'm not ready to settle down just yet. You know, like have my own job, my own house, my own car, my own wife and my own kid. I'm just not ready for that. Christ, I'm thirty-six years old, only four away from the big four-oh, and I don't know what I want to be when I grow up. Do you ever feel that way? Like something inside is not fulfilled?"

"Right now, everything is up in the air. I feel like I'm still dealing with the loss of Sandy and my parents, and now, my relationship with Maggie."

"Yeah, but Maggie is a good thing, right?"

"Yeah, she should be, but then the question is, is she going to stay? Is she going to leave? I don't have any control over these things."

"But you do have control over how you react to things. Have you ever talked to her about this?"

"I've been meaning to, I just haven't had a chance with everything that's going on around here now."

"Like what?

"Like this damn body showing up—"

Frenchy looked at Hank from behind the sunglasses. "You want to tell me about the body?"

Hank felt his jaw drop and could see his own startled reflection in Frenchy's sunglasses. "The body? You mean the body they found at the mill?"

"Come on Hank, I know you're involved with this body in one way or the other. It's written all over your face."

"I think the guys said something to me about something they may have seen at Pettiford's, but I—" Hank watched himself in Frenchy's dark glasses. *Shit, he knows I'm lying.* "Oh hell with it, here is what happened that night..." Hank went on to tell the same story about the night at Pettiford's that he had told to Maggie.

Frenchy let out a long low whistle and removed his dark glasses, "And you lived with this all these years?"

"Well, no, except for this recurring dream of an ugly face, which now I know is Pettiford's; I guess I had blocked it out completely. Most of it has come back now that the body was found. I just wish I could remember what happened between the time I passed out by the pool and when I was standing over the body with the rifle."

"So, my good friend what are you going to do now?"

"I contacted all the guys and they have agreed to come up for deer season. Then we'll figure out what to do."

"What's to figure? Shouldn't you just go to the police and tell them?" Frenchy finished his can of beer, crushed the empty into a small ball of aluminum, and opened a new one.

"I was hoping that we could re-construct the crime, maybe if we go through it enough, I can find out what exactly happened that night. I might be able to recall the missing pieces. It bothers me that I can't remember what happened between the time I fell asleep and woke up standing over the body with the gun. Besides, we kinda made a pact that we would all be in this together and we would resolve it together. We'll spend a week out at the hunting camp like we used to, that way it won't be suspicious."

A snicker broke from Frenchy. "Camp? You guys call that falling down dump a camp?"

"Hey, watch it; we fixed up that place ourselves!"

"That's obvious," Frenchy said, lighting a cigarette. "I hope you don't use that excuse for a camp as advertising for your carpentry business."

Hank started to correct him, but thought for a moment and said, "We all lived with this Pettiford thing too long. Maybe it's for the best that it came out. It's time to resolve it."

They sat looking out over the Millpond watching the clouds and sun play at making patterns of light and shadows over the town and the last few leaves of the year floated downward on the slight breeze.

Frenchy was smiling at him, "I gotta get going, and I'm out of beer." Then seriously, "If you need any help at all, I'll be here."

"Yeah, thanks Frenchy, and good luck with your women problems."

Twenty

"Hank, come in, it's really cold out there." Maggie held the door to her apartment open. "Just how long have you been waiting?"

"About three or four minutes," he lied. He was shivering and his teeth were chattering from the cold.

Once inside her apartment, Maggie started a pot of coffee, an automatic reaction when Hank came over. "Why didn't you wear your heavy coat? God, you guys have to be so macho! You'll never admit you're too cold."

Hank ignored her comment. "I was feeling lonesome at the house. You know, it really needs a lot of work. I'll probably end up re-doing most of the place."

"Tell you what Hank, I'll be more than happy to help you pick out whatever you want." Maggie hesitated, hiding a small grin. "And we could buy some new kitchen cabinets."

"Maggie, that's what I do, I make cabinets, I am a cabinet maker.

"Gee, really?" Her grin widened.

"Yes, really, I can make much better cabinets than you can buy." Hank could feel the irritation in his voice.

"Just teasing. I know yours would be better." Maggie's face lit up with a smile.

Hank felt its warmth from across the room and felt bold enough to ask. "Maggie, why'd you stay in Fairhaven so long?" He was sitting on the floor, Orphan on his lap. "I knew you came up to write an article on the lynx, and then the moose over in Michigamme, but I thought you would leave after that one. But now you stayed to do the story on the wolves."

Maggie paused, went to the kitchen and returned with a cup of coffee for Hank and a large glass of red wine for herself, as well as the bottle. She was wearing a faded white and blue University of Michigan sweatshirt easily three sizes two big for her and a pair of men's gray lounge pants. Her hair, pulled back, was held with a large clip. She was curled up cross-legged in the big overstuffed chair that dominated the small living room. Hemingway was on her lap in one leap.

Maggie slowly stroked the big cat, "I thought about going back after Sandy died, but Sarah needed a lot of help with the mill restoration project and my publisher asked me to do the story on the wolves. They paid well for the article on the moose and sent a healthy advance on the wolf story."

"Do you ever miss California?"

"Yes, yes I do. God, I hate the thought of winter this year. It seems like it lasts forever up here. Just one big gray snowy long, long winter." She shivered and tucked her feet under her. "I miss the warm weather and sometimes I even miss the noise and the hustle and bustle. But what I think I miss now is just being able to walk down a beach..." Her sentence faded off into deep thought, the only sound was Hemingway, purring loudly.

Hank smiled, "Yeah, and all those loonies out in L.A.? How can that possibly compare to all there is to do in Fairhaven?" The sarcasm was greatly exaggerated.

"Loonies in L.A?" Maggie's abruptness startled

Hemingway, "How about ice-fishing, snowmobiling, or deer hunting? God, I never did understand ice fishing! You guys sit in that little shack all day watching a hole in the ice. Even if you catch one of those little perchy things, you can't eat it anyway, it's full of bones."

"Perchy things? Wow, that's really good coming from a nature writer." Hank smiled at her. "Anyway, it has nothing to do with fishing, and everything to do with drinking beer. It's the greatest excuse there is to drink beer."

"Hank Duval, when does anyone up here need an excuse to drink beer?" Maggie waved her hands in the air in an exaggerated air of disbelief. "And then there is snowmobiling! What a sport! Spend a couple of thousand dollars to buy this huge toy, strap a six-pack on the back and run into a tree at fifty miles an hour, then spend thousands of dollars in medical bills, or a funeral. Then there is deer hunting. Thousands of armed beer drinkers running around the woods with big guns shooting at anything that moves. No thanks, give me L.A. with its loonies anyday. At least it's warm."

"Wow Maggie, why don't you tell us how you really feel about the U.P.?"

Hank and Maggie exchanged smiles, the room fell into silence and Hemingway returned to Maggie's lap. Hank watched Maggie as she sat stroking the large cat, taking in small nuances he hadn't noticed before. A tiny scar beneath her left eye, holes on her ears that once held earrings, small reminders of her life before he met her. "You know Maggie, I've known you for over three years now and I don't think I really know very much about you at all."

"I don't think," Maggie said, seeming far away, "that I really ever talked very much about myself."

Hank sipped his coffee, waiting for Maggie to continue.

She sat slowly petting Hemingway. "I think I'm finally over it. The relationship, I mean."

"Relationship? What relationship? You don't mean our relationship?"

"Brandon."

"Hah, it is about a man. I thought so. I wondered why such an intelligent, beautiful woman like you was still running around single and hiding up here in Fairhaven."

"Well, yes and no. Yes, there was a man. Brandon. A handsome, very bright young man who had, I mean, has everything going for him, he was one of the leading nature photographers in California. He did a lot of work for National Geographic and we worked together on a number of projects. Well, to make a long story short, it turns out that he was fooling around with one of my best friends." Maggie poured herself another glass of wine. "I couldn't face my friends, my world had turned to shit and I had to get out of there.

And no. I took the assignment to do the magazine article on lynx, met Sarah and Sandy, stayed to do a follow-up story on the moose, and as they say, the rest is history. And I think I have fallen in love."

Hank felt his heart skip a beat, but remained silent.

Maggie continued, "Yes, I've fallen in love with this country and the people. The people are the kindest, most wonderful people in the world."

"So what do you think you'll do? I mean about moving back to California?" *And what about us?*

"Honestly Hank, I don't know. There are so many things to think about, my job, my career, you—"

"Me?"

"Yes, you lunkhead. Of course about you, I mean us. I have to consider us also. It would be so much easier if you were to move out to California, go to school there and we could be together."

"Or, you could stay here, Maybe?"

"I know Hank, but all my life I've had this dream. I want to write for The National Geographic's magazine, and I can't do that from here."

"Yeah, I understand..."

"Don't you have any dreams? I mean like with your art?"

THE LAST DEER HUNT

"Maggie, I haven't really thought that much about art since Sandy died. I've tried getting back to it, but it's really been hard."

"Hank, promise me you will keep working at it. And really think about california, okay?"

"But, my art isn't that good."

"Promise me Hank, promise me that you will try and work at it."

"But—"

"Promise?"

"Yeah, okay, I promise." *Yeah, but there's a long way between trying and being really good at something.*

"Thanks Hank, that's all I ask, just try." Maggie was up, "I'm hungry." She took two pieces of leftover pizza from the fridge, heated it, and they ate in silence.

Maggie broke the quiet. "Is your sister Diane still in California? She seems like a really wonderful person. I met her at Sandy's funeral and I would love to see her again."

"Yeah, that was the last time I saw her too. She's still living in California, north of San Francisco. After she had a big fight with Mom and Dad over going to college, she left home to live with an aunt in Ohio, then went to college down there. Anyway, Diane kept me up on her life through post cards. They went something like this:

" 'Accepted by Kent State University, will start this fall.'

" 'Changed major to Psychology.'

" 'Graduated! Moving to Chicago.'

" 'Met Mr. Right. Life is beautiful.'

" 'Getting married, hope you can make it to the wedding..'

" 'Working for University of Chicago Medical School.'

" 'Getting a divorce. Turns out Mr. Right's first name was 'Always.''

" 'Moving to San Francisco. Doing sculpting.'

" 'Moving to Mt. Shasta to do pottery.'

" 'Met Miss Right. Life is beautiful.'

" 'We have a small place on a river and are thinking of

starting a family.'"

Maggie sat petting Hemingway. "Why don't you ever go out and visit her?"

"Don't know. I guess I never felt that I was that close to Diane, she always had her own life. She didn't come back for Dad or Mom's funerals. Not that I blame her. After they passed away, I found all the letters Diane had written them, unopened."

"I never met your parents. I believe your father died in 1976, the year before I moved here and your Mom died the following spring.

"Yep, Pa passed away in November, 1976." Hank was sitting on the floor. Orphan came over and laid his head on Hank's lap. "Pa was inconsiderate enough to die and have his funeral during deer season. All the men came to the wake in the afternoon directly from hunting still dressed in their hunting clothes. While dad was lying in his coffin, everybody stood around drinking coffee and discussing the morning hunt. Who saw a deer, did the deer have legal antlers, who shot at what, and all of the ones that got away. Everyone was quiet during the homily, but as soon as they closed the lid on the coffin everyone left to go back to hunting."

"I don't think they meant to be disrespectful Hank, in fact, I would think that was just what your father would have wanted."

"You know Maggie, I didn't even cry at his funeral. I was so angry with him about everything."

"That's O.K. Hank, that happens to a lot of people, they just have to have time to grieve."

"But it's been a long time since he died. Shouldn't I have gotten over this by now?"

"Not if you haven't dealt with it, Hank. You really need to talk about it and deal with it before you can move on." Maggie moved over and sat next to him. "If you ever want to talk about it, you know I am here."

The apartment was quiet again, Hank sat on the floor

slowly scratching Orphan's ears. He was hoping that Maggie could not see his eyes blur as pent-up emotions gave way and he finally found the tears for his father's funeral.

Maggie watched, but chose not to go to him, allowing him to be alone with his thoughts.

Time passed slowly, the only sound was Hemingway's intermittent purring. Hank signaled he had reached a level of comfort by standing and stretching.

Maggie moved over to him and embraced him. "How would you like to take Orphan back?"

Hank rubbed his eyes and looked at her, trying to understand what she was saying. "Why? He seems really content right here with you. Seems like he's worked out a territorial treaty with Hemingway."

"I meant if I should move back to L.A." Maggie was looking down at her feet.

Twenty-One

What did she mean, if she moves back to L.A.? Then after she had dropped that bombshell, she didn't want to discuss it so Hank decided to walk home.

Sleep came hard, tossing and turning until nearly three-thirty. Maggie's comment stuck in his mind and the intensity of his feelings surprised him. Anger over her leaving, frustration and a sense of helplessness over not knowing what to do, and deep sadness from just the thought of losing her.

When sleep finally did come, the dream was back, more vivid than usual. The vision from the grave wouldn't be stilled and for the first time, he could make out the face in the dream as a little piggy face with the small beady eyes. Pettiford! And a gunshot. Then slowly, Hank shook off the sleep and stood up to face the day.

He mullled the dream over in his mind as he managed to get down a couple cups of coffee and some cinnamon toast. *The gunshot was part of the dream.* He found the cleanest clothes from the pile of laundry at the foot of the bed and got dressed.

THE LAST DEER HUNT

It was nearly one-thirty when Hank arrived at Frenchy's Diner. Although it was near closing time, the diner was quite full. He did not recognize many of the people. *Can't blame the regular customers for staying away. Between the reporters and the curiosity seekers, no one has any privacy left.*

Lucy was in high gear, "Hey Hank, you just missed Frenchy. He just left." wearing a Frenchy's Diner apron over a knee length red skirt, red blouse and her red beret.

"He left you to take care of the place all by yourself?"

"Yup. He won't be gone long." With a sweeping gesture, she asked, "What do you think?"

Looking up, all the old beer cans were gone, replaced by framed pictures of Parisian landmarks. Hank frowned.

"Yes, you're right." Lucy shrugged. "They aren't really appropriate here." Then with a twinkle in her eye, she added, "I would love to put up some of your artwork in here."

"I'm flattered Lucy, I'll see what I have laying around."

"Okay, dokie, that would be like, really great." Lucy was off, waiting on a customer.

Hank finished his coffee and called to Lucy, "Guess I'll head over to the shop. If Frenchy comes back, have him give me a call."

As Hank walked out the door, the lady reporter from Channel Four pushed her way next to him, followed by her cameraman. "Hello, Mr. Duval, my name is Karen Casey, may I have a minute of your time before you leave?"

Before Hank could answer, she had a microphone near his face. "I hear you have lived in Fairhaven all your life, is that true Mr. Duval."

Hank looked at her. She had been the third reporter to approach him in the last two days. At first, he had tried to be civil with them, to answer their questions, then he saw himself on the evening news and what he had said packaged into other interviews that lead someone to perceive Fairhaven as some sort of sordid Payton Place.

"Yes, that's correct."

"So, Mr. duval, what can you tell me about Mr. Pettiford." The microphone waved almost against his face.

"I'm sorry miss, but I really don't have anything to say."

"But surely you must remember Mr. Pettiford? He was one of the area's leading citizens, was he not, Mr. Duval?" She moved her face within inches of his face. The smell of her perfume overwhelmed him and he moved away, feeling awkward with the closeness.

"No, actually, I don't." Hank realized he sounded angry, but right now, he did not care. He just wanted the lady to go away and leave him alone. "Pettiford didn't have anything to do with mill workers."

"What about the kids? Didn't Pettiford hold parties up at his house for young boys?"

Hank looked at her. "I'm sorry lady, I have to leave now." As he walked away, he heard the reporter say to her cameraman, "I think Mr. Duval knows a lot more than he is saying." The cameraman was busy rolling up cables. "We'll see him again."

"Hank, can you wait up a minute?" Sheriff Andy McCarthy was moving his heavy body down the street in Hank's direction, his gun belt around his wide girth was pulled down by the weight of all the little pockets and gadgets hanging from it. "Wait up a minute, got to talk to you."

What the hell now, Hank thought, still irritated by the lady news reporter. He had to shade his eyes against the brilliant sunlight, "Oh it's you Andy," he waited until the sheriff was able to breathe again. "What's up?"

"Thanks for waiting Hank," Andy McCarthy said, gasping for breath. "Gosh Hank, looks like you could use some sleep."

"You chased me down the street to tell me that?"

Sheriff McCarthy wiped his face with a handkerchief. Even on this cool day, the sweat rolled down his face. "Hank, would you mind coming down to my office for a few minutes, Mr. Smith and Mr. Powers from the State Police Crime Investigation Unit are investigating the murder and they would like to ask you a few questions. Do you know them? They just about live at Frenchy's Diner."

"Yeah, I saw them at the diner." *And was not looking forward to seeing them again, especially the one with the lean face.*

The short walk to the sheriff's office did not give Hank the time he needed to try to rehearse his answers. Sheriff McCarthy's office was a messy combination of electronics and paper scattered around in random piles.

The thin man's slate blue eyes pierced through Hank's brain. "I am Frank Powers from the State Police Crime Investigation Unit." He was dressed in his leather jacket over a white shirt and tie. "This is Harold Smith." He nodded towards the man sitting at the sheriff's desk.

The disheveled man looked up from a large pile of papers and nodded towards Hank. He was still in his wrinkled sport coat and flower tie. He took a pencil out of his mouth and gestured towards a chair. "Thank you for coming Mr. Duval." The heavyset man's voice was deep and pleasant. "I'm sure you will be able to assist us."

Frank Powers continued to stare at Hank, his voice high and nasal, his words were crisp and articulate, the tone accusatory "This is just routine, we are talking to just about everyone and anyone in town. We're just trying to find out what you could tell us about the body that was uncovered at the mill."

Hank's immediate reaction was to deny everything, say as little as possible, and not to lie.

"Cup of coffee Hank?" The sheriff was pouring a cup from a coffeepot in the corner.

Hank shook his head.

The sheriff moved in front of Hank. "Could you tell what you know about Pettiford?"

"Excuse me." Frank Powers had moved in front of the sheriff, placing himself between the sheriff and Hank.

Power's voice carried no emotion or feelings. Sheriff McCarthy moved back behind his desk and sat down.

Powers moved close to Hank. "What do you know about this Pettiford thing?" The blue eyes locked with Hank's.

Hank returned the stare. "I'm sorry, I don't think I can help you. I never had anything—"

"Mr. Duval," the thin man studied Hank closely, speaking deliberately, "do you recall hearing of any parties at Mr. Pettiford's house?"

Hank hesitated, as if thinking. "What do you mean, parties?"

Harold Smith rolled his shirtsleeves to his elbows. "Parties, you know, like this Pettiford guy would lure boys up to his house for food and beer and to use his pool."

"I'm not sure I know what you mean?" He was starting to feel defiant, irritated with the questions.

"For sex." Frank Powers put his hands to his forehead in a gesture of frustration. "He would lure boys up to his house for sex."

Hank could feel all six eyes in the room looking directly at him. "Now that you mention it, I remember that some of the older boys did mention parties up there once or twice," *well, that was the truth, didn't need to lie on that one,* "but no one I knew would ever think of going there." *Well, maybe a little fib there.*

Smith sipped his coffee, "Hank, do you remember any names of the boys who mentioned the parties at the Pettiford place?" His rich, friendly voice belied the purpose of the question.

"I'm not sure, but you might want to ask a guy named Fuzzy Walstrom or some of his friends. They were real party animals." Inwardly Hank smiled, *revenge is a dish best served cold.*

Frank Power's face was very close to Hank's face. "Come on Duval, let's not play games. You're no goody-two-shoes. You used to belong to a gang called the Omega Gang and your leader was this bad ass, what's his name, Victor Pollo?"

Hank could feel Power's hot breath on his face. "We weren't a gang. It was just a bunch of us kids hanging out together."

"Hank, I mean Henry Duval was not a bad kid," Sheriff McCarthy said from behind the desk, "he just kinda run around with the wrong crowd for a while."

Frank Powers gave the sheriff a glaring look. "Yeah, right." Then picking up papers from the desk, his mouth formed a pencil thin smile. "Well, it looks like you and your gang-banger friends used to raise some hell. Your gang leader, Vic Pollo has a rap sheet a mile long and spent three months locked up in reform school for being a wise-ass in school. Then he was back in reform school for almost killing some woman in Duluth. That guy really got around."

"I can't help you with that, I wasn't there." *Geez, I didn't know anything about that. And that's the truth.*

"Yeah, I betcha you never were there when anything bad happened." Powers remained right in Hank's face. "And this one, stealing the final exams and passing them out to the students."

"Why would I want to steal them, they were eleventh grade tests, I was only in the tenth grade." *Heck, I didn't even know about that one, and that's the truth.*

Powers read page after page of charges against the boys in the Omega Gang. Fighting, shoplifting, breaking school rules, and many more. "What's this about the graffiti on the water tower?"

Hank put up his hand, "I wasn't up on that tower. I never painted anything up there." *No lies there.* He looked in the direction of the sheriff.

Sheriff McCarthy leaned back. "Duval is right about that. He was not up on that tower that night, but we sure nailed that bugger Pollo and the rest of that gang." The sheriff put a hand on the side of his head where remembered he had been kicked by Vic.

Hank could only sit, looking at his feet.

The thin detective stopped reading and looked at Hank, a tight smile on his face, and asked, "What's this? You tipped over Percy Twill's outhouse?"

"Yeah," Hank answered, "I guess we did do that. But it was supposed to be a Halloween prank."

Smith let a small laugh escape. "With Percy in it?"

Frank Powers pointed to the paper in his hand. "And this, Involved with the burning down of Paul Bunyon? What the hell is that?"

"That was an accident!" Hank shook his head, *That was the truth, sort of.*

"I'll bet." Powers sneered.

The sheriff lifted his weight into a standing position "Yep, whole thing went up in flames, fifty feet into the air." Then looking directly at Hank. "Was the God-awfulist thing." McCarthy was breathing heavy, "That statue was like the symbol of the lumber industry in this town. Never did actually find out who started the fire, but we had our suspicions."

"Yeah, looks like your gang were the leading suspects again." Powers continued to stare intensely at Hank.

Hank pointed to himself. "Wait a minute, I was the one who pulled that blue ox out of those flames by myself. Tell them, Sheriff."

"Yep, that's right."

"But doesn't it seem seem strange that you just happened to be right there when old Paul Bunyon burned down?" Powers finally turned and walked away.

The room was quiet as the three men looked at Hank waiting for him to answer. Finally, Hank shrugged, "It was an accident."

Harold Smith came over and put his hand on Hank's shoulder. "Maybe young Henry here was right, maybe it was an accident. Accidents will happen."

Frank Powers shook his papers at Hank. "Accidents hell! Larceny, destruction of property, vandalism, the list goes on and on. Don't you think it's odd that the guys you hung around with were always in trouble, but you seem to have never been there when trouble happened?" The thin man moved back towards Hank, speaking deliberately, "Where were you on the night that Mr. Pettiford disappeared?"

"I'm not sure, just what night was that?"

"Saturday, August 22nd, 1965."

"Gosh, that was soooo long ago, it's really difficult to remember."

"Eighteen years ago." Power's glared at Hank, frustration in his voice. "Weren't you hanging out with that 'Omega Gang' down at the old mill that night?"

"I wasn't a member of that so-called gang then." *The truth, nothing but the truth.*

Frank Powers and Harold Smith looked at each other and walked over to the coffeepot and poured a cup of coffee. Hank heard Frank Powers say, "We got us a smart ass here."

Smith answered, "Let me try."

Harold Smith moved over and placed his hand on Hank's shoulder. "Now Henry, you boys had access to guns?"

"Yeah, everybody does up here. Everybody hunts. They even close school during deer season."

"I understand, Hank," Smith smiled, "I can call you Hank, right?" Without waiting for a response, he continued. "You know anyone who has a 7mm rifle?"

"Yeah, lots of people. It was a very common hunting rifle." Hank realized his voice was sharp.

"Thank you Henry." Harold Smith backed up.

Frank Powers moved close to Hank, his hands nervously fiddling with a pencil. "How about your buddy, Vic Pollo, did he have guns?"

"Vic was not my buddy." *And that was the truth.* Hank pushed back away from Powers. "Like I said, everybody up here has guns." *True again.*

"It's just a simple yes or no question dammit." Powers stood up and threw the pencil onto the desk, his face twitched, the veins on his forehead sticking out. He glanced over in the direction of Harold Smith.

"Just a minute." Smith said, walking over into a huddle with Powers and the sheriff. Then turning to Hank, Harold Smith spoke softly, "Work with us here Hank, Pollo did have a gun, didn't he?"

"Ah, yes," Hank responded automatically. "He had some sort of German pistol that he got from his uncle. *Too many people knew Vic had a gun to lie about it. I hope Gus hasn't told them he has it or that I knew about it.*

"Hmmm," Harold Smith looked at his notes. "That's interesting,"

Why does he want to know about Vic's gun?"

Frank Powers looked at his papers, then at Hank. "And you were with Vic Pollo when he shot and destroyed the headstones in the cemetery in July of 1967?"

Hank pushed back away from Powers, surprised by the question. "Cemetery? No way. I wasn't with them."

"So you are saying that they were the ones who shot up the cemetery."

"I didn't say that, I meant I wasn't there."

Frank Powers shook his head, "You're never are there, are you?"

Powers turned to Harold Smith and the Sheriff and just above a whisper, said, "Can you believe this clown?" The three men all looked at Hank, then each other.

Harold Smith broke the silence. "What did Pollo do with the gun?"

"He said he threw it in the middle of Luther's Swamp." *And that's no lie, that's what Vic said he did with it.*

"That's one hell of a big swamp, how do you expect us to find it?" Smith sneered sarcastically.

"That's not my problem, why don't you ask Vic?" Hank responded, matching the sarcasm.

Do they know Gus has the gun? No, if Gus would have told them he had it, he would have told me that—wouldn't he?

Again, Powers, Smith and the Sheriff huddled together. Hank could not hear the rest of their conversation, but from

THE LAST DEER HUNT

the gesturing and expressions, it seemed they were arguing. The sheriff sat down at his desk shuffling a pile of papers and appeared to be pouting.

Powers, Smith and the Sheriff passed silent signals to one another, and the Sheriff hooked his fingers in his belt and said, "I think that will be all for now. Stay in the area, we will probably have to talk to you again. Thanks for being cooperative and if you think of something, call us."

"Yes, thank you Mr. Duval." Mr. Smith was already back at the desk with the pile of papers, writing quickly on a note pad. The thin man nodded at Hank, his face betraying nothing.

Without saying anything, Hank nodded back as he walked out the door into the warm evening air. Something was tugging at his mind, something about the questions the detectives were asking that bothered him. Why did they ask about Vic and his guns? *Why did I say anything about the Luger? What if Gus tells them he has it?* Hank knew he had dodged a bullet today at the sheriff's office, but it was only a matter of time before they would ask him the question he would have no truthful answer for and they would know if he was lying.

Twenty-Two

The twenty-fifth of October brought the first snow of the year. It started in early morning as small flakes that melted before they hit the ground and by noon, large wet flakes were quickly building up on lawns, bushes, and trees.

By early afternoon, the temperature had dropped into the low thirties and wind swirled the snow around buildings, down the streets and into the faces of the people who were out walking. By early evening, the temperature had dropped to below freezing driving the wind-chill down to close to zero degrees and the snow was sticking to driveways and automobiles.

Hank finished his coffee and put the cup in the sink with the other coffee cups. *I think I'd better get out to the hunting camp pretty soon*, he thought, *see if it's still standing*. He took a rolled up blanket from the hall closet and slowly unwrapped it to reveal an old Winchester Model 68. The 210 grain slugs were so heavy that the gun was modified to only hold three rounds. Hank This had been his father's who used it for many seasons until Uncle Andre upgraded it for Hank. Hank continued to use it until the ammunition for the old gun became difficult to find and too expensive and he replaced it with a newer 30-30 Winchester Model 94.

Hank sat at the kitchen table and moved a long rod with an oil impregnated patch through the barrel of the rifle and his mind drifted back to the sheriff's office and the two men that questioned him. *Damn, they were getting a little too close with some of the questions.* He thought. *At least I didn't have to lie. Well, technically, I didn't lie.* Hank put small drops of oil on the different mechanisms of the gun and worked them to distribute the oil. *Well, maybe just one little fib.* Taking an oil soaked rag, he slowly and carefully rubbed oil into the wood parts of the weapon almost caressing the curves of the shoulder stock and front grip. How many times had he sat and watched his father clean and oil this same gun?

Those state police are really good at asking questions. Sooner or later, they're going to trip me up...Jesus, the thought went through his mind, *I wonder if they would use a lie detector? I hadn't thought about that! Then what do I do?* Hank carefully wrapped the gun back in the blanket and put it back in the closet.

Outside, Hank decided to stay away from downtown and Frenchy's Diner. There were still many reporters around town.

A sudden thought came into his mind. Something that he had been thinking about for a while, something that he should have done a long time ago, *Why not today?*

The walk felt good. He took a left on Potters Landing Road along the river and turned onto Cedar Street with its long winding hill. It had been a long time, a couple of years since he had walked down this street and the snow, highlighted in the glow of the street lights, was falling in giant flakes slowly floating down and quickly covering Hank's coat and gloves. It brought back visions of himself as a young boy with his friends starting their sled run at the top of the hill, belly-flopping onto their Flexible Flyers and racing to the bottom where they quickly stopped their sleds before they could leap the snowbanks and end up in the river.

This part of town had been one of the nicer areas during the 1950s but had deteriorated with the exception of the little white house he was standing in front of. This house, unlike everything else on Cedar Street, was still well maintained.

Standing by the little white fence, the past flooded back in his mind to when this house, always pristine, boasted the most bountiful gardens in town. He could remember closely clumped tomato plants, severely pruned of most of their leaves, filled with masses of bright red tomatoes, strained against the stakes and wires that held them up. Long trailing vines of large leaves snaked around the back yard of this little house, every one concealing numerous zucchini, squash and egg plants. Beans covered the fences surrounding the yard and neat little rows of onions, lettuce and radish took up whatever room was left. It was a garden that even the Italians would come and admire.

A small dim light glowed through the window in the front of the house as Hank knocked softly on the door. It was one of those quiet knocks that he almost hoped would not be answered. Just as it seemed that it would not, the door opened and a grizzled head of gray hair and a face in want of a shave looked out at him.

Hank removed his snow-covered hat. "Uncle Andre, how have you been?"

"Hank, why, it's so good to see you boy! It's been too long, come on in."

Hank walked into the house and back twenty years in time. Uncle Andre had lived in this little house, a bachelor all his life, and memories flew at Hank from every shelf and furniture top, every photo, and every knickknack. Memories of days and sometimes weeks when Hank would stay at this house. The past blurred his recollection of that time, but he could remember being packed up and left with Uncle Andre during times when Mom was sick and unable to care for him. This ordeal was tempered by the many special times when he would sit and watch his Uncle work his trade as a gunsmith in the small workshop in the basement. Uncle Andre would allow Hank to assist in repairing and renewing the weapons and would patiently explain in depth every intricate detail of his work. In the evenings after supper, Uncle Andre would entertain Hank for hours with wild stories about when Fairhaven was just a frontier town.

As Hank stepped into the house it took a while for his eyes to become accustomed in the dim light. Uncle Andre was an old man. Since he had broken his hip in a fall over a year ago, his body was bent and stooped and his knees wobbled as he clumsily attempted to maneuver. But when Uncle Andre talked, his mind was sharp, his memory concise and his speech strong.

"It has been a long time Uncle Andre, and for that I am sorry."

"No need to apologize son, let's not dwell on the past. Would you like some coffee?" Uncle Andre asked as he shuffled towards the kitchen.

Back with the coffee, Andre sat down, slipped a pair of glasses from his shirt pocket and put them on. "You're looking good these days Henry. What's new with you, young man?"

Hank looked at his uncle sheepishly. The resemblance between Uncle Andre and his father was clearly evident. In the right light, Andre could be mistaken for Paul.

Hank spent the next twenty minutes filling Andre in on his cabinet making business and his work on the cabinets for the Huron Mountain Club as well as the work he had planned for the house. He spoke about the coming hunting season and what he had heard about how good it was going to be. Then he sat back and waited.

Andre rubbed his whiskers. "I don't suppose you came over here to listen to an old man talk about his boring life and his ailments. What can I help you with?"

"Uncle Andre, you know, Gus Lundgren was telling me about a fire and Pa being a hero. I never heard anything about this."

"That was your father! Risks his life, goes into a blazing building twice, has major burn scars and a bum leg to show for it, and what does he do? He wouldn't allow anybody to thank him. What happened as best I can recollect is that back in 1957, I guess you were about five, your Pa was on his way home when he stopped for a beer or two down at the Fairhaven Bar, that's all gone now, closed years ago. Well, your Pa left the bar and when he got to High Street, he could see Gus' house in flames over on Bluff Street. He ran about a quarter-mile lickity-split, right past people standing and gawking, and right into that burning house. He pulled one boy out and heard the other boy crying for help. By now the whole house was in flames and starting to collapse, but your Pa went right back in for the other boy. When the fire brigade arrived, they found your Pa just inside the front door, his body covering the boy. But it was too late, both boys died. Gus' wife Molly also perished in the fire. Your Pa spent four weeks in the hospital over in L'anse and his leg never healed quite right."

Hank shook his head, "How come I never knew about this? Why's it been kept such a big secret?"

Andre motioned towards the coffeepot, but Hank shook his head. "Your Pa never considered himself a hero—"

"But he was a hero, even though he didn't save those boys."

"Yes sir, even the State of Michigan thought so too. Your Pa received a letter of commendation from the Governor, and a certificate delivered to your father by a state senator. I don't know what your Pa did with them. I asked him once whatever happened to them, and he told me he didn't know where they were, and anyway, he said he had not done anything to deserve them. He also said he didn't want anyone to ever mention it again. Made me and your Ma swear to it."

Hank sat trying to grasp this new perspective on his father. *All these years and not a single word. All those years*

THE LAST DEER HUNT

that he just wanted to be a hero, to be somebody special— "Uncle Andre, how come he didn't feel like he deserved the recognition?"

"He felt that if he hadn't stopped at the bar that night and had those beers, he would've been able to save those kids. He felt responsible for their deaths and all of the words on all the recognition awards in the world could not erase the memory of those dead children. He never did get over it. I guess that's when he took up drinking as a way to try to forget." Uncle Andre sat back and talked slowly. "That was a time when your father was having a very difficult time. He was drinking too much and couldn't find any work. When CMPC re-opened the mill, he worked there for a week and got fired. Oh, Gus tried to help out what he could, especially when your Ma got sick. After Paul lost his job at the mill in 1960, Gus gave him a job remodeling his office over in Hancock with the promise that your Dad would not drink. Your Pa worked up there fourteen months without having a drink." Uncle Andre sighed. "It didn't take long once he got back here before he picked up that next beer though." Andre's lower lip quivered as he spoke. "I guess I was part of that problem cause I was always ready to help Paul with a beer."

Hank said thoughtfully, "I remember all the times I would come and stay at your house when Ma was so sick. That must have been when Pa was working in Hancock."

"Yeah, it was really hard your Pa working up there when Marie was so sick, but he needed the job and earned enough to open his own cabinet-making shop."

"You know I realized I don't know that much about my mother and father when I was really young. I don't think I even have any pictures of them from those days."

Andre was back with six shoeboxes full of photos. Coffee was refilled and the photos were handed back and forth and looked at and remembered with an occasional question.

Innumerable pictures of family get-togethers, relatives,

picnics, car trips and holidays. So many memories of his own youth that he had stuffed into the recesses of his mind and had lay dormant for so many years now covered the floor and tables of the room.

Uncle Andre sat back in his chair holding a picture of men in hunting clothes wearing Detroit Tiger baseball caps. "I can remember your father and I working as guides up at the hunting lodges. You know, during the forties, the Detroit Tigers would come up every year for deer hunting and your Pa and I would stay out at the lodge with them and we could sit and listen to the players talking about their baseball at old Briggs Stadium. That's what they called Tiger's stadium in those days." Uncle Andre's composure brightened as he talked. "We knew all them players then, Pinky Higgins, Hal Newhouser, Dizzy Trout, Dick Wakefield. Oh so many, I can't remember them all. Of course, that was in the days when the teams stayed together and there weren't all these trades and changing teams like there is now. These days, players are only interested in the God-almighty buck!"

"Yeah, I agree." Hank smiled. "Things sure have changed."

Andre sat back, looking thoughtfully at Hank. "And your mother, she was a saint. Did you know while she was sick, she wrote poetry? She had three articles and a short story published in Readers Digest. Now, I know that Readers Digest is not the New Yorker or the Atlantic Weekly, but they were published just the same. They're around somewhere, I'll see if I can find them."

"Yes, I would like to see them, I didn't know that about Ma. I didn't find much of her stuff over at the house."

Andre stood and stretched. "And what's this Pete Peterson tells me about a certain young lady you've been seeing?"

Hank blurted out, "I do have a new girlfriend. Her name is Maggie and she's from California. She's writing a magazine article on wolves." The quick outburst sur-prised Hank. *Girlfriend? Did I say girlfriend?* "I mean she's really a nice lady and she helped me with some of my drawings." *God, why don't I just shut up.* "I'm sorry, I didn't mean to go on." Hank felt a slight blush of embarrassment warm his cheeks.

Andre nodded and gestured with his coffee cup.

"No thanks Uncle, no more coffee. I really have to get going. But before I do, I believe I remember you working on a particular model rifle. They were 1918 German Mausers I believe."

Why yes, that's right. I converted a number of them to sporting rifles. After world war one, the market was flooded with them. Very fine weapons, but one drawback for a military rifle, It's clip could only hold five rounds.

Andre met Hank at the door with his coat. "You take care now Henry, and thanks so much for coming. It was so good to talk to you, let's try to do this more often."

"Yes Uncle, we really need to do this more often and if there is anything I can do for you, please let me know. Okay?"

The hug felt good. Uncle Andre's frail body and thin arms held on tightly and when they let go he backed away. He looked into his Uncle's face and his father's face smiled back at him. It would take more time to come to peace with his father, but tonight was a good start and somehow everything looked a little brighter in the falling snow of the late October afternoon.

Twenty-Three

More snow had fallen. About eight inches covered the ground and the weather stayed cold. It was the last day of October and Halloween was canceled due to inclement weather. At least the parade had been moved to the school auditorium. For trick or treat, all the costumes were buried under layers of winter coats, snow pants, hats, and mittens.

Hank pulled up his collar against the cold and headed down Main Street towards Maggie's. He was feeling good. He had worked all week on the cabinets for the Huron Mountain Club, finished them and now hopefully would get the last ones over to the club and installed.

Orphan started barking before Hank had a chance to ring the doorbell and Maggie's voice could be heard through the door. "Come in Hank, but don't let Orphan out."

Maggie opened the door and under her coat, she was dressed in an oversized pair of men's bib overalls over a T-shirt.

Orphan leapt and danced around Hank as he came through the door carrying several large books. "I brought

THE LAST DEER HUNT

some books of wallpaper samples for you to look at. I marked the ones I thought looked good."

Maggie looked at the large books of samples. "I'll look at them Hank. Then we can get over to Marquette and get the ones you like." It would be best to have Hank agree with the ones she already selected and let him think he picked them out.

"Good idea." He took his coat off, threw it over the back of the large chair in the living room and sat down.

"Can you believe this weather? It's like the middle of winter already." It amazed Maggie how much weather related topics dominated the conversation in the U.P. However with the severity of the weather, it was understandable. Maggie walked towards the bedroom, "I think I'm going to change, it's been one of those days." Glancing over her shoulder, she blew curls from in front of her eyes, "I'll be back in a minute."

Hemingway was on the arm of the chair in one jump and stood watching Hank through green slits of eyes. Orphan walked back to his bed looking rejected.

Maggie came back into the living room wearing a pair of men's red boxer shorts and a T-shirt that read UCLA and revealed the outline of her breasts.

As he watched her he slowly ran his hand down Hemingway's thick fur. "Looks like I have a new friend."

Whack. Hemingway turned and walked away slowly.

Maggie bent down and slowly petted the big cat. "Sometimes it takes time before a cat becomes friends with a person. You just need to have patience." Hank could feel the the closeness of her, the heat of her body and the faint scent of something musky and erotic and a feeling stirred inside of him. He reached up and softly stroked her cheek.

Maggie took his hand and kissed it gently, then backed away from him. "Hank, I am so overwhelmed right now, I don't know if I am coming or going. I am just so frustrated."

Hank reached out for her, but she backed up just out of reach and stood rubbing her temples. "Oh damn it, Hank, I don't know what to do. I'm way behind on my article about the wolves and now I have all this stuff to read on the mill renovation, pointing to a large stack of papers on the kitchen table.

Hank walked over and picked up a stack of papers. "What're these all about?"

"Oh hell, why don't you read it your-self. I don't have time for that right now, I have to worry about my own things."

Hank sensed the tension in her voice. *Not tonight, I'm going to stay out of arguments with her.*

Sitting at the small table in the living room, a pencil in her mouth, her hair a profusion of curls, her typewriter was in the middle of a mess of papers and photographs. She took the pencil out of her mouth, looked at Hank, and flipped the hair from in front of her face. "Christ, if I don't get this installment back to the publisher, they'll probably use some other story." She ripped a sheet of paper out of the typewriter, wadded it up in her hands, and threw it on the floor already littered with balls of discarded paper.

Hemingway, looked up at the sharpness in her voice, and jumped up onto the windowsill.

Orphan retrieved his pet stick from the corner by his bed, dropped it in front of Hank's chair and looked up at him with a pleading look. Hank gave it a small toss across the room and Orphan skittered after it.

"Not now! In case you guys can't see, I am a little busy here." Another sheet of paper was ripped from the typewriter. "Damn Hank, where do you think the wolves are? They released the four of them two months ago, and no one has seen even a footprint of one since then. They can't just disappear like that, can they?"

"Don't know, I haven't heard a thing. There was a deer killed over near Big Bay the day before yesterday, but that could have been coyotes."

"Well, I'd better come up with something soon or my boss will cancel my contract." Another ball of paper fell to

THE LAST DEER HUNT

the floor.

Hemingway watched the paper ball and leapt, scattering paper everywhere.

"Hemingway! Get out of here."

The cat was out of sight into the bedroom and Orphan fled onto his bed, his head buried under his blanket.

"Hank, I thought you were the great white hunter around here. If it moved, you'd know where it was. Why don't you go..."

Hank looked towards the door, not sure of the wisdom of staying.

"No Hank, I didn't mean for you to leave now, I meant, go and find the wolves for me." Maggie picked up a handful of papers, let them fall to the floor, put her head in her hands and began to cry.

"Sorry Maggie, I really haven't been out in the woods all that much myself." He should give her a hug, but wasn't sure if he would get a hug in return or the typewriter over his head. "But I have an idea, why don't you ask the Dolittles? If the wolves are out there, the Dolittles would know."

"Ooh, I couldn't do that, they all look like hillbillies right out of the Ozarks." She made a face like 'yuck'.

"How about that, little miss diversity loving liberal; did we find a chink in your armor? Love everybody but prejudiced people and hillbillies?"

Maggie blew the hair from her eyes, "Hank, be serious, I really do need to get moving on this."

"Maggie," he almost called her honey, "I hear the Dolittles can even talk to the animals." He grinned widely, smug with his sense of humor. "Just last month they found a two-headed llama for some Englishman."

"Haaaank!" The papers flew at him; she was up from the table, "You are a rat," and she was in his arms.

He returned the embrace and as time slipped by, neither of them dared to move, neither wanting to spoil the moment. The snow continued outside the window, swirling in the wind and picking up a faint blue, white and red tinge from the Eiffel Tower sign flashing at the end of the next block.

Hemingway, sensing that it was safe, resumed his watch in the windowsill and Orphan crawled out from under the blanket.

Hank slowly and gently pushed away from Maggie, to find her looking deeply into his eyes. "Hank, there's something we have to talk about."

He looked at Maggie standing in front of him, her red curls hanging down in disarray and she looked as if she were going to cry again. Hank had never seen her lose her poise before.

"Hon ...I mean Maggie...okay, I will talk to Luther Dolittle tomorrow and find out for you, okay?"

He could see a redness and puffiness in her eyes, half hidden now between a mass of curls. Here it comes he thought, the conflict, start of an argument, anything to get us to move away from each other. He did not speak, waiting for the other shoe to drop.

"Hank, there is a good chance I might have to move back to L.A."

He pushed away from her, her words hanging in his mind, the shock starting to turn to resentment and then to anger. He pushed the anger back, trying to think, *I'm going to lose her, she's going to leave.* And with those thoughts, the anger quickly faded. He took her into his arms and hugged her, at first lightly, and then firmly. He felt her body respond to his and quietly whispered, "I don't want to lose you now." *Nothing is going to come between us, not this time, not tonight.*

On this night, nothing, absolutely nothing came between them.

Twenty-Four

Maggie was still sleeping when Hank dressed and left. A quick stop at the diner for a cup of coffee and Hank was at Waino Matson's Garage to pick up his truck.

Waino shrugged. "I did what I could for the transmission. The cost to replace it would be more than this old truck is worth. You might want to think about a new truck."

"Yeah sure." Hank rubbed his hand over the hood of the old Ford. "Been a mighty good truck."

"Yeah sure, you bet. But you know, we all wear out sometime.eh?

"I'll think about it. If you ever see a good deal on a truck, give me a call."

"You bet."

"Gotta get going. Time to get out to the old hunting camp and make sure it's ready. The old gang is coming back for a few days." The transmission was worse, really starting to slip badly, but the old truck started on the first try and Hank knew this would be a good day. Now he had to get his clothes washed and his kitchen cleaned

It took him a while to layer himself against the cold

weather. The red suspenders were needed to hold up the heavy woolen pants that covered the longjohns underneath. The polypropylene undershirt would wick any moisture away from the skin, and this was under the cotton shirt with a woolen shirt over that. Then cotton socks were covered with woolen ones that would go into waterproof boots lined with felt inserts.

Hank laughed when he thought of when, as a small boy, his mother would dress him to go outside in the winter. After it took forty-five minutes to get fully dressed, he would stand, a roly-poly ball of clothes, a large woolen hat, and huge mittens tied together with a string through the sleeves, hardly able to move, and needing to go to the bathroom.

Fully dressed, Hank decided to take a gun with him and selected a Winchester model 12-gauge pump shotgun from the half dozen guns in the gun cabinet. He didn't have a small game hunting license and didn't need a weapon, but having the shotgun nestled in the crook of his arm while he walked through the winter woods brought back many fond memories.

From the garage, Hank took an old sled with wooden runners and loaded it into the back of the truck. This was the same sled he had used when he was a lttile boy, racing down the road from Mansion Hill into town, and was his father's before that.

He arrived at Frenchy's Diner late. Most of the regulars were still hard at work trying to solve the mystery of the 'body at the mill,' as it had become known.

Frenchy was nowhere to be seen. Lucy was cooking up stacks of pancakes as well as eggs and bacon.

"Morning Hank." She called out cheerfully. Today she had on a white blouse and a black skirt, neat but still short, covered by a very large cooking apron and her new bright red hair, cut very short was peeking out from a floppy chef's hat.

Hank moved a small vase of flowers from in front of him on the counter. Looking around, he found all the booths had flowers in little vases. "Nice touch. Have you seen Frenchy today?

Lucy brought him his coffee. "He left about an hour ago. Had to pick up a new menu board over in Marquette. He should be back really quick."

"New menu board? The menu hasn't changed in three years."

"Then it's about time, don't you think?"

"Does new menu board mean higher prices?"

Lucy didn't answer, she was back at the grill, piling pancakes, eggs, bacon and sausages onto dishes.

Hank picked up his coffee cup and walked over to where Homer Perrin and Bill Robertson were quietly sipping on coffee. "Morning folks, What's up?"

Nothing much." Bill replied, looking at Homer.

"Nope, nothing much." Homer echoed.

"Hear anymore about the body?"

"Nope, but heard they took those Sloan boys in for questioning." Homer said, buttoning his coat. "But them cops are barking up the wrong tree. There ain"t no way those brothers killed Pettiford."

"Those two boys wouldn't hurt a flea." Bill added.

"Yeah, I agree." Hank responded, and waved as the two men headed towards the door.

"See you later Hank." Homer and Bill waved back.

"Can I get you anything else?" Lucy asked, standing in front of him at the counter, then she added, "What's Maggie up to today?"

"No thanks. Maggie went with Sarah over to Marquette. They had a meeting with someone up the college and then they were going to a concert at the Unitarian church. It's too bad that they didn't know Frenchy was going, they could have had lunch together or something."

"Yeah, that would have been nice." She picked up some coffee cups from the counter and put them in a large bus container. "Except that Frenchy and Sarah don't see each other very much anymore."

"I don't wonder why." Hank said under his breath. He Finished his coffee and turned to go. "I had better get a move on, it's getting late."

Jostling a large wrapped package, Frenchy came through the door.

"What the heck you got there?" Hank asked, bursting with curiosity.

"New menu signboard, one you can read." Frenchy was busily unwrapping the large package.

In a minute, Lucy was at his side helping to tear at the paper covering the large sign. As it was unwrapped, Hank could make out a large red and blue Eiffel Tower run-ning up the center, with 'BREAKFAST' written on the top left and 'LUNCH' written across the top of the right side.

The three of them stood back and looked at the new menu board. Hank scratched his head, "Frenchy, why didn't you just get menus printed?"

Before Frenchy could answer, Lucy injected, "Because then it wouldn't be Frenchy's Diner, would it?"

Hank was about to answer that it was beginning to look less like Frenchy's diner anyway, when Frenchy said. "You know, I kinda like it, what you think?"

Lucy stood looking at the sign. "You know Frenchy, maybe we should have left room on the menu to add dinners."

"Whoa, hold on," Frenchy shook his head, "we been making so many changes I can't keep up with them. How we gonna pay for all these?"

Hank scanned the new menu board, "With higher prices?"

"Inflation." Frenchy answered.

"Catch you guys later," Hank started to button up his coat. "I'm going out to the hunting camp to make sure everything is ready when the guys get up here. I gotta bring some apples and check the blinds around the salt lick and make sure there's enough wood for the stove." He was mentally checking off a list of things to do, but said it aloud.

THE LAST DEER HUNT

"Apples? Salt lick? What the heck is a salt lick?" Lucy asked as she helped Frenchy move the sign onto the counter.

"It's a large block of salt that farmers use for the cows to lick, guess it gives them the salt they need, deer like it too. We put one out near the edge of the swamp with apples so the deer will get used to coming to that spot."

"Oooh, what great sportsmen!" Frenchy said, "Do you serve milk and cookies too?"

Lucy joined in the teasing. "And what do you do with the cute little deer in the evening, put them in a little barn to keep them warm?"

Hank threw his hands up in the air, "You guy—"

Lucy squealed. "Do you give them cute little nicknames? Maybe like Billie Buck, or Darlene Doe?"

Hank adjusted the bill on his cap. "Stop it you two, you're both acting really stupid."

Frenchy was enjoying Hank's uncomfortableness. "Or maybe you snuggle up with them so they learn to love you and come back again so that you can blow their little heads off."

"I hope you both get locked in here for a month and have to eat your own lousy cooking. See you around." Hank stepped outside to the sounds of laughter coming from the diner.

The temperature was still trying to push up to 20° and the freezing rain had stopped. The ice covering the trees, buildings and cars gave an eerie crystal forest scene to the landscape as he walked down Main Street.

The marquee from the old Chippewa Theater hung over the sidewalk with dirty icicles and strips of old paint hanging from the edges. The letters 'ST_R W__RS' still hung from the marquee from the last movie that had played at the theater. *Star Wars, 1977*, Hank guessed.

Lots of memories from this old theater. Many monsters tamed by Bud Abbott and Lou Costello, and many cowboys shot off their saddles by Gene and Roy. *How many times did we hoot and holler when a full orchestra would break out and Gene Kelly would tap dance his way down the street with a beautiful woman.*

There was also the first date with Sandy at the theater, putting his arm around her, then walking her home after the movie, and then, their first kiss. *I wonder what it could take to restore this place?*

Downtown Fairhaven appeared bleak in the flat colorless light of the cloudy day. The ghosts of J.J. Newberry, the Woolworth Five and Dime and the hardware store were still present among the peeling paint and decaying trim of the old brick facades. The side of old Hoffman building still held red paint that spelled out the name of the Piggly Wiggly Market whose windows once held signs advertising pork chops for fifty nine cents a pound, strictly fresh apples, oranges and vegetables or farm fresh eggs. Now the windows were filled with pictures of young men and women in various poses of Kung Fu or Tai Kwan Do and large photo cards of Babe Ruth, Al Kaline and other athletes.

Better get out to the hunting camp, Hank thought, and turned and headed towards the IGA Store. *You know, with a little work, this town has possibilities.*

With the back of the truck loaded with provisions, Hank drove out of town. The sun had started to melt some of the ice and the crystal forest was slowly dripping off branches and the eaves of buildings.

Hank turned off the highway at the sign indicating the location of 'The Antlers Hunt Club.' The road into the camp was crusty and slippery. After fighting the icy road for a hundred feet, he stopped the truck and unloaded the provisions onto the sled Then taking the shotgun and a belt with shells, he locked the truck and put his keys on top of the right front tire. He loaded three shells into the pump shotgun, and pulling the sled, walked down the road through the open field towards the deep woods and the old camp.

At first, the walking was difficult as the rain had left a

coating of ice that crunched as Hank's boots broke through and the ropes to the sled dug into his shoulders.

The snow was half way up the sides of the camp and it took a while to dig down enough to get the door open. The inside of the cabin was cold, much colder than the outside air, but Hank let the door open to let in light and air out the mustiness from being closed up so long. It took a few minutes for his eyes to become accustomed to the dim light. He removed the cardboard from the three windows and lit a kersosene lantern. Outside, he dug into a large drift of snow and brought back an armful of logs.

The stove was a large barrel that someone had cut a hole in the side, welded on some hinges, added a door, then welded four legs on the bottom. Hank loaded the stove with paper and logs and after banging on the metal chimney to assure it was not plugged, started a fire. At first smoke came out of every opening in the stove filling the room until it caught a draft and the smoke started up the chimney.

With the fire going, he put away the provisions and while a pot of coffee was brewing, he checked the rest of the cabin. Porcupines had chewed through the corner of the cabin right under the roof, but not so bad that a large chink of rags would not fix it. He cleaned off the rest of the woodpile, and brought in wood and kindling to have it ready when the guys get here. He then cleared the walk from the camp to the outhouse.

Finally, after having his coffee, he took the shovel from the woodbox and walked down to a small pond about a quarter mile from the camp. At the edge of the pond where springs kept the ground from freezing, the shovel dug quickly into the bog.

Not too deep, he thought, *won't take long*. After a few minutes, the blade of the shovel hit something. "That's it!" Hank said aloud, then stood quietly, looking around to see if anyone could be watching.

A couple of shovels of dirt and Hank uncovered a rock.

More digging, more furiously, deeper and deeper. Nothing. Deeper yet, and still nothing. Far deeper than he had buried it. A double check of the exact location checked out. Right in the middle of the two cedar trees and the birch. *This is the right spot!*

Hank Duval sat in the snow, wet and cold from sweating, water dripped down from the trees on his head and soaking his clothes. "It's gone! Where the hell is that damn rifle?"

Twenty-Five

The first week in November brought more winter weather. The snow banks along the roads now were over two feet deep and sub-zero nighttime temperatures were common. Hank pulled up the collar of his Mackinaw jacket against the cold afternoon air and walked out of the house.

The diet Maggie had suggested for him was working. His pants were definitely looser and he had more energy. He sensed a little more spring in his step as he trudged along Main Street towards Frenchy's Diner.

Hank was feeling good that work on the house had finally started. A new range and refrigerator were on order and Maggie had even suggested a dishwasher. *Yeah, the dishwasher that Sandy always wanted.*

The small gold charm bracelet in his pocket he had found behind a heater vent in the master bedroom while the room was being re-done. It was a very special bracelet that Sandy had lost about two months before she died and they had searched for it without success. Thoughts of Sandy started to drift back into his mind but were interrupted by the sounds of voices moving towards him. Homer Perrin and

Roger Greenlee walked the snow-covered sidewalk, from the direction of the diner.

"About the worst weather we've seen this early in the year." Homer commented.

Roger nodded his agreement. "With all this snow, the deer are going to be down in the middle of the cedar swamps come hunting season."

Hank had to agree with them. *This was going to be one heck of a winter.* "Anything new at the diner?"

Homer chuckled, "With Lucy there seems like everything's always changing."

Roger nodded his agreement.

Hank had to agree with them.

Frenchy's Diner had the large 'Closed' sign hanging in the window when Hank arrived at two-thirty. The last of the lunch customers had already left and Lucy had gone home early today so Hank and Frenchy would have the diner to themselves.

Frenchy opened the door. He was wearing a green and black plaid flannel shirt and camouflage military style pants. His red beret was pushed back on his head and Hank noticed the pigtail was missing, the haircut short.

Hank took off his coat and sat down on a stool. Frenchy sat down on the stool next to Him, reached over behind the counter for two cups, and filled them from the pot.

"Place looks good," Hank said, looking around the diner. "Your new menu sign really perks the place up." He frowned at Frenchy, "Even with the new higher prices.

"Hey, we have to pay for the sign."

Hank wanted to ask about Lucy, but quietly sipped his coffee as he watched Frenchy pulling things out of each of his pockets and putting them on the counter next to the cup in front of him. When the contents of his pockets were on a pile on the counter, he picked out a cigarette paper and with one hand made a half tube. From a small plastic bag, he poured out what looked like basil into the tube. In one fluid motion, he licked down the paper completing the tube.

THE LAST DEER HUNT

A match appeared and Frenchy lit the end of the makeshift cigarette.

"Holy shit, it that what I think it is?"

"Yep, a joint."

Hank looked at Frenchy with astonishment. "Where the hell did you get marijuana in Fairhaven?"

"Hank, where the hell have you been? You can get marijuana, coke, heroin, LSD, or anything else you want in Fairhaven." Frenchy took a long drag on the joint. "Don't tell me you never used."

Hank just sat looking at Frenchy. "No man, never. I've never even been anywhere where people smoked marijuana...or anything else for that matter."

Exhaling slowly, Frenchy handed the joint to Hank. "Here, I think you could use this."

Hank pulled back his hand as if the joint was a hot poker. He sat looking at the funny cigarette for a few seconds then reached over and took the joint.

"Hank, are you going to take a drag, or you going to let that thing just go up in smoke?"

The first inhale was quick and Hank broke into a rasping cough and started to hand the half-burned joint back to Frenchy. Frenchy waved him off. "Go ahead, go for it. This stuff is Super Skunk #1, imported from Canada."

This time Hank took in a long drag and held it before exhaling as he had seen Frenchy do, and handed the joint back. For the next few minutes, the joint passed back and forth, both men taking deep breaths of smoke.

Hank finished the tiny end of the joint and put it out in an empty coffee cup. "This stuff doesn't work, I don't feel a thing." *Except my head feels like it's stuffed with multicolored cotton candy.* He took the charm bracelet from his pocket, turned it over in his hand, and put it on the counter.

"Watcha got, Hank?"

"Charm bracelet. It was Sandy's." He slowly moved each of the small gold hula dancers through his fingers. "Found it when we re-did the bedroom."

Frenchy reached over and gently took the bracelet. "It's the one thing she always wanted, to get over to Hawaii. How come you guys didn't go?" He handed the bracelet back and lit another joint.

Hank took the cigarette from Frenchy and took a deep drag. "Because I didn't know that..." Hank felt the heaviness build up inside. "If I had only known that it was her last..." The multi-colored cotton candy swirled around inside his brain.

Frenchy's turn to take a long slow drag. "You can't always know; that's why you gotta do the right thing."

"Yeah, but how does one know what's really important? I mean like, before it's too late?"

"It's like we should live each day like it was our last. You sit down and say to yourself, 'I only got one day to live, how do I want to live it, and what do I want to do?'"

"What would you do Frenchy?" Hank took the joint from Frenchy, "If you only had one day to live?" He inhaled deeply.

"I'd try to find peace with myself. How about you?"

Hank blew the smoke out slowly. "Maggie mentioned she might have to move back to LA." He looked at Frenchy for any reaction.

"L.A.'s fine, but it ain't home." Frenchy responded, trying to think of the singer who recorded that song. "What do you think you'll do?"

"I don't know; I like having her around. I think I'm getting used to her..."

Frenchy waited for Hank to continue, and then said, "Maybe you should tell her that." He pulled the smoke deep into his lungs, held it and slowly released it through his nose and handed the joint to Hank, "Neil Diamond, that's who sang that song."

It was Hank's turn to draw the smoke deeply inside. "Frenchy, you got to help me with this one. What do I do if she goes back to LA?"

Frenchy sang, "LA Lady, Blue Jean Baby...that was Elton

THE LAST DEER HUNT

John, Tiny Dancer, I think." Another deep drag on the joint.

"Frenchy, you're no help."

"Hell, I can't even deal with my own problems." Frenchy released the smoke from his lungs and watched it rising in little circles. "It's over between Sarah and me. We decided to call it quits."

"More like you decided to call it quits. I mean like, you and Lucy have become quite the item."

"Sarah is so busy lately between her job at the school and the mill restoration project. Do not get me wrong, she is a beautiful person, intelligent as hell, but I don't know what she is doing up in this neck of the woods. With her talent and brains, she could be in New York, Detroit, or anywhere. Hell, she could up and leave any time she wants."

"Yeah, a lot like Maggie."

Frenchy nodded. He slowly turned the stool, listening as it screeched in protest. Just as slowly, he turned the stool the other way and it continued to wail. "This whole thing between Lucy and me just happened. It wasn't supposed to happen, but I didn't stop it from happening either."

"Yeah, a lot like Maggie." Hank tucked his chin into his chest.

Frenchy took a long drag on the cigarette and put it out. Both men sat side by side on stools in silence watching the deer head staring at them from over the counter. Frenchy took out another paper, filled it, and rolled it. Slowly he lit it, inhaled and passed it to Hank.

Hank inhaled and went over to the deer head, staring at it. Slowly he walked around the diner looking at the deer. "Yep, it sure does, follows me everywhere I go in the diner." Hank squinted, trying to focus on the deer head. "Did I ever tell you that I screwed up a deer head?"

"No my friend," Hank inhaled and passed the cigarette back to Hank, "How does one screw up a deer head?"

"I had ruined my Pa's chances of being a hero. He thought if he did something special like get a trophy for shooting a deer with a big rack he would be this big person.

193

That was important to him, that he would have been a hero. But it didn't matter because I found out he was a real hero, but he didn't want to be a hero, so he wasn't."

"I am so confused."

"Yeah, that's true you know. My Pa ran into a burning house to save a boy, and then put his life at risk again to run back in a second time to try to save the boy's brother. The two boys died, their mother died and my father almost died, but he felt that he should have saved them. He thought it was his fault he didn't. People tried to tell him he was a hero, but he would not accept that."

"That was Gus' Lundgren's house, right? I heard about that, but I never knew who tried to save the kids. So that was your Pa, you must be proud of him."

"I'm confused. I spent so much of my life seeing my father punishing himself, I never knew this story." Hank picked up the joint that had been put out, motioned to Frenchy for a match, and re-lit the cigarette. Taking a long drag and exhaling. "Now here's a real lulu for you. I'm sure you have heard who saved Ol' Babe the Blue Ox, right?"

"Yeah, that was you, good buddy. You pulled her out of the fire when Paul Bunyan burned down." Frenchy took the joint, inhaled and held the smoke, "So you are a genuine hero."

"Wrong, wrong, wrong. My Pa was the hero who is, and I, Mr. Frenchy; I am the hero who ain't."

Frenchy wrinkled his nose. "Now I am confused. Is you? Or is you ain't?"

"I ain't. I mean, I am the one who incinerated Paul Bunyan. I started the fire. I am the villain, not the hero. I have been living a lie, a big fat lie."

"But you risked your life to drag that big wooden cow out of the fire, didn't you? So I say that makes you a hero, a genuine certified hero."

"Nah, you can't be a hero if you're just trying to fix something that you screwed up."

Frenchy drew down on the cigarette until there was

nothing but ashes, burning his fingers. Stuffing out the ashes, he held the smoke in his lungs, and then very slowly released it.

"Yeah, but you, Mr. Frenchy, you are a genuine certified hero. Green Beret, Vietnam, you must have seen a lot of action over there, right?"

"Wrong. Sorry to disappoint you, Hank old buddy."

Frenchy was desperately searching through his pockets, turning them inside out. A small bag fell to the floor and Frenchy was off his stool and onto the floor where he proceeded to fill another joint. Hank joined Frenchy on the floor and watched as Frenchy rolled the joint.

Lighting the cigarette, Frenchy sat back, inhaled deeply. "I ain't a Fricken hero." He took another extra long drag and held it in his lungs for an eternity. When he finally let it out, he leaned back and told his story.

"I grew up in Williamstown, a small town in western Massachusetts where my father and mother were both professors at a small college. My mother taught psychology and my father taught economics. I was seventeen and was to start college at the University of Massachusetts in 1964 when Vietnam was just starting to become an issue. I was bored and restless. All I wanted to do was play guitar in a rock band, but my parents, of course, wanted to see their only son become a lawyer or doctor.

I spent the summer of '64 hanging around with a wild rock group touring the country trying to make the big one. It was the usual scene, drugs, girls, too many gigs, and too many towns. I was out of my league and before I knew it, I found myself on the streets, broke, and out of work and with a pregnant girlfriend.

Good old Mom and Pop turned their back on me, told me I made my bed, now I should sleep in it, or something like that. The pregnant girlfriend got an abortion and disappeared. Just to piss off my folks, I went in the army in sixty-five.

JERRY SARASIN

I volunteered for the Special Forces, went through training at Fort Devens, and then went directly to Vietnam as a 'military advisor.'

I was sent up to Plauku on a shotgun tour, green as hell. The first night I was there, I was put in a barracks at Fort Hollaway. During the night, the Vietcong infiltrated the camp and blew up the barracks. Eight G.I.s were blown to hell and over a hundred were wounded along with a bunch of civilians, a lot of them kids.

I woke up lying buried beneath bodies listening as the last groans and sobbing of the dying slowly faded away and I passed out. I don't know how long I lay there unconscious, but when I came to, I could hear right above me, "Hey Sarge, over here, there's someone still alive!" Just as I passed out again, I heard, "Holy shit, it's a GI, and he's still breathing!" When I woke up, I was in a MASH unit with so many tubes and wires, and shit, the pain. Christ, the pain was unbelievable.

"That was my big war story. First night, I got blown up, never fired a shot. Now all I get are fricken headaches and nightmares that never go away." Another long drag on the joint, "After Nam, I was in and out of hospitals trying to recuperate and get my life back together. I kicked around doing odd jobs, then went back to school, got a degree in social work, and worked in homeless shelters with vets and with adolescents at risk. I was working in a shelter in Sault Ste Marie when one of my army buddies who owned the Black Bear Diner here in Fairhaven got sick and I came over to help him run the place until he died. With your able assistance, we rebuilt the diner and now it's Frenchy's Diner and that's how I ended up in Fairhaven."

Sitting on the floor in the diner, both Hank and Frenchy passed the joint to each other and smoked it without speaking. Taking a long drag, Hank pointed to Frenchy, "Wow, I always thought you were this real cool guy, you know, like that Fonzie guy." Hank puffed on the joint again without

THE LAST DEER HUNT

thinking about it.

"Wrong, sorry to disappoint you, Hank old buddy."

"Or a hero. I always thought of you as a hero."

"Hank, you do a lousy job of picking role models."

"Nope, you're wrong about this one Frenchy. You are a hero." Hank paused, then smiled at Frenchy. "For being a friend to me when I needed you, you are my hero."

Twenty-Six

Two more days to the 15th of November, the first day of deer hunting season. Hank was still in his pajamas sitting at the kitchen table trying to understand how the rifle could be missing when the loud knock on the door hammered through his thoughts.

Maggie's face peeked around the half-opened door, "Hope I'm not disturbing you Hank, but I had to talk to somebody."

"What's up?" Then seeing the distress in her face, asked, "How's the mill restoration going?"

"It's a disaster; all of our funding sources seem to have dried up. Lyle Burke was supposed to have procured additional funding, but he never came through. He really let us down.

"Maybe it's not that bad, after all—"

"Coming from you that's a laugh. Where were you when we needed you? You should have been there yesterday, we...I needed you." Maggie sat at the table, her hands in her lap. "I'm sorry Hank, I am just so frustrated. Can we do something today? I mean go somewhere and do something fun?"

THE LAST DEER HUNT

Hank moved to her, taking her hands in his. "I'd love to, but I have to go and pick up the guys at the airport and bus terminal in Houghton today and drive them out to camp. I had planned to spend the night out there with them." Then watching the rejection cross her face, quickly said, "No, I will come back into town after I drop them off."

"Are you sure? That's a long drive and the weather's moving in."

"Not a problem, but could I use your Volvo? The truck won't hold everyone." *Besides the damn thing is down at Matson's garage again.* "I should be back by three thirty and whatever you come up with will be okay with me. Sound good?"

"That's fine." A small smile formed. "Thanks Hank, I'm sorry I blew up at you, I'm just really frustrated with this whole thing. Especially that ratfink Burke."

"Yeah, but he has art hanging in a gallery so he must be okay, right?"

"Touché Mr. Duval. But I would take your art work any day." Maggie blew him a kiss as she moved towards the door.

The wind picked up and the sleet and snow moved from the vertical to the parallel as Hank rounded Huron Bay and headed for L'anse and then north to Houghton. He would pick up Gino, Eddie, and Tom at the airport, and then on the way back, pick up Bob at the Greyhound Station in L'anse, then pick up Ollie at his sister's house on the way to the hunting camp.

At the airport, the wind continued to increase in intensity and the snow and sleet came down heavier, darkening the day and giving it a look of late evening.

The scheduled arrival time came and went. The whirling snow nearly obliterated the runway and Hank doubted that the plane would even attempt to land in these conditions. The lone airline employee stood nervously watching the window when the phone jangled startling everyone. The employee said yes into the phone at least ten times before putting it down and announcing the plane would be landing in about twenty minutes.

The new arrival time came and went. Hank could have used another cup of coffee, but the coffee booth had closed for the evening.

The phone jangled again, echoing through the empty terminal. The North Central employee answered and informed the other three that the tower had called to inform him that the flight was on its final approach. About the time he hung up the phone, the loud roar of aircraft engines increasing power could be heard and Hank could make out the landing lights of the small propjet as it raced past the front window pointed its nose upwards and disappeared back into the snowy sky.

The young man in the uniform of North Central Airlines shrugged, "Musta missed the approach." and disappeared into his small office.

Hank sat at the window staring at the wind-driven snow, and as he watched, the plane loomed back into view, raced past, its propellers kicking up blasts of snow and disappearing down the runway.

The employee appeared outside, dressed in a parka just as the plane reappeared, and as it parked, rolled a stairway up to the plane. The door to the plane opened and people moved from the plane down the stair. Eddie and Tom were off first, followed by Gino. No one else deplaned.

Inside the terminal, the men, shaking snow off, greeted Hank openly.

"That was one hell of a ride." Gino offered, holding up his shaking hands. "Christ, I didn't think we were going to make it, all we did was bounce around all the way from Chicago."

"Yeah," Eddie piped in, "That was scary, and I thought we missed the runway the first time. I didn't know they were allowed to land in this kind of weather." The green tinge on Eddie's face gave tribute to a decidedly bad day flying. Tom looked a little peaked but managed a smile. "Good to

THE LAST DEER HUNT

see you again Hank."

"Yeah, same to you guys," Hank replied. "Welcome to God's country."

"God can sure as hell keep it." Gino shook his head and slowly stretched. "This place could use a bar."

"Yeah, I could sure use a drink." Eddie added.

The men picked up their luggage. Gino, decidedly having gained weight, picked up a gun case along with a suitcase. Waving the gun case, he said, "Wait till you guys see this beauty."

The drive from Houghton was quiet and uneventful which was okay with Hank who wanted to concentrate on navigating in the driving snow that now packed the roads.

Bob had waited over three hours at L'anse and had gone down to a small restaurant for a pasty, the first one he had since he was in this area five years ago. He grabbed Hank's hand with a hearty shake. "Good to see you guys. Hank, what's going on, I mean with Pettiford and all?"

The men gathered around Hank, who spoke quietly, "Nothing much new since I talked to you. The state police had me in for questioning."

Hank could feel a surge of concern from the men around him. He continued. "I think they're just fishing, they didn't have anything specific and they've been talking to everyone. We'll have time to talk about it more at the camp. Ollie drove over yesterday. We can pick him up at his sister's place just outside of L'anse. I suggest that we change clothes here at the bus station so we can go directly to the camp, there are too many cops in town."

Hank made a stop at Bill's Corner store and picked up provisions and the men picked up liquor that was jammed into the Volvo, already packed tight with bodies and the luggage that would not fit in the trunk. A quick stop at Ollie's sister's, more greetings, and back into the overloaded Volvo for the rest of the trip back to Fairhaven and the hunting camp. The ride started quietly, interrupted only by an occasional grunt, snore or gripe as someone shifted position.

Suddenly, a series of quick movements coincided with the strong smell of whiskey and Gino, from the back seat, "Christ Eddie, can't you wait until we get to camp?"

"Quit pushing, now you made me spill it, you asshole."

"Come on you two," Tom, also from the back, in the middle, "Shut up and sit still; we're almost to the camp."

"Shithead," Gino called back to Eddie, "If I could reach you, I'd punch your stupid face in, you—"

"Come on guys," Hank broke in, "we only got another few miles to go, and then you can fight all you want."

From the front seat, Bob laughed, "Nothing ever changes."

As the Volvo moved silently down the snow covered road, the quiet returned as the men dozed off or helped Hank stare at the large flakes swirling upwards in front of the windshield.

Hank parked at the cut-off to the camp and after a brief glaring contest between Gino and Eddie, the men loaded with luggage and provisions, followed Hank single file through the snow to the hunting camp.

"Christ it's cold," Tom said, looking around the camp as Hank lit the two kerosene lanterns and light filled the dusky camp.

Bob slowly gazed around the cabin, "Same as always, nothing ever changes."

Hank was busy putting paper and logs in the barrel stove that sat in the middle of the camp, then dropping in a match. After a short burst of smoke from the stove into the camp, the draft caught and the stove roared to life. "Yeah, everything's pretty much the same as always, but the whole place is settling some. The porcupines had chewed a few holes through the logs and a few glass panes were broken, but it's pretty much the same. I washed all the bedding and cleaned all the dishes and stocked firewood back in the wood box, so you guys should be okay for tonight."

"Where are you going, Hank?" Eddie asked, pouring a large glass full of whiskey.

THE LAST DEER HUNT

"Well, I promised I would see Maggie tonight."

"Oh hell, did you hear that," Gino laughed, "Hank prefers spending the night with Maggie to being here with us."

"Yeah," Ollie added his laugh, "So would I."

"I gotta go back in anyway; all my stuff is at my house," Hank said, putting on his coat and gloves and heading for the door.

Outside, the snow was still falling in large flakes that were quickly filling up the footprints from their walk into the camp. In fifteen minutes, Hank reached the Volvo. A loud click was the only sound when the key was turned. More clicks, but the engine would not turn over. "Damn battery is dead."

The men were in various stages of getting into nightclothes when Hank, snow-covered, opened the door.

"Ah, see there," Gino laughed, "Hank really likes us better."

"What happened?" Tom asked

"Dead battery." Hank replied, "Maggie never does anything to that car. It's a wonder it still runs at all. I'll go out tomorrow and maybe someone will come by and give me a jump-start."

A brief period of chatter tapered off as one by one, the men climbed into their assigned bunks and pulled the heavy quilts up into warm cocoons. Hank, banked the fire with ashes to keep it smoldering all night, turned the lanterns off, and then created his own cocoon.

At dawn, the men were still sleeping when Hank left to head back to the car hoping that some early morning deer hunters were on their way out to favorite hunting sites.

Twenty-Seven

After standing by the car for over an hour watching the large snowflakes pile up, a Good Samaritan finally stopped and offered a jump-start.

Cold and wet, Hank stopped off at his house for a quick change and pick up his hunting clothes. It was good to get out of the dirty clothes he had slept in all night and the warm shower water washed away the dirt and smells from his body.

After he made a fire in the small woodstove, had his coffee, and made a quick check of the television for news and weather, Hank decided to call Gus. "What's up Gus? No, I haven't heard anything either...and yes, the guys came in yesterday and are out at the hunting camp. Gus, things are getting complicated and I'm not sure I know what to do. I think it's time I took you up on your offer and talked to somebody about what happened that night at Pettiford's."

A hesitation, then Gus responded, "Maybe it is time. You can fill me in later, but Pat Johnson, the attorney from Marquette will be in L'anse for a couple of days, and I suggest that you should talk to her."

"Thanks Gus, I will talk to the guys and get back to you."

THE LAST DEER HUNT

As he hung up, a loud sharp knock rattled the kitchen door

"Okay, Mr. Duval, just where the heck have you been all night?" Maggie stood outside the door, scowling, her voice filled with disappointment disguised as anger, "I waited up for you until one this morning."

"Your Volvo is over at Matson's Garage getting a new battery."

Maggie pointed into the house. "It's cold out here and I could use a cup of tea." Hank opened the door to allow her to enter.

"You know, you should have—" They said in unison, Hank standing, arms folded tightly across his chest, Maggie wiggling a finger towards him.

"Tried getting a ride in last night..." Maggie continued

"Taken care of your car, have it checked once in a while. I stood out there for forty minutes freezing my tush off." Hank finished.

"Ha, you're one to talk, look at that piece of junk you drive. Everything on it is falling apart. It's probably at Matson's right now."

Hank suppressed the urge to yell back knowing it would just be putting more fuel on the fire.

The sharpness in her voice softened. "First of all Hank, I am happy and relieved that you're all right, I was worried about you." Maggie took the cup of tea from Hank, "I really wanted to go over to L'anse last night. There was a dance at the Finnish hall. I don't know how to polka, but it looks like it is so much fun." Then sadly, "I...we haven't danced in so long, it would have been fun."

"There will be other dances; they have them every other week. Maybe we could try for the next one."

"Yes, that would be nice." Maggie said, then doing a quick survey of the room, "Gosh Hank, this is the first time I've seen the whole house back together." "This place really looks great. I especially love the kitchen. You did such a good job building the cabinets." She settled on the couch in front of the fire.

Hank opened the front of the stove, put a screen across the opening creating a small fireplace, and sat down next to Maggie. Basking in the warmth of the fire, Hank was happy to be away from the hunting camp.

"Penny for your thoughts?" Maggie broke into his dreaminess.

"Those guys out at camp are driving me crazy. We can't seem to ever talk about anything important."

"Of course, they're guys."

"Oh Maggie, give it a break, they're just not facing the issues, it's like they don't want to deal with problems."

"That's what I said, they're just guys." Maggie moved further into the blanket until only her curls showed.

Shadows and light played on the walls from the open fire as Hank sat down on the couch next to Maggie and they turned to each other. "I've got some big news for you." Both Hank and Maggie blurted out as one, looked at each other, and broke into laughter.

"You first." Hank offered.

"No, please Hank, your news must be more important."

"I bumped into Moses Dolittle on my way into town today and he said three of his kids tracked a family of wolves for about half mile down in the swamp. Thinks there might be four adults and two pups and they may have been stalking a sick deer. Would that work for your article?" Hank waited for a reaction. *This is the news she's been waiting for.*

Maggie sat wrapped up in her own thoughts.

"Hello Maggie, are you in there?" Then with more concern, "You okay?"

"Oh yeah, I'm sorry Hank, I guess that's good news, I mean about the wolves..."

"I guess I'm confused, I thought you would be happy about that."

"I guess I am but, I mean, oh I just don't know."

"Does this have to do with your news?"

"I think I would like another cup of tea please, if you

don't mind."

"Okay, one tea coming up, and I think I'll have a cup of hot chocolate."

The tea brewed and the cocoa made, he put another birch log on the fire and the flames leapt and danced. Hank waited.

Maggie was sitting on the couch holding her teacup, knees tucked up under her chin, legs covered by her extra large Green Bay Packers sweatshirt, curls cascading down both sides of her head, almost covering her left eye. "Everything is moving so fast, I wish it would get over."

"Don't worry about this Pettiford thing; it will all work out now that—"

"Oh Hank, it's not that." Maggie nestled against him. "I hope you don't mind, but I sent some of your wolf sketches into the magazine hoping that I could use them with my new article."

"You didn't! God, those things are bad, I bet they won't even look at them. I wished you would have asked."

"I know Hank, I should have asked first, but I thought you would have said no."

"Darn right I would have said no!" Hank thought a minute, and then added, "Well?"

"Well what?

Hank watched Maggie, a question on his face. "Well, what did they say about the sketches?"

"They liked them a lot, but..." Maggie's voice trailed off.

"But what?"

"Well, they said they want to use photographs on this story, you know, to make it look more professional."

Hank did not answer, but his face must have said enough to have Maggie continue. "What I meant was that they are trying to change the look of the magazine." Slowly, Maggie reached over and took Hank's hand. Very softly, she said. "They are going to send Brandon up here to do the photoshoot."

She said this so softly, Hank was not sure he heard her

correctly. "Brandon? You don't mean your Brandon?"

Maggie nodded.

The thoughts raced through his mind. *Brandon will be here in Fairhaven?* "Damn Maggie, I hope…"

"Hank, it's no big deal, Brandon was a long time ago."

He studied her face, wanting desperately to believe her. "I don't know what to think right now."

"It's okay Hank," Maggie pulled him back down on the couch with her. Her face was inches from his, he could feel her warmth and smell her soft scent, and for a minute, he lost his thoughts. She was looking at him, holding his gaze. "There is nothing to worry about, it's over with Brandon." As the light and shadows from the bright birch fire played across the walls, Maggie slowly pulled Hank down into her arms and pulled the quilt over them.

Twenty-Eight

It was nearly noon when Hank picked up his truck from Waino's, wrote a check for the bill, and headed out to camp.

The light from the two dirty windows filtered through the smoke escaping from the barrel stove and danced around the dimly lit interior of the hunting camp.

Bottles, glasses and disassembled hunting rifles covered the old metal kitchen table. Ollie Bjornson and Gino Grappone sat at opposite sides of the table cleaning weapons while Tom Peters and Eddie Mahoney, cards in hand, were intent on a game of cribbage. Bobby Lindstrom was nearly invisible in the hazy camp air as he sat on a bunk at the back of the cabin fully absorbed in his Bible.

Ollie looked up, squinting at the layer of smoke growing across the top of the cabin, "Christ Gino, did you forget to open the damper on the stove again?" He slowly caressed the heavily oiled walnut stock of his rifle as he ran an oil-soaked patch on a long rod through the barrel.

Gino reassembled his rifle taking extreme care. "I told you I opened that stupid damper, didn't I? Duval musta missed something when he checked out the camp." He glanced over at Hank as he worked the rifle mechanism, listening intently to each metallic sound from the gun. Satisfied, he moved away from the table and put the new Remington 7400 automatic along the wall with the rest of the hunting rifles. He gave his gun an extra nudge to assure it would not fall and made a long slow wipe of the telescopic sight, making sure the other men were watching.

Hank poured himself a cup of coffee from the blue and white speckled metal coffeepot on the stove. "No way man, the stove has been working just fine. Did you check the damper Gino?"

"Hell yes, what do you think I am, stupid?"

Hank reached up, gave the damper several twists, and watched as the smoke cloud slowly abated. "Looks okay to me, the damper just needed to be opened."

"Yeah, yeah, okay." Gino snorted, counting cartridges out of a box.

Hank turned to watch Tom and Eddie play cribbage; he reached over and pointed to the obvious discards in Tom's hand.

"No helping him!" Eddie said, looking up at Hank.

The hand played, Tom put his cards on the table, counted his score quietly, and moved his pegs on the cribbage board. "Your count Eddie."

Eddie put his cards down and counted out numbers in terms of fifteen-two, fifteen-fours, and other coded language that only cribbage players understood, and then moved his pegs around a corner and towards one end.

Tom rubbed his hands together against the cold draft that fought its way in against the heat of the stove. "Hey Eddie, looks like I have two counts to your one, you should just give up."

"No way man, you might just get a nineteen." Eddie replied, taking a long drink of straight whiskey and shaking his head.

"Can't get nineteen, Eddie, you know it's the same as zero." Tom continued to rub his hands together. "God, it

THE LAST DEER HUNT

seems like we say these same things whenever we get together."

Hunting clothes hung to dry around the perimeter of the interior of the camp added the smell of wet wool to the other smells of the camp

To the room in general, Hank said, "Deer season opens tomorrow. Did you get a chance to get out this morning and look around?"

"Saw some fresh tracks up on the ridges." Tom said, changing the lens on his camera.

"I didn't see anything moving," Ollie was looking up through the barrel of his rifle. "Gino said he saw a buck and a doe down by eleven point grade, but he sees that same buck and doe every time he goes there."

"I said I thought I saw the buck." Gino answered defensively. Then turning towards Hank, "How's the weather look out there now?"

"Lots of snow coming in." Hank sipped his coffee. "An Alberta Clipper has moved in from Canada and the weather channel said the wind might shift to the east and if it does, we'll get a heck of a lot more off the lake."

Ollie was at the stove moving the pans around. "Hey fellas, I could use some help getting the table cleaned off. Eddie, why don't you quit sulking and get us some dishes and I'll fill them up here. God I love your meatballs Gino, it's the only reason I come back here, what's your secret?"

Gino laughed, uncorking a bottle of Chianti. "First of all Ollie, you gotta be Italian. You just gotta know what goes into the meatballs. Hell, the only thing you Swedes eat is white sauce on dried fish that comes in little wooden boxes."

"Hell, you never heard of Swedish meatballs?" Ollie laughed, taking dishes from Eddie and stacking them on the table.

Gino wrinkled his nose. "Swedish what? You don't mean those little white anemic things, do you?"

The food was piled on dishes and put on the table, bread was cut in large chunks, and butter and grated cheese put on the table. Gino poured red wine into five plastic tumblers decorated with cartoon characters. He handed Eddie the Bugs Bunny glass, and Ollie took the Woody Woodpecker glass. Gino held up a tumbler with a picture of Tweety Bird and offered it to Hank.

"No thanks," Hank waved the glass off. "I'll stick with coffee."

"Still on the wagon?" Ollie offered. "I have to give you credit. With everything that's happened, I mean, Sandy and all..."

Hank's look told Ollie that it was okay. It was okay to talk about Sandy.

Ollie nodded his acknowledgement.

Gino's meatballs lived up to their reputation and the spaghetti went quickly. The drinks lasted longer and the evening grew mellow. The snow outside continued and the path to the outhouse had refilled with snow up to the knees.

The usual discussions and arguments about guns, ammunition, muzzle velocity versus trajectory versus impact energy pursued. Stories followed about fish that got bigger every year, or deer that had more points on their antlers every time the story was told. And laughter over childhood stories that never get old.

Hank stood near the stove listening to the ebb and flow of the conversation, occasionally throwing a new log into the stove. *Tom's right, same thing every year. Nothing ever changes.* He wanted to start discussing the Pettiford situation, but he knew the guys needed this time to talk and get caught up with each other.

He could pick out Eddie's shrill voice, using volume to make his point. He was always working on his insecurities, feeling out each of the men to assure himself that he was still accepted.

Gino's low baritone was easy to pick up; it was always accompanied by his usual loud guffaw of a laugh. Ollie, Tom, and Bob were the quiet ones. Ollie would offer up his unique, if sometimes incomprehensible logic, quick to drop

THE LAST DEER HUNT

out of the conversation if his point was not validated early. Tom would sit back waiting, and when he had the opportunity, would try to form alliances. Bob had become more introverted over the years, seemingly absorbed in his religion, but not comfortable talking about it with his old friends.

Tonight, Tom was quiet, sitting on his bunk writing in a journal between long pauses of deep thought.

Bob put down his bible and rubbed his eyes. "Tom, it looks like you have a new lens for your camera."

"Yeah, this is a new 500mm that should help me get some nice close-ups."

Bob picked up the lens, fondling it and slowly rotating it. "Yeah, someday I would love to have something like this. All I have is my old Argus C3. But it will have to do for now. You got some really good pictures the last time we hunted together, especially of the deer hanging up down at Waino's garage. Thanks for sending them."

"I hope you guys didn't tell people those were deer we shot. They were shot by the Dolittle boys."

"Hell yes we did." Gino said, drinking red wine out of the Tweety Bird cup, "we needed to have something to show the guys back home what great hunters we are. Shit, we never even get to shoot at anything anymore." Looking at Hank, he added. "You'd think our local boy here would at least be able to help us find a deer."

"Damn Gino, what's your problem?"

"No problem Hank," Gino lay down on his bunk, head back on his folded hands. "No problem at all. Just seems like someone who's lived here all his life would be able to find a deer or two, at least something we could shoot at."

"Gino," Hank wanted to say, *you couldn't hit the side of a barn if you were standing inside of it...* "Let's hope you get a chance to use that cannon you brought this year."

"Whatever." Gino said, taking another long drink from his Tweety Bird glass.

"Hey guys," Hank motioned for their attention. "Before you all get too drunk, I got to ask you something. Is there anything you guys aren't telling me?"

All faces turned towards Hank. Silence. A few glances back and forth between the men, more silence.

Ollie coughed out a quiet "What do you mean?"

"Hell, I thought it was a pretty straight forward question. Is there something you men aren't telling me?"

"About what?" Gino asked reaching for a bottle of wine.

"About the Pettiford killing of course, what the hell else do you think I mean?"

More silence. Finally, Tom asked, "Is there something specific, maybe if we knew what you were looking for..."

Hank felt his anger rising. "Oh hell, you guys are something else, you know that? It's the rifle, it's missing, and we were the only ones who knew where it was."

Gino sat straight up on his bunk. "What the hell do you mean, the rifle is missing?"

"The rifle is missing?" Eddie sat, looking at his feet. "So what?"

"So what? The rifle, the gun, the Mauser from Pettiford's house! It's missing, that's what!" Hank answered. "When I came to check the camp a few weeks ago, I went to the bog to dig it up just to see if it was still there. It's gone."

"Who the hell would have taken the gun?" Ollie looked around at the men hoping one of them would have an answer. "We were the only ones who knew where it was, weren't we?"

"As far as I know." Hank looked down at the coffee cup he held in his hands. "I don't have any good ideas."

"That's the problem Duval; you don't have any good ideas." Gino said sharply. "It was your job to take care of the gun, dammit."

"Yeah, and who was supposed to take care of the body?" Hank snapped back. "Putting it under the floor of the maintenance building turned out to be a dumb decision!"

Eddie filled his glass with whiskey. "Come on guys, let's all try to get along. Hell, ain't we the old Omega Gang?

THE LAST DEER HUNT

You know, one for all—"

The men all peered at Eddie through the thick smoky haze and the silence returned, making the small cabin feel oppressive.

Hank stuck his head out the camp door and breathed in the cold air, trying to clear his mind. "Anybody got any great ideas?"

"I don't know." Bob rubbed his hands together. "Maybe it's your buddy, you know, the guy who keeps showing up when you're in trouble?"

"Gus? No, I don't think so, he would have said something."

Eddie took a long drink, "Don't worry about it, it'll show up somewhere."

"That's what worries me." Hank shook his head. Then looking at each of the other men said, "I think it's time we faced up to our responsibility in this thing. I think we need to talk about what happened that night."

"What happened that night is that we all ran into the room and Pettiford was dead and you were standing over him, your head bleeding, with the rifle." Gino slowly scanned the faces in the cabin.

Hank looked up to see the five men staring at him through the haze, every one of them frozen at that point in time. "I didn't shoot him, I know I didn't."

"Didn't say you did," Gino answered, "I just said you were standing over the body with a rifle in your hands."

"I guess the question is, what do we do about Pettiford?" Ollie said, stripping out of his long johns.

"What's to do about old Ronnie? I hear he's quite dead." Tom had moved away from the bunk towards the other men.

"And may he rest in peace." Bob added.

"Pettiford got what he deserved, justice was served." Ollie hung the long johns on a line over the stove.

"Yeah," Gino filled Tweety Bird with red wine. "Someone did this town a big favor."

Eddie sat with Bugs Bunny full of whiskey, his face twisted at the sound of Pettiford's name. "We could all go to jail!" He gestured, throwing his hands in the air. "Do you realize we all could go to jail?"

"Oh shut up Eddie." Gino took another drink from Tweety bird, "I think we should just go home after hunting season and forget the whole thing."

Hank felt the irritation growing. "That's okay for you to say, I live here."

Gino interrupted. "That's your problem; you never had the guts to move outta here."

"I think of it more like you guys running away." Hank said, "Just like you did every time we got into trouble. You always left someone else holding the bag."

Eddie motioned with his hands. "Yeah, you guys left me holding the bag, you didn't—"

Hank ignored Eddie. "How did we get into this mess in the first place?"

"If you wouldn't have begged and whined to go up to Pettiford's with us, this wouldn't have happened." Gino said.

"I don't think so Gino." Hank replied, "First of all, you guys were already at the mill when I got there and secondly, you had already decided to go up to Pettiford's, nobody twisted your arms to go."

Gino drank from his Tweety Bird mug. "Well if you didn't kill him, then the only other person in that room was Eddie—"

"Go to hell, you guys." Eddie was standing, his finger waving furiously. "I'll be damned if I'll let you make me the scapegoat. You guys used me—"

Gino cut him off. "Eddie, why don't you quit your whining? We didn't let you down at Pettiford's."

Eddie sat back on his bunk. "Then where were you when I needed you?"

Silence filled the interior of the small cabin again while outside, the wind howled as it whipped around, moaning as it tried to force its way through the crevices in the walls of

THE LAST DEER HUNT

the old hunting camp.

"Hah, see, just like I said, you guys let me down."

"Shut the fuck up," Gino said, almost snarling, "Didn't we all shoot that fat bastard with you?"

The mention of shooting Pettiford filled the room with a heaviness that became almost suffocating. Realizing that this conversation would not continue on its own, Hank took a deep breath. "The rumors in town are that the cops think the Sloan brothers are responsible for killing Pettiford. If we don't say anything, they could be accused of murder."

"What's wrong with that?" Gino said quickly, "They would become local folk heroes."

"Yeah," Ollie added, "They could have their fifteen minutes of fame."

"But it's not right." Hank shot back. "We know they didn't do it."

"Maybe, but then, we don't know who did kill him." Tom said.

Gino filled his Tweety Bird cup. "Yeah, but we were there that night." He took a long drink.

The other men looked at Gino. They knew he was right. They would be the main suspects.

Bob came over to join the others. "There has got be lots of suspects, lots of people who must have hated this man."

"Yeah, you're right," Tom nodded, "but once they thought it was us, they wouldn't even bother looking any further for the real killer."

Eddie took a long drink from Bugs and sat back; thinking for a minute, then quickly pulled himself up to the table. He stood, his face turning to a grayish green from the alcohol and the heat in the room. His hands covered his mouth as he moved quickly towards the door, but not quick enough and the nauseous smell of vomit filled the small cabin. Before Eddie was out the door, Gino and Ollie were quick on his heels, releasing their sickness as they ran.

The smell of vomit mixed with the hot smell of the wood stove and wet wool was overwhelming. Within minutes,

Hank watched as all the other men had succumbed and stood in a line in the cold evening air, retching. Back inside, he opened the door and windows, letting the cold night air push through the small cabin. As the cold sobered up the shivering men, fatigue started to set in, eyelids started to flutter and heads to nod.

Hank knew the conversation had ended. There would be no more discussion about the body tonight. The conversation slowly died away as each of the men withdrew back into their thoughts. The snow outside was still falling heavily and Hank decided he should spend the night here at the camp and go into town tomorrow after hunting. He banked the fire and turned down the kerosene lamps.

"We better get some sleep, got a big day hunting tomorrow." Hank said to no one in particular. *Maybe it would be O.K. if the Sloan brothers were accused. Hell, they would be heroes for getting rid of old Pettiford.* Hank crawled into his sleeping bag, and tossed and turned himself to sleep to a chorus of random snores.

Twenty-Nine

The first day of deer season brought a beautiful, sunny, but very cold morning with bushes and trees hanging down under twelve inches of new snow.

Inside the camp, the men were busy attacking stacks of pancakes and piles of bacon in preparation for the day's hunt. The cabin was steamy from the red-hot barrel stove as Ollie and Bob worked feverishly trying to keep the serving platters full.

No one was talking as they ate quickly, each anticipating the excitement of the hunt and the possibility that today they just might get lucky and bag a buck. Not just any buck, but a trophy buck.

Gino leaned back and slapped his stomach with both hands. "That was really a good breakfast you guys. You should cook every morning."

"No way." Bob and Ollie replied together. "Everybody gets a turn, them's the rules."

Gino put his plate in the sink and walked over behind Hank who was still eating and placed his hands on Hank's shoulders. "I'm sorry about yesterday, Hank, I know I was a pain in the butt but it didn't have anything to do with you and I apologize for being such a jerk." He gave Hank's shoulders a hard squeeze. "Just before I came up here, I was really fed up with my job and I did something really stupid." Gino put his head back and laughed. "I can't say I'm sorry, but it probably cost me my job." Gino gave Hank another hard squeeze. "I shouldn't take it out on you, buddy."

"Yeah, I understand and I'm okay with that. I hope everything will work out for you when you get back home."

Gino laughed, "It gets worse. When Marsha finds out about what I did, she'll leave me so fast, but only after she makes sure she gets everything she can squeeze out of me."

"Speaking of squeezing, Gino, you can let go of the shoulder anytime, okay?"

"Sorry guy." Gino let go of Hank, walked over to a large pile of clothes, and started picking out his cleanest hunting clothes.

"Hey, this is great!" Eddie wiped the food from his face. "See, we can all get along if we try." He looked around at the other men for their response and found none.

"I want to visit my Mom and her sister while I'm in town." Tom said, putting his dishes into the sink. "She's not doing well, her memory is really starting to go, and she hurt her hip. I might have to move her to another place."

"I haven't seen my Mom or Dad since they moved to Phoenix." Ollie moved over to the sink to help Bob with the pots and pans. "I guess they play a lot of golf, play cards every night, and are always going somewhere. They live in this retirement village and ride around on golf carts on streets that have names like Twilight Drive, Sunset Lane, and Trails End."

"My Mom and Dad are doing God's work." Bob said, piling up cooking utensils in the sink. "They are running a mission in Zacapa, Guatemala working with the Mayan Indians. I don't hear from them too often, but I get a letter about every couple of months."

Eddie emptied the coffeepot into his cup. "At least your folks write. Hell, I don't even know where my Pa and Ma

THE LAST DEER HUNT

are. They both left after they split up. I think Ma moved to Iron Mountain, but she's never tried to call or write." He said, staring down at his plate.

"Geez Eddie," Ollie stood up from the sink, "did you ever try calling them, or writing them?"

Eddie's look suggested that the thought had never crossed his mind. "Yeah, may-be I should do that."

The men were up and busy. The cabin became a beehive of activity as their thoughts moved to the days hunt. They were busy preparing for it, putting on long johns, heavy woolen pants, suspenders, three layers of shirts and two of socks that took some time to wiggle into after a big breakfast and too many cups of coffee. Hats and coats were delayed as each of the men made the required, but unpleasant trip through the deep snow to the frigid outhouse.

Outside, while the guns were checked and loaded, the petty bickering started between Eddie and Gino. "You know Gino, that cannon you brought ain't worth a darn up here in these woods. You ain't never gonna get a shot off over 40 yards in this thick brush, and that makes your scope worthless, picks up nothing but brush."

Gino leaned close to Eddie. "Oh listen to mister deer hunter here, I bet you couldn't shoot a buck—"

"Hey, that's a good idea," Tom broke in, "why don't we all put fifty dollars into a kitty and the first one who shoots a deer gets the kitty."

"Yeah sure," Bob laughed. "Hell, since Tom and I aren't hunting, that gives you four a better chance to win."

"Well, you guys might as well say goodbye to your money," Gino was speaking directly to Eddie, "you ain't got a chance."

Before Eddie could answer, Hank broke in, "Save it guys. Christ, can't you two just go out, and hunt without having to get into a meaningless argument?"

Hank's stinging comment made all the men stop and look at him. Looking at the men for some help, Hank asked,

"Where does everybody want to hunt today?" When no one volunteered, Hank continued, "I think the railroad grade would be a good spot, down by the opening where we put the apples."

Tom took his camera and moved over next to Gino. "Why don't I go with you down to the grade?"

Bob would take his camera and he and Ollie would hunt on the bluffs down near the river while Hank and Eddie decided to try the ridges near the edge of the swamp.

Hank had Eddie stay on the edge of the first ridge while he would walk up and around a half mile loop over the second ridge, hoping to scare up something and drive it towards Eddie. Hank fought with himself for a few minutes and then decided not to say anything to Eddie about his large flask of whiskey. *None of my business.*

The first sweep over the ridge brought Hank along a trail he knew the deer had been using earlier in the year and as he suspected, he found the tracks of three different deer in the fresh snow following the trail towards the swamp. *Looked like a buck, a doe and a yearling.* Hank always liked the woods where in the silence of the snow-covered trees he could lose himself in a world of solitude. He walked the quarter mile towards the river to the next ridge where he found a large opening. He chose a place to sit on the ridge, just at the dividing line between the maples and oaks above him, and the pines, balsam firs and spruce below him. From here, he could see up and down the ridge from the river to the edge of the swamp.

Twenty minutes went by when his eye caught the movement on his right, just down the ridge. Out of instinct, the rifle went to his shoulder and the safety clicked off. He sat motionless, his finger working its way out of the heavy glove onto the cold metal of the trigger. There! He sensed the movement again; a head, no antlers, a doe broke out of the trees about seventy-five yards down the ridge. The wind was coming towards him, so the doe would not pick up his scent. Quickly, but cautiously, the animal moved into the

THE LAST DEER HUNT

opening, followed by a smaller deer. *Yearling*, Hank thought. He aimed at the doe, just behind her front leg, directly where her heart was, and Hank knew the 220-grain slug in the rifle would be lethal. The doe's head came up and she looked right at Hank with her very large dark eyes. She knew Hank was something alien to her, but without the wind, she could not tell if he was a threat. The smaller deer, following the doe's lead, was also looking directly at him.

Hank had a permit to shoot the doe; the department of conservation had given out a good number of them this year hoping to thin the herds. The paper companies were decrying the fact that the overabundance of deer was destroying the woodlands. *Profits more like it*, Hank thought. He kept the bead of the front sight at the same spot behind the front leg of the deer.

The doe stood at the edge of the opening sensing danger. Still watching Hank closely, she dug her pointed front hooves into the snow and in her stiff-legged dance, blowing condensation-laden air from her nostrils. *She's trying to make me move, make me commit myself*, Hank thought, half aloud. The rifle pointed directly at her heart, all Hank had to do was squeeze the trigger. *I've never shot a doe, and I'm not going to start now.* He clicked the safety on and swung the gun in the air. "Go, go, git, git out of here." In one leap, the doe was gone, chasing through the woods after her yearling. She had not gone more than a couple of yards into the snow covered pines and the silence was back.

A few snowflakes were falling and the clouds covered the sun creating a flat dull light with no shadows. Hank poured himself a cup of coffee out of his thermos bottle and sat shaking in the cold. *Yes, I've shot deer, but I never enjoyed it. The only reason I hunted was so Pa and my friends would like me. Around here, hunting and killing for food is what men do, it's a way of life. At least, it used to be a way of life.*

Sitting quietly intensified the cold, but it always seemed

to bring his thoughts into sharper focus and his father came to mind. In many respects, he was his father. Many of his values were his father's values. He had chosen to stay in Fairhaven, to live his life here. Like his father, he married his high school girlfriend and worked in the mill alongside his father and other young men who stayed in the area. Like his father, he turned to drink. He found the tavern and sought out companionship and familiarity there. Unlike his father however, he chose not to stay on that path. Maggie and Frenchy, sometimes with gentle persuasion, and other times, with blunt reprimands and open condemnation kept him from falling into that chasm when he was hanging on the edge by his fingers.

A sharp report, muffled as it was by the snow, shook Hank out of his thoughts. "Sounds like Eddie's 257 Roberts...Damn it's that doe." He quickly headed down the ridge towards where he had left Eddie.

The doe was lying in the snow, still alive and thrashing painfully in an ever-widening pool of red. "Hank, I got one! After all these fricken years I finally got one!"

"Yeah Eddie, you shot a doe, and she's still alive, would you put her out of her misery for Christ sake?"

Eddie looked at him, disgust etched into his face. "Me? You want me to kill it?"

"Oh Jesus Eddie, you are a loser, you know that?" Hank took the safety off, pointed his rifle right behind the deer's front leg, right at the heart, and fired. The young doe jerked violently and lay still.

"Eddie, you don't have a doe permit."

"You got one; you can give it to me."

"No way Eddie, it's your deer, you take care of it."

Eddie was circling the deer, poked it with his rifle to assure it was dead. "Hey Hank, help me gut it?"

"Nope, Eddie, you shot the damn thing, you clean it out."

"Hell, I don't know how! You got to help me clean this thing."

"Eddie, you carry that big hunting knife on your belt, now

THE LAST DEER HUNT

it's about time that you used it." Hank walked back over his tracks towards the camp. He looked back to see Eddie standing over the deer with his knife in hand.

Gino and Tom had returned to the camp when Hank got back. "You guys have any luck?"

"Nope, just tracks. I heard a shot. That come from you?"

"That was Eddie." Hank poured a cup of coffee from the pot on the stove.

Gino and Tom waited, but when Hank did not continue, Tom asked, "Well?"

Hank had to laugh, thinking of Eddie standing over the deer, not wanting to gut it. "Eddie got himself a doe."

Gino poured himself a large glass of red wine. "Eddie doesn't have a doe permit, how the hell could he do that?"

"Guess he didn't need it," Hank rinsed out his cup and headed for the door. "And I don't know what he's going to do with that doe...I'm sure as hell not going to keep it at my house. Especially with all those cops running around."

Bob and Ollie returned and Hank retold the story of Eddie and the doe.

"You had any time to think about what we should do?" Ollie addressed the question to Hank, but he looked around the room for any answer. "I mean about the body?"

"No, I haven't." Hank was still in his hunting clothes, the other four men were in long johns.

Noticing that Hank was still dressed, Tom inquired, "Going into town tonight?"

"Yeah, I guess I'd better go back in and see what's new." Hank headed for the door, but turned around and went over to where the four men were standing near the stove. "I'll be back tomorrow, and then we settle this whole matter once and for all."

Thirty

Hank reached over and softly touched Maggie's cheek as she slept. Last night had been a beautiful evening and even the news about Brandon coming to Fairhaven had done nothing to dampen the mood. He quietly slipped into his clothes and blowing a kiss back to Maggie, went out into the darkness of early morning and walked through the alleys to Frenchy's Diner to elude any police or reporters who might be out and about.

"What's up?" Frenchy called from behind the counter, sliding out a cup of coffee and a plate filled with scrambled eggs, toast, and bacon in front of Hank.

"I'm on my way back to the camp."

"Just as well, this place has been a zoo for the last couple of days. People are coming in from all over just to gawk and reporters are interviewing everyone they can find. And, oh yeah, the cops are everywhere.

Frenchy leaned over the counter "The police confiscated a number of weapons from the Sloan's house, a Remington .22, a couple of shotguns, a twelve and a twenty gauge, and a German military rifle, I believe."

Hank did not want to ask the question and he was not

THE LAST DEER HUNT

sure he wanted to hear the answer, but asked. "Did the police say anything about the German rifle?"

Frenchy hesitated slightly. "No, but from what I heard, it was in bad condition. I believe it's down at the state police lab undergoing ballistics testing right now."

"Thanks Frenchy."

Only a few regulars sat around the diner trying to resolve worldly issues and Lucy was scurrying around straightening, dusting, and wiping down everything she could reach.

"Frenchy, let's get a booth, there's something I'd like to talk about."

"What's up buddy?" Frenchy asked.

"This whole thing about shooting Pettiford is bothering me."

"Yeah, that's understandable, all you turkey's went and shot him, one at a time."

"But Pettiford was already dead at that point. Someone already had shot him."

"And you don't know who that was, right?"

"No I don't." Hank was reaching back, brushing away mental cobwebs, trying to reach back to that night. "If I could only remember what happened between the times I passed out by the pool until I was standing over the body with the gun."

"Okay Hank, let's take it slow, maybe we can get you to recall what happened. What was the last thing you remember before falling asleep?"

"I felt sick and when I went over to lie down; I tripped and hit my head on something, then I lay down in a lounge chair. I must have passed out."

"And the next thing you remember is?"

"I heard a gunshot. And the next thing I knew was that I was standing over Pettiford with the rifle."

"How did you get there from the pool into the house?"

"When I heard the gunshot, I must have gone into the house."

"Do you remember anything about how you did that?

Really focus."

The cobwebs in Hank's mind started to flutter, as if driven by the air currents created by his intense concentration. "I remember now, the door to the house. Yes, I am inside the house and yes, I remember, I could hear somebody crying in the room to the left."

"That's good Hank."

The cobwebs fluttered more wildly and Hank could see himself inside a large room, yes, it was a library. "

"Think now Hank, think hard. You are standing there not knowing what to do. Can you recall what happened next?"

Hank squeezed his eyes tightly, pushing aside the remaining cobwebs. "The room was decorated in red wallpaper; the walls are filled with books. There are large works of art on the walls, statues, and knights standing like guards."

"Good, that's good Hank, and then what did you do?"

"The rifle, it was laying on the floor with a bunch of other stuff. I just went over and picked it up. I don't know why, and then...I can't remember..."

"Focus Hank, Really focus hard. What happened next?"

"Yes, that's it, I saw him..."

Frenchy waited for Hank to continue.

"Pettiford, it was Pettiford, I remember his piggy face. He was lying in the middle of the floor with a lot of things around him on the floor and I was standing over him."

"And that's when the rest of your buddies came running in?"

"Yes, wow, this is something, after all this time, I remember. I remember!"

"You know what this means Hank."

"Yeah, it means I can finally remember what happened that night."

"Well yes, but it also means that you didn't shoot Pettiford because the shot you heard was the one that killed him. So someone else shot him."

"That makes me feel better." Hank thought for a minute. "But then, who did shoot him?"

THE LAST DEER HUNT

"Why didn't you just ask John Deer?"

"Wouldn't have done any good."

"Why not?"

"Because I didn't know the answer. But thanks for helping out, good buddy. At least I know now what happened, and I know I didn't do it." Hank was up, ready to go. "I better hit the road, and I would appreciate it if you didn't mention to anyone that we're staying out at the camp."

A mixed sense of relief and apprehension filled Hank as he drove towards the hunting camp. The large snowflakes were dizzying as they curled upward, almost blurring out the road.

Perhaps now, those dark suppressed memories would no longer be capable of influencing every aspect of his emotions without him being aware of it. But the question remained. Who killed Pettiford?

A snow covered Hank walked into the cabin startling the five men sitting around the small table.

Ollie peered at him through the dimly lit cabin. "Hey, you just missed lunch. We had beans and franks."

"Thanks for warning me. Didn't anyone get out hunting today? What's the matter, too cold?"

"Nah, we took a vote and decided we want to go into town today." Eddie said, leaning over, putting dishes and silverware into the sink.

"Yeah, we're getting cabin fever. We gotta get out of here for awhile." Gino was washing out the dishes in the sink.

Hank filled his coffee cup. "Don't know if that would be a good idea, the town is crawling with reporters, sightseers, and cops."

Tom was gathering dishes from the tables. "Was there anything new about the body?"

"No, but they found a German rifle at the Sloan's home."

"Do you think it's the same gun?" Tom asked.

"It was a German Mauser and it was covered with mud. It has to be the same gun."

"How the hell...?" Gino was shaking his head. "How could they know where it was? Did they see you bury it, Duval?"

"I don't know; I'm just as confused as you are."

"Well, if they saw you bury it Hank, then everyone will know it was you."

Gino leaned forward, slowly looking at each of the men. "So once again, Hank Duval has got us all in trouble."

"Wait a minute," Eddie waved his arms, "we don't know that for sure. I mean there has to be lots of different explanations of how they ended up with the gun."

"Okay Eddie," Gino faced him, "let me hear one explanation."

Silence.

Tom tried to reason it out as he spoke. "Maybe they could have discovered it some other time by accident."

"I don't think so." Bob shook his head. "I didn't think anyone in the world knew about the bog or ever went there."

"Oh sure Lindstrom," Gino scowled. "It was your idea to bury that stupid gun in the bog." Mocking Bob's voice, he continued. "'I know a place where nobody will ever look,' you said, 'Not in a million years,' you said! Good choice Bob."

"Shut up Gino." Bob shot back, scowling. "At least I have the ability to have an idea once in a while. That's more than I can say about you."

"Screw you, you dumb Swede." Gino scowled back.

Ollie was on his feet. "Hey, watch your mouth, Gino. Christ, you don't have the I.Q. level of the Sloan brothers put together."

"You should talk, Ollie," Gino smirked. "If it wasn't for your Italian girlfriend you'd probably starve to death while trying to figure out how to use a can opener."

He gave two-thumbs up gesture to Eddie, who silently mouthed, "All Right Gino, way to go!"

Ollie shook his head. "Hey, what you think Bob? Should

we take that kinda crap from this greasy WOP?" Stepping towards Gino, "Especially a big ugly hairy one like you."

"Yeah," Bob had joined Ollie in front of Gino. "Probably can't even see your pecker under that big WOP stomach. I doubt if you could even throw a punch anymore, you fat ass."

One of Gino's smirky smiles grew across his face. "Would you care to find out?" He motioned Bob and Ollie to move forward.

Hank moved quickly between the four men. "Whoa! You guys are getting too serious."

Tom followed, "Yeah, you guys are supposed to be friends. What ever happened to one for all and all for one?"

"It'll be one smooshed for all and all smooshed together if I get my hands on those two shitheads." Gino yelled, trying to reach past Hank and Tom.

"Enough already!" Hank pushed Gino back into Eddie.

Gino, Eddie, Bob, and Ollie looked at Hank with astonishment, surprised by his strong remarks.

"Damn, when did you get so assertive?" Tom whispered.

Hank replied, grinning. "I've been practicing."

Tom was still standing between the four men. "Come on guys, let's cool it. Shake hands and be friends."

Gino and Ollie, Bob and Eddie shook hands reluctantly and moved back towards the table, stills staring at each other.

Hank stretched his arms trying to work out the tension. "I think we still need to be talking about what to do about Pettiford. It's not going to go away and we need to deal with it." He was standing, hands on hips, looking hard at the men.

"Who the hell died and made you the Boss?" Ollie snickered.

"You guys don't seem to get the point; we need to come to a decision on what we're going to do about this."

"Personally, I don't give a damn who did what to who but I'm tired of this shit." Gino blurted out, "I got to get out of here for a while. I'm getting claustrophobic stuck out here in this little shit-box of a camp."

"Me too." Eddie said, moving over beside Gino. "Why don't we get out of here for a while. Maybe we can go into town or at least to the tavern."

"We're not going anywhere until we figure out what we're doing." Hank felt the frustration building up. "Sit down. The town is crawling with cops. They would pick you up in five minutes."

"Hank is right." Tom gestured towards the door. "We need to agree on what we're going to do about Pettiford."

Eddie was busy opening a new bottle of whiskey. "Why don't we just draw straws and the loser takes the blame?"

Gino shot an angry look at Eddie. "Why don't you just shove the straw up your butt? Just for the hell of it, let's just say you did it. You were alone with Pettiford when he was raping you—"

"He didn't rape me!" Eddie took a step towards Gino. "He didn't rape me, Dammit!" He stepped back, slumped into a chair and found his glass of whiskey. Taking a long drink, barely audibly, he repeated, "He didn't rape me." Then Eddie stood, visibly shaking, his voice, high and sputtering. "No way, Gino, you're not gonna do this to me again. You didn't come and help me at Pettiford's; you just waited and let that creep..." His voice trailed off in a series of quick breaths.

"Yeah, okay Eddie, whatever." Gino took another drink of wine.

Yeah, whatever yourself, you fat ass." Eddie stuttered. "All I know is that Pettiford stood up, said "what do you kids think you're doing," and then the shot. Christ, it was so fricken loud, and even with my eyes closed, I saw the muzzle flash; it had to be right next to me."

"Well, if we don't believe Eddie did it," Gino pulled the cork out of a bottle of red wine and drank from the bottle, looked around the room at the other men, stopping at Ollie. "Did you shoot Pettiford?"

THE LAST DEER HUNT

Ollie just looked at Gino, shaking his head. "I was with Bob."

"How about you Tom? Where were you?" Gino took another drink.

"I was with you Gino."

A long drink of wine, same crooked smile, Gino said. "Well then, maybe old Pettiford was so racked with guilt over diddling Eddie that he went over, got the rifle, and somehow shot himself in the heart." Gino looked around at the men, "No? Well, gee whiz now, that kinda narrows it down to Hank and Eddie, doesn't it? And by process of elimination, Little Eddie was over in the corner crying like a baby...that leaves you, Duval." One more drink of wine. "You standing over the body, bloody head, makes sense to me," Gino gestured, "what do you think?" To the other men, "Doesn't it make sense to you?"

A few heads nodded and a couple of "Yeah sure" were mumbled. "Then that's that," Gino raised Tweety in a salute. "Hank Duval shot and killed Pettiford."

"You guys are something." Hank said, the tone of his voice harsh and accusatory, "When it's convenient, we are all part of this all for one shit, but when it's not, some of us are not included." He slowly scanned the faces of the silent men, "I think that's enough of this horse-shit about me shooting Pettiford."

Gino threw up his hands in frustration. "Then how do you explain the fact that you were standing over Pettiford with the rifle?"

Hank leaned forward and looked directly at each of the men. "I am going to say this once, and this is the last time I am going to say it. I did not kill Pettiford. I did not fire that rifle—"

"Yeah, what about—" Bob injected.

Hank glared at him, "No! I know I did not kill Pettiford that night. I can now remember every second from the time I heard the gunshot until I was standing over the body and I certain, without a doubt that I did not kill him."

"So, what does that prove?" Gino shrugged.

Hank spoke, slowly and deliberately. "It proves that you guys are trying like hell to convince me I shot and killed Pettiford, because if I didn't do it, then one of you did."

The room fell into dead silence, the men wilting under Hank's glare.

Ollie broke the silence. "But, we all—"

"No more bullshit!" Hank said, almost menacingly. "Just the truth."

More silence, glances, furtive looks, and then Eddie cleared his throat. "If good ol' Vic were here," looking around at the others, "he'd know what to do."

Hank's laugh startled the men. "Sorry good buddies, but good ol' Vic can't help you this time. Good Ol' Vic is dead."

"You're serious?" Bob muttered.

"Dead serious," Hank laughed again, "No pun intended."

No response from the men, Hank shook his head, "Come on guys, what's up? Don't you even want to know how he died?" Without waiting, Hank continued. "Seems like his abused wife finally had enough and she gave him a warning shot with a 350 Magnum...right between the eyes."

Eddie poured a drink and downed it in one swallow. "I always figured someone would get him."

Gino, standing by the stove, took a long drink of wine. "Shit, damn Vic Pollo."

"You are sure that Vic is dead?" Ollie asked, moving over near Gino.

"That's what I've been told." Hank replied.

Bob and Tom both stood and moved near the stove. Hank watched the men, their sidelong glances, and small nuances, and feeling something unsaid passing between them as they stood in silence.

Gino took one long drink and looked at Hank, "Truth?"

"Truth." Hank answered. "I want the truth."

"Vic did it." Gino lifted his bottle to drink, but only a few drops came out.

THE LAST DEER HUNT

"Vic did what?" Hank looked at Gino, trying to comprehend.

"There is no need to keep this a secret." Digging through a large cardboard box next to the sink, Gino pulled out another bottle of wine. "Vic was at Pettiford's that night." Gino uncorked the bottle and took a drink. "He followed us up to Pettiford's and while we were busy playing games, he was robbing the place. He figured that we would distract Pettiford and that he could get in and out without anybody ever knowing. He said that as he was leaving, he surprised Pettiford, who yelled at him, so he shot him with the rifle, dropped it, and ran out."

"What?" Hank sputtered, "And all this time you kept saying I was the one who shot him?" He quickly looked around at the others who stood in silence.

"We couldn't tell you, Vic said that—"

"That's horse shit," Hank growled, "You could have told me. I am not just anyone off the street. I'm supposed to be part of this gang." Hank glanced around the room. "Are all you part of this conspiracy?"

Eddie stood up, glaring at the others. "Not me, I didn't know anything about this...how come you guys didn't say anything to me about Vic?" Eddie's voice was touched with anger.

"You didn't know about Vic being there either?" Hank asked, looking at Eddie.

"No, nobody told me anything, damn it."

"Looks like we're the only two who don't seem to know what's going on." Hank said. "How come none of you guys told Eddie and me about this before?" His attempt to make eye contact with Ollie and Bob was met with each man looking away.

Gino took a long drink from the wine bottle, "'Cause we were protecting you, like you were little brothers or something. We figured the less you and Eddie knew, the less chance you had of getting into trouble. Vic told us that if we said anything, he would have say we were all involved in his plot."

Hank shook his head. "If Vic were still alive, you would be still trying to blame me."

"Come on Duval, you don't think we would let you take the blame for this, do you?" Gino was up, pulling his suspenders up over his dirty undershirt, "What the hell do you take us for?"

"Yeah," Bob gestured disbelief, "you didn't believe we would do that, did you?"

"Yeah Hank, we would never do that," Ollie joined in, "You're one of us, a buddy, a pal. There is no way we would let you take the blame."

"What about me?" Eddie whined. "You guys woulda never told me about Vic?"

"Nah little buddy," Ollie said, "Not till Vic was dead and couldn't tell on us."

Gino tipped the bottle and drank deeply, a small trickle of wine running down his chin that he wiped with his sleeve. His large frame sat heavily in the chair, his muffled voice, a whisper. "Yeah, if Vic would have said we were all part of the plot, we woulda all been charged with murder."

Bob sat shaking his head. "None of this would have happened if we ever—"

"Not now Bob," Ollie said, cutting Bob short.

Hank looked at the men, "If we ever what? What are you talking about?"

"Nothing." Ollie said quickly, still looking at Gino. "What Bob meant was why we ever got involved in this whole mess in the first place."

"That's for sure." Tom nodded, putting a log into the old barrel stove.

Gino, Bob, and Ollie nodded.

The fire caught and the heat started to push back the cold. Fiery images danced around the walls and ceilings from narrow openings in the stove while the men stood lost in their own quiet thoughts.

Hank stood and stretched, trying to release the tension in his neck and back. "I don't know about you guys, but I

THE LAST DEER HUNT

am absolutely confused. So okay, we say Vic was there that night, why would anybody believe us?"

Gino answered, "Because he is Vic Pollo."

"But," Hank said, thinking aloud. "How do we convince the police that Vic did it?"

Gino flashed one of his quirky smiles. "That's easy; we all swear that Vic was there that night. He had means, motive, opportunity and he was Vic Pollo who everybody knows was crazy. We all stick to that story, and we'll be okay."

"Yeah but," Eddie squeaked, "Hank and I didn't know that Vic was there. We would be lying...and the cops would know that right away."

Tom stood, stretching. "Then, little buddy, you and Hank just tell the truth and say what you saw that night. That would work."

"Okay then." Bob headed outside towards the outhouse. "We have Pettiford's killer."

"Yeah," Gino's speech slurred. "I like this solution. It only affects two really rotten people, Pettiford and Pollo."

"I just want this whole thing to go away." Eddie was sitting, his head in his hands. "I just want the demons to let me alone."

"Yeah, I know, I'm frustrated too." Hank could hear his words from a distance, as if he were outside his body. "I have these dreams where this ugly dead man with this piggy face tries to catch me and drag me away with him. Some nights I wake up completely covered with sweat."

"You too?" Ollie lay on his back on his bunk, his head on his hands. "Damn, I thought I was the only one."

Bob lay on his bunk. "Every day I would pray that Hannah wouldn't find out that I've been living this lie. Now she'll know that it was Vic."

"Hey look," Eddie said, pointing, "Gino's sleeping. He must feel good now that the truth is out about Vic."

Ollie walked over to Gino's bunk and leaned over. "Nah, just too much wine."

"What about you Tom, how are you feeling?" Hank asked.

Tom sat on the edge of the top bunk, legs dangling over the edge of Eddie's bunk, below his. "I got my own demons. I had to deal with this stuff, and growing up gay in Fairhaven was not fun and games either." Tom shifted uncomfortably. "Yeah, that's right; I'm coming out of the closet!"

"Yeeow! You mean like you're gay?" Eddie was sitting on the lower bunk looking up at Tom's legs, dangling over his bunk. "Get your gay legs out of my bunk!"

"Finally decided to come out of the closet, eh?" Hank said, laughing. "What took you so long? Did you think we didn't know? Hell, I've known since you were a junior."

"Yeah, we all knew." Ollie laughed. "You dropped so many hints, you know, like your choice of lingerie, especially that cute little pink item."

"Yeeow! How come you guys never told me?" Eddie was still staring at Tom's legs.

"Tom, it didn't make any difference," Bob said. "Still doesn't. Not to us anyway."

"Well, how about that," Tom sat, his head moving slowly from side to side, not sure if what he had heard was good news or bad news. "I spent all that time worrying I would be found out and all which time, it didn't matter."

"Yeah, it really doesn't matter does it?" Eddie lay down on his bunk. "But you can still get your gay legs out of my bunk, and for Christ sakes, you should at least shave those ugly things."

"So, why don't we wake Gino up and go into town." Eddie said, looking for approval from the others.

"Great idea," Ollie was at Gino's bunk, shaking him.

Among great snorts, wheezes, snarls and swearing, Gino sat up. "What the hell? What are you idiots doing?"

"It's four o'clock, let's go into town?" Ollie was digging into the clothes basket, looking for clean underwear.

Gino rubbed the sleep from his eyes. "You guys are

THE LAST DEER HUNT

nuts." More snorts and grunts. "Did you come to any conclusions?"

"Yes we did." Eddie hoisted his two thumbs in the air. "We all shot him."

"Yeah, after he was already dead." Ollie said, putting new wood into the stove. "We all agree; our late and great friend Vic was killer."

Tom added. "Then we just continued to kill him."

"Yeah," Eddie said, laughing hard, "Were we ever stupid." His laughter was bringing tears to his eyes, "And they can't convict us for stupidity!" His smile faded, replaced by a frown. "Can they? I mean, do you think we could go to jail?"

"That couldn't happen?" Tom spoke softly, phrasing his words into a question. "If we all stick together and tell the truth, they won't be able to convict any of us, right?"

"To truth!" Eddie raised an imaginary glass in a toast.

"Hear, hear. To truth." Tom echoed.

"Yeah, to truth." Ollie raised an imaginary glass. "And to the Omega Gang!"

"You're with us on this, aren't you Hank?" Bob asked

Hank hesitated, his mind still trying to grasp this new information. He scanned the faces of the men around him who were watching him, looking for an answer. "I don't know, I mean yeah, I guess so, it kinda makes sense." *Actually, it feels good not be the prime suspect.*

"One for all, and all for one." Eddie drank from his imaginary cup.

Cries of "Hear, Hear," and "One for all," filled the little cabin.

Thirty-One

Evening was settling in the woods and the lights of the small hunting camp flickered through the windows and into the darkness outside.

The mood of the camp had definitely changed. Bantering had replaced complaining. Petty arguments had turned into playful teasing. Hank had joined Tom, Gino, and Bob at the table taking turns talking about their lives and listening intently to the others.

Hank watched the men getting ready to go and contemplated the events of the day. He was not totally comfortable, especially the disclosure about Vic being the killer, or the fact that they guys had kept it secret all these years. Yet, it did make sense, and it was good that everyone agreed with it. He stuck his head out the door and watched the snowflakes swirling in the light from the doorway. "Are you guys really sure you want to go into town tonight?"

Eddie buttoned up his union suit and with a smug grin, said. "Yeah, that's what we all agreed on."

Gino added, "We decided that we gotta get out of this place for a while."

"I don't know if that's such a good idea." Hank argued,

THE LAST DEER HUNT

"Those cops are probably looking for you."

"Hell, if we wait here, they're gonna come out after us anyway." Ollie said, putting on his cleanest old shirt.

Bob interrupted with a nervous laugh. "Yeah, it's only a matter of time."

"Yeah, Hank," Eddie squeaked. "We figured you were going back into town anyway to see Maggie."

As one, the men hurriedly finished getting dressed and that done, stood by the door ready to go.

"Oh what the hell," Hank laughed, "This is the second time you guys all agreed on something, but we can't all fit in the pickup. I'll have to drive you in two at a time. Let's go!"

"No way," Eddie was slipping his coat on. "We'll ride in back of the pickup."

Hank looked at him. "You're all out of your freakin minds; it's got to be 10° below zero out there."

The door flew open and the men spewed out into the early night. Cries of 'Yahoo!' and 'Let's go Omega Gang!' Then Eddie's voice, "One for all, and all for one!" Gino's low voice followed. "Put a lid on it Eddie."

Hank led the way with his flashlight. The walk to the truck was punctuated with snowballs and horseplay. The men arrived at the truck, gasping and panting, half-exhausted, but in good spirits.

The bed of the pickup was cleared of snow and Ollie, Tom and Bob jumped in. Hank could only shake his head. "It's your funeral guys."

Gino and Eddie squeezed into the cab with Hank. The truck started on the third attempt and moved slowly down the road towards the Bayside Tavern, the blowing snow obliterating the three men in the back.

Eddie leaned towards Hank. "You're going to join us at the bar?"

"I thought I would go over to Maggie's for a couple of hours."

"Oh come on Hank, we really need to stick together right now." Eddie said, sounding almost like a plea.

"All right, I'll call her from the bar and fill her in on what's happening. I have to call Gus too and see about getting together with the lawyer."

The parking lot at the tavern was full. The area was full of hunters and hunters were a thirsty bunch, especially after hunting deer all day. The three men in the back of the truck hopped out, all looking like abominable snow creatures.

Inside, the bar was filled with a high intensity noise level as hunters tried to out-talk the other with their tales of the day's hunt. Pitchers of beer filled the bar and every table and the inevitable cigarette smoke filled the air.

"Hey Hank, how's it going? It's good to see you." Harry's voice came from behind a veil of smoke that hung over the bar. "Did you have a chance to do some more sketches? We could sell em before we even put them up."

"Nope, haven't had a chance. Mind if I use the phone?"

"Help yourself." Harry briefly came out of the blue smoke cloud, put another pitcher of beer in front of the young man on Hank's old stool, and disappeared again.

Hank quickly dialed before somebody else could request the phone. "Hi Maggie, what's up?" The question was asked in apprehension, hoping the answer would be a simple 'nothing.'

"Nothing.—"

"Nothing. That's good." Hank responded.

"Nothing is not good. I mean nothing is going right over here." Maggie's voice was filled with frustration.

"What do you mean, nothing is going right?" Again, he wasn't sure he wanted to hear the answer.

Maggie's voice came over the phone as if she was mentally checking off a list. "First, I have to finish working on this article, and then I have so much to do around here to get ready for Brandon. Then your Uncle Andre stopped by to leave off a package and..." A long pause.

Hank waited, Maggie's frustration was transferring to

him and the cigarette smoke in the bar made his eyes water. "And what?"

"Oh nothing. It just seems like everything is happening all at once. And oh yes," after another short pause, she continued. "Frenchy called to let you know that the Sloan boys told the police that they had found the rifle along the tracks down by the river about seven or eight years ago."

Now it was Hank's turn to pause. *How the heck did it get there?* Thinking aloud, he said. "So they don't know who buried the rifle." For just a brief second, he held the notion that maybe they shouldn't say anything. *Nobody would ever know if we just kept our mouths shut.*

Maggie was reading his mind over the phone. "You guys can't just keep quiet and let the Sloan boys take the blame for this."

Hank caught the worry in Maggie's voice. *Yeah, too many people already know too much to keep it quiet...*

Maggie's voice broke through his thoughts. "Brandon will be here before Thanksgiving." She hesitated, "He wants to start..."

Hank's mind was racing. *Then again, if the Sloan brothers don't know anything, maybe, just maybe..."*

Maggie's voice broke through his thoughts, "Hank, you're not even listening. You don't even know what I'm saying, do you?"

Hank heard Maggie, but his thoughts were on his own problems. "Yes, of course, you said Brandon was coming." *Could we get away with this? I wonder...* Then aloud, "How...?"

"By plane, he's coming by plane into Marquette...Bye Hank." The dial tone burned in Hank's ear.

"Damn." The realization of what Maggie said finally sank in. *Brandon will be here by Thanksgiving.* "I'll call her back right after I talk to Frenchy."

The phone rang twice before Frenchy picked it up. "Glad you called Hank. Did you hear the news about the Sloan brothers?"

"Yeah, Maggie told me. I don't know how anybody would believe that story about them finding it down by the tracks."

"Yeah, it's hard to know what to believe with those two." Frenchy said, a spark of excitement entering his voice. "I've got some really great news, but I'll wait to tell you when you get here."

Hank could sense the energy in Frenchy's voice and promised he would be over as soon as possible. He hung up and started to dial when Gino, Tom, and Eddie were beside him.

"My turn." Tom said, taking the telephone from Hank. "I'd like to give my Mom a call."

"Come on Hank, join us." Gino was tugging on Hank's coat.

"Yeah Hank, come on over. We're really having a great time." Ollie said, holding two pitchers of beer.

"I'm sorry guys; I need to get over to Maggie's. Something's come up and I need to talk to her. You guys take it easy while I'm gone, okay?"

"Yeah sure." Eddie said, carrying two glasses of whiskey and a bottle of red wine towards the booth. "You be careful out there, eh?"

Tom hung up the phone, and waved to Hank. "Hey buddy, if you get hung up at Maggie's, not to worry, we can always crash at my Mom's house. She's not there and there's enough room for all of us."

Hank waved thanks and was out the back door. The truck started quickly and as he pulled out of the parking lot, the sheriff's car pulled in, followed by a police car carrying the two detectives from the State Police Crime Unit. Hank fought off the urge to go back into the tavern.

With his mind full of guns, Pettiford, Maggie, and Brandon, he headed towards Fairhaven and Maggie's apartment.

Maggie let Hank in. Orphan greeted him with his circle dance and alternate jumping and pawing the rug. Hemingway sat in the window looking indifferent.

Hank shook the snow from his coat as he took it off and put it over the back of the chair.

Maggie took Hank's coat off the back of the chair, smelled it and wrinkled her nose, then hung it in the closet near the door.

"I really do apologize, Maggie, for being so out of it on the phone. I don't know where my mind is at half the time anymore."

"I'm sorry too. I had just hung up after talking to Brandon and I was not in a good mood. God, I am not looking forward to this!"

"Come here Orph." Hank knelt and scratched the dog's back. Orphan responded by rolling over on his back, exposing his stomach and pleading for Hank to scratch. Hank obliged. Maggie sat on the couch, Hemingway sitting on her lap, his purring the only sound in the room.

"Hank?"

"Maggie?"

"I told Brandon that it would be better if he didn't come. I told him that the weather was too bad and that we probably wouldn't have any opportunities to get any pictures, but he insisted and I've never been able to say no to that guy."

"Never?" Hank heard his voice squeak. "You could never say no to him?"

"Oh Hank," Maggie laughed, "Don't be silly, you know what I meant."

"Oh, yeah sure, as if I don't know what never and no mean."

"Honestly Hank, It's been four years since we've seen each other."

"Maggie, do you still have feelings for him?"

"I, no, I mean, yes, no, I don't, that is, no, I don't."

"Boy that sure was definite." Hank slowly shook his head.

"Come on Hank, it's just that so much is going on right now that it's confusing. Of course I don't have any feelings for Brandon, how could I?"

"Why are you asking me?" Hank shrugged.

Maggie stood, reached over, picked up a brown paper package, and handed it to Hank. "I almost forgot, Uncle Andre brought this package for you." Maggie, Hemingway, and Orphan watched intensely as Hank slowly unwrapped the package and removed a nine-by-twelve black framed certificate.

"What is it Hank? Please read it."

Hank sat looking at the plaque, slowly moving one hand over the surface. "It says, 'To Paul Duval. In recognition of your heroism and disregard for your own safety on April 14, 1956. For your gallant attempt to save the Lundgren family, the Governor of Michigan and the State of Michigan award you this plaque and Medal for Bravery.'"

The packaging fell to the floor, a two-inch medallion attached to a red, and blue ribbon fell out. Hank picked it up and handed it to Maggie along with the framed certificate.

Maggie held the certificate and moved her hand over it as she read. "I never knew this about your father. Why didn't you ever tell me?"

"Maggie, I just found out about this myself from Gus and Uncle Andre. It was Gus' house, his wife and his kids that Dad tried to save. He wasn't successful, but he tried and was burned and his leg was badly hurt."

"And for all these years, you never knew?"

"No, nobody ever told me. I guess Dad never wanted anyone to know and Mom would never say anything if he didn't want her to. I don't think he ever considered himself a hero, in fact, he felt it was his fault those people died. There are a lot of things I didn't know, or didn't remember about my father, or my mother, that I'm just starting to find out."

Maggie stood and Hemingway went back to his window. "That's so sad. I mean for your father not to accept that and to live all his life feeling guilty." Maggie left Hank alone with his thoughts while she went into the kitchen in search of something to eat. A quick check of the fridge and the pantry revealed nothing. "Hey Hank, I'm really starved and haven't had dinner yet, would you mind if we sent out for a pizza? And I must apologize, but tonight I really have to go over my article and have it ready when Brandon..." Maggie wrinkled her nose, "gets here."

"A pizza would be good. But after, I can take Orphan over to the house so he won't bother you." Hank hoped his disappointment didn't show.

"No, you can stay here. I'll just work at the kitchen table. I don't plan on spending all night on this stupid article, believe me! Brandon can take his pictures and I can write around what he has. Of course, that means all the work I've done so far may be for nothing."

The pizza finished, Maggie was back to her typewriter. Hank switched quickly through the four snowy channels before settling on a documentary about some small rock found in Texas that some scientist claimed came from Mars. "Can you believe that, how can they know this rock came from Mars?"

"Sorry Hank, I'm busy. Maybe if you watch the program, it'll tell you."

The television turned off, Hank tried solitaire. Six games later, he realized the deck was two cards short. "You could use a new deck of cards.

"That's nice." Maggie answered without looking up.

Finding a pencil and some paper, Hank sat drawing, copying from nature books lying around the apartment. He worked deftly and quickly and before he realized it, he had completed three sketches of a family of wolves.

"Those are really beautiful." Maggie said, having stood to stretch, "You do that so easily, you have such a great talent."

"Does this Brandon work in black and white, or color?"

"He can work in either or both. Sometimes he uses more than one camera. Now I really have to get back to my work."

Hank shrugged and returned to his drawing. One more sketch and the lead on the pencil broke. Time moved slowly, Hank skimmed through magazines and books, checked the refrigerator and every drawer and cabinet in the kitchen and tossed and turned on the couch out of boredom. "Maggie, I'm being abducted by space aliens and they are taking me back to their space ship to conduct sexual experiments on me!"

"That's sweet honey, have a good time." Then looking up, blowing the curls from her eyes, added, "If you don't stop pestering me, I'll never get done in here, and you will have waited all this time for nothing."

The television back on, the documentary on the Mars rock was still humming along at a snail's pace and just as it was to be revealed how the scientists had concluded they knew the rock had traveled from Mars, Maggie switched off the television.

"Darn Maggie, now I'll have to spend the rest of my life wondering how they knew this little one inch rock came from Mars and ended up in Texas."

Maggie sat down next to Hank. "I give up. This article will have to wait." She leaned over and kissed his cheek. "It's too bad you have to go and get the guys and bring them back to the camp."

"They're okay. They can spend the night at Tom's mother's house."

"Great." Maggie placed her hand on Hank's knee and slowly ran her hand up his thigh. "Now show me what those aliens did to you up there in their little space ship."

The next morning, Maggie was already up when Hank woke up with Hemingway lying on the couch next to his head watching him closely. Hank went to reach over and pet the big cat, but thought better of it and sat up. Maggie had just come into the room with two cups of coffee when Orphan leapt up, barking, just before the loud knock on the door startled them.

Sheriff McCarthy stood in the door, his massive bulk filling the entire doorframe. "Is Henry Duval here, Maggie?"

Maggie moved away from the door as the sheriff shuffled into the apartment.

"Morning Hank, sorry to bother you." Sheriff McCarthy said in an official voice.

Maggie was holding Orphan by the collar. Hemingway stood and arched his back, trying to look as menacing as he could.

Hank pulled the blanket up to his chin, feeling very naked with only underwear on. "It's okay Sheriff, what can I do for you?"

"I'm sorry Hank, but I'm going to have to take you over to the Baraga County jail in L'anse."

"Why?" Maggie asked. "Is Hank under arrest or something?"

"No Ma'am. Just need to bring him in for questioning."

Hank, wrapped in the blanket, went into the bathroom, and came out dressed in jeans and a sweatshirt. Pointing to the plaque and medallion on a small table, he said to Maggie, "Take care of these for me." Then to the sheriff he said. "Let's go Sheriff."

Sheriff McCarthy, his uniform straining under the stress, was trying to reach around his large frame with great difficulty. "Hank, can you give me a hand?"

Hank reached behind the sheriff and produced a pair of handcuffs.

"Good grief. You don't really need those things do you?" Maggie stood in front of the sheriff, looking up at him. "It's not like Hank is a criminal or anything."

"No Ma'am, it's just procedure. It's for Hank's protection."

Maggie glared at the sheriff. "You try to put those on Hank and you'll need protection from me!"

Sheriff McCarthy was not sure what to do. Slowly he stuffed the handcuffs in his belt and motioned for Hank to follow him.

Hank nodded to her. "It's okay Maggie. You can you

call Gus and tell him what's going on and that I need that lawyer now."

"Hank can be reached by calling the Baraga county courthouse." the sheriff said, tipping his hat to Maggie.

Followed by the sheriff, Hank walked towards the door and as he reached it, he pulled up his shoulders in his best Edward G. Robinson impersonation, "Okay, baby doll, will you visit me when I'm in the big house?"

"Hank, this is not funny. Do you want me to go with you?"

Hank did not hear her question. He was already down the stairs when he saw the crowd of people standing around the sheriff's car with its flashing lights.

Sheriff McCarthy, taking Hank by the arm and using his great bulk, pressed on through the crowd of reporters. "Make way, in the name of the law, let us through."

"Sorry about this Hank." Sheriff McCarthy said. "Hell, I've known you all your life and I know you're a good kid, but I got to do my duty." The car roared off, sirens screaming and lights flashing and turned down Skanee road, heading towards L'anse.

Thirty-Two

Hank followed the sheriff through the dull green halls of the Baraga County jail, passing empty cell after empty cell, each footstep echoing the length of the hall.

"Hey Hank, what took you so long?" Tom was standing with his face and hands hanging through the bars. "We missed you last night."

"Hey buddy! Good to see you." Eddie's shrill voice cut through the bars on the cell. "You here to get us out?"

Hank shook his head. "Nope."

Inside the cell, Gino lay sleeping on one cot while Bob sat on another, reading his Bible.

Sheriff McCarthy unlocked the door and stepped back while Hank, squinting in the dim light, entered the cell. "How long have you guys been here?"

"Hell," Eddie answered, "the sheriff and those two goons came into the bar right after you left, put us in cuffs and dragged us out. We had to spend the whole night here without any dinner. Probably just as well, breakfast was lousy."

Gino was awake, sat up, and rubbed the sleep from his eyes. "Jesus Hank, what's happening? Are we going to get out of here or what?"

"Don't know Gino. I sure hope so. Maggie is going to call Gus and see about the lawyer and hopefully he'll show up here today. What's been going on here? Where is Tom?"

Bob had put his Bible down. "Tom is in being questioned right now. They've been taking us out one at a time to different places and questioning us individually. I think they're trying to find contradictions in our stories. They've even been saying that we are blaming each other. Divide and conquer I guess."

"But we all stuck with our story about Vic being there that night." Gino said.

"Yeah, they'll keep this up till they find us guilty of something." Eddie's voice was strained. "It really hit home when they took me down and fingerprinted me and took my picture. Christ, now I'm a criminal and..."

"No you're not," Ollie interrupted, "you haven't even been accused of anything yet."

Sitting back on a cot in the cell, Gino broke into a smile. "Hell, we're not even guilty of anything. Christ, we shot a dead man then we buried him."

"It is funny when you say it that way." Eddie laughed, then uttered a sigh.

"Henry Duval?" The voice came through the bars of the cell.

Hank peered through the bars, "Yeah?"

The cell door opened and Tom walked in, followed by Detective Powers and two state troopers. "Henry Duval, would you come with me?"

"Watch out for the rubber hoses." Tom's laugh followed Hank down the hall.

"Just tell the truth, they don't have anything on us." Eddie yelled over Tom.

Hank was in a small room with a desk, Sheriff McCarthy and the two detectives. "Please sit down Mr. Duval." The thin faced detective said. His steel blue eyes conveyed no emotion.

THE LAST DEER HUNT

Sheriff McCarthy shifted his body and waited until the various parts stopped moving. "Hank, you remember Frank Powers?" Pointing to the thin detective, "And Harold Smith?" Indicating the heavyset man.

Hank sat silently. This time he was not going to say anything more than he had to, just stick to the truth.

Harold Smith moved in front of Hank, his face inches away, and his breath heavy with the smell of garlic. "Mr. Duval, you are in a lot of trouble."

Hank just sat. He could feel the heavy man's breath on his face and see the beads of sweat on the man's face.

Frank Powers sat across the desk cleaning his fingernails. "Do you understand the seriousness of this, Mr. Duval?"

Hank just sat. He had an urge to ask Mr. Smith what he had for breakfast.

"Come on Hank, work with us here," Sheriff McCarthy was wheezing. "We can wrap this whole thing up—"

An icy stare from Harold Smith cut the sheriff short. Smith moved in very close to Hank's face. His voice was smooth, but all business. "Henry, may I call you Hank?"

Hank just sat trading stares. Harold Smith stood straight, his hands on his hips. "Okay, let's cut through the shit." His voice turned menacing. "Just for starters, we have you on manslaughter, obstruction of justice, destroying evidence, and if we try hard enough, we can probably add murder."

Smith moved back in close to Hank's face. "You're buddy's have set you up. They told us that you were standing over the body holding the rifle when Pettiford was shot, you buried the body, and you hid the gun. This looks pretty bad for you. Unless you cooperate with us, you're going to be the scapegoat and take the fall."

Bastard. I don't believe him. They are just trying to trick us, divide, and conquer, Gino said. Hell, I don't know, so I don't say anything.

Harold Smith walked over to the desk and turned on a recording device. "Now why don't you tell us exactly what happened that night?"

Slowly Hank told his story exactly as he remembered it.

Smith moved back, his face close to Hank's. "So this Pettiford was dead already when you walked into the room?"

"Yes, as I have said, I heard a shot, then I entered the house. Before I saw the body, I picked up the rifle. It was pure instinct. Then I saw the body and heard Eddie crying. Then the other boys came into the room."

Detective Smith made notes on a pad of paper. "And you saw no one else. Is that correct?"

"That is correct."

"I'm sorry," Detective Powers said, rubbing his hands together, "But you said that you did not shoot Pettiford, didn't you?"

"Yes, that's true, I did not shoot Pettiford." Hank spoke slowly. *Damn, they're trying to catch me in a trap.* "I heard the gunshot and then I went into the house. "I didn't even fire the rifle."

Power's face was inches from Hank's. "We know there were six of you at the house that night. Ballistics shows that Pettiford was shot six times with that same rifle. How do you account for that?"

Before Hank could answer, Powers leaned forward. "Your buddies said you had already shot him, meaning you were the first to shoot Pettiford."

Again, Hank answered slowly, "That is what they thought at first because I was standing there with the gun when they came into the room, but they said that as they were leaving the house with the body, they ran across Vic Pollo. They told me that Vic had told them that he shot Pettiford with the rifle."

Hank felt Powers piercing blue eyes looking right into his mind, and he spoke slowly and deliberately. "Did you see Vic Pollo at Pettiford's house that night?"

"No."

"Don't you think it's strange that two of you did not see this Pollo character?"

"No, I came in from outside and Eddie was a little busy."

Frank Powers leaned forward. "You were the one who buried the body and the rifle used in the killing, is that correct?"

"No, the other guys took the body and buried that. I took the rifle and buried it."

"Where?"

"At the bog behind my Uncle's camp."

"And you don't know how it showed up at the Sloan Brothers house?"

"No."

Harold Smith moved and stood behind Hank's chair where Hank could not see him. "Hank, did you know that on the night that Pettiford disappeared, a number of items were stolen from the house, among them were a number of World War II souveniers."

Hank was startled. "No, I truly did not know that." He watched as the other three men glanced at each other, each waiting for someone to continue.

From behind him, Harold Smith's voice took on a menacing tone. "You are not being very cooperative here Mister Duval." Smith snarled, "If you don't help us here, we won't be able to help you."

Frank Powers pencil thin smile crossed his face as he motioned to Smith to meet him at the water cooler, then said quietly, but loud enough for Hank to hear, "I think this wise ass is our Numero Uno suspect."

Smith looked at Hank, "Now let's get back to what happened that night at Pettiford's."

Hank pushed back away from Smith. "What am I being charged with?"

"Nothing, not yet." Harold Smith reached across the desk, picked up a large sandwich, unwrapped it, and took a bite out of it.

"I think I'll just wait until my lawyer gets here." Hank said, folding his arms tightly in front of him.

"You don't need a lawyer; this is just a goddam preliminary questioning session." Harold Smith snarled, spitting out parts of the sandwich.

The small room settled into silence, the only sound was the wheezing of Sheriff McCarthy. Harold Smith wadded up the sandwich and tossed it into a waste can. Frank Powers sat across the desk shuffling through a large pile of papers. Hank watched the clock over the door, 11:30 A.M.

The silence continued. The clock read 12:15 P.M. when the door opened and a young woman dressed in a gray business suit with a rainbow colored long scarf and briefcase was escorted into the room by two state police officers.

Each of the men's gazes settled on the shortness of her dress and the leg that was exposed.

Quickly, Hank looked at her face. Jet-black hair, straight cut bangs and shoulder length, and a gorgeous smile. Hank thought, *about thirty-two, thirty-three years old, maybe.* Then a thought hit him. *The lawyer must have sent his damn secretary.*

"Gentlemen." She waited until their stare moved up from her hemline. "Gentlemen, I am Ms. Johnson, Pat Johnson. I am an attorney representing Mr. Duval and the other men involved in this case." She looked towards Hank.

Hank looked at the young woman. *She's the lawyer. Pat's a she?* He felt the redness working up his face. *Damn, do I ever feel stupid!*

Frank Powers and Harold Smith both stood and introduced themselves. The sheriff attempted to rise, but just nodded.

Pat Johnson handed each of the men a business card, looked directly into each of their eyes, and took a step back.

Frank Powers gaze moved down Pat Johnson's dress until it found the hemline again and the toothpick he had been chewing splintered. Spitting out pieces of wood, he tried to compose himself. "Ms. Johnson, it is Ms., isn't it?" he snarled. "I don't think there is a need for a lawyer here. Mr. Duval and his buddies haven't been charged with anything."

"Oh," her dark eyes danced, "then why are you holding

and questioning them?"

Harold Smith stood shuffling his feet, his hands stuffed in pockets. Frank Power's eyes narrowed. "We can hold them for questioning for twenty-four hours."

Her gaze shifted from one detective to the other. "Have you advised Mr. Duval of his rights?"

Harold Smith stood flipping Ms. Johnson's business card in his hand. "Mr. Duval has not been charged with anything, or accused of anything, at least not yet."

Pat Johnson moved her body and her dress moved slightly up her leg. Pat waited until the men's gaze had dropped down and asked, "Did you inform Mr. Duval that he, and the other men have a right to legal counsel?" She shook her head. "And did you say to Mr. Duval that he did not need a lawyer?"

Every look went back to her face. She shook her head and wiggled her finger back and forth in front of her like a scolding. "Now, now gentlemen, you should know better than that."

Mr. Powers and Mr. Smith put their heads down.

Speaking deliberately, she moved her gaze from one detective to the other, "Now that we have settled that, I suggest that either you charge Mr. Duval and his friends, or you let them go." The smile quietly lit up her face, "But then, I don't have to tell you men about the law, now do I?"

Sheriff McCarthy had managed to extract himself from the chair he was sitting in and said with a measured sense of authority. "I believe Ms. Johnson has a valid point, do you gentlemen agree?"

Powers and Smith glared at the sheriff, nodded grudgingly, and then turned their gaze to the lawyer.

Pat Johnson closed the clasp on her briefcase. "Then I suggest that Mr. Duval and his friends are free to leave with me." When no one moved, her smile faded and she added. "If you do not release them now, I will call the district court judge and get a court order." Her smile returned.

As he followed Ms. Johnson out of the room past Frank

Powers, Harold Smith and the sheriff, Hank heard Smith say, "I hope that little cutie from Marquette doesn't think she has a chance in hell of winning this case. These backwoods yokels from up here don't stand a chance. When the big boys from downstate get here, they'll eat her up and spit her out."

"Yep," Frank Powers added. "The only way she could win a case up here is if she hiked that hemline up another eight inches."

Hank and Pat Johnson met Tom, Gino, Eddie, Ollie, and Bob in the lobby of the courthouse. After introductions, Pat agreed to drive the men back to Maggie's apartment where Hank had left his truck. Tom decided he would stay in Fairhaven with his mother.

"What will happen next, Ms. Johnson?" Ollie asked.

Pat's smile was quick and infectious. "If they charge you, I will request a preliminary hearing from the district court. With the exception of Henry, you men all live outside of the area and a grand jury could take forever. I believe there is a good chance we can get this thrown out without a trial."

"Trial?" Eddie said, gesturing his deep concern. The others returned Eddie's look of alarm.

Pat Johnson laughed. "I wouldn't worry so much, the case is so old, and you guys were all minors when this happened. Besides, these two clowns from the State Police have made a mess of the investigation." She waited, and when no one responded, she continued. "I will be representing Henry, but it would be in everyone's best interest to have your own lawyer." The men shuffled about looking at her, faces filled with anxiety.

She continued. "If you don't have a lawyer already, I can recommend a couple of good law firms in Houghton and Marquette and if you like, I would be happy to contact them for you."

"Thank you, I would appreciate that." Tom looked toward the other men, who nodded agreement.

A few minutes of silence, then Bob shrugged his shoul-

THE LAST DEER HUNT

ders. "I'm not sure that I can afford this." The men looked at each other, apprehension starting to build with the thought.

"Don't worry about that, Gus Lundgren has taken care of everything. And please call me Pat, 'Ms.' sounds so formal."

The truck ride back to camp was crowded. Tom had left with Pat Johnson to visit his mother in town and Eddie had opted to ride in the truck bed. The other four men were squeezed in the cab with Hank and at the request of Gino, Hank stopped at a party store in L'anse. Gino, Eddie and Ollie made a quick trip inside for wine, whiskey and beer. Back on the road, Gino was drinking his red wine and Ollie opened a beer. Eddie sat crouched down in the bed of the truck by himself drinking his whiskey from the bottle.

"Christ Hank, this thing is blowing out cold air; can't you turn the heat on?" Gino's muffled voice came from inside the pile of bodies and hunting jackets.

"Can't help you." Hank shouted over the sound of the truck. "The heater don't work."

"Nothing in the truck works." Gino mumbled, his head hidden in a large scarf. "Why don't you just shoot it and put it out of its misery.

Geez, now I got a cramp," Bob mumbled from somewhere under the pile of bodies. "Can you stop the truck? I have to stretch this leg."

"Great idea...I gotta pee." Ollie started to open the door until he realized the truck was still moving. "Stop this damn thing."

The four men stood in a row facing the snow bank. "Wow," Gino said, looking skyward, waving his wine bottle. "You don't see that around where I live." The other four heads all turned upwards.

"That's some show! I haven't seen Aurora Borealis since I lived here in Fairhaven." Ollie said, shaking him self off.

"No, they're not the aurora whatever you said." Gino was sweeping his arm across the sky. "Those are Northern Lights."

Hank laughed, "They're both the same thing."

"I knew that!" Gino zipped up. "What do you think, I'm stupid?"

Just then, all the heads turned around together at the sound of singing coming from the large heap of snow in the back of truck. "Show me the way to go home, I'm tired and I want to go to bed..."

"Hey Eddie, you okay back there?" Bob said looking at the other men. "We forgot about Eddie."

The singing stopped, and the pile of snow stirred slightly. An arm and hand holding a whiskey bottle appeared followed by a muffled voice. "Damn, wasn't that some show back there." The pile of snow in the back of the truck stood up and Eddie shook the snow from his head and shoulders, "Those idiots from the state police sure looked stupid as hell."

"Yeah, but now they're going to be mad as hell." Hank blurted out. "They'll be out to hang us if they get the chance."

"Whatever." Gino threw his empty wine bottle into the snow, took the bottle of whiskey from Eddie, and took a long drink. "What they gonna get us for? Hell, they should give us a freakin' medal." He handed the bottle back to Eddie, who sat back down in the pile of snow on the back of the truck.

"Yeah, like we rid the world of this terrible evil." Ollie headed back towards the truck and another bottle of beer.

"That would be true if we were the ones who really killed him." Hank said.

"Yeah, you're right Duval, if we were the ones who killed him." Gino followed Ollie towards the truck. "Give the freakin medal to Vic."

The others followed and the truckload of men headed back towards the hunting camp. Parking at the camp road, the men, out of the truck, walked single file, following Hank back towards the cabin.

The walk to the camp was cold and difficult in the deep snow. At first, the talk was about the day, being in jail, and being questioned. As they wove their way towards camp, the discussion became more optimistic and soon the men were reinforcing each other's viewpoints until by the time they reached the camp, they were all in good spirits.

The cabin was cold, the fire had gone out, and Hank's breath was visible as he stuffed paper and kindling into the stove. For a minute, as usual, a layer of smoke drifted to the ceiling and then the draft caught and the stove roared to life. Ollie stood by the stove beating his arms together trying to fight off the cold and the others joined him.

The fire finally going, the stove glowed red in spots, and as soon as the heat had pushed back the cold, the men were out of their coats and seated at the table.

"I don't know about the rest of you guys," Ollie opened a beer, and took a sip, "but I would really like to get home now."

Hank sat with pencil and paper doodling. "But, you can't leave town yet, not till after the court hearing anyway."

"Hell, I don't even know if I have a job." Gino opened the bottle of red wine and took a long drink. "Come to think of it, I don't even know if I have a wife. Nobody ever answers the phone."

"Hannah said she was going to come over as soon as she could find somebody to watch the kids." Bob took his worn Bible out of a backpack, went over, sat on a bunk, and opened it. "I'd just as soon she stayed home, there's nothing she could do here except hang around that little motel."

Ollie took out a deck of cards, shuffled them and played solitaire in silence, then stood up and stretched. "Hell, can't beat the devil, might as well turn in."

Hank sat up startled, "Hey, I completely forgot! Eddie, what did you do with the doe you shot?"

The room was silent as the men looked around. "Eddie?"

"Eddie, are you here?"

"Eddie? Where the hell are you?"

The men looked at each other, shook their heads, and as

one, called, "Eddie!" No answer. They were in their coats and out the door.

Giant flakes of snow were piling up on each other and accumulating quickly as they raced back to the truck. Nobody said a word as they stumbled and fell, pushing their way back up the trail.

Gino jumped on the back of the truck and swept away the pile of snow. As the men watched, Gino shook his head and gestured that he was confused. "He ain't here!"

The tracks leaving the truck were being covered quickly by the snow and the men all walked in line following the beam of light from the flashlight Hank had taken from the truck. The tracks wound around in circles through the big field across from the camp, each circle getting bigger. "Eddie! Where the hell are you?" Each of the men took turns calling out to him.

The beam of the flashlight moved back and forth and stopped on an empty whiskey bottle attached to an arm. "What the heck are those things?" Ollie asked, looking at the strange imprints in the snow.

"They're angel wings." Bob was half laughing, half in panic. "That little shit has been out here making angels in the snow."

Thirty-Three

Outside, the eastern sky was forming a thin red line across the horizon as the morning sun inched up over the big lake. Inside the Baraga County Memorial Hospital, the men sat huddled together on uncomfortable metal chairs in the hallway of the emergency ward where they had been waiting through the night to hear some word on Eddie.

Hank had just nodded off when Gino tapped him on the shoulder and pointed to the door to the emergency room where they joined Tom, Bob, and Ollie who stood, hands jammed in pockets, standing in front of a short dark-skinned doctor.

Doctor Bogojavellian waited until Hank joined the group. He stood with his left hand in the pocket of his hospital jacket and his right hand holding a clipboard. His gaze went from one man to the next, stopping at each to shake his head.

The doctor scanned the clipboard, then mouthed a silent "Tsk, tsk." "We really don't know the extent of the damage. As you know," the doctor scanned the faces of the men in front of him, "Mr. Mahoney was allowed to be exposed to sub-zero temperatures for quite a considerable period of time, and the frostbite is quite severe." There was a strong emphasis on 'Allowed to be.'

The doctor continued. "There is tissue loss in his fingers, but we think we can save them. We are most concerned about his left ear, and we suspect he will lose most of it." He lowered his eyelids and peered at the men. "Tsk, tsk."

The men stood with heads hung, shuffling their feet. Tom asked. "How long will he have to stay in the hospital, doctor?"

"We think he will be able to go home by Thanksgiving if all goes well, but it will take a couple of weeks for a full recovery. Tsk, tsk." The doctor snapped his clipboard shut and joined a group of nurses.

"What are they laughing at?" Gino asked, looking at the doctor and nurses.

"I suspect they're laughing at us for being so dumb." Ollie replied.

"Stupid doctor," Gino scowled, "with a name likes Bobojackoff or whatever it is, he should talk, hell; he's not even an American."

Hank scowled back at Gino. "Come on, admit it, it was a really dumb thing to do, leaving Eddie outside for so long." Motioning to a nurse, Hank asked, "Is it possible to see Eddie for just a minute?"

"Of course sir, but only two of you and please keep it very short."

Eddie lay in the bed with tubes running out of his arms and nose and wires running from his body to a set of monitoring machines. His head was bandaged and his breathing was short and raspy.

"Hi Eddie, how you doing?" Hank asked softly, seeing if Eddie was awake. "Tom is here with me."

The only sounds were the equipment beeping and Eddie's breathing. Then almost inaudibly, "Hank, come here, I have to tell you something."

Hank moved close to Eddie, Tom backed away.

"Hank," Eddie rasped, "it was me."

THE LAST DEER HUNT

Hank leaned closer. I don't understand, what do you mean, it was you?"

"Yeah," Eddie coughed lightly, "It was me. I took the rifle from the bog."

Hank looked at Tom and shook his head. "It's okay Eddie; you don't need to talk now if you don't want to."

More rasps, "Yeah, it was the summer four years ago when I came back to visit. I was feeling really bad and I decided to kill myself. I dug up the gun to use; but it was all jammed up. There was a live round stuck in the chamber, but the bolt wouldn't work and I couldn't get it out. I buried it under some brush down by the railroad tracks thinking I would bury it back in the bog later." A short pause, then almost silently, his lips moved, "I'm sorry Hank, I never got back to it." Eddie's head relaxed back on the pillow, his breathing becoming slower and slower.

"I think he's asleep." Hank whispered to Tom, "let's go."

As they were leaving, Tom asked, "What did Eddie say in there?"

Hank stood up still trying to comprehend what Eddie had said. "I'm not sure I understood. He was mumbling, probably all the drugs he's on."

Ollie and Gino came over and Hank put his finger to his mouth, signifying quiet. "He's sleeping now. He'll be okay."

Not sure what to do, the men stood around or sat on the metal chairs for a couple of hours until Gino sat up and slapped his thighs. "I don't know about the rest of you guys, but I am really hungry."

"I agree." Tom stretched. "Where should we go?"

Hank held up his hands, "I would suggest that you men move into the new Northwoods Motel out on Skanee road. They have a small café and you should be near town in case the lawyer needs to get in touch with us."

"Think they'll have any rooms?" Bob asked. "There are a lot of reporters and other people around."

"I don't think that will be a problem, we're expecting some bad weather to move in and lots of people are bailing out before it gets here. As soon as I can, I'll head out to the camp and pick up whatever you guys need. If anyone wants to go, you're welcome." After dropping the men off at the motel, Hank waited until they checked in then drove back to Fairhaven and headed towards Frenchy's Diner.

The usual crowd shared the diner with hunters and others that Hank did not recognize. The two detectives from the state police sat in the end booth and glanced up quickly as Hank entered the diner.

"Hey Hank, good to see you." Lucy stuck her head out from behind the counter. She had on a red beret and a T-shirt with 'Frenchy's Diner' written over a picture of the Eiffel Tower.

Frenchy, wearing his red beret appeared behind Lucy, "Where the hell you been Hank? Geez, I was worried about you when we heard you were brought over to the jail in L'anse." He came around the counter and sat next to Hank.

Hank was hungry. When Lucy brought him coffee, he ordered the special, two eggs, bacon, sausage, and two flapjacks.

"Hey Hank, how was jail?" Homer Perrin called across the diner.

Pete Peterson was kneeling on the booth bench, coffee in hand, "We heard they tried to pin old Pettiford's murder on you guys."

"Yeah, but we hear that young lawyer kicked some butt." Bill Robertson raised his coffee cup and a chorus of approval went up from the regulars in the diner.

"Yeah that hadda be something, all right." Kurt Hurla nearly spilled his coffee in his enthusiasm. "Sure wish I could have been there to see that young lady attorney take them two state cops down a peg or two!"

"Yeah, musta been embarrassing to be shown up by a dumb Yooper," Pete Peterson said in his loud voice, then turning towards the booth where the two detectives were sitting, he added, "Oops, sorry about that, didn't know you two were there."

THE LAST DEER HUNT

Quiet laughter moved through the diner. The two detectives stood, put money on the table and put on their coats. Moving towards the door, the larger man, Harold Smith, stopped in front of Hank, reached into his pocket, took out an envelope and handed it to Him. "This isn't over yet Mr. Duval. We will have our day in court. You've been served. We're are on our way to the Northland Motel to serve papers to your buddies, then we will stop off at the hospital and give you friend his papers."

"What the..." Hank stood holding the envelope watching the door slam as the two men left the diner.

"Whatcha got." Frenchy asked, joining the group of curious men around Hank.

"Looks like a subpoena to appear in court," Hank re-read the paper. "To face charges of murder." He slowly folded the letter and put it back in the envelope. "We need to be in court at 8:30 on Monday morning, November 21st."

"Oh no." Someone mumbled softly. "They can't do that...Can they?"

"Looks like they can...and did." Frenchy put his hand on Hank's arm. "You better call your lawyer."

The call to Pat Johnson was answered by an answering machine that gave the office hours and would have Ms. Johnson call back. Hank left the diner's number and hung up to find everyone watching him intently. "They needed to page her. She'll call back."

Hank made another quick call. "Gus, first of all, thanks for taking care of the lawyers for us. And just to say that Pat Johnson is really something."

"It's no problem Hank, the lawyers are friends of mine and they are doing this work Pro Bono, but I wanted to help out anyway I can. I never got to repay your father for what he tried to do for me."

"Secondly Gus, when those police were questioning me while I was in jail, they seemed to be very interested in a German Luger that Vic Pollo had."

"Did you tell them I had the weapon?"

"No, I told them Vic told us he threw it into Luther's swamp, because that is what he told us he did with it."

"Okay, I think what I need to do is to turn the Luger over to the police. I won't tell them that you had any knowledge of the gun being with me,"

"I appreciate that." Hank hung up the phone and tried to understand what this all meant. Then he redialed.

"No way, Maggie!" He shouted into the telephone and every head in the diner snapped towards him. He turned his head to the wall, covered the phone with his hand, and now very quietly said. "You can't do that Maggie. I do not care and no, it is not right. I'll call you later and we will talk about this."

He sat in silence and listened as Maggie talked, then continued. "We almost had a tragedy, we forgot about Eddie and left him outside last night and he almost lost an ear to frostbite." A small pause, then, "I know Maggie, it was dumb, and no, we really didn't leave him out there on purpose." Another small pause. "And no Maggie, I don't need a lecture right now."

A long period of listening, Hank nodded continuously, and then spoke. "Yeah, we heard about the big storm coming in from Canada around Thanksgiving, and yes, I did remember about ordering the turkeys. And yes we definitely need to talk." Hank slowly put the phone back into its cradle.

"Gotta second, Hank?" Frenchy motioned to the booth vacated by the two detectives. "Gotta talk to you." He called back over his shoulder towards Lucy, "Be back in a minute, Hon."

Sitting in the booth vacated by the two detectives, Hank looked at his friend, sitting across from him, his head in his hands. *Great, now I can talk to Frenchy about Maggie and Brandon.*

Frenchy rubbed his hands together. "I talked to Sarah last Wednesday..."

"Is this about Sarah?"

Frenchy glanced up at Hank. "No. It's not about Sarah. Sarah and I are still good friends and I'm still very fond of her."

So much for talking about Maggie and Brandon. "Yeah, I guess with you and Lucy being an item..."

Frenchy shook his head.

"I mean, with Lucy moving into your apartment over the diner and all..."

"No Hank, this isn't about Lucy. This is about me." Frenchy was rubbing his hands together nervously.

"You? What do you mean, you?"

Frenchy looked directly at Hank and said quietly. "I'm leaving."

"What do you mean, you're leaving? You're leaving what? You're leaving the diner?"

"Fairhaven, Duval, I'm leaving Fairhaven."

Hank sat back, his mind trying to accept what he had just heard.

Frenchy continued to look directly at Hank. "I got a call Tuesday from Mel Tuttle from my old unit in 'Nam. Mel and a couple of the guys are going back to Vietnam to set up and run an orphanage at Plauku. I'm going to go with them."

Slowly, Hank realized what his friend was saying. "You're not kidding are you?"

"I'm afraid not. This is something I have to do for myself. Maybe it will help me make peace with myself and maybe, just maybe, the nightmares of 'Nam will go away."

"But what about the diner?" Hank could see the anguish in Frenchy's face. "How can you leave your diner? Everything you worked for is here."

"Lucy's going to run it. We'll share the profits until she has enough to buy it outright. Hell, she's doing a better job than I ever did. Look at this place, it's clean, it smells good, it's always full, and it's profitable."

Sitting in silence, watching Lucy move around the diner and customers come in and leave, a realization of the inevitable passed between the two men. Not an acceptance of their separation, but the knowledge that what they had shared would always be a bond between them.

Hank finally broke the silence. "I better get going, I have to get out to the camp and bring the guy's stuff back for them. They decided to stay at the Northwood's Motel."

Frenchy wrinkled his nose in disapproval. "How's Eddie, I just heard about his frostbite. Christ, how did that happen? Did he fall asleep in the outhouse?"

"That would have been better, that way he would have frozen something that wouldn't show. No, he decided to take a quart of whiskey and go make snow angels in a field." Hank's face flushed red. "We kinda forgot about him."

Frenchy broke into laughter. "You're kidding me?" The look on Hank's face convinced Frenchy that he was not. "You and your hunting buddies are something else, you know that?"

Hank could only manage a weak embarrassed grin.

Frenchy stood. "I better get busy and help Lucy finish up. Tell you what, give me a call when you get home tonight and maybe we can talk some more. You can fill me in on what happened in L'anse and what's going on with the whole Pettiford thing."

"Sounds good. It's been one hell of a week. I'll catch you later." He buttoned his coat. *And now the news about you leaving Fairhaven just about beats everything.*

Lucy called out over the noise. "Phone call for you Hank; sounds like the lady attorney."

The diner became hushed and every head in turned to follow Hank as he walked over to the phone.

"Hi, Ms. Johnson..." Hank stood silently nodding as he listened. "Thank you Ms. Johnson, I understand. Yes, goodbye and thank you."

Every face was staring at him, waiting in silence. "What?" Hank shrugged.

"So what did she like, say?" Lucy asked, gesturing her impatience.

THE LAST DEER HUNT

Everyone in the diner waited for the answer. "Yeah, what'd she say?" Pete Peterson asked for everyone in the diner.

"She said that I have to appear at the arraignment Monday to answer to charges."

"What about the other guys?" Frenchy asked.

"She contacted them and let them know and she also has found defense lawyers for them, a law firm from Houghton, Kaarla, Kaarla, Graves, Graves, and Riddle." Hank shrugged. "Anybody ever hear of them?"

Kurt Hurla raised his hand. "Yeah sure, you bet. "They're the biggest outfit in Copper Country. They've been there for a long time. How you guys afford them folks?"

Hank could only shrug.

Thirty-Four

Monday, November twenty-first, eight thirty in the morning and Hank sat in front of the large window in the lobby of the law offices of Kaarla, Kaarla, Graves, Graves, and Riddle looking at the town of Hancock clinging precariously to the steep banks on the far side of the Portage Canal. The silhouette of the old large Quincy Mine shaft and other relics of the long-gone copper mining era on the horizon stood in stark contrast to the brightening skies.

Eddie was absent, still recovering in the hospital and Gino, Tom, Bob and Ollie had gone into the office area to meet with the members of their defense team, the lawyers who would represent them.

Pat sat watching the dark cumulus clouds break up as they raced across the sky and as the sun broke through, she lifted her face to the warm rays. "This country is so beautiful; I could never live anywhere else. I love living in Marquette where I get a chance to be alone, take a walk by myself, and see the Milky Way. And if I am lucky, I might get to see a deer or bear or even a moose out in the wild. When I was at the University of Michigan in Ann Arbor, my life was usually restricted to workouts at the health club. My astronomy was limited to the star show at the planetarium and with the exception of possums and raccoons; the only wildlife I saw was in zoos."

"Two different worlds," Hank sighed. "I wonder if a person could live in both."

The door to the offices opened and the men filed out, each followed by a lawyer. Introductions completed, the group moved to a large conference room where Pat Johnson presided.

"Today, at 9:30 A.M., you will be arraigned in the Baraga County District Court in L'anse for your initial hearing. Someone will inform you, the defendants, of the charges brought against you and conditions of bail will be discussed. They may or may not ask for, or accept a plea of innocence or guilt, but if they do, we will enter a plea of not guilty. From there, depending on what happens, will decide where we go."

Edwin Kaarla Sr., representing Gino, stood as well as he could. His 88 years of life had left him with a back that was perpetually bent in the shape of a question mark. Leaning on his cane, the senior Kaarla spoke, his voice raspy, but strong. "We will not waive a preliminary trial and let this go into a grand jury or directly to trial. We believe that Ms. Johnson has put together a very strong case and we feel we can get the charges dropped."

Edwin Kaarla Jr., representing Tom, stood up next to his father. Except for the lack of wrinkles on his face and the stooped posture, he could have been his father. "I echo what my father has said. We just need to be sure that we stick with the truth."

The other lawyers in the room nodded in unison. Janet Riddle, representing Eddie, stood next. "Even in the event that this would go to trial, we will have a solid defense and we are positive that the prosecution will never be able to prove guilt beyond a reasonable doubt."

The junior partner in the firm, and representing Ollie, David Graves, a slender young man in his late twenties stood next. "Our main goal for now is to get over this hurdle. Once we are done with this, we can get down to working on the preliminary hearing." This time every person in the room nodded in unison.

Even with the soothing words of encouragement from the lawyers, the defendants sat stiff with tension.

Robert Graves, representing Bob, stood next, a rumpled old man in a rumpled old suit and a face as fierce as that of a bulldog. He cleared his throat and behind an intimidating glare, he said in a gruff voice. "I suspect by now, you folks have heard the story about the shoplifter in Calumet that we represented who ended up getting five years of hard labor. Well, let me tell you as I stand here in front of you, that story is not true—he only got two years of hard labor."

With the laughter that followed, Hank sensed the tension easing and a change in the mood of the meeting. Coffee was served with cinnamon buns. The meeting was adjourned to drive to the County Court House in L'anse for the arraignment.

The courtroom was intimidating. Hank stood next to Pat Johnson in a line with the other men and their lawyers. Frank Powers and Harold Smith stood behind another table talking with a dark swarthy young man identified as the assistant district attorney. Behind him stood three men and a woman dressed in business suits that turned out to be members of the prosecution team brought up from Lansing. Smith and Power, gesturing and pointing towards Hank and his friends were alternately looking serious and laughing. Hank decided he preferred it when they looked serious.

The bailiff stood in the front of the courtroom. "Hear ye, hear ye, the County Court of Baraga County is now in session. The Honorable Judge Philip Peterson presiding." The judge, six feet, eight inches tall ducked his way through the door into the courtroom and seated himself behind the judge's bench.

"All be seated."

Everyone seated, the bailiff read the terms of the arraignment. "It's okay," Pat whispered, sensing Hank's anxiety. "This is just standard procedure."

The word murder echoed in his head as the interchange of conversation alternated between the lawyers and the judge. As 'Calculating killers' followed by 'In cold blood,' and other words followed, Hank reacted with an involuntary flinch. *They're not talking about us, are they?*

Ms. Johnson stood and addressed the judge. "Your Honor..."

Again, the conversation between the defense lawyers and the judge flowed over Hank's head with key words working into his mind.

"Yes, Your Honor," Edwin Kaarla rasped. "We do not waive the right to a preliminary hearing."

"We need to expedite the hearing Your Honor." Edwin Graves addressed the court. "My client will face both personal and financial hardships if this case is not adjudicated quickly."

The Judge leaned forward, his head nearly over the front of the desk. "We will set the date for the preliminary hearing for December 5th, 1983."

The young District Attorney interrupted. "We are asking the court to refuse bail. Most of these men are from out of the area and there is no guaranty that they would not leave."

"Bail?" The defendants sucked in their breaths in unison and Hank felt his body tighten. *They want us to remain in jail?*

One by one, the defense lawyers stood and pleaded the case for their clients and one by one, the judge ruled on $1,000 bail, citing that he could see no real threat of these men leaving, and one by one, Hank could sense the men starting to breathe again.

The arraignment was over. Ms. Johnson settled the bail with the bailiff and the judge offered a stern warning with dire consequences if any of the men decided to leave the area without notifying the court.

Hank shivered. The realization of what had just transpired finally hit him. *Damn, I'm accused of murder! Jesus, I cannot believe this. What were we thinking all of these years; that this would just go away?*

Tom's voice broke through his thoughts. "How you guys feeling?"

"Like shit."

"Me too."

"I'm scared."

"Me too."

"Okay guys," Pat Johnson addressed the group, "We are done with the first step and we did well and we got what we wanted. We are scheduled for the preliminary hearing here in the courthouse on December 5th. If anything comes up before then, I will be in contact with Mr. Kaarla Sr. and also with Hank and if you need anything, you can get in touch with Mr. Kaarla." Turning to Hank with a smile, "I am truly sorry that I will have to miss your Thanksgiving dinner, but I have a good deal of work to catch up on back at the office and I have to get back."

Hank nodded his disappointment.

Pat Johnson walked away in conversation with the other members of the defense team, their breath condensing in the cold morning air.

"Hey Hank," Tom came over. "Who paid the bail for us?"

"Gus Lundgren."

"What the hell does he get out of this?" Gino grunted.

"Nothing. He's just trying to repay an old debt, something that happened a long time ago. I'll tell you about it someday."

Ollie waved over to Hank and Tom. "How'd you like to run over to the motel, get something for lunch, and then maybe head over to the bar?"

"Thanks Ollie, but it's still early and I think I'm going to run over to the Huron Mountain Club to double-check some things with the new cabinets."

"Sounds good, buddy, but if you want, you can meet us

over at the tavern later." Tom said, ducking a snowball that had been launched from the small group of men.

The tension broke, snowballs flew freely, most missing, some hitting while a group of people gathered around in a circle watching these men-boys playing their game.

Hank quietly left the group, got into the Ford pickup and turned north on Skanee Road. The snow intensified and just before he came to the Huron River, the snow began to accumulate on the windshield.

"Damn truck!" Now the windshield wipers decided to quit.

Thirty-Five

The ride back to Fairhaven took over an hour. The back of Hank's neck was stiff with tension and his arm sore and cold from leaning out the window and cleaning the windshield with his snow brush as he drove. Matson's Garage was closed so Hank left the truck in front with a big note on the dashboard. 'Please fix windshield wipers!' and left the keys in the ignition. *Maybe if I'm lucky, someone will steal the darn thing.*

Frenchy was sitting on the floor of the diner by the large sink, surrounded by various pipes, elbows, tees, traps and tools, his face a mask of total frustration. "Damn plumbing. Nothing works like it's supposed to. I've soldered this joint three times and it still leaks. What the heck am I doing wrong?"

Hank looked at the joint, covered with gobs of solder. "I think you're supposed to flow the solder, not try to build it up around the joint. Let me try."

Frenchy flinched, burning his finger. Shaking the finger to cool it, he handed the torch to Hank and moved aside. "I got your message. How come you didn't get out to the Huron Mountain Club today?"

"Darn wipers quit on me up near the tavern."

"You haven't given up on that truck yet? God you should have that thing condemned."

"Well, when I finish the Huron Mountain Club project, I'll have a few bucks," Hank held the flame from the torch on a joint, melting the solder, "I'll think about it then."

"How did the arraignment go today?"

"The lawyer said it went okay. I think she's doing a great job. We got a court date for a preliminary hearing on December 5th and we're out on bail. Can you believe that? Me, out on bail. God, I feel like some sort of criminal."

"Well, good buddy, you and your friends are involved in the death of a person...and you did shoot him."

"Yeah, I guess so." Hank was busy with the torch melting the solder. "You're not really leaving are you?"

"Yep, I've made up my mind." Frenchy handed the roll of solder to Hank. "I've been thinking about this for a long time and it was really a hard decision. I'm sorry to be leaving Fairhaven and I'll miss the diner, but most of all, I'll miss all of you guys." He was watching closely as Hank applied the solder to the joint.

"See Frenchy, you don't glob on the solder, you heat the inner part, and the solder just flows in. It's called capillary action." Hank turned the torch off. "Think you'll come back to Fairhaven?"

Frenchy began picking up the various parts and tools. "I don't think so buddy, although I might come back to visit when I get back in the states.

"I will miss you Frenchy."

Both men worked in silence cleaning up the area and checking the work.

Frenchy turned the water on and waved both thumbs in the air, a signal of success. "No leaks!"

Frenchy sat back and lit up a cigarette. "Now buddy, what about you and Maggie? What's she going to do?"

"Oh, I forgot to tell you, Brandon is coming here."

"Brandon? Who's Brandon?"

"Brandon is, I mean, was Maggie's boyfriend back in

California. They broke up a while back. He is a very good nature photographer and the magazine wants him to do a photo shoot on the wolves in winter. I'll admit, it would be a big plus to Maggie's story."

Frenchy shrugged. "When does this Brandon get here?"

"Any day now I guess. Maggie says he wants to go and get pictures as soon as he gets here."

"You have a problem with him coming here?"

"Yeah, you know what, I guess I do. I guess it does bother me."

"That's good. It means you care about Maggie."

"But I didn't need this guy to show up to get me to figure that out."

"I wouldn't worry about it Hank. This cool California guy gets one look at the hostile environment up here and he'll skedaddle out of here faster than a scared rabbit."

"Yeah, you're right." Hank let out a small laugh. "Can you imagine this guy in Luther's swamp in a blizzard? Thanks Frenchy. As usual, you come through when I need you."

"No problem buddy, thanks for the help with the plumbing."

Hank sat in silence and finished his coffee, "Gotta go."

His knock on Maggie's door brought the usual flurry of barking and scampering sounds from inside and the door opened.

Before he could get in the door, Maggie asked, "How did it go at the arraignment this morning?"

"Oh, it was just a formality. You know, we were accused of murder, called cold-blooded calculating killers and now we are marked men out on bail. Other than that, we are doing well. We do have a court date, December 5th. Ms. Johnson said not to worry, everything will be okay, but it is kinda scary, not knowing what's going to happen." Dressed in her oversized man's white dress shirt, sleeves rolled up to the elbows and cut off blue jeans and wearing Winnie-The-Pooh bedroom slippers, she leaned against the doorframe, one hand on her hip, the other straight up over her head.

THE LAST DEER HUNT

"TA- DAAA!"

"Jean Harlow, I presume?" Hank said, taking off his coat and putting it over the back of the couch.

Maggie picked it up and hung it in the closet. "No silly, do you see anything different about me today?"

"That's a trick question, right? Men hate to be asked that. However let me guess." He rubbed his chin as he slowly walked around her. "Hmmm, this is a tough one." Suddenly, he threw up his hands in an exaggerated gesture. "I've figured it out! You've had breast implants?"

"Hank! No, not even close." Maggie re-assumed the Jean Harlow pose. "You get one more guess."

Hank studied her intently, his hand cupping his chin, "Hmmm, this really is a tough one. Yes, that's it, you had a chin tuck."

"Hank, quit teasing. I just had my hair re-done. How do you like it?"

"Oh yeah, it looks really good." *And I was about to say she was having a bad hair day.*

From the look on his face, Maggie was sure he didn't mean what he had said. "Well I like it, so there!" She picked up Hemingway from the window and sat on the couch. Orphan had finally tired of jumping and pawing at Hank and lay on his bed. Maggie rubbed Hemingway under the chin and Hank could hear the purr from across the room.

"I made some great new herbal tea Hank, would you like some?"

"Coffee, please."

"Hank, you drink way too much coffee. It can't be good for you."

Hank ignored it. "Hon, I have to apologize, I guess I was a bit jealous of Brandon. At first, I thought you had said that he would be staying here with you. Isn't that silly of me?

Her eyes twinkled, "And how do you know that's not what I meant?" Hank looked at her, confused by his feelings.

"You're kidding, Right?"

"God yes Hank. He's my ex-boyfriend, there's nothing between us now. Don't be silly."

"Darn it Maggie, quit your kidding." Hank pushed his hair back on his head.

"You know," Maggie smiled, "you are so cute when you're jealous." She covered her small smile with her hand.

"Now you're teasing me."

Maggie stood, Hemingway jumped to the floor, then the window. "Of course I'm kidding; I'm going to be staying with Sarah while Brandon is here."

Hank's feeling moved from irritation to relief and back to irritation.

"You know Maggie, sometimes when you tease; I'm not sure how to take you." Hank swung the couch pillow hitting Maggie softly on the head. "You know you're a big pain in the neck."

"Probably a lot lower than that. Would you like some herbal tea now?" Maggie's face was one broad smile from side to side.

"Coffee." Hank still was irritated. "The windshield wipers on the truck died again."

"When are you going to give up on that old thing? Good grief, you can see the road through the rusted out floorboards." Maggie poured herself a cup of tea. "How's Eddie?"

"It looks like he'll be okay. He might lose one ear. He was lucky."

"First you guys leave him out to freeze to death and then he'll lose one ear, and you call him lucky?" Maggie shook her head. "Coffee's done, I'll get it."

"It wouldn't have happened if he..." Hank realized the futility of trying to blame Eddie. "Yeah, it was really dumb of us. We were tired, and the guys had too much to drink." Hemingway stood and stretched, then in two jumps was on the arm of the couch watching Hank. The big cat rubbed his head on Hank's arms, lay down, and with eyes closed to slits, began purring and Hank could feel his frustration melt away.

THE LAST DEER HUNT

"Hey, I think Hemingway likes me now." Hank reached over to pet the big yellow cat.

Whack. Hemingway shook his head as if to say, 'Not yet, buddy.' He looked back at Hank with contempt and leapt up to his window ledge.

"How are the guys doing out at the motel?" Maggie handed Hank a coffee cup.

"Okay I guess. They just want to go home."

Maggie was busy going through some papers. "Hank, I hope you don't mind, but I took the liberty to send the sketches you did for the magazine to the California Institute of Art in Valencia, California. They're one of the leading art schools in the country."

Hank frowned, got up, and walked over to the window. Maggie walked over to him and took his hand. "I thought you would be happy about it."

Hank pulled his hand back. "You should have asked me first. There were other sketches I thought would have been better."

"Yes Hank, I understand. And you can send those also." Maggie confronted him. "Is there something else? You seem too upset."

"When does Brandon get here?" Irritation crept back into his voice.

"Ah yes, Brandon." Maggie said, putting the palm of her right hand to her forehead. "Of course, I should have realized." Then, with hands on hips, she continued. "He'll be here tomorrow. He wants to do the photo shoot as soon as he can, probably the day after Thanksgiving. We have one of the Dolittle boys lined up to take him out to where the wolves have been seen."

"We have a big storm coming this way?" Hank's face reflected his concern. "You know how fast they can move in up here. Where did you hear the wolves were sighted?"

"I think Mr. Dolittle said it was the old Johnson's logging site in Luther's Swamp."

"That's not a good place to be with a storm coming in.

Are you sure Brandon should be doing this?"

"Do I sense a little jealousy Mr. Duval?" Maggie said with a hint of sarcasm. "Brandon has shot pictures in Alaska and the Colorado Mountains in winter. He's been in the Himalayas and Greenland. I would think he would know what he is doing."

"Yeah sure," Hank said, feeling frustrated, *I better shut up before I get in any deeper. What the hell, if he wants to go into the swamp in a storm, that's up to him.* "I gotta go now Maggie. It's getting late."

"Oh Hank, I have a small favor to ask. Do you think you could watch Orphan while Brandon is in town? I think it would be better if the dog weren't in the apartment bothering him. You know what a pest that dog can be."

"Yeah sure." *Now I get stuck taking care of the dog just so poor Brandon doesn't get bothered.* "I probably won't see you tomorrow, you'll be so busy getting ready for Brandon, and I need to do some work at the shop." *Yeah, and I'll be busy being upset over Brandon being here.*

The silence crept between them as Maggie moved back to her papers and the only sounds were Hemingway's deep purr. Hank sat in stillness and when the cat's purring quieted his mind, he stood, opened the door, whistled softly, and with Orphan running in front of him, quietly left.

Thirty-Six

The door opened and Maggie stared at Hank. "What are you doing here? You're not supposed to be here this morning!"

Hank could feel the surprise and annoyance in her voice, he took a deep breath. Then slowly letting the air out, he said, "I'm sorry Maggie if I surprised you. I forgot to take Orphan's food and bed with me last night and thought I better come over and pick them up." *Yeah, sure, I just want to see what this Brandon guy is really like.*

"I'm sorry Hank, I didn't expect you." Her hair was pulled back and tied, the slightest hint of eye shadow and she was dressed in a navy blue suit, open down the front over a low cut white blouse showing a large amount of cleavage.

"Expecting Brandon, I presume?" Hank was looking directly at Maggie's exposed chest. "Perfume's a little too obvious."

"Not as obvious as you showing up here today." A frown filled her face with concern. "He was supposed to be here an hour ago. I don't know what happened."

Inside the apartment, the silence grew awkward as Hank sat on the couch and watched the clock and Maggie was busy going through her notes on her magazine article.

Maggie looked over at Orphan's bed and the bag of dog food for the third time. "Is that the only reason you came over?" Then looking at Hank, her eyes pleading with him, "You shouldn't be here, I have too much work to do."

Ignoring her, Hank picked up copies of Maggie's article and sat on the couch to read them. Hemingway came running full speed across the room, jumped on the couch, and settled on the papers on Hank's lap.

Maggie looked at Hank, then the dog food and back at Hank, frustration written across her face. Hank put the papers on the coffee table and sat with the purring cat on his lap. "Are we friends yet Hemingway?"

The cat looked up at him and before Hank could move his hand; whack!

"Damn that cat." Hank pushed him off his lap and Hemingway fell into an undignified heap on the floor. "I give up; you are never going to like me are you?"

Maggie went over, picked up Orphan's bed, and set it down in front of Hank. She picked up the bag of dog food and handed them to him. "There, you have your dog food and Orphan's bed, now would you please..."

The knock on the door startled both of them. Hank stood quickly. Maggie glared at Hank but remained silent as she crossed the room and opened the door.

A young man stood in the door in a green L.L. Bean Gore-Tex ski jacket, an orange Tommy Hilfiger ski hat, and a gorgeous smile.

God, he is beautiful. Hank thought, *how do I compete with that? And look at that dimple!*

Offering his hand to Hank, his smile turned to a charming grin and the dimple grew more pronounced. "Hi. I'm Brandon, Brandon Howard."

Oh shit, listen to that deep baritone. Christ, doesn't he have any faults? Hank took his hand, and felt the powerful grip. *Geez, perfectly clear eyes, not even a trace of red, and what a grip.* "Glad to meet you, I'm Henry Duval. I forgot the dog food." *Dumb, that was really dumb!*

THE LAST DEER HUNT

Brandon let Hank's hand go and stepped back, the wide smile returned. Hank's hand was sore.

"Hi Brandon." Maggie walked over and gave Brandon a small hug and kiss on the cheek. "It's been a long time. It's good to see you again."

Brandon was out of his ski jacket showing a skintight shirt revealing a taut stomach that rippled when he moved. *Damn, he is so thin! There's not one once of fat on that body.*

"Wow," Brandon said, rubbing his hands together. "They weren't kidding when they talk about the snowfall up here. They had this big sign coming from the airport that looked like a big thermometer and said something about a record 220 inches of snow. Is that correct?"

"That's 320 inches," Hank corrected.

Brandon's face broke into a wide smile. "You can't even see over the snow banks and gosh, it's not even Thanksgiving yet. Is this normal?"

God, even his teeth are perfect. Hank managed a thin smile, no teeth showing.

"Yep, pretty normal. We usually get over two hundred fifty inches a year, but around here, we don't think much about it. We only have two seasons up here, shoveling season and swatting season. It's just kinda the way of life around here, we get used to it—"

A hard tap on his ankle from Maggie's foot told him he was talking too much. Hank stopped talking and gave Maggie and Brandon a sheepish grin.

"Right." Brandon was grinning. "I'm hoping to be here for only a week, so I think I should try to do my photo shoot as soon as possible. I had planned to have a young man, Samuel Dolittle, help me go out the day after Thanksgiving, but he called and said he couldn't do it."

"That's too bad," Hank said. "Sam knows the woods as good as anyone. Especially Luther's Swamp."

Brandon's smile was warm and formed quickly. "Well, it's okay, I managed to get a Fuzzy Walstrom to guide me. He was recommended to me by Percy Twill, your township supervisor, so I expect he's quite good."

Hank looked at Maggie. *Good grief, not that idiot, he couldn't find a chicken in the chicken coop, but then, Percy was never a good judge of character.* He looked directly at Brandon. "I would be careful. It's still deer season and there might be a few hunters still out. And that swamp can be treacherous. We're expecting a storm sometime in the next couple of days. It's supposed to be a big one and they do come up quickly around here—"

"Not to worry Henry," Brandon waved Hank off, still grinning. "I am not naive. I have photographed in the Swiss Alps in winter, in Alaska and in Northern Greenland. I expect that Fairhaven, Michigan can't be that harsh."

Hank was unsure how to respond. "I'm sure you know what you are doing, but like I said, the storms up here can be dangerous."

Hank felt the slight kick in his ankle from Maggie. "Hank, you needn't worry about Brandon. He's very capable of taking care of himself." Maggie smiled at Brandon and he grinned back.

Hank was up. "I better get going." *So much for this guy turning tail and running.* "Got to get over to Matson's to pick up my truck."

Brandon extended his hand. "It's been nice to meet you Henry, I'm sure we'll see each other again before I leave. You have such a quaint little town here; I would like to know more about it."

Hank took the offered hand, but before he could answer, Maggie handed him his coat and nudged him towards the door.

"I will see you later, Henry Duval." She said, then moving close to him, she whispered softly, "Aren't you forgetting something?"

Hank leaned his head close to hers, expecting a kiss.

She moved her mouth close to his cheek, and in a whisper said, "Hank, you forgot the dog food."

THE LAST DEER HUNT

Outside, clouds had moved across the sun and the drab dull light did little to make Hank feel better as he walked along with the bag of dog food. *Wow, did I screw up, made a jerk of myself. I wouldn't blame Maggie if she never talked to me again.*

He swung the bag of dog food at a small oak tree standing at the edge of the sidewalk. The bag burst and dog food scattered over the sidewalk and a large chunk of snow fell from the tree, right down the back his neck.

That was really dumb. Sitting in the snow, Hank scooped up wet dog food trying to put it back in the bag. The snow down his back was working its way further down every time he moved. "That's all he does is grin. He never stops grinning."

"Hey Hank, who is grinning all the time? The Cheshire Cat?"

"Oh, hi Sarah." Hank looked up, embarrassed, and waving his hand over the dog food lying on the ground. "This was me getting mad and letting off steam...I met Brandon today."

"Oh good, Brandon finally made it. Maggie was worried when she called last night, she didn't know if he would get here or not. What's he like?"

"Sarah, he's beautiful."

"I wouldn't worry about it; Maggie tells me he's ancient history, besides she told me..."

Yes, told you what? Hank waited in anticipation.

"Oh, what I meant to say," Sarah shifted the heavy bundle of papers in her arms, "Maggie called last night and told me about your story about Pettiford. I didn't know if I should believe it, at least not at first. How did you poor guys live with this all these years?" Her raven black hair and her bright yellow ski jacket and hat highlighted her cheeks, bright red from the cold. "If you want to talk to anyone about this, just let me know, okay? I do counseling and maybe I can help."

"Thanks, Sarah. I just might do that. And yeah, I'm glad

that it's finally going to be out in the open. It's been too long." He put a handful of wet dog food back on the ground, stood up and gave Sarah a small hug. "I'm sorry about you and Frenchy breaking up."

"Thanks. It will be okay. I have so much to do; I don't know where I'll find the time for it all." Sarah took a deep breath. "Well, I do have to run; I'm going to meet with Patti and Lyle Burke over at the library. Remember what I said, if you need to talk, please give me a call."

"Will do, Sarah." Hank said, picking up the dog food bag. Grabbing a handful of wet dog food, let it slip through his fingers, threw up his hands in frustration, and walked towards home. Having a few hours to kill, He picked up Orphan and walked over to the shop. He turned on the heat, put on an extra large pot of coffee, and finished the pasty he had brought with him. He opened the book on the desk and read. The more he read, the more intriguing it became. Labeled "The Art of Marquetry," it described a method of creating modern-day masterpieces in wood using an ancient technique of wood veneer inlay. He tacked a large diagram of a mosaic inlay onto a large message board, turned on the machines of his trade and went to work.

The time flew by, but Hank had to pick up Eddie at the hospital and bring him over to the motel. He quickly brought Orphan home and stopped by Matson's Garage. It was closed again. *When does this guy ever work?* The note on the windshield of Hank's truck said: 'Wipers fixed. Had to pull the dash to get to the wiper motor, but found a rebuilt one so saved a few bucks. P.S. Strongly suggest you think about a new truck.'

Eddie as ready to go. "God, it's so good to get out of that hospital." His head swathed in a large bandage covering his left ear, Hank wheeled him through the lobby in a wheelchair and out the door of the hospital.

"Hey, look it's Eddie," Ollie said, pointing to the truck.

Eddie waved, the guys waved back, and the men moved to Greet Eddie with words of welcome and glad you're back.

"A lady from the television station is here already," Tom said. "She showed us an article they wrote about us in the newspaper. I guess it was even in the Detroit Free Press."

"Yeah," Bob said, looking up from the paper he was reading. "She interviewed us and we're gonna be on television news tonight on channel four."

"Yeah, we're famous," Eddie giggled.

Ollie looked at the others. "Yeah, but now we all have to call home and let everyone know what's going on."

Gino walked towards the lobby. "Yeah, I might as well get this over with."

Bob nodded in agreement and handed the newspaper to Hank. "I called Hannah this morning to let her know. She might come out this week."

Sitting down, Hank opened the paper. Large headlines said:

'VICTIMS OR MURDERERS. THE STRANGE TALE OF 6 YOUNG BOYS AND A BIZARRE KILLING.'

Hank read slowly. The story detailed the account of Hank and the men, drawing on the coverage of the hearing and anecdotal stories from around town. It asked more questions than it answered. Why did six very young boys go up to Pettiford's house that night? If there were six boys, and Pettiford was shot six times, who really killed this man? And why? Was this killing justified? Or was it an act of murder?

A second article was headlined as 'Sex scandal in the small town of Fairhaven.' It chronicled a three-year period when Pettiford had lured young boys up to his house. It included interviews of anonymous men who had been abused by Pettiford as well as a number of men who revealed their identities, including Fuzzy Walstrom. The article also included interviews of ministers, doctors and some teachers; all who had suspicions that something had been going on, but never took action.

Yeah, Hank shook his head, *"I guess we are famous...or is that infamous?*

Thirty-Seven

Thanksgiving Day broke clear and bitterly cold. Here and there, lights blinked on in houses as people awakened to meet the day. Outside, the town lay quiet under a blanket of new snow and tendrils of smoke from wood and coal fired homes rose straight into the air for a quarter mile before flattening out into a canopy of smoky haze. In the east, the rising red ball of the sun was transforming the dark colorless sky into gossamer layers of delicate pinks.

Hank put on a jacket over his pajamas and stood in the cold morning air watching his breath as he waited until Orphan signaled he was finished with a wag of his tail.

"Sorry Orph, it's too cold for a walk. Besides, we have a lot of company coming over for dinner today and we need to get ready."

Orphan agreed and raced Hank back inside the house.

Hank grabbed a large pile of mail lying on the small table by the front door and flipped through it, picking out a large white envelope with a return address from the Art Institute of California. Running his hand over the unopened envelope several times, he tried to envision himself in California. Not just California, but Southern California. *And not just southern California, but Los Angeles!*

The telephone jangled him out of his thoughts and he picked it up to hear Maggie's voice. "How's it going? Everything ready? Anything you need?"

"Yeah, how about a six-pack of beer. You and I can go out on the lake ice-fishing and forget about all of this."

Maggie was laughing. "Yeah sure Hank baby, anything you say. Except it's too cold in that little shack to take our clothes off...I really got to run. See you in a little while."

"Yep." A smile spread across his face.

"Bye."

"Bye." Hank listened to the dial tone for another minute before he hung up. He sat looking at the unopened envelope. *Nah, never happen, not in a million years.* He put the envelope back on the pile of mail and went into the kitchen. Thoughts of California living did not last long. *Hell, we haven't resolved this Pettiford thing yet.*

The doorbell rang, startling Hank, and he looked at Orphan in surprise. It was the first time the doorbell had rung in years. *Nobody uses the doorbell around here; they just pound on the door.* Orphan was up and standing guard. He had never heard the doorbell ring either.

"Wow, Sis? Diane, what are you doing here?" Hank stood holding the door, his brain trying to understand.

"Hi Hank, you going to invite me in? It's kinda cold around here for a California girl."

Hank motioned his sister inside, shut the door, and pulled her close. Stepping backward, Diane reached out and took Hank's hand in hers, and they stood, looking at each other.

Orphan went back to his bed. This new person was no threat.

"It's so good to see you Sis. What are you doing here?"

"When Maggie called to tell me what was going on with this Pettiford thing, I called the airline and managed to get a seat. "No way Sis, you're going to stay here, we have enough bedrooms. I'll get your luggage later."

THE LAST DEER HUNT

"Thanks Hank."

"Is everything okay with you Sis? I haven't heard from you in quite a while. I hope that means everything is all right."

"Yes, everything is fine with me. I am writing fiction now and teaching pottery and art at a local school. It gives me enough money to live on. My dear friend Susan and I are still an item and she would have loved to come with me, but we couldn't find another ticket on such short notice."

Diane had a beautiful smile, perfect teeth, dark eyes, and wearing a turtleneck sweater striped in every possible color. Her lean body filled the designer jeans. "Gosh Hank, I couldn't believe it when I heard what was going on with this Pettiford thing. And you lived with this all these years." Diane moved her head to take the long blond hair away from one eye. "How do you think it's going?"

Hank sat in the rocker opposite his sister. "Pat, I mean Ms. Johnson feels like it'll be thrown out if we have a probable cause hearing and we won't have to go to trial. I sure hope so; I am so tired of it. Would you like a cup of coffee?"

Diane nodded. "You know Hank, I had heard rumors about Pettiford when I was in school, but I just thought it was boys exaggerating, or bragging."

For the next hour, Hank and Diane drank their coffee and talked about being young and growing up in Fairhaven, until Hank looked at his watch. "Folks will be showing up soon. We better get ready. Where are your things?"

"They're out in the rental car. I plan to get a room at the Northland Motel."

"No way sis, you're going to stay here. We'll get—"

They were interrupted by a loud banging on the door.

Tom, Ollie, Gino, Eddie, and Bob came through the door carrying various bags and packages.

"I think we rented the last thing left at the car rental agency," Ollie said. "All they had left was this monster Ford pickup truck."

"Where do you want this stuff, Hank?" Tom said holding several packages.

"Kitchen."

"Oh, Oh," Gino and Ollie said together, noticing Diane standing by her chair. Gino continued, "Does Maggie know about this?"

"Guys, this is Diane, my sister. You remember her, don't you?"

"No, this isn't that skinny sister of yours?" Bob said.

"Can't be, no buck teeth or pigtails." Tom said.

"Yeah, no knock knees or band aides." Ollie added.

"Hi guys," Diane smiled broadly, "Yes, me, that big sister who used to give Hank hell for running around with you guys. I used to say you would get him into big trouble some day."

The four men looked at each other. Gino shrugged, "What do you mean, get him into trouble? Heck, I thought it was the other way around!"

Diane scanned the men, "Speaking of who was the trouble-maker, where's your other buddy, that crazy person, what's his name?"

"You mean Vic?" Hank asked, putting the coats in the hall closet.

"Yes, Vic," Diane thought for a minute, "Vic Pollo. God, he was something else. It seemed every time you were with that guy, you were in some kind of trouble.

"Didn't Hank tell you?" Ollie asked quickly.

"Sorry Sis, I didn't have a chance to tell you. Vic was killed. Shot by his wife whom he had been abusing."

"I don't wonder." Diane looked at the men standing in front of her, shuffling their feet. "I just hope all this stuff with Pettiford works out for you guys," looking at Hank, "And my little brother Henry."

A small knock on the door and Diane opened it to find Sarah and Brandon. "Come on in, everybody is welcome."

Orphan had decided there were too many humans in the house and found refuge under Hank's bed.

THE LAST DEER HUNT

"Hi everybody," Sarah waved, "I'd like you to meet Brandon."

"Hi folks." Brandon grinned.

From somewhere, Hank heard Ollie say, "Yeah, I can see why Hank was concerned."

Sarah introduced Brandon around and soon they were absorbed into the flow of conversation. A number of people gathered around Brandon to hear his stories of his photography assignments around the world and he did not disappoint them.

"Is there anything I can do to help you Hank?" Diane said.

Hank put a match to the wood, paper and kindling in the small woodstove, and watched it as it leapt to life. "Thanks Sis, yeah, check the kitchen and see if we're set on drinks."

Everyone turned to a loud knock on the door. Gino opened it and Gus and Patti Culpepper came in. With introductions done and coats put on Hank's bed, the conversations started up again. Gus and Diane moved away to the woodstove and were engaged in a conversation of their own.

Patti joined Hank in the kitchen and checked his hands. "Can I be of any help?"

"Yeah, that would be great. Can you get the oven going? I haven't had a chance to use it yet."

"The place looks really good; you put a lot of work into it." Patti moved dials and checked the oven.

"Yeah, but Maggie picked out almost everything."

Patti was closely examining the cabinets, running her hand over the surface and checking each handle and hinge. "My goodness, Hank, you made these cabinets? You do beautiful work."

"Hank, can I see you a moment." Gus motioned to Hank to follow him. Alone in the back of the kitchen, Gus spoke quietly. "Did you hear the results of the ballistics test? It seems like all six slugs found in the body of Pettiford were fired from the German Mauser rifle that was found at the Sloan's."

Hank's mind flashed back to the night when he was crawling around frantically trying to locate all the shells on the floor at Pettiford's, as if trying to find a missing piece to a puzzle. "Thanks Gus, I'm not sure what that means, but I'm sure it will come up again."

A knock on the door and Tom moved across the room. "I'll get it."

Maggie, her arms full of pans and bowls came in. Hank took pans from Maggie and they headed to the kitchen.

"What's this?" She was holding the large envelope from the California Institute for Art.

"I haven't had a chance to open it."

"Well, we're going to open it right now!" Maggie was dragging Hank towards the bedroom.

The conversations stopped. "Hey, can't you two wait?" Gino called out.

More remarks followed as Maggie closed the bedroom door. "Now open it."

The envelope opened and the contents fell onto the bed, Hank and Maggie traded papers as they read in silence.

"Well?" Maggie said, holding up sheets of paper. "What do you think?"

Hank took the papers and quickly scanned them. "It says there aren't enough art samples for them to make a decision."

"No Hank, what I read was that they were impressed with your work, especially the sketches you did for the magazine article and they just need to see some recent works."

"Did you send the ones that I gave you?"

"They're already mailed."

"That's good." Hank looked over the papers from the envelope. "You know Maggie; I'm really struggling with this whole thing, like having to leave Fairhaven. I know what I have here in Fairhaven and I don't know what would hap-

THE LAST DEER HUNT

pen in California."

Maggie sat watching him as he picked up the papers and returned them to the envelope. "What bother's you about going to California?"

"What if I fail at the art school?

"You will do just fine, believe me. So why wouldn't you go?"

"I couldn't afford it?"

"Gus said he would help you."

"I can't do that."

"Yes you can. You can't afford not to go."

"Where would I stay?"

"With me, of course."

"I can't do that."

"Yes you can Hank Duval." Maggie said, with a deep sense of frustration. "You will find every reason not go to California. Think about it, this may be your last opportunity at pursuing your art. You are very good at what you do and you should have this chance. Besides Hank, California will have one thing that Fairhaven won't have…"

"What's that?" Hank asked.

"Me."

"Sorry folks, but I need to put these coats somewhere." Patti said, bursting through the bedroom door, arms filled with coats, hats, scarves, and gloves. "Lucy and Frenchy are here and you should see all the food. God, the turkeys look sooooo good."

Maggie quietly moved towards the living room, a look of sadness on her face.

"Dinner will be ready in about twenty minutes!" Gino called, shuffling large platters covered with aluminum foil from the front door into the kitchen. Sarah and Lucy were following with smaller bowls and dishes.

The conversation ceased and everyone joined in the work. Chairs were gathered up and put around the tables. The kitchen hummed as Lucy and Frenchy removed foil, uncovered dishes, put bowls in the microwave, and took them out of the oven. All of these were then passed out the door to people who took them and placed them on the table.

A loud "Coming through," followed by two large platters bearing turkeys being passed through the door and then put in the center at either end of the table.

Hank sat at one end of the table looking out over the vast array of food. Without a word, everyone at the table took the hand of the person next to them and lowered their head.

Hank looked around at the people sitting at the table. *These are the people who have touched my life and made it better, Gus, Frenchy, Diane, Sarah, Lucy, Uncle Andre, Gino, Eddie, Ollie, Bob, Tom, Patti, Gus, Maggie and —yeah, Brandon.* Then he spoke words that he had not uttered in many years, "Dearest God, we are gathered here in your presence...Amen."

Echoed by all, "Amen."

"And get this damn Pettiford case closed." Eddie added.

"Amen to that." Everyone replied.

"And just one more," Hank looked around the table. "A special thanks to Gus for the bail money, without which, we wouldn't be here today."

"Amen to that." Everyone replied.

Thanksgiving dinner was over. The turkey carcasses were picked clean and all the side dishes were empty.

"Great food!" Tom commented, leaning back with both hands on his stomach. "My compliments to Frenchy and Lucy."

"Thanks, it was a labor of love." Frenchy covered the last of the leftover turkey and put it with the other pans, pots, bowls, and dishes.

Lucy was busy scraping and cleaning the last of the plates and putting them into a large plastic bag. "Yes thank you. And just to let you know so you can tell all your friends...Oh hell that won't work, all your friends are here already. Anyway, I want you to know that I'm starting up a

THE LAST DEER HUNT

catering service. I'm thinking of calling it 'Lucy's Luscious Larder.'"

A chorus of laughter, boos and jeers rose from the room followed by various suggestions.

"All right you guys, I guess I'll go back to plan B, How about 'Frenchy's Fine Foods?'"

"Good choice, Lucy." Gus said, reflecting the nods and approvals from the room.

"You got it." Lucy gave thumbs up.

"Good luck, Lucy." Sarah moved to hold the bag for her. "You do Bar Mitzvahs too?"

"You got it." Lucy smiled back at Sarah.

"Hey guys," Eddie's voice squeaked, "let's make a pact to stay in touch. I mean after this is all over. Just so we know where everybody is and what they are doing."

"Yeah, and the rest of us too." Tom, Ollie, Bob, and Eddie nodded. Gino poured another glass of red wine.

Hank laughed, "Now, that won't be a problem, we'll all be in adjoining cells at the state prison."

"That won't happen." Gus said, reassuringly, "I'm sure Pat Johnson will take good care of you."

Uncle Andre held up an unsteady hand and with quivering voice said, "I should head out now, but I wanted to give you these papers. I found them while cleaning out a closet. They're from your Mom and Dad." He handed Hank a wrinkled envelope. "You can have them."

Hank took the envelope. "Wait Uncle," Hank quickly went and returned from the bedroom with a large package. "Before anybody leaves, I have something I would like to share with you."

. He opened the flat package and held up a framed picture made from different colors and grains of inlaid woods in a mosaic pattern.

When looked at from a distance, Frenchy could distinguish the figure of a man holding a child up in his arms while flames swirled in a wooden background. "Your father?" Frenchy continued to study the picture. "My God, this is beautiful. My friend, this is a beautiful work of art, you are indeed a gifted artist."

"Yeah, it's my Pa. It's just something I wanted to do for him." Hank ran his hand over the plaque. "It's not done yet, there is quite a bit of work left."

Maggie peered closely. "How did you do this? Where did you learn this technique?"

"Out of a book I picked up. I used red maple, white oak, birch, and cedar. I don't think it's that good. It was my first attempt. The technique is called Marquetry. I found out about it from a place called Hudson River Inlay in New York State.

Lucy came over to see what Hank and Frenchy were looking at. "Oh, Hank, it's beautiful. If you want, when it's done, we'd be happy to put it in the diner, right Frenchy?"

"Yeah, no problem." Frenchy was still staring at the inlaid plaque. "We'd be proud to show it there."

The other people moved over and looked at the plaque. They all nodded their agreement with Lucy's proposal.

Uncle Andre slowly drew his hand across the plaque. Putting on his coat, he smiled. "Your Pa would be proud of you boy. That's mighty nice work."

"Thanks Uncle. If you need anything, please call me. Okay?"

"I'll be okay Henry, you take care of yourself."

Hank watched with sadness as the old man turned to walk away.

Gus was up, "Wait a minute Andre, I'll go with you and see that you get home."

"I think we're leaving too." Gino said, following Tom, Eddie, Bob, and Ollie who were taking coats out of the closet.

"Thanks for coming guys." Hank looked at each of the men and they nodded as their eyes met. "We've been through a heck of a lot recently and I just want to let you know that I really appreciate and thank you for being here."

As the men left, Hank went to the door and called after

them. "Hey fellas, don't forget about Eddie this time. He only has one ear left!"

Sarah and Brandon came from the bedroom with their coats on; Sarah came over and gave Maggie a small kiss on the cheek and a hug for Hank. "We'll be going too; I want to take Brandon over to Michigan Tech to see the ice sculptures. They are so beautiful at night."

"Thanks for everything." Brandon extended his strong handshake to Hank, then taking Maggie in both hands said, "And I'm sure we will have more time together before I leave." Then seeing Hank watching him, continued. "To work on the article of course."

"Wait up a minute, I'll go with you." Patti said, wiggling quickly into her coat. Patti, Sarah and Brandon waved goodbye and turned to leave with Brandon's grin seeming to just hang in the air.

"Cheshire cat." Hank mumbled

"Cheshire cat." Maggie agreed.

Heading for the door with Lucy, Frenchy said. "We got everything picked up and we're ready to shove off." "Let us help you," Hank grabbed his coat and handed Maggie's to her.

Outside, Frenchy's van was loaded and after handshakes and hugs, headed down the road. The late afternoon shadows were lengthening as Hank and Maggie walked back to the house. Their breath condensing in the cold air and the snow crunching under their feet. Memories of long ago welled up inside him, memories of snow forts, sled rides down snow covered streets, and skating down at the town rink in the evenings with friends.

Hank reached into his pocket and felt the charm bracelet with the hula dancers. "You know, I should go over to the cemetery. I would like Sandy to finally have her bracelet back."

"Hank, you are nuts. There is four feet of snow on the ground; you wouldn't even find headstones. It can wait until next spring." She gave a playful tug of his sleeve back towards the house.

Letting go of Maggie's hand, Hank backed up, scooped a handful of snow, and tossed it in her direction.

"You dirty rat." Maggie squealed, scooping up a handful snow, packing it into a ball and hurling it at Hank. It glanced off his head with a large puff of snow. "Hah, gotcha Duval!" Then she quickly ducked as two missiles came in her direction. The snowballs continued until they reached the house and they burst through the door, filled with laughter and covered with snow.

Diane was sitting in front of the woodstove reading a book, Orphan curled up at her feet. "You two kids been playing outside again?"

Out of their wet clothes, they sat on the couch next to Diane, each sipping on a cup of cocoa, their cheeks still bright red from the cold. Hank went into the bedroom while Diane opened the envelope from Uncle Andre.

Hank, back from the bedroom, handed Diane the certificate of heroism from the state indicating their father's bravery. She studied it for a moment, "Yes, Gus was just telling me about this today, isn't it amazing? I cannot believe that Dad kept this secret all those years. You know, it is amazing; it seems that everyone in our family had some sort of a secret. You, with Pettiford, me with my sexual preference, Dad, with being a secret hero, and Mom, with her fling with that traveling salesman."

"Ma had an affair?"

"Yes, I always suspected it, but now I'm sure of it. Look at the papers in that envelope that Uncle Andre gave us."

Hank picked up the envelope, opened it and slid out the contents; a number of papers, and what looked like a military medal. Shuffling through the papers, he picked one sheet and put the rest down. "It looks like you were right Diane, I mean about Ma." He looked at her, shaking his head. Listen to this."

It was Maggie's turn to be curious, but she just watched as Hank held up a paper from the envelope and read.

THE LAST DEER HUNT

5/12/1960

In the month of May,
My man had left
To seek a new endeavor
A new love came, stole my heart,
And changed my life forever.

5/23/1960

A flying hero brave and bold,
He came as stranger, left as lover.
A span of time
 Too short to measure
He filled my life with joy,
And memories to treasure

Hank picked up the medal and studied it.
"What is it Hank?"
"Some kind of military service medal. All I can make out is 'RCAF.'
Diane was going through more of the papers, more poems and entries in a journal, which she shared with Hank. Putting the papers down, Hank and Diane looked at each other, then as one, burst out in laughter.
"Can you believe this?" Hank said, looking at Diane, still laughing.
"Care to share?" Maggie said, sitting and watching.
"It's appears, Diane replied, "That our dear, shy and introspective mother was guilty of an indiscretion."
Hank picked up the rest of the papers from the envelope and read them. "Looks like there is more of Ma's poetry about this man." He handed them to Diane. "And a copy of an old Readers Digest with some of her poems."
Diane leafed through the pages and sighed, "I'd give

anything to know who this guy was."

Hank slowly turned the military medal repeatedly in his hand. "I think I know who it was, and as soon as I am sure, I will tell you."

The room turned quiet as the fire flickered and danced around the walls.

Diane stood, yawned, and stretched. "I think it's time for me to hit the sack. You two can sit here and watch the fire go out."

Thirty-Eight

The morning was mild and overcast with no sign of the foreboding storm. Hank was up early and, after his usual cup of coffee, filled a large portfolio case with just completed sketches and drawings. He had been planning to bring these to the cabinetmaking shop for about a week but could never find the time. Maggie and Diane were still sleeping and this morning would be a good time to get this done. It would give him a good excuse to walk down Main Street...and to go past Maggie's apartment.

An old flatbed truck with a snowmobile chained to its bed was sitting in the street just in front of Maggie's blue Volvo. Fuzzy Walstrom was busy loading large cases into the truck and Brandon was walking out of the building carrying camera equipment, one hand wrapped in a bandage.

"What happened to your hand?"

"That cat Hemingway, took a whack at me. Got me good."

Hank suppressed a grin. *I think I finally like that cat.*

"You're up early this morning." Brandon said his face a wide grin. "I can't wait to get started. It looks like it's going to be a great day."

"Storms come up very—" Hank stopped, *Hell with it, I am*

not going to preach anymore. "I was just going over to Frenchy's Diner for some breakfast; you're welcome to join me."

"No thanks, I already ate." Brandon said, putting the camera equipment in the truck. Then, stopping what he was doing, he turned to Hank and the grin grew into a full smile. "You know Henry; I had forgotten how beautiful Maggie really is."

"Yeah," Hank fought to keep his emotions in check. Well you guys better be careful out there today, this storm's supposed to be the big one."

Fuzzy opened the driver's door on the truck. "Don't worry Hank, I've lived around here as long as you have I ain't gonna do anything dumb. We'll be in and out before the snow hits."

"Yeah sure, you just can't be too careful, you know." *I'm preaching again...*Hank could almost feel the kick in the ankle from Maggie.

As the truck pulled away from the curb, the passenger's window rolled down and Brandon's smiling face appeared. "Oh yes Henry, if you see Maggie today, remind her that we have a date for dinner tonight over in Houghton." The old truck moved down the deserted main street leaving Hank standing on the snow covered sidewalk.

The truck out of sight, Hank, portfolio under his arm, started down Main Street towards the shop. *Yeah sure Brandon. Anything you want Brandon. You bet, Brandon. You can take that plastic grin and you can go straight to..."*

The cabinetmaking shop was biting cold. Hank turned the heat on and started a pot of coffee. *Still too cold to work, can see your breath.* The radio was predicting that the snow should start falling about mid-morning.

Hank busied himself picking out certain sketches and putting them in one pile, then changing piles and moving sketches between piles, his mind somewhere else. He forced a fake grin and moving his head from side to side, mocked Brandon. "We already had breakfast...I can't remember how beautiful she was...yeah, yeah, yeah...Remind Maggie we have a date tonight...yeah, yeah, yeah.

Well, you had your chance buster, do not think you are just going to waltz in here and take her home with you! No way! I don't care how beautiful, smart, rich, and talented you are! Hell, take away all your good looks, your brains, your money and your talent and what do you have left? Me!

After fifteen minutes, he realized he had accomplished nothing. Speaking out loud in the empty shop, "None of these sketches are really very good. There is no way I'm ever going to get into that art school. I just don't understand why Maggie keeps pushing me to do this. Even if I get into that school, there's a good chance I won't be able to get through it." Hank ran his hand through his hair, picked up one small pile of sketches and flipped through them. "What if I get out there and it's too hard? Oh heck, I haven't even been accepted yet...but what if I am?"

The telephone jangled Hank out of his thoughts.

"Hi Gus. Yeah, things are going okay."

Gus' voice came over the phone, "They ran ballistics tests on the Luger and they have found a match between the German Luger to bullets found in the destruction of headstones in the Fairhaven cemetery in 1967.

Hank shook his head. "Good old Vic.

"Can't help you out Henry, need to run." Gus hung up.

Hank hung up the phone. "Now I need to find Maggie. She's supposed to be at Sarah's." Dialing Sarah's number, he was interrupted by a knock on the door.

"Maggie, what are you doing here?"

"Hank, how could you let Brandon go out today with this storm coming up?"

"Me? Heck Maggie, I was the one who—"

"Hank Duval, you know how the storms can come up really quick and—"

It was Hank's turn to interrupt. "Whoa, you were the one who told me to back off. I tried to say something—"

Maggie was in his arms. "I'm sorry Hank. I've been so confused, I wasn't sure of my own feelings. But now I know I'm over him."

"Oh Yeah, then what about your date tonight with Mr. Smiley?"

"Henry Duval," Maggie backed up a step, tilted her head and put her hands on her hips. "Do I sense a little hint of jealousy?

"Don't call me Henry." *Damn, I hate it when she's right.* He picked up the mailing envelope. "These are the sketches I selected for the Art School in California; I'll get them sent as soon as I can." He was still fretting over Brandon when he added sarcastically, "Is that okay with you?"

Maggie reached over and took the envelope. "I'll mail these for you today. Hank, I hate to change the subject, but Brandon...I mean, could you..."

"I'll look into it. The radio said the snow would start about mid-morning."

"Is it supposed to be bad?"

"Yeah, the air feels thick out there. I think it's really gonna come down."

Maggie's face turned into a deep frown. "I guess I'm worried..."

"It's okay Maggie, I'll watch the weather, and if it gets real bad, I'll check on him."

"Thanks Hank." She moved away from him, but held each of his hands and watched his face.

Hank stood looking deep into her eyes, "Maggie...doesn't that guy ever stop grinning?"

The tension released, Maggie laughed. "No, never, even in the shower..." Seeing Hank's face drop, she added, "But you got to love that cute dimple."

Hank shook his head. *I know what I would like to do with that damn dimple!*

. "I have to run." She kissed Hank's cheek and waved the envelope. "I'll make sure these are mailed today." A quick wave and she was out the door.

THE LAST DEER HUNT

The day had turned dark and drab. The first snowflakes had started to fall, giant flakes that were quickly lowering visibility. It would not take long for the snow to accumulate. Hank crossed the street and walked towards Matson's Garage.

"Good grief Waino, your garage is actually open, how the heck did that happen?"

"Yeah, I gotta work sometimes you know. Gotta pay the rent."

His bill for his truck wipers paid, Hank asked. "Waino, would you mind if I borrowed one of the snowmobiles you got out back?"

"Yeah, you can do that. What you want it for? You're not planning on going out today, not with this storm coming in are you?" Waino wiped his large bald head with a grease-covered bandanna. "It's gonna be a real bad one."

"Fuzzy Walstrom took a photographer out to Johnson's old logging site in the swamp looking for wolves. I thought I better go and check on them."

Waino put his bandanna back in his pocket. "Johnson's is about a mile into Luther's Swamp. Fuzzy Walstrom was never the brightest lamp on the porch, but this is downright dumb. Yeah Hank, take the SkiDoo. Keys in it and it should be full of gas."

"Thanks Waino, I owe you for this one."

"Hell Hank, you already put my grandkids through college with what you spent on that old truck of yours. It was just about worn out when you got it from your Pa."

Hank did not answer. He was halfway through the garage and out the back. The red and white SkiDoo started and Hank carefully edged it forward across the road and headed in the direction of Luther's Swamp.

The wind had picked up and the snow was coming across rather than down when Hank turned off River Road onto the old grade. Hank drove up the grade for about a mile and a half until the faint lights on the left marked old man Paget's homestead and the end of the plowed road.

Fuzzy's truck was parked and the snowmobile was not on the truck.

Gusts of wind blew from all directions swirling the snow and cutting visibility to nearly the front of the snowmobile. The goggles were useless in the blowing snow and Hank stuffed them in his coat pocket.

He knew the grade ran perfectly straight for another three-quarter of a mile, and then dropped steeply down to Birch Creek. Right after the creek, a large oak had fallen across the grade and marked the trail through the swamp to Johnson's old logging camp.

Hank kept the nose of the machine straight ahead. Suddenly, the engine coughed and sputtered. *Damn thing had better not die out here.*

The snow was accumulating rapidly, about four or five inches so far. *By tonight, it will be over a foot, maybe even two feet.* The nose of the snowmobile tipped down. *We're on the hill to the creek. Not far now.*

His eyebrows and eyelids covered over with snow every few minutes and needed to be cleared off. A bump. The oak tree! *Okay, need to turn left here and follow the creek.*

Hank stopped the SkiDoo and checked ahead to assure himself that he was in the right place. *Yep, need to turn between the two spruces, but beyond that, I'm going to have to feel my way.*

The snowmobile moved slowly between the spruces but on the other side, the front tilted sharply towards the brook. "I better leave the snowmobile here and walk."

With difficulty, Hank turned the vehicle around and parked it on the grade. Talking to himself, he felt his way forward, one step at a time. "Why didn't I take the snowshoes? Now what the heck do I do? This storm may keep up all night." The vision of the lost hunter leaped into his mind. The bluish face, the frozen smile. "I wonder if Brandon is still grinning."

"It's less than a half mile to Johnson's camp, oh what the hell, I've come this far, I can make it the rest of the way." The

THE LAST DEER HUNT

going was slow, feeling his way from tree to tree, he counted his footsteps. *Just stay at the bottom of this ravine. Don't go up either side.*

"Six steps, a spruce on the right, ten steps, and another spruce, this one on the left. Three steps," *shit, just about poked my eye out on that small aspen.* "Now twelve steps." Something in the path. "Damn, it's a snowmobile! Must be Fuzzy's."

"HELLO, HELLO, ANYONE OUT THERE?" *Hell, nobody would hear that more than five feet away in all this snow.* A touch of panic passed quickly through his mind. *What do I think I'll find when I get to Johnson's logging camp? They could be anywhere. No, maybe they're smart enough to stay put.*

"Have to keep going, seven steps, another spruce, fifteen steps, and another spruce. Thirty-two steps, no tree." *This has got to be Johnson's clearing. Should be the stump of the big white pine ahead and just to the right. Yeah, that's it, I'm here!*

"HELLO, BRANDON! FUZZY! HELLO OUT THERE!"

Nothing, not even an echo. *Listen. Nothing. What do I do now?*

Go around the perimeter of the opening. Hank felt his way along, calling every three steps. "Hey you guys, you better come out, it's going to get down to minus thirty tonight."

More steps, "OLLY OLLY OXENFREE!" Standing, trying to catch his breath. *Damn, walking in this deep snow is work.*

One more time, "THAT'S IT GUYS, I'M GOING HOME!"

Then, through the blowing and twisting wind, a voice, "Henry?" That you Duval?"

"Yes. Is that you Brandon? God you scared the hell out of me." Quickly, Hank was digging through the snow helping Brandon free his arms. "How are you doing?"

"Careful Hank, my leg, I think it's broken." Brandon was not grinning.

"Okay. Just sit there a minute." Hank said, wiping snow from himself and Brandon. "Where's Fuzzy?"

"He went back to the snowmobile to go for help. Didn't

you pass him coming in? You must have just missed him.

"No, I didn't see him, but then again, I could have been right next to him in this blizzard and not seen him."

Brandon was struggling to stand, and although he was only a foot away from Hank, he was almost obliterated in the wind driven snow. "No, just sit for a minute Brandon, we need to think. Do you have any rope?"

"There's some nylon rope in one of the bags next to me. Do you think we should just stay here? I'm sure they will come looking for us soon."

Hank dug out the bags and found the rope. "The temperature could be down to thirty below tonight and this storm might last until tomorrow evening." The vision of the frozen hunter still hung in his mind. "And the clothes you have on aren't going to keep you warm for very long."

Working with difficulty in the blowing snow, Hank was able to find two sticks large enough to make splints and tied them to Brandon's leg. Using the rest of the rope, Hank tied himself to Brandon and with a large branch Brandon could use as a walking stick; they started walking.

With the large white pine stump as a reference, Hank measured off the steps towards where he hoped the path was that led back to the grade and the snowmobile.

It was nearly dark by the time they reached Fuzzy's snowmobile. Hank kicked around but could not find any sign of Fuzzy or the snowmobile keys.

"I'm exhausted." Hank said, leaning against the snowmobile.

"Christ, this leg hurts." Brandon's face was covered with snow. "I don't know if I can make it."

"Come on guy. It's not too far now." Hank stood, pulling Brandon with him.

"Six steps." Hank counted aloud. "There's the spruce. Now nine steps to the next tree."

The wind howled through the trees. The snow was blinding, coming from all sides. Hank could feel Brandon's body sagging against him.

THE LAST DEER HUNT

Darkness had fallen and even the snow was not distinguishable, but Hank could feel the stinging flakes wherever they could find bare skin.

"Six steps, we should be in the clearing. Yes! This is it guy, we made it!" Hank kicked at the drifts of snow. "No, no, shit no. It's got to be here, right here!"

"What is it?" Brandon sounded weak. "What's wrong?"

"The SkiDoo. It's gone. I left it right here and it's gone!"

Brandon sagged lower. "You must be mistaken. Maybe we're not in the right place."

"No...It's gone! Damn! Fuzzy took it. Damn that Walstrom, he took the fricken snowmobile."

Brandon wiped the snow from his face and looked at Hank. "We better be getting on, old buddy."

Brandon is grinning. Maggie was right, he never stop grinning! "Okay fella," Hank secured Brandon onto his side, "let's go."

One step at a time in the darkness and biting snow. *No idea what time it is. What difference does it make?* Brandon was nearly dead weight now.

I'm strapped to this grinning fool, and I'm probably going to die with a grin on my face like that frozen hunter. Every step was a major effort, more difficult than the last one. *Up the steep hill and follow the grade straight ahead.*

Hank tripped over the bump in the grade and the two men fell to the snow. *Jesus, my fingers are froze, I can't untie the rope.* "Come on Brandon, help me."

Brandon moaned, "Don't know, don't know." Another moan, "Look at her, isn't she still beautiful?"

Geez, now he's hallucinating! It would serve him right if I just left him here. The rope worked free and Hank pushed himself to his knees. Slowly he crawled towards the faint yellow light shining through the trees and whirling snow. "Paget's. We made it to Paget's. Brandon; we made it." His voice was swept away by the winds as each word left his mouth.

Thirty-Nine

Hank tried to smile but his face muscles refused. His head hurt, and he blinked his eyes trying to focus on the small furry creature on his pillow. "Holy cow Toto, I'm in Kansas!"

Maggie, Frenchy, and Uncle Andre, standing by the side of the hospital bed, turned in unison and looked towards him.

Hank blinked at the line of people. "Look Toto, there's Dorothy, the cowardly lion and the tin man," and seeing Gus behind the others, "and oh look, it's the wizard. So where the heck is the brainless scarecrow?"

"Hey buddy, how the heck are you?" Eddie, his left ear wrapped in bandages, was sitting on the other bed.

"Ah, the scarecrow." Hank felt the stab of pain and pushed the button for the pain relief medicine. As the medicine flowed down the tube into his arm, he looked at Gus, "Oh great wizard, send me back to Oz where it's safe, there is no intelligent life down here." Hank held up both of his hands, studying the large bandages. "How long have I been here in the hospital?"

Maggie moved next to the bed. "Since last night. God Hank, we thought you were dead!" Maggie put her hands

THE LAST DEER HUNT

on his bandages. "Don't worry; you're going to be all right."

Slowly, Hank's vision came back and he could focus on the small creature on his pillow, a small stuffed dog, with a tag, "Get better quickly, love Maggie."

Slowly, yesterday's events filtered back into his brain and he tried to sit up, to look around. "Where's Brandon, how is he? Is he okay?"

"Easy buddy," Frenchy was moving pillows under Hank's head. "Brandon is in the next room. Except for some frostbite and broken leg, he's O.K."

Hank tried moving his fingers, but the bandages were too tight. "Looks like the end of a promising career in art."

"Hank, you will be okay. You have some tissue damage and will lose a little skin, but that's all." Maggie moved her hands slowly over each bandaged hand.

The door to the room opened and Sheriff McCarthy came into the room followed by loud conversation and an obvious great amount of people trying to follow him.

Uncle Andre approached the other side of the bed, "It's good to have you back son. When Fuzzy got back and told us that you and Brandon were lost and - well, we thought you two were goners."

"Fuzzy Walstrom? Where is that shithead?"

The sheriff pushed the crowd of people back and closed the door. "Morning Hank, everything is going to be okay. I just talked to Brandon and got his story. Fuzzy Walstrom came back to town with all these bruises and a cockamamy story about how you showed up at Johnson's logging camp and in a fit of jealousy, beat him and Brandon, and left them stranded out there to die." We were trying to launch a search party to go out first thing in the morning when old man Paget showed up about midnight and told us you and Brandon were at his place."

Hank tried to push himself up, but the pain in his hands stopped him. "If I get my hands on Walstrom, I'll..."

"Don't worry about Walstrom," Sheriff McCarthy patted Hank's shoulder, "I'll find him, and when I do, I think we can charge him with stealing a snowmobile or endangering lives or whatever else we can pin on him."

Maggie and Gus moved away, heading for the door. "We're going over to check on Brandon, we'll be back in a bit." Maggie said softly and they left the room.

Frenchy pushed his chair up to Hank's bed. "Well my friend, how's it feel to be a genuine hero? Now that word is out that you saved Brandon, everybody in town is talking about you."

"Funny, I don't feel like a hero, I was just trying to get out of that swamp."

"Buddy, we really thought you had had it. Old man Paget couldn't get his truck out so he walked all the way to town in the blizzard. It took him over three hours to get here. Good thing he did; probably saved your hands."

"Then he's the hero. God, that guy is ninety years old."

"Come on buddy, what you did was incredible. You walked nearly a mile out of there without being able to see your hand in front of your face and a man with a broken leg strapped to you. Don't tell me that was nothing."

"Frenchy, all I could think of was the face of that frozen hunter and kept going. Do you know how long I'll be here?"

"You will be out by Monday." Frenchy was moving towards the door. "I have to get back to check on the diner. We lost power for about three hours and I need to make sure the freezers are okay." As he reached the door, he turned and said. "Hope you didn't finish the inlaid plaque for your Pa, you need to add yourself to the plaque now that you're a hero."

"Hero? Come on Frenchy, I was just trying to survive."

"Hank, if all you were trying to do was survive, you could have left old Smiley back there in the swamp." With that, Frenchy was gone.

Uncle Andre came back over to Hank's bed. "You're going to be all right young man. Your Ma and Pa would be very proud of you if they were here today."

"Heck, if that's all it took to make them proud of me," Hank smiled, "I should have done this about thirty years ago!"

"Hank, I think they're up there right now looking down on you and I know they're proud. I know I am proud of you. Yep, you do have some of your old man in you." Uncle Andre squeezed Hank's arm. "I have to go now, I'll stop in and make sure Orphan's okay."

Hank heard his name and looked up at the television. "This is Karen Casey, Channel Four News from outside the Baraga Memorial Hospital with this nights leading story. We are happy to report that Mr. Duval is doing fine and will be released from the hospital in a couple of days. It seems that the earlier reports that Mr. Duval had left Fuzzy Walstrom and Brandon Howard to die in the swamp was incorrect. We have just talked to Mr. Howard and it seems that Mr. Duval is the hero here, not the villain. If the name Duval is familiar, it's the same Henry Duval who only recently divulged his involvement in the death of Ronald Pettiford nearly twenty years ago. And now, we are going to interview Mr. Paget, who at ninety-four years old, walked out five miles in the raging blizzard to get help for Mr. Duval and Mr. Howard."

"Hey Hank old buddy, you're getting to be famous." Eddie was standing watching the television.

"Will everyone please stop already, I'm not any damned hero."

Old Mr. Paget sat sheepishly in front of the cameras, bright lights in his face, making him squint. Tiny beads of sweat moved down his forehead as he nodded in response to Ms. Casey's many questions.

An intense jolt of pain surged through his hands and Hank pushed the button for the pain medication. Quickly he felt himself drifting off into a welcome sleep.

From somewhere he heard a voice break through the fog. "I really do love you Hank, I love you very much."

Through the layers of drugs and exhaustion, he could

make out the face surrounded by the long red curls. "Thank you Dorothy, I love you too, take care of Toto for me." He wanted to reach out for her, but, exhausted, fell back into a deep, welcome sleep.

Forty

It was the 5th of December and a small crowd milled around the entrance to the county courthouse enjoying the early December thaw. Temperatures were heading for the forties and cars were threading their way down streets and around pedestrians picking their way through large puddles and melting snow.

Even the bright sunshine glistening off the snow could not take away the damp chill that Hank felt as he watched his friends in conversation with Pat Johnson. *Yes, we had all agreed that Vic was the killer. They had said so, right?* Ollie and Tom stood talking. Eddie was engaged in an animated conversation with Gino that looked like another of their frequent arguments. Bob stood by himself holding tightly to his Bible.

When the men saw Hank watching them, they stopped talking, nodded, and waved to him. *And yet, there are questions that are unanswered. I didn't see Vic at Pettiford's that night. But I got to believe it was Vic, because if I don't, that would mean that my buddies is lying,* He shook his head; *and I would be the chief suspect. The only thing I'm sure of is that I didn't shoot the old bastard...and there are times I'm not sure about that.*

Pat Johnson's voice broke through his thoughts. "Hank, it's good to see you, you look like you have fully recovered from your ordeal." Then gesturing to include all the men, she said. "You all look really nice today." Her black hair framed her face and her dark eyes sparkled, reflecting the bright sunlight. "How are you all doing?"

"Nervous." Gino answered. He pushed his hands further into the pockets of his red down vest. "I'll be glad when this is over."

"Same here." Tom said nervously, looking at the lawyer, seeing if he could read anything in her face.

Pat Johnson returned Tom's look with a small smile that revealed nothing. Slowly she scanned each of the men's faces looking for any small sign that would help her understand the inner working of each of them a little better.

Tom's brown corduroy sports coat hung loosely around his shoulders and the tie was dated, a little too wide with a red and green plaid design whose time had passed. Holding on to one of the too long sleeves, Tom said, grinning shyly. "Borrowed it from Hank."

Eddie stood, head lowered, hands stuffed deep into the pockets of dark brown corduroy pants. He was visibly shivering under his thin brown plaid sports coat buttoned tightly around his body.

Pat Johnson nodded towards Bob, studying the man's face as he shifted his Bible from hand to hand and kept looking at his watch. "Bob, I thought Hannah was going to come today."

Bob looked at his watch, shaking it to make sure it was correct. "She should have been here by now. She said she would try to make it."

"Don't worry, she'll be here," Pat smiled again, and again her expression revealed nothing. She looked back at Gino, already thinking ahead, "How about your wife?"

Gino shook his head and shrugged. "Nah, she's going up to visit her mother for a couple of weeks. Guess she didn't want to deal with this."

THE LAST DEER HUNT

Tom put his hand on Gino's left shoulder, Ollie patted his back, and Eddie lightly hit Gino's right arm.

Gino nodded, "Thanks guys."

Pat Johnson studied the men's display of support for Gino and seemed to be checking off a mental list. She also made a mental note of Eddie standing off by himself and Hank Duval by himself, away from their friends.

Ollie, looking slightly embarrassed, pulled his hunting jacket closed over his desperately wrinkled dress shirt. "I couldn't fit into any of Hank's things." He explained.

Pat Johnson did not respond, but made another note on her checklist.

Tom shook his head and laughed, pointing to the Channel 4 Television truck and the four or five reporters gathered around it. "Looks like we're yesterday's news. Wow, only one television news team and two local newspaper reporters to cover the most sensational trial in the history of Baraga County!"

Hank glanced quickly towards the group of reporters. "Yeah, what the heck is going on?"

Pat Johnson laughed. "You mean none of you guys heard the news this morning?" She studied them, her face a sincere look of amazement. From the looks on the men's faces, she knew they had not, and continued. "Early this morning, a large male moose fell through the ice off Keweenaw point and there are many fire engines and police out there trying to rescue it."

"You mean," Tom chuckled. "The trial of the century in Baraga County has been upstaged by a stupid moose."

The beep, beep from Frenchy's old Volkswagen van announced their arrival. Frenchy hopped out of the driver's side, Lucy, the passenger's side. The side door slid open, and Maggie, Gus, and Diane hopped out.

Feeling a small tug on his arm, Hank turned to find Maggie had moved next to him and put her arm through his. "You look nice today Hank, that blue blazer and red tie fit you nicely."

"Of course they do Maggie, you bought them." He felt the warmth of her presence and was happy she was there.

"Sarah brought Brandon to the airport yesterday. He felt bad that he didn't get any pictures of the wolves, but the good news is that the magazine is now willing to use your sketch work. Isn't that great?"

"Yeah sure, but I'm going to have to get to work on them." *But I don't want to go back to Johnson's old logging camp in that swamp.*

Frenchy and Lucy joined Maggie at Hank's side. "How's it going, guy?" Frenchy asked. "You know everybody is rooting for you."

"Yeah, thanks, everybody for coming today." He clasped Frenchy's hand.

Lucy was dressed in a dark suit and her red beret. "We came all the way over here to give you moral support, what do you think of that?"

"Yeah, we thought you guys would need some character references." Diane said. She seemed overdressed for this warm weather in her oversized yellow ski jacket. Sarah just looked at the men and gave them a two handed thumbs up sign.

"Yeah sure, with you folks for references," Ollie said shaking his head, "we'll probably get twenty years to life at hard labor."

Diane moved in front of Hank, and he took her hand. "Thanks for staying around Sis, you know you didn't have to, but I'm glad you did."

Diane squeezed back. "Anything for my little brother." She said, smiling at him.

Two Lincoln town cars pulled up and stopped. The car doors opened and Edwin Kaarla Sr., Edwin Kaarla Jr., Richard Graves, Robert Graves, and Janet Riddle made their way to their respective clients and were quickly engaged in greetings and conversations.

"Time to go." Pat Johnson said, starting up the steps of the courthouse followed by the large group of men. Halfway up the steps, she was confronted by reporters and a television cameraman. "Not now," she said to them, "I will give you a prepared statement once we are inside." And the small entourage entered the courthouse.

Once inside, Hank, Tom, Gino, Ollie, Bob, Eddie, and the Kaarla Law Firm followed Pat to a table in front of the judge's bench. As more people shuffled into the courtroom, the men sat in silence watching Pat and the other lawyers removing papers from briefcases and holding small discussions.

At the other table in front of the judge's bench, the sheriff, the two state police detectives, Smith and Powers, and a man identified as being from the state police crime lab were in a head-to-head discussion with the prosecuting attorneys.

The courtroom became hushed in anticipation of the start of the proceedings and the only sounds were paper being crumpled, an occasional sneeze or sniffle, and the ticking of a large clock.

"Hear ye, hear ye, the circuit court for the county of Baraga is now in session, all rise, " the court clerk called out from the front of the courtroom. "The Honorable Judge Sylvia P. Murphy presiding."

Judge Murphy entered and sat behind her bench. Her gray hair was pulled back sharply and she wore her reading glasses halfway down her sharp nose. "You may now all be seated," she said with authority, then took a moment. "We will now take up our first hearing of the State versus Grappone, Mahoney, Duval, Bjornson, Lindstrom, and Peters. This will be a preliminary hearing to establish probable cause that one, a crime has been committed, and two, that there are reasonable grounds to believe that the accused committed the crime."

The attorneys identified and introduced themselves. Judge Murphy, who leaned forward, adjusted her glasses and looking towards the prosecutor. "Mr. Chavez, I believe that it is customary for the prosecution to present on behalf of the state, the evidence which you feel will meet the burden of proof required to show probable cause."

The handsome, young Luis Chavez, Assistant District Attorney, stood behind the prosecution's table. "Yes your Honor." He moved with ease and addressed the court with self-assurance. Speaking slowly and pausing frequently to allow certain points to be grasped, the lawyer told the story of six young boys being invited over to Mr. Pettiford's home to enjoy his hospitality. And how did they repay him? By attempting to rob him, then killing him when he caught them in the act. By their own admission, these young men shot Mr. Pettiford not once, but six times in the chest then buried the body and disposed of the murder weapon.

The Assistant District Attorney paused, watching the faces around the room for reaction, then continued. "We can prove they went to Mr. Pettiford's house on this night in August of 1965 with the specific intention of robbing him and in the process of that robbery, shot, and killed Mr. Pettiford."

Another pause, a small sip of water. "We can prove opportunity. Again by their own admission, and through corroborating witnesses, we can place these men on or near the Pettiford home on the night in question." The young attorney paced back and forth in front of his table, measuring every word.

Hank watched as Pat Johnson sat writing. *Why doesn't she challenge that? Or say 'I object' like they do all the time on television?*

"Finally," the young assistant District Attorney added, "We can prove motive. We can show that on the night Mr. Pettiford disappeared, a good number of valuables, money, jewelry, personal effects, and war souvenirs were missing from the Pettiford residence. We can prove through the exhaustive and meticulous investigation of the state police crime lab," Mr. Chavez motioned towards the two detectives. "That we have been able to trace some of those valuables back to the defendants."

Hank glanced quickly at his fellow defendants who were all looking at each other, shrugging.

THE LAST DEER HUNT

Luis Chavez walked back to the prosecutor's table, turned and looked directly at Judge Murphy. "We can prove through ballistics testing that the rifle found at the Sloan's residence was the gun used to murder Mr. Ronald Pettiford and we will show that this gun was fired at the victim by each of the defendants and buried by one of the defendants." The young prosecuting lawyer, looking smug, walked back to the prosecution's table.

The prosecuting attorney addressed the Judge. "I would like to now call the witnesses for the prosecution."

"Please proceed," Judge Murphy replied, sitting back in her chair, her glasses off, rubbing her eyes.

Dr. Whatley from the county coroner's office was quickly sworn in and testified that due to the decomposition of the body, time of death and cause of death could not be concisely established. Six 7mm bullets had been found in the chest cavity and damage to the rib cage indicated that all six shots had entered through this area.

"Ms. Johnson?" The judge nodded towards Pat. "Ms. Johnson, do you have any questions for this witness?"

"Yes Your Honor." Then to the witness. "Can you ascertain which shot actually killed Mr. Pettiford?" Ms. Johnson asked, writing on a piece of paper.

"No. There would be no way of knowing that."

Hank glanced over at the paper in front of Ms. Johnson. He could barely make out a series of squiggles and shapes on the paper. Looking closer, he could see a number of doodles and the words, 'The prosecuting attorney is a doll!' More doodling, then 'He's to die for.' A stick figure that looked to be running was drawn next. 'What a great body, must have fantastic abs.' *Geez, she's got the hots for the prosecution!*

Ms. Johnson smiled, "That will be all for this witness."

Hank looked at her. *Isn't she going to do anything?*

More witnesses followed each other, technical witnesses with dry technical data. Hank was sleepy from the heat and lack of air in the room. A few witnesses were called who had recalled seeing the defendants near the Pettiford home the night in question.

"The prosecution calls Mr. Harold Smith to the stand."

Smith identified himself. "Harold Smith from the State Police Crime Investigation Unit."

Sitting in the chair, Smith appeared confident as he glanced from Mr. Chavez to the judge, then back to the young prosecutor. Hank looked at the other men sitting at the table with him wondering if they felt the same tension and feeling of hopelessness that he felt. He was trying to recall his conversations with Mr. Smith.

Mr. Chavez moved towards the witness stand, "Mr. Smith, you were present at the questioning of the defendants on November 17th of this year."

"That is correct."

The Assistant District Attorney handed the court clerk a small stack of papers. "Here is a copy of that report for the court record."

"So received."

The Assistant District Attorney moved to the witness stand. "Now Mr. Smith, could you tell us what the defendants told you during this session?" Mr. Smith took out glasses and put them on, opened a binder, and looked at Ms. Johnson.

She smiled back. She had resumed her doodles. Hank glanced over and could make out the stick figure of Mr. Chavez being chased by a female stick figure. *Geez, now she's chasing him.*

In a business-like manner, Harold Smith recounted the stories each of the defendants had told during the questioning. It was the same story, going to Pettiford's, playing hide and seek, the shot, finding Eddie, the body and the gun, shooting Pettiford's body and burying it. Mr. Smith wrapped up his testimony, with, "These boys, I mean men, were all at that house that night, they all had been drinking and all of them shot the victim, but one of them killed him. If they had not been there, he would not have been killed. They have a joint responsibility in this man's death."

"Do you care to cross-examine, Ms. Johnson?" Judge Murphy asked.

Pat Johnson approached the witness stand. "You didn't mention anything about Vic Pollo being at the house that night did you?"

"No."

"Wasn't that brought up when you questioned these men?"

"Yes."

"And didn't at least four of the men testify that they had knowledge of Vic Pollo being up at the house that night?"

"I believe that to be the case, yes."

"But you didn't seem to think it was relevant?"

"No, I thought it was a bunch of kids trying to shift the blame from themselves."

"Did you pursue an investigation into the activities of Mr. Pollo on or about the time this incident took place?"

"No, we did not."

Ms. Johnson looked at the defendants. "Is that because you had already made up your mind that these young boys were guilty?"

"No."

"Mr. Smith," Ms. Johnson pointed to the six defendants, "Did you read these men their Miranda rights prior to questioning them?"

"No, at the time, we were just asking them some questions about the crime."

"When did you read them their rights?"

"Well, it was sometime later in the day."

"How late? Was this after you had completed the questioning?"

"No, we still were questioning some of them. It was only after that we realized that these men were actual suspects..."

"And, Mr. Smith, did you inform the defendants that they had the right to legal counsel?"

"No, like I said, we were just—"

"No more questions." Pat Johnson looked across at Mr. Chavez. "I would like to enter a motion to suppress all the statements of the defendants on November 17th based on the fact that they were not read their Miranda rights, they were not told they could speak to an attorney or that they had the right to counsel."

An almost inaudible sigh went up from the back of the room.

The judge took off her glasses, sat back in her chair, and looked over the hushed courtroom. "This is only a preliminary hearing and normally I would not accept a motion to suppress evidence, but I will address this at a later time."

Mr. Chavez smoothed back his black glistening hair and announced. "The prosecution calls Mr. Durfey from the state police ballistics lab in Lansing."

Mr. Durfey, the lab technician was sworn in and sat in the witness chair, sweating and nervous. He testified that all six bullets, marked peoples exhibit 'A' had been removed from the remains of Mr. Pettiford and tested at the police lab in Lansing and found to match a bullet fired from rifle taken from the home of the Sloan brothers. The rifle was labeled peoples exhibit 'B'.

"Now Mr. Durfey, how did you conduct this test?"

"We fired a round from the rifle, exhibit 'B', and compared this slug to those that were taken from the body."

"But did you not have difficulty in firing this rifle?"

"Yes sir."

"And can you tell the court why that was."

"Yes sir. The rifle was in poor condition. The mechanism was completely encrusted in dried mud, as if it had been buried for a long time. We cleaned it up and managed to extract a live round from the chamber. We then reassembled the mechanism and were able to fire the weapon."

Hank sat straight up. *Live round. There was a live round left in the chamber? Then the ballistics test has to be wrong!* He whispered, "Psst, Ms. Johnson!"

"One moment Your Honor," the lawyer said, and then to

THE LAST DEER HUNT

Hank, "What's up?" She listened to Hank as he whispered in her ear. Ms. Johnson turned to the judge. "May we take a fifteen minute recess, your Honor?"

The men stood in a small circle in the hall outside of the courtroom. "What's up Hank?" Gino asked.

"I just realized that the rifle could not have killed Pettiford. That proves I could not have killed Pettiford."

"What do you mean?" Tom scratched his head, looking puzzled.

"You must be mistaken." Eddie's voice was rising. "Didn't ballistics show that the rifle was the weapon that fired all the shots in Pettiford?"

"No, listen to me." Hank gestured for patience. "You just heard that there was a live round still in the chamber of the rifle."

Eddie became excited. "Yeah, Remember Hank, that's what I told you."

"Gino looked at Eddie, then at Hank. "What do you mean, you told Hank? What the hell did you tell him?"

"That's not important." Hank gestured for silence. "What's important is that round had to have been left in the gun from when we fired it.

The men looked at Hank, every face a question mark.

Hank continued. "You guys shot him five times right?"

The men nodded agreement. Ollie still had a question, "But you shot once before we did, yes? Wouldn't that make six?"

"No, I didn't fire it first. The one unfired round in the chamber; that is the sixth round. The gun only holds five shots in the clip and one in the chamber, that's six. So nobody could have killed Pettiford with the rifle since all six rounds are accounted for."

"Somebody could have reloaded it." Ollie injected.

"There wasn't time. I was in that room in seconds after I heard the shot; and why would anyone reload after firing one shot? Besides, there were no other shell casings on the floor."

"But the testing showed that all the slugs were from the rifle." Bob said, biting his lower lip.

"Then the tests must be wrong, that's why I asked Ms. Johnson to request they look at the tests again."

"I don't think this is a good idea." Gino was rubbing his hands rapidly, nervously.

"What's the matter with you guys?" Hank shook his head. "This proves that we didn't fire the killing shot. Don't you guys—"

A bailiff's head appeared through the door. "Recess is over, please return to the courtroom."

The court was called to order. Mr. Durfey was called back to the witness stand. The judge leaned forward. "You may proceed Ms. Johnson.

"Thank you, Your Honor," Ms. Johnson said, "May I cross-exam this witness?"

The judge nodded. Ms. Johnson continued. "There were six bullets found in Mr. Pettiford's remains, is that correct, Mr. Durfey?"

"Yes, that is correct. They were all exactly the same types. 7mm, copper coated. Yes sir. Excellent bullet for deer hunting." He smiled and nodded, smug in his certainty; and all the men in the courtroom nodded their agreement with him.

"And you found an unfired round in the chamber of the rifle, is that correct?"

"Yes Ma'am."

"And you ran ballistics on all six, is that correct?"

"Well, I mean, I..."

"That was a yes or no question. Did you test all six bullets?" Ms. Johnson stood with her face a foot from Mr. Durfey's.

"Yes, but...."

Pat Johnson leaned towards the witness chair. "But, but what? Just what do you mean, yes, but? Did you or did you not test all six bullets?" She glanced at Hank.

"We tested four of the slugs, they were all 7mm, and all

tested the same so we assumed..."

"You assumed? Is that the way you run your testing down in Lansing? You assume things?"

"No Ma'am, I mean..." Mr. Durfey looked at the young district attorney and shrugged his shoulders. "There were new people conducting the tests. They had misplaced two of the slugs at the time of the testing. When the two missing slugs showed up later, we assumed that they would all be the same so they were not tested.

Ms. Johnson looked towards the bench. "I suggest then, that we re-run the tests and this time, we test all six slugs."

"It is late in the day." Judge Murphy appeared uncomfortable in the heat. "I suggest that we stop for the day and reconvene in the morning. Ms. Johnson, the defense has the right to run new tests on the bullets as you see fit. I will make the appropriate arrangements. Ms. Johnson, do you have anything to add at this time?"

"No Your Honor, not at this time."

The court adjourned. Outside the courthouse, Gino, Tom, and Ollie caught up with Hank.

"Wow Hank," Eddie was pacing. "That was really smart of you to have figured that out. But if the rifle didn't kill Pettiford, what did?"

"Hell Eddie, I'm not that smart. All I know is that there was no way that rifle was the weapon that killed Pettiford."

"Yeah," Ollie shook his head, "We were surprised about those test results too."

"Yeah," Tom added, "There's no way they could have come up with those results."

Gino lit up a cigarette. "I just hope you didn't open a can of worms in there."

Hank was tired. "Well, I guess we'll find out tomorrow. Sorry guys, but I think I'd like to just get home."

Forty-One

The next morning, the crowd outside the courthouse was larger with more reporters. "Guess no moose fell through the ice today." Gino muttered as the men were hurriedly escorted inside the courtroom.

Mr. Chavez called the first witness of the day for the prosecution, The Reverend Waldo Trapper.

Mr. Chavez approached the witness booth. "Reverend Trapper, Can you recall what transpired on the night of August 22, 1965?"

"Yes sir," the reverend answered thoughtfully, looking very pious, I was walking home after a meeting with Mr. Pettiford about his donation to build a new steeple on my church, which is the First Methodist Church, when I encountered six boys running up the hill Mr. Pettiford's house on Mansion Row."

"And," Mr. Chavez turned towards the defendants table. "Do you see those boys here today?"

"Yes sir," pointing towards the defendants table, "That's them."

"No more questions." Luis Chavez returned to his seat.

Pat Johnson stood, "Reverend, did you see the boys actually go to Pettiford's house?"

"Well, no, but they were heading in that direction."

"And, Reverend," Ms. Johnson looked at her notes, "how is it that you remember that night so clearly, so long ago?"

"Well, it was because as they ran past me, those little monsters started calling me names."

"And what names would that be, Reverend?"

The reverend cleared his throat and looked at the judge.

The judge looked back, "Please answer the question, Reverend Trapper."

The reverend cleared his throat again, and then very quietly said, "They called me a faggot."

"For the record," Pat Johnson repeated, "The witness said faggot." Then turning to the Reverend, "Are you one?" The buzz in the courtroom grew loud.

"Order, order in the court." The judge rapped her gavel.

"No, no," The reverend cleared his throat once again, wiping his brow. "Heavens no, absolutely not."

"Objection." Luis Chavez was on his feet. The buzz increased.

"Objection sustained." Judge Murphy's stern admonishment quieted the courtroom.

"No more questions." Ms. Johnson sat down.

Samantha Biggers, who was introduced as a high school classmate of the defendants.

"I enter as exhibit C, this small brooch." The assistant district attorney showed it to the witness. "Let it be shown that the prosecution exhibit C, a brooch, was the same pin that was reported stolen from the Pettiford home the night he disappeared."

"Do you recognize this pin, Miss Biggers?"

Miss Biggers responded with a nervous nod.

"And do you remember who gave you this brooch, Miss Biggers?"

"Yes, it was Ollie Bjornson," but she added quickly, "Bobby Lindstrom had some too."

Hank looked at Ollie and Bob, silently mouthed, "What the hell is this?"

Ollie silently responded. "I don't know."

Bob shrugged.

Mr. Chavez leaned close to Miss Biggers, "And when did Mr. Bjornson give you this brooch?"

"It was the first of November, 1966, I remember because it was my fifteenth birthday."

Hank sat, bewildered. *Dammit Ollie, where the hell did you and Bobbie get that jewelry? How come I didn't know about this?*

"Your witness." Mr. Chavez sat down.

Pat looked over to Ollie's lawyer, David Graves, who stood and asked. "And where did Mr. Bjornson tell you that he acquired this piece of jewelry?"

Samantha Biggers looked quickly at Luis Chavez, and then at Mr. Graves, "I think he told me that their friend Vic Pollo gave it to them."

"No more questions for this witness." Attorney Graves sat down.

Luis Chavez looked towards the defendants. "I call Rose Prentice to the stand.

"Miss Prentice, you received a gold locket from Bob Lindstrom, is that true?"

"Yes sir."

Chavez handed Miss Prentice a locket and gold chain. "Is this that locket?" To the court, he added, "Exhibit D."

"Yes sir. It sure looks like it."

Luis Chavez took the locket back to the exhibit table. "This item of jewelry was also identified as belonging to the estate of Ronald Pettiford."

Attorney Graves stood. "And where did Mr. Bjornson say he got that locket?"

And the answer was the same. "From Vic Pollo."

Luis Chavez stood and looked at the men seated at the defendant's table. "So what we have here are two of the men who were at Pettiford's house that night who had possession of jewelry that came from that house. Luis Chavez took a few minutes straightening papers on the table in front of him. Composed and smiling towards the defendant's table, he said, "And now I call Mr. Toivo Niemi to the witness stand.

Toivo, dressed in a very new suit took the oath and sat down.

Chavez approached him, Mr. Niemi; do you recall when the floor of the maintenance building was filled in with concrete?"

"Yeah sure, I do remember, August 24th 1968. I was da night watchman at the mill back den."

"And Mr. Niemi, can you recall for us, what transpired at the mill just a night or two before that date?"

"Yah, like I said to you before in your office, Mr. Lundgren and me, we saw a bunch of kids running from the maintenance house with a wheelbarrow and shovels."

"A bunch? Can you be more specific?"

"Yah, I think four."

"And Mr. Niemi, do you see those boys here in this courtroom today?"

Toivo scanned the room. "No sir."

"No?" Mr. Chavez gestured towards the defendants table, "Are you sure you don't see those boys here?

"No sir, there ain't no boys here." Giggles and laughter emanated from around the room.

"Yes, we know that, but do you see the men you thought you saw that night as boys?"

"Yeah sure, I kinda think it was dem," pointing to the defendants table. "Yeah, dat would be Gino, Tommy, Ollie and Bobby."

"Thank you that will be all, Mr. Niemi. Chavez gestured to the defense lawyers.

Robert Graves rose and with his deep gravelly voice asked, "Mr. Niemi, You kinda think it was those men, I mean boys? Are you not sure?"

"It was kinda dark out and dey were way over by the maintenance shed. But those boys, dey hung around the mill all the time and it sure looked like dem."

Mr. Graves crossed his arms and leaned forward. "But could you swear it was these men you saw that night back in 1968?"

"No sir, dat I couldn't do, I couldn't swear exactly dat it were dem."

"That will be all." Robert Graves sat down.

Luis Chavez stood. "I now call Paul Sloan to the witness stand."

"Do you swear to tell the truth, the whole truth and nothing but the truth?"

"I sure do." Paul Sloan smiled and waved at the defendants.

Mr. Chavez picked up the rifle from the exhibits table and presented it to Paul Sloan. "Is this the rifle you found?"

"Yes sir. But it's been cleaned up really nice now."

Mr. Chavez leaned on the railing of the witness box. "Mr. Sloan, can you tell us exactly how you came to be in possession of this gun?"

"Yes sir. We found it down by the railroad tracks near the river. You know where the lumberjacks sleep sometimes when they had too much to drink. Peter, and me, we go down there with our metal detector and look for money that falls out of the lumberjacks pockets. That's how we found the gun."

"And when did you find the gun?"

"Musta been about ten years ago. Peter and me, we took that gun home but we never used it though 'cause there was a round in the chamber and the bolt was jammed and we couldn't get it free." Paul Sloan's face broke into a worried frown. "But we don't have it no more because those police came and took it away to make it an exhibition B."

"Your witness." Chavez said, bringing the rifle to the court clerk.

Ms. Johnson stood. "Paul did you or your brother or anybody else ever work the bolt on the rifle and were you ever able to eject the live round from the chamber?"

"No Ma'am, we could never get the bolt to work."

"No further questions of this witness."

The judge addressed the witness. "Thank you Paul, that will be all, you can step down now." The bailiff handed the judge a note, which she quickly scanned, then held up her hand. "Before we continue with witnesses, Mr. Durfey is back and informs me that he has the new ballistics tests on all six bullets."

Mr. Durfey took the witness box, informed that he was still under oath.

"We have re-run the ballistics test on all six slugs this time."

"And what did you find?" Ms. Johnson approached the witness stand.

Mr. Durfey coughed into his hand, looking down. "Five of the six bullets were 7.92mm that were fired from the Mauser rifle. It turns out that one bullet was a 7.65mm. And the 7.65mm bullet matches a bullet test fired from a German Luger that was brought in voluntarily by Mr. Gus Lundgren."

The Luger was presented as evidence, exhibit E.

"Shit." Came very quietly from where Gino and Ollie were sitting.

"So, if I have this correct, five of the bullets came from the rifle, and one came from this German Luger, is that correct?" Judge Murphy asked.

"Yes Ma'am, that is correct." Mr. Durfey replied.

"Mr. Chavez, do you have anymore witnesses?"

"No Your Honor, the prosecution rests."

Pat Johnson returned to her chair. Hank glanced over at her. She was doodling again, drawing a characteristic likeness of Mr. Chavez, only this time, he was hanging from a gallows.

"Then would the defense call their first witness?"

Pat Johnson looked at the Judge and Mr. Chavez. "We would like to call Mr. Gus Lundgren if the prosecution has no objections."

Gus was sworn in. Ms. Johnson approached the box and handed him the German Luger from the exhibit table. "Is this the gun that you gave the police for testing?"

"Yes," Gus studied the Luger. "There is no mistaking this gun; it is a very unique piece."

"Mr. Lundgren, how did you come into possession of this weapon?"

"I took it away from Vic Pollo when he shot my dog with it. That was in September of 1968. It has been in my possession ever since."

"Thank you Mr. Lundgren. That will be all."

The judge faced Luis Chavez. "It says in this report that this gun, the German Luger has also been implicated in the destruction of headstones at the Fairhaven cemetery in July, 1967, is that correct?"

"Yes, Your Honor."

"And," the Judge continued, "Do you know who is responsible for the shooting of the headstones?

"No Your Honor."

"Well then, it would seem that if you can find who shot up the headstones, you could possibly find who killed Ronald Pettiford, or vice versa. Do you agree?"

"Yes, Your Honor. I agree."

Judge Murphy took off her glasses and rubbed her nose. "Ms. Johnson, does the defense have anything else to add?"

"Yes Your Honor, we would like to call a number of witnesses that will show these young men were not the only ones who were lured up to the Pettiford mansion on the pretext of a good time."

Nine men, all about Hank's age or a little older testified to being enticed into going up to Pettiford's for a promise of a good time, only to find Pettiford had much different plans for them.

Ms. Johnson walked back to the table, looked at the other lawyers, one by one, and received a nod of approval from all of them. To the judge, "The defense rests."

"Then," Judge Murphy said. "Would you do a summation?"

THE LAST DEER HUNT

Pat Johnson walked around to the front of the defendant's table. "We," she motioned to include all the defendants and their lawyers, "firmly believe the prosecution has not established probable guilt of murder. What they have presented is a case based primarily on circumstantial evidence gathered by law enforcement individuals who overstepped their authority in the questioning of the defendants and from sloppy work by the police ballistics test lab. They failed to establish that the defendants fired the shot that killed Mr. Pettiford, they have failed to prove that my client buried the rifle; they have failed to prove that the defendants stole any property from the victim's home. In summation, they have failed to prove there is any probable cause that the defendant's are guilty of any crime. And, they have repeatedly failed to follow up on other suspects, Mr. Vic Pollo in particular, in their rush to judgment."

Ms. Johnson leaned back against the table and looked directly at Frank Powers and Harold Smith. "I believe that we should now address the issue to suppress the statements of the defendants during their questioning and the issue of the defendants being denied the right to counsel, and they were not read their Miranda rights prior to questioning.

Judge Murphy rubbed the back of her neck, turning her head to relieve the tension. "Would the lawyers for the defense and the prosecution please join me in my chambers."

When the lawyers for both sides returned to the courtroom, Luis Chavez did not look happy. Judge Murphy called a twenty-minute recess during which the courtroom became oppressive as seconds dragged into minutes as the large clock on the wall moved ever slower with each tick.

Apprehension and pent up emotions flooded the spectators as Judge Murphy returned to the bench.

The judge leaned forward, her two hands together in front of her, peering down her nose through her glasses. "We have an incident that happened eighteen years ago, by boys who were thirteen or fourteen at the time. Personally, this case should have been held in the juvenile courts and is a waste of this courts time and my time. I find that the prosecution has not established probable cause and I do not find sufficient evidence against the defendants to proceed to trial. From what I have seen, this case was bungled from the beginning with sloppy investigating, questionable interrogation techniques, a breach of the Miranda act and slipshod laboratory procedures. This case does not warrant a charge of murder. At best, it should have been a charge of conspiracy to commit murder. But that has a ten-year statute of limitations. I therefore dismiss the charges in this case. I must caution the defendants however, that double jeopardy does not apply in a probable cause hearing and that if a grand jury so finds, this case could be re-opened at a later date."

At first, a collective sigh of relief moved through the courthouse, and then the galley broke into loud applause. Tom, Eddie, Bob, Ollie, and Gino grasped each other. Hank stood, reached over and grasped Ms. Johnson's hand.

Forty-Two

Hank, Tom, Gino, Bob, Eddie, and Ollie sat in the middle booth at Frenchy's Diner as the cacophony of diner life swirled around them. Conversation, loud comments, laughter, and congratulations mixed with the noise of Lucy delivering dishes full of food and picking up empty plates. Lucy had been good enough to get back from L'anse early enough to open the diner for the people returning from the hearing.

"TA DA!" Lucy called out loudly as she turned on the brand new television set in the corner of the diner and every head turned to watch.

"Good evening ladies and gentlemen; this is December 7th and this is Karen Casey, Channel Four reporting to you live from outside the county courthouse where a preliminary hearing was completed today into the death of Mr. Ronald Pettiford who was killed some eighteen years ago...."

"Hey look you guys," Kurt Hurla was in front of the television pointing at the images on the screen, "you're on television again. You sure are popular."

Cries of 'Shhhhhh' and 'Hold it down' and 'Sit down Hurla,' rose throughout the diner.

An image of Karen Casey filled the screen as she interviewed various people until; finally, Hank's face appeared.

"So, Mr. Duval," Karen Casey stood with microphone in hand, "Are you happy with the outcome of the trial? It seems like you and your friends have won."

"I'm sorry, but no one has won anything. All we know is that we did not kill that man. Right now, all we want is to put that part of our lives behind us."

"Way to go Hank!" Kurt Hurla yelled.

"Kurt, for the last time, shut up, we're trying to hear this." Homer Perrin put a large hand on Kurt's shoulder and pulled him back down into the booth.

The television camera moved on past a number of other interviews. Harold Smith, wearing a very tight smile across his face for the television camera said, "No Comment."

Mr. Chavez responded to Ms. Casey's question with a curt, "No, this isn't the end of this case. We plan to take this case back to a grand jury. We believe we have enough new evidence to..."

The camera moved over to a close up of Pat Johnson, her eyes hidden behind very large sunglasses. She slowly removed the glasses revealing her large dark eyes and giving Mr. Chavez a wry grin, spoke. "We believe the outcome of the hearing speaks for itself and I am sure if Mr. Chavez had any new evidence, he would have brought it up at the hearing. I think I can safely say we have heard the last of this case." The large dark glasses went back on her face leaving only a smile.

The television camera panned slowly around the courthouse and the diminishing crowds. Ms. Casey's sparkling smile filled the television screen. It appears this preliminary hearing ended with the judge ruling there was not sufficient evidence to hold this case over to trial. It does not say the case is closed, nor does it mean that we are any closer to finding out just what happened to Ronald Pettiford that night. It just says that there was not enough evidence to hold this case over for trial. We have also learned that one of the weapons involved in the killing of Mr. Pettiford has been linked to the destruction of gravestones in the Fairhaven cemetery in the summer of 1967 by a person or persons unknown. And so, ladies and gentlemen, that concludes our broadcast from outside the Baraga County Courthouse in L'anse." The television set faded to a commercial.

Lucy turned the sound off and the diner went back into one large noisy conversation.

"May I interrupt you men?" Pat Johnson was standing at the side of the booth, a large briefcase in hand. "I have some news."

The six men, crowded in the booth all tried to stand at one time and ended up in a half crouch, barely able to wave.

Ms. Johnson motioned for them to sit back down. Sitting, they watched the lawyer closely, not sure if they should smile or frown.

As she spoke, her face broke into a wide smile "It turns out that Vic's Uncle Pasquale never was in the army. All of the souvenirs that Vic said he got from this uncle were really stolen from Pettiford's residence. They were never reported stolen because Mr. Pettiford never registered the guns. I would guess that he didn't want people to know he had the weapons since they was brought into the country illegally."

Eddie spoke first. "So Vic must have used the Luger to kill Pettiford."

"Yes, It's just like we said," Ollie mused. "Vic was at Pettiford's house that night. When Pettiford surprised him robbing the house, he shot Pettiford with the Luger and then took it with him."

Ms. Johnson nodded in agreement. "Looks like that's what happened."

"So what does this mean for us?" Tom asked, looking at Pat Johnson.

"Well, I think this is good news for you men. This information muddies the waters still more and it looks less likely that the state will pursue this case any further. Because the preliminary hearing found for the defendants and the state chose not to pursue the case at this time, it doesn't mean that the state could not bring it back up at a future date, but that doesn't look likely. And with that," Pat Johnson said, waving to each of the men, "I must say goodbye. I have to leave to catch the four-thirty plane out of Houghton. If you men ever need anymore help with this case, please call me, or you can call the other lawyers."

The men were up, and each shook hands with Pat Johnson, followed with a hug of thanks. After a short round of good-byes, she turned and left Frenchy's Diner.

"So," Hank sat with his head resting on his hands, propped up on his elbows. "I'm still confused. Back at camp, you guys told me that Vic shot Pettiford with the rifle."

More silence. Finally Gino, speaking quietly said. "Yeah, well that's what Vic told us."

"Why would Vic have said that? It doesn't make any sense, since he couldn't have shot Pettiford with the rifle."

"Well, maybe we just misunderstood him." Tom said, looking down at the floor."

Ollie pushed forward, "Yeah, it was really chaotic that night, we probably misunderstood Vic."

Hank felt a shadow of doubt start to build. "You know, I'm not sure you guys have been honest with me."

"Yeah well, you didn't tell us that Gus had the luger." Gino said. "We all thought Vic had thrown it into the swamp." The other men nodded agreement.

Hank shook his head. "And you, Ollie and Bob, you didn't say anything about the jewelry you were handing out to the girls."

"We didn't think you needed to know about that." Ollie reached over and put a hand on Hank's shoulder. "The less you knew the less trouble you could get into."

Gino twisted around to face Hank. "And what was that about Eddie and the rifle?"

Hank looked at Eddie and waited. Eddie shrugged okay. Hank talked quickly and quietly. "Eddie was the one that

THE LAST DEER HUNT

moved the rifle and put it by the river bank. He thought it would be safer if it was somewhere that was not connected to us."

"Yeah, that's right Hank," Eddie said, "Like you said, I was looking out for all of us. You know we got to stick together on this, just like the old times, right?"

"Whatsamatta," Gino laughed, squeezing close to Hank, "How come you didn't tell us? Don't you trust us?"

"Give me one good reason why I should?"

"Hank, trust us." Tom said, putting his hands on the table, palms together, "You've always been like a little brother to us and we always tried to protect you. You know that."

"Yeah, that's right," Ollie chimed in, "You were like our little brother."

"We would have never done anything to get you into trouble." Bob joined the others around Hank. "We were only looking out for your best interests."

"And the destruction of the headstones," Hank glanced at the men surrounding him, "did you guys know about that?"

"No, no." Ollie said quickly. "I didn't know anything until we just heard about it. God's truth."

"Me neither," Bob asserted, "I would have said something if I knew."

"Yeah, Vic was a vicious bastard." Eddie said, "Especially when he damaged all those Italian gravestones with pictures on them."

"Wow, what's all the arguing going on here?" Frenchy interrupted, "Aren't you guys supposed to be one for all and all for one? How about some more coffee? Maybe some left-over doughnuts or muffins?"

From the negative looks in the booth, Frenchy decided to take the silence as a 'No' answer and he moved on to another booth.

Tom moved forward. "Look guys, it's over. It's behind us. For whatever reasons, it all worked out for the best. Let's stop the bickering. At last we can get back to our lives."

Ollie gave the others thumbs up. "You're right Tom, Pettiford was a pedophile, and the world's better off without him"

"Yeah," Gino laughed, "Just think of how many boys were saved because Pettiford ended up under the floor of the maintenance shop."

"Yeah," Bob forced a smile. "This couldn't have worked out better if we tried."

The men looked at each other, nodded agreement, and then looked to Hank.

Hank shrugged. "Yeah, I guess so." *The unanswered questions were probably better off unanswered,* "Looks like Vic did everyone a big favor."

The men threw Hank thumbs up and wide grins of agreement, then headed for the door to go back to the motel for the evening.

Forty-Three

It was close to noon by the time Hank picked up the men and brought them back to Fairhaven in Frenchy's van.

Lucy was standing in the middle of the diner. "Just to let you all know; starting next spring, Frenchy's Diner will be serving a full line of vegetarian dishes along with our regular menu."

"Oh Geez, what you going to change next about this diner?" Waino Matson's voice carried across the room. "Probably going to start serving that God awful expensive gourmet coffee from Seattle?"

"Yeah," Kurt Hurla broke in, "that Grande' latte, cappuccino stuff that only comes in giant and super giant sizes."

"What about pasties?" Pete Peterson asked, "When you going to have pasties?"

"No way," Lucy stood with her hands on her hips, looking defiant. "Everybody in town already sells pasties."

"Hey Lucy, how about cinnamon buns?" Someone yelled from the back of the diner.

"We already have cinnamon buns."

"No, you know, the great big ones; like them they sell over at the Hilltop Restaurant in L'anse."

"If you want giant cinnamon buns like they have over in L'anse, then go to L'anse. If you want Frenchy's small but incredibly good cinnamon buns, come to Frenchy's." Lucy whirled around and headed back behind the counter.

The diner buzzed with an animated exchange of views about gourmet coffee, cinnamon buns and new menu offerings. Homer Perrin stood and motioned for silence. "We all agree Lucy; we don't want you to change anything else."

Lucy, hands on hips, swung a towel over her shoulder. "Okay you guys, if that's what you want, I'll keep serving the same lousy coffee that Frenchy's been giving you all these years. Heck, all I need to do is leave it cooking in the pot overnight."

Another round of laughter and discussion from the diner until Kurt Hurla yelled out, "Oh hell, if that's how you feel about it, get the stuff from Seattle!"

"Yeah, but don't change anything else." Waino Matson replied to no one in particular.

Sarah and Patti came bursting through the door, Sarah waving a paper, "Did you hear the news? We got the state funding for the mill renovation."

"Yes indeed," Patti squealed, "Now we can really get going on the restoration. Sarah's face reflected her enthusiasm. "And Ben Epstein has agreed to come up here and work with us. Isn't this so exciting?"

"Stay tuned folks," Patti's face was flushed with excitement. "We have so much to do."

Sarah waved her paper, drawing the attention of the diner once again, "We'll be looking at putting people to work very quickly."

At the talk of jobs, everything in the diner had stopped. As the message sank in, people turned to people, mumbles became words, then words became conversations that reflected the excitement and enthusiasm swirling around the two women.

"I've got to run." Patti blew kisses around the diner as

THE LAST DEER HUNT

she headed for the door.

Questions and comments swirled around Sarah as she melted into the back of the diner and the conversations spoke of opportunities and optimism.

Hank let his mind wander around the diner trying to imagine it without Frenchy. The old Bosch Beer clock had been replaced with a new one advertising a microbrewery not available around Fairhaven. Shelves and other surfaces around the diner had started to collect old artifacts from the old wood product mills and sawmills that had existed throughout the area. The walls, which still showed the outlines of where beer cans were lined up, now had signs announcing companies that had been out of business since before Hank was born. The only vestige of Frenchy's artifacts in the diner was John Deer, who smiled on the patrons of the diner as he observed them from where he hung on the wall, looking each in the eye, following them around the diner.

Tom's voice cut through Hanks thoughts, bringing him back to the booth and his friends. "I've decided to move back to Fairhaven." Tom's face was a mask of total resolve. "And don't try to talk me out of it."

"You're what?" Five men said in unison.

"You're crazy, you know that?" Gino scratched his head, looking at Tom.

"Christ, what's someone like you going to do in this little town?" Eddie pulled at his hat, making sure it covered his half-ear.

"My plan is to move into Mom's old house on Main Street, fix it up, and with Tobias, open a bookstore there."

"So, you're gonna bring your boyfriend, huh?" Eddie smirked, poking Tom in the arm.

Tom started to continue his story, but stopped, thought, and looked at Eddie. "Tobias is my cat."

Bob cleared his throat. "Hannah called today and left a message. Seems like our boy Zeke took a turn for the worst and the fever is over 103°. I'm not sure what to do. Hannah kinda believes that if we pray enough, Jesus will answer our prayers. But, I'm kinda thinking we should get him to a doctor. But if I do that, I would be rejecting my faith."

Ollie was the first to speak. "Bob, you gotta do what you gotta do, but maybe it wouldn't hurt just to get a doctors opinion. After that, then you might have enough information to make a better decision."

Hank was trying to think of what he could add, but could come up with nothing, and that was okay too. Somebody else could have the answers. He nodded his agreement with Ollie.

"Yeah Bob," Ollie continued, "I think you need to do that, because if you don't and something happens you would never be able to forgive yourself...you need to put your faith in Jesus, pray to him and if you take Zeke to the doctors, then that must be what Jesus wants."

Gino shifted his weight in the small booth and stretched, trying to act casual. "For me, I'm gonna have to find something else to do when I get back home, I sure as hell won't have a job with all the downsizing going on and the stunt I pulled."

Hank held his coffee cup up for Frenchy. "What about you Ollie? What are you going to do now that all this is over with?"

"You know, I've been so busy working as a counselor with kids and families over there in Duluth, I haven't had time to think about it."

"Just a suggestion Ollie," Tom said. "You know you're pushing thirty-three and time is going by. Maybe when you get back home, it might be good to cut back on work. Could be you're working all these hours because it doesn't give you any time to think about life, or anything else for that matter."

"Yeah," Gino nodded, "Sometimes, you gotta just stop and smell the roses."

The other men in the booth nodded in agreement. Hank put his hand on Ollie's arm. "Just go where your

THE LAST DEER HUNT

heart leads you."

"Darn it, you guys are right. I just can't let Katie walk out of my life. I have to quit burying myself in my work. "

Eddie blurted out. "I never had that problem; I never buried myself in any work, just in a bottle! Ever since that night at Pettiford is...the nightmares don't go away, they just get worse. I can't hold a job, I can't keep a girlfriend, and I don't have any friends..."

Hank reached over and put his hand on Eddie's shoulder. "It's okay guy, it's going to get better. The nightmares will go away now. You'll see."

Ollie handed Eddie a napkin, "You're going to be okay, you've taken the first step. You are willing to acknowledge that you have a problem. You're one of us, remember, one for all, and all for one?"

Eddie wiped his nose with the napkin, "That's just really dumb kid stuff."

"No, it isn't Eddie," Tom said, giving Eddie a hug from the other side. "It's real, and don't worry, we won't forget you or ignore you anymore."

"Ooooh, I been hugged by a gay," Eddie's laugh broke through the tension and infected the other men and soon they were all doubled over, the laughter loud and spontaneous, each new laugh brought on more laughter and it rippled around the booth until at last it ended with the men exhausted.

"You guys going to be okay?" Frenchy was back at the booth with the coffeepot.

The men nodded. Now silence took hold of the men. Each one trying to find the right words to bring them back into conversation.

Finally, Tom took a deep breath and said, "So Hank, you've made up your mind yet?"

Hank looked at Tom, not understanding the question. The other men waited as Hank slowly grasped the meaning. "You mean stay here in Fairhaven? Heck, I haven't even thought about that."

"Come on Hank," Gino said, "being accepted by that prestigious art school in California? Don't tell me you haven't thought about it."

Hank was uncomfortable. "I could go to an art school around here."

"Yeah, but Hank," Eddie gestured with his hands, "Maggie will be in California."

"But I've really just started to feel comfortable here in Fairhaven."

"What was that advice you gave me?" Ollie asked. "Sometimes Hank, you got to go where the heart is."

The booth grew quiet, the men lost in their own thoughts. Gino put both his hands on the table, "I'm gonna really miss you guys."

"Yeah, me too." Ollie put his hands on Eddie's.

"And it goes double for me," Tom said, adding his hands to the others.

Eddie put his hands on top of Tom's. "Yeah, just like it used to be."

Hank felt the others looking at him and he looked back at them, one by one, not sure what he was looking for, and put his hands on top of theirs, conscious of a flow of energy between them.

Sarah stuck her head over the top of the booth. "Now, don't tell me this is male bonding for new age sensitive guys?"

Maggie stood beside Sara, trying to suppress a smile. "Whatever happened to all the chest beating, butt grabbing, and primordial screaming?"

Diane joined Sarah and Maggie. "My, my, what do have here, the last of the great white hunters?"

Maggie started to laugh. Why are they looking so sad?"

Sarah's laugh grew louder. "Gee, do you they feel bad about Bambi?"

Diane started to double up with laughter and grabbed Maggie's arm to keep from falling. "Heck, with these guys hunting, Bambi doesn't have to worry."

Gino managed a furtive glance at the three women. "Okay ladies, cut it out, enough is enough already."

"Yeah," Eddie's face a sheepish grin, "Come on, we've had a really tough week."

"Oooh, poor babies." Sarah said, pointing at the men, causing them to sink lower in their seats. The three women were now contorted with laughter, tears running down their cheeks.

Frenchy was standing next to the booth. "Looks like these ladies are giving you a pretty tough time?" His face broke into a wide smile, "You big strong virile hunters need some help?"

Tom tried to stand in the crowded booth, but fell back into a heap with Eddie and Bob, bringing another round of laughter from the three women.

"Come on Frenchy, don't encourage them." Ollie managed a smile and poked Hank with his elbow, causing a small grin on Hank's face. The grin widened into a contagious smile, which spread to the other men. Once the tension was released, the smiles continued to expand, first into small giggles, then louder, until it grew into strident laughter that doubled the men over and brought tears to their eyes.

Life in the diner was suspended as every person watched as the six men, their eyes bleary from crying with laughter, crawled and helped each other out of the booth.

The men, still full of laughter, headed back to the motel, Frenchy locked up the diner after everyone left, and Hank and Maggie walked slowly down Main Street towards his house. The snow was falling gently in giant flakes as Hank stopped under a streetlight and held Maggie close to him. He wondered how much she had heard him say about not going to California, but decided not to ask, not wanting to break the magic of this moment.

Hank stood back and looked at Maggie. Large flakes of snow caught in the curls of her long hair and on the collar of her coat and she smiled at him, a smile that made Hank feel like he was an adolescent again who was in love for the first time. If Maggie asked him right here, right now what his decision would be, he would race home to pack for California.

Forty-Four

"Thanks Hank, for everything." Diane took the last dishes out of the dishwasher and put them in the cupboards. "This trip has been good for me. I'm so glad I had this chance to spend time with you and to get to know you again."

"Same here Sis. It was good that you could be here while all this stuff was going on. It was a big help, believe me." Hank picked up the dishes and cups from the kitchen table and put them in the dishwasher. "Wasn't that something about Ma? I would never have believed it if I didn't see it myself."

"Yes," Diane said wistfully. "But it helps me. It was important for me to know that she was more than the one-dimensional woman I remembered.

"All these years, all I could think of was this woman who always had supper on the table for Dad, always made sure his clothes were washed and his house was clean...and to take his abuse and keep it inside like she did. I don't know how she did it; God knows I could never do that."

"Yeah, I remember the time you stood up to him when he was coming after me with his belt for some dumb thing I did." Hank shook his head and shivered as the memory that he had buried so long ago came creeping back into his brain.

"Isn't that amazing, I had forgotten all about that. But then, there are probably a lot of times I don't remember. Like I don't remember any of our Christmases. Believe me, as much as I've tried, I cannot remember any. And I've gone through all the boxes of pictures that Ma and Pa had, and I cannot find one about Christmas."

Diane looked sad, "Our father could be a very unpleasant person when he was drinking."

"Yeah, it's taken me a long time, but you know, I believe that I finally have been able to come to terms with Pa. If I had left Fairhaven, I never would have been able to come to terms with whom Pa was. I think it helped me to be able to be here and go back to the places where I spent time with him in the woods hunting and along the rivers fishing. I'm not sure I'll ever understand why he did some of the things he did, or even if I will ever be able to accept them, but it helps me to understand that there was more to Pa than just an angry man who drank too much."

"I think it's a wonderful thing you're doing, making that inlayed plaque honoring him for what he did. It is absolutely beautiful."

"Sis, I think I'm doing that more for me than for him."

Diane stood and looked at her watch. With a touch of sadness in her voice, she said softly, "I think it's about time for me to hit the road."

Without speaking, Hank and Diane moved her luggage from the house and once it was in the rental car, Diane turned to Hank, "Maggie is a wonderful woman. I hope you know that. And I hope everything works out between you."

"I know she is Sis."

"Do you think you will come out to California?"

"I don't know, there's so much to do here now that the mill project will take off."

"Are you sure that you're not just finding reasons to keep from going out there? You have to ask yourself why you do

THE LAST DEER HUNT

not want to go. What are you afraid of?"

"If I wanted to go, I would. What the heck would I be afraid of?"

"That my dear brother, you would have to ask yourself, or the ugly old John Deer."

Hank took Diane's hands in his and they stood looking deeply into each other's eyes, sharing the closeness that had once been their childhood and family, good times and bad.

Hank gave his sister a hug and they stood looking at each other one more time. "You stay in touch now."

"And you promise me that you will come out to California and visit. I know you would just love Susan, she's such a beautiful person." Diane dug through her wallet, brought out a small picture, and handed it to Hank. "What do you think?"

Hank looked at the picture of a young woman, pixie haircut, freckles, and a large mouth smiling from a very expressive face. He nodded, "Beautiful. She's a very beautiful woman." A smile spread across his face as he passed the picture back to Diane. "Yeah, for sure. She would be worth going to California for."

"Hank, she's taken, besides, I don't think she's your type." Diane smiled back and was in the car. Starting it, she threw Hank a kiss and moved away slowly down the snow-covered streets of Fairhaven.

Fortified with a last cup of coffee, Hank walked down the street to Matson's car repair shop. "Yeah sure. It's time I do this."

Hank stared at the little red truck. "Ford Ranger?"

"Yep, it's a 1980. A very reliable truck: and it's four-wheel drive. You got yourself a great deal young Hank." Waino took the check from Hank and put it in a cigar box on the top of the desk. "You remember now, you have any problems, you call me right away." He handed Hank a set of keys and an envelope.

"Thanks Waino. I'm going to miss my old truck. Pa took

good care of it and it took good care of me, at least until this winter."

Hank sat in the driver's seat of the Ranger looking at all the gauges. It started on the first try.

Hank shifted the truck into 'drive' and turned onto Upper Skanee Road, headed towards L'anse and the Northwood's Motel.

Tom was waiting for him when he pulled up. "Morning Hank, nice looking truck."

"Yeah, just picked it up. Where are the guys?"

"They went over to Houghton. I think they wanted to take in a movie this afternoon. Thanks for asking me to go out to the camp with you."

"No problem, Tom. Glad you could come."

"Heat!" Hank played with the various controls on the dash as the truck moved past downtown Fairhaven and headed up River Road towards the hunting camp. Suddenly the radio came on as Hank pushed buttons and twisted knobs until the radio stopped on a station playing an old Hank William's tune. Hank went to push the button to find another station, but Tom gestured to let it stay. "It's been a long time since I heard country music."

"You move back here, you'll have to get used to all this snow and cold again." Hank moved the truck back and forth across the empty road. "Love this four wheel drive."

"What's up with Maggie?" Tom asked.

"You mean California?" Hank moved the windshield wiper controls through different speeds. "I put together some more and will send them to the Art Institute. I'm almost hoping they will reject them. It would make my decision easier."

"No, I meant Maggie. What's happening with her...and you?"

"We're doing a lot of talking. Things are complicated, she has her career, and I have so many things going here. Maybe next spring we'll be able to figure it out."

The truck pulled up to the road leading into the camp.

THE LAST DEER HUNT

There were no signs that anyone had used the entrance road since they last used it and it lay nearly indistinguishable in the large unbroken field of snow.

It took a few minutes to strap on snowshoes and the two men were moved through the snowfield towards the camp carrying shovels and pulling a small sled.

The camp lay buried under three feet of new snow and it took twenty minutes for Hank and Tom to dig down enough to try the door.

"No luck." Hank said. "Looks like under the weight of the snow, the camp started to cave and the door frame is bent." Hank thought a minute. "Oh the hell with it."

Three hits with the shovel and the door broke open. Inside, the roof had buckled down a foot and the men had to hunch over to fit. The stovepipe had bent and had come apart in the middle. "Good grief, this thing may collapse at any second!" Tom was busy picking up the rifles, ammunition, and a number of personal effects.

The camp groaned and settled another inch. "Oh, oh. We better hurry." Hank had to kneel to get out of the small opening in the door. He put the armful of guns in the sled and as he turned to go back in the camp, the air was rented by a sharp CRACK followed by "Christ!" Coming from inside the camp.

"You okay?" Hank yelled through the door.

"Yeah, that was a window that cracked when the frame bent."

The camp groaned and settled again. Hank yelled, "Get the hell out of there!" And Tom pushed his way out through the door just as the camp gave off a sorrowful cry of anguish and the roof collapsed in a cloud of snow.

They both looked at the camp, shaking their heads. "That was too close." Tom said, shaking off the snow.

Hank managed a weak laugh. "Yeah, even the camp figured this was the last deer hunt. I guess we got most of the stuff out." A quick inventory of the gear lying on the ground, "Oh hell, Gino's gun is still inside the camp!"

Hank let Tom off and headed home where he called Maggie. "How about dinner tonight? Your place or mine?'

"My place, 7:30."

Carrying a large package, Hank walked slowly to Maggie's apartment, enjoying the cold night air. Wreaths and Christmas lights hung from every light post in an attempt to give the downtown a holiday flair, but the street was mostly empty. In the last five years, there hasn't been much reason for people to come to town. Most stores were closed and folks headed out to malls to do their Christmas shopping.

Outside of Maggie's apartment, Hank could hear Orphan barking before he knocked on the door.

"Come in." Maggie's voice could be heard over the barking.

Orphan went through his welcome dance, jumping, running, and leaping over furniture. Hemingway stood up and yawned.

"Be right out Hank." Maggie called from the bathroom.

His coat off, Hank no sooner sat down than Hemingway leapt on his lap looking up at him. Hank quickly moved his hands away, expecting the usual whack. Instead, the big cat nuzzled down on Hank's lap purring and licking his hand with its tongue.

"Looks like you have a friend." Maggie called from the doorway. "It's very special when a cat picks you as a friend."

"Yeah, friends at last." Hank slowly stroked Hemingway and the purring grew louder.

Maggie came into the room. No, Hank thought, she didn't just come into the room, she made an entrance. She was captivating. There was something sensuous in the way she moved. Dressed in jeans and a T-shirt, her long red curls streamed down. Outlined against the lamp behind her head, there was something special in the way she looked tonight.

"I brought some of the sketches of wolves I did for the article. I hope they're okay. I used photographs at the library." Hank moved Hemingway from his lap, picked up the large package and juggled it three times before it fell, scattering sketches all over the floor. "OOPS, all thumbs tonight."

Maggie was close to him, he could smell her body mixed with the scent of lavender. "It's okay Hank, I love to see your etchings." Now Hank could feel her, standing right next to him. Orphan watched them from his bed in the corner and Hemingway sat on the window watching them through half-closed eyes, paws hanging over the sill.

"We have a real problem tonight Hank." Maggie's voice was husky. Her breath was warm on the side of his face.

What now? What problem? What's she talking about?"

He felt her lips on the side of his face. She spoke softly and slowly, reached up, took his hand and moved towards the bedroom. "I didn't cook any dinner tonight."

The morning light filtered through the big bay window. Hank blinked his eyes open, and was greeted by the large yellow eyes of Hemingway lying on his stomach. Cautiously, he stroked the large cat, and was rewarded by a loud purr.

Hunger pulled at his stomach and slowly last night came back to him. The memories of last night filtered back into his mind and warmed him.

"Good morning Mr. Duval." Maggie said, leaning against the frame of the kitchen door dressed only in an extra large man's shirt. "I trust you slept well last night."

"Yes, I did. I slept very well." He sat up, rubbing the last bit of sleep from his eyes and attempted to sit up. "Excuse me Hemingway."

Maggie disappeared back into the kitchen. "Great. Breakfast will be ready in about fifteen minutes. Hope you're hungry."

"Starved!" Hemingway jumped off as Hank stood and headed for the kitchen.

"Here Sweetie." Maggie said, handing Hank a cup of coffee.

"Maggie, is Los Angeles as crazy as everyone says it is?"

"Some of it is but a lot of it is really very beautiful and the weather is always really great."

"What about all the twelve lane freeways and a bazillion cars and all the smog?" Hank walked over and patted Orphan. "And what about all the crime?"

"Hank, you've been watching too much television. Why don't you set the table while you're waiting? Where I lived, it was beautiful. Hills, winding roads. We had a little town center with a bakery, coffee shop, grocery store and just about everything else you would need within walking or biking distance."

"Is it true that where you lived in California, you could see the Pacific Ocean?"

"Yes, I was about six blocks from Huntington Beach State Park. You could see the most gorgeous sunsets from the apartment and I just loved walking down the beach as the sun was setting and seeing all the people and enjoying the warm breeze coming off the ocean. When I woke up in the morning, I could smell the hundred different kinds of flowers and lush plants right outside my door."

Hank sat on the floor petting Orphan. "Oh Maggie, I don't know if..."

"We'll take Orphan for long walks on the beach and go camping on the Baja and just sit and watch the sun set. We'll go to some of the best art museums in the country and there are always plays and music and you'll be able to sit and paint and..."

"Hold on," Hank interrupted, laughing, "Enough already. You're beginning to sound like the L.A. Chamber of Commerce."

Maggie came out of the kitchen carrying two bowls of oatmeal and put them on the table. "So what do you think?" Maggie went back into the kitchen. "Of California that is."

Hank stood looking out the window at the snow. "It does sound really nice."

The telephone ring startled them and Maggie went to

answer it. "Hank, it's Frenchy, for you."

Hank held the phone, listened, and turned to M_ gotta go, it's Uncle Andre, he just had a stroke and t taken him to the Baraga County Memorial Hospital." put the phone back on the wall. "They don't know how _e-rious it is yet."

Forty-Five

Hank fought off the sleepiness with his third cup of coffee. It was time to go and see the men off to the county airport.

He had been at the hospital with Uncle Andre until three-thirty in the morning, not wanting to leave until he knew for sure that Andre was going to pull through. The stroke had been bad enough, but not paralyzing. Sight and speech did not seem to be too badly damaged, but the affects on his cognitive functions were unknown. Hank sat by the bed for almost three hours watching the monitors and listening to the steady drip of the IV bag. Uncle Andre lay surrounded by tubes and wires with only an occasional moan indicating any sign of life.

Tom, Gino, Eddie, Ollie, and Hank stood in Frenchy's Diner waiting for Waino, who had volunteered to drive the men to the county airport. "Well guys, I guess this is it. Time to go home." Ollie said, looking down at his feet.

All the men nodded, Bob came into the lobby and dropped his suitcase down with the others, then seeing Hank, said, "This has been one hell of a hunt hasn't it? I'm glad it turned out the way it did. You don't think we'll hear from the district attorney's office anymore, do you?"

"Pat Johnson doesn't think so." Hank sipped on a cup of coffee. "By the way Eddie, what ever happened to that doe you shot?"

Eddie had replaced the large bandage on his ear with a small piece of gauze. "Well, you know, I was standing over that deer with my knife when this guy comes along. I thought, oh shit, I'm caught killing this doe without a permit. But this guy is not a DNR officer. He says his name is Joey Dolittle and if I didn't care, he would take the doe and get rid of her. Well, I'll tell you, it didn't take me long to figure he could have that doe."

"Way to go Eddie." Bob said, "You're the only one who got a deer this trip."

"So I get the two hundred fifty dollar prize for getting the first deer, right?

"Hell no," Gino snarled, "that doe don't count."

Ollie joined in. "Yeah, besides it was illegal, you didn't even have a doe permit."

"Wait a minute you guys," Tom help up his hand, "the rules did say the first deer killed, it didn't say it had to be a buck, or that it had to be legal. What do you think Hank?"

"Tom's right. I think we all throw fifty bucks into the pot and give Eddie his prize."

The money was counted out and given to Eddie, who laughed. "Yeah, I got the first deer from our camp...and the last."

"Yeah, I guess this is it." Bob said quietly, "I won't be coming back next year. I will miss you guys. Let's keep in touch okay?"

All the men nodded agreement and went outside to wait for their ride.

"Hey Gino, we're sorry about your rifle." Tom stood stamping his feet against the cold. "We managed to get some stuff out, but the darn camp collapsed before we had a chance to get your gun out. I'll be back here and next spring, Hank and I can go back out and get it."

"Hey, don't worry about the damn thing. I'm not going

to need it anymore. Donate it to charity or something."

Hank blew into his cupped hands, "I guess I'll have to get rid of the camp and the land. It's still in my Uncle's name." He looked at the other men. "Anybody interested in buying it?"

"What the heck for?" Ollie laughed. "Retirement?"

Hank joined the others in laughter, then paused, looked deeply at the other men, "I'm really going to miss everybody. You guys take good care of yourselves, okay?"

"Yeah sure."

"You bet, and you too."

Tom stepped forward, "I would like to say a special thanks to Hank here. I think he did a heck of a good job getting us through this."

A collective nod, then the men stood in shared silence reflecting on their own thoughts when the horn announced the arrival of Waino's station wagon. Hank, Ollie, Bob, Gino, Tom, and Eddie reached for each other's hands.

Lucy stepped outside and called out, what is it with you guys, you gay or something?"

"Yes, I am." Tom replied, holding up one thumb.

"Yeah, and we love him." The men spoke as one.

Hank motioned the men into the van. "Better get going guys or we might start that slobbery stuff all over again and you'll miss the plane."

Eddie was the last to get in the station wagon, stood for a moment, still clutching his two hundred fifty dollars, and called out, "One for all, and all for one."

The station wagon moved slowly down Main Street, over the bridge heading towards the county airport.

Frenchy's Diner was empty. Lucy was busy doing some last minute cleanup. "Can I get you anything else before I close up Hank?"

"No thanks, I think I had all I need for one day." A quick look around, his friends still fresh in his memory.

More snow fell on the following Tuesday. Hank sat in his cabinetmaker shop reading the blueprints for the mill. More blueprints and planning notes were scattered over worktables throughout the shop.

"Orphan, why don't you come over here and keep me company."

The dog walked slowly over to Hank and lay down near his feet.

"Hey dog, what am I going to do? Uncle Andre is doing better, but he'll never be able to live on his own again. I can't leave him at home without help, and we can't afford to have someone come in all the time to take care of him.

Orphan looked up at Hank, but had no suggestions. Reaching down, Hank stroked the dog's ears. "But, Orph, that means I stay here and California is out of the question. In fact, Andre might live for years. God, I hope I'm not sitting here wishing that old man would die." Orphan tilted his head, looking at Hank. "Dog, you've got no answers, you're no better than John Deer."

A cold draft woke Hank from his thoughts. Somebody had opened the door. "Okay, close the door, you born in a barn? You're letting all the heat out." The draft stopped.

"Sorry Hank," Patti Culpepper was dragging a large box of papers towards his desk. "I've got great news! It turns out that Cora Anderson had her office in Fairhaven and we got approval to put the mill and the town on the National Historic Register and got additional funding for restoration from the Michigan Legislature."

"Who the heck is Cora Anderson? I've never heard of her."

"She was the first woman in the Michigan Legislature. That was in 1925. Can you believe that? Not only that, but she was an Ojibwa Indian, so that makes her the first Native American in the Legislature and I would think the first minority. How'd you like them apples?"

"That's something all right; I've lived here all my life and never heard of her."

"You and a lot of other people, but we're going to change all that. Patti Handed Hank a large packet of papers, "These are some more plans and proposals for the restoration. We're gonna restore the mill and this little town back to where it was in its heyday."

"I'll look over this stuff you brought as soon as I get a chance, and then I'll get together with Charlie LeBlanc. He's been maintaining most of those buildings for many years."

"Thanks Hank, anything you could do would be a big help. Oh, by the way, how is Andre doing? He is such a sweet old man. I brought these old magazines from the library for him to look through, if he wishes."

"He's doing better Patti, thanks. And I'll read the magazines to him." Hank shuffled through the box of books and magazines, many of them showing what the downtown looked like when he was a young boy.

"Did you hear from that art school in California yet, Hank?"

"Nope, haven't even thought about it yet." Then to himself, *that's all I ever think about, that and Maggie.*

"Well, we would miss you around here, but I think it's a chance of a lifetime for you and Maggie." Patti looked at the distress on Hank's face, "It's your Uncle Andre isn't it? That's what's got you down. You don't know what to do about Andre, do you?"

"I haven't had a chance to think about it much. I'm not sure what I can do about it."

"Well, if you ask me," Patti was heading back towards the door, "Uncle Andre would want you to go to the art school in California." With an enthusiastic wave, she was gone.

"Hey dog," Hank reached over and rubbed Orphan's head. "You know Maggie's leaving and Frenchy's gonna be gone. Pretty soon the only people left in town will be you and me." His coat on, he shut off the light, waited for Orphan to go outside, and closed the door behind them. "Time to go and see Uncle Andre."

Uncle Andre was sitting up with his eyes closed listening

to the television, tuned to a daytime talk show.

"Hello Uncle Andre, how are you doing?"

"Hello?" The voice was frail and weak. A multitude of hoses and tubes ran from Uncle Andre's body to various bags and machines. The machines glowed as green lines squiggled across a small screen and beeped every time the green line peaked. The bags dripped fluid into a tube connected to the old man's arms.

"It's me, Hank, your nephew." It did not seem like a good idea to ask Andre how he was feeling.

"Oh Hank," the voice quivered, "You shouldn't have come all the way out here tonight, not with the terrible storm and everything."

What storm? It's clear as a bell outside. "It's okay Uncle Andre, I went over and checked your house tonight, and everything is okay."

"Who's taking me home tonight?"

Hank decided to let that pass. It would be a long time before Uncle Andre went home, and there is a good chance he would never go back to that house. "Everybody said to say 'Hi' to you and tell you that you are in their prayers."

"Where am I?" The voice was weaker.

"You're still in the hospital Uncle. We're not sure how long..."

"Is your father going to come and get me to take me home?"

He's really out of it tonight. Hank thought. "Uncle Andre, your brother Paul died many years ago." Hank watched the green line and spikes move across the screen beeping at regular intervals.

"Paul is dead? Nobody tells me anything around here. I want to go home. Who's going to take me home if Paul is dead?"

The regular beep from the monitor became erratic. Alarms and lights went off and three nurses rushed into the room, the male nurse turned to Hank, "Please sir, you're going to have to leave now."

Hank looked back at his uncle's hospital room now filled with activity as nurses ran in and out and were doing something to Uncle Andre.

Yeah, this is going to be a long, long winter. Hank moved into the hall and stood, leaning against a wall watching the activity swirl around him. It brought back memories of standing here in this same spot waiting to hear about Sandy. *Now, that seemed so long ago. There's been so much that's happened, Maggie, Frenchy...Oh God, I almost forgot about Frenchy! I'm supposed to be driving him to the airport in Houghton.*

The little Ranger pickup moved slowly through traffic but once outside L'anse, picked up speed over the snow-covered roads. Orphan was thoroughly enjoying the ride, his feet up on the dash, his head turning at everything that passed by outside and his tongue hanging from the corner of his mouth.

Finally, turning onto Main Street of Fairhaven in the early evening light, the lights were still on in the diner. "Sorry I'm late Frenchy."

Frenchy was sitting at the counter, cup of coffee in front of him. "Not to worry, we have plenty of time, you're actually early." Frenchy reached over and took the coffeepot off the heating plate. "Sit down; join me in a cup of coffee. Don't look so worried Duval, the plane's been delayed by half an hour. Damn thing never lands on time up here in the winter."

Hank declined the offer to sit, instead paced nervously behind the stools.

Frenchy poured the coffee. "Didn't you hear what I just said? The plane has been delayed. You don't need to worry. Okay?" He pushed the coffee in front of Hank. "Ah geeze, you're worried about your Uncle aren't you? How is he doing?"

Hank slid into the stool next to Frenchy. "Not too good right at the moment. He was having some sort of problem

THE LAST DEER HUNT

when I left." Hank shook his head. "I don't know Frenchy. I just don't know. I hate to say this, but there are times when I wished he would just quietly go, you know what I mean?"

"I think I do, but, I don't know what to tell you. Yeah, you're going to have to figure this one out all by yourself."

"How are you flying to Vietnam?"

"I go from here to Detroit, then to Tokyo, then to Hanoi. The leg between Detroit and Tokyo is twenty-three hours and a whole bunch of time changes. I think we land there the next day or something."

"I can't believe you are really leaving." The words came out slow and barely audible. Hank waited, but there was no reply. He slowly turned his head and looked at Frenchy.

Frenchy was looking down into his coffee. Feeling Hank's gaze, he slowly looked at his friend and their eyes met. "Christ Hank, I am really terrible at long good byes."

Hank could feel the sadness welling up and had to turn away, to break the tension, and found himself staring at the large deer head over the counter. "Frenchy, did you ask John Deer what you should do about going to Vietnam?"

Frenchy glanced at his friend, his face questioning. "Yeah, yeah I did, but I already knew the answer. Did you ask John about your dilemma?"

"Yes I did, but he doesn't know, as usual." Hank's face grew a smile from the silly idea that just came to him. "I think John Deer would be the next thing Lucy would get rid of. What do you think she'll do with it?" Hank asked.

"What do you care for? You don't want that ugly thing." A small laugh from Frenchy. "Do you?"

"Well, I got a hunch that I know that deer head. I think it's the deer my father shot. Remember I told you about the head I screwed up. I believe that is John Deer. I believe that Percy Twill stole that buck's head and had it mounted, but had the taxidermist change the face so we wouldn't recognize it."

"So the head comes home, so to speak. What are you going to do with it?"

"I don't know what, but – Hey, can you imagine that thing over my woodstove?"

The vision of the deer head over Hank's stove was enough to have both men start laughing.

"Can you imagine," Hank said between chuckles, "Maggie coming over and seeing John Deer staring at her?" More laughter, then Frenchy looked at his watch and Hank followed Frenchy's glance towards his duffle bag. They sat in silence and gazed slowly around the empty diner taking in the memories. There were the many cups of coffee the two men shared and the stories passed between them. Frenchy took in a lung full of air and expelled it forcefully, releasing his tension. "It's time to go."

"Yep."

Frenchy picked up his army duffle bag, followed Hank to the door, turned out the lights, and locked the door to Frenchy's Diner.

Forty-Six

It had been only four days since Frenchy left and Hank was walking to Maggie's He had promised to help her pack. The lights were on in Frenchy's Diner and he could see Lucy working inside. He decided to go in for the first time since Frenchy left. A tap on the window and Lucy unlocked the door.

Hank took off his coat, sat on a stool at the counter, looked around and for a moment listened to the echoes of times past. *Life seems to just go on after somebody leaves as if nothing changed, as if the person never existed.*

"Hey Hank, good to see you." Lucy was standing behind the counter wiping her hands. "Can I get you a cup of coffee?"

"Yeah, that sounds good."

"You hear from Frenchy yet?" Lucy said, handing Hank a cup ?"

"Nope." Hank took the coffee from Lucy. "He's probably really busy, getting started and all."

"Yeah, I guess." She stood quietly, somewhere in her own thoughts.

"You have been putting in a lot of work lately, what's up?"

"I'm getting ready to start serving dinner here." Lucy managed a smile. "I told Frenchy that serving dinner would work, but you know Frenchy, he wouldn't hear of it."

"Well, from what I see so far," Hank quickly surveyed the diner, "It's really coming along nicely." *Oh no. The deer head! John Deer...is missing! That moth eaten, smiling deer head isn't staring at me. Lucy must have thrown it out.* "What'd you do with John Deer?" Hank pointed up to where the deer head had been.

"That thing had to go." Lucy laughed, then seeing Hank's serious face, asked, "Why, did you want it?"

"Yeah, actually, if you don't want it, I would like to have it."

"You got it. It's out in the back room; I was just about to chuck it in the trash."

"I'll get it in the next few days. Thanks."

"By the way, how's your uncle?"

"About the same, but it doesn't look like he'll be able to go home again so I'm not sure what's going to happen."

"That is a bummer," Lucy said, walking towards the booths with a large bundle of place mats and containers of silverware. She was still wearing her Eiffel Tower apron, which covered black slacks and a black blouse. Her hair was now blond and was cut straight, bangs across her forehead.

"Yeah, I guess I'll have to figure out what to do with him. Hank waved goodbye, left a dollar on the counter, picked up his coat and walked out into street. He paused under a lamppost with a Christmas wreath and colored lights. *Two weeks to Christmas and I haven't even thought about buying presents.*

Hank stepped over the snow bank into the street towards Maggie's apartment. A small U-Haul trailer was parked just behind Maggie's old blue Volvo, the car loaded with boxes, lamps and other pieces of household furnishings. Hank walked past the Volvo and up the stairs. Orphan's bark announced him before he knocked.

THE LAST DEER HUNT

"Hi Maggie, how's it going?"

"Dandy, just dandy, Hank." Maggie, dressed in bib overalls and a T-shirt, was busy filling, sealing and marking boxes. Blowing curls out of her face, she put down her marking pen and sat in the large chair. Hemingway wended his way between boxes and jumped on her lap. Orphan danced, jumped, and ran around the boxes coming back to Hank carrying a leather bone.

Hank unconsciously threw the bone behind some boxes and the dog was gone, searching for it. "Looks like you'll have good weather for driving. You sure you are up to this? I mean LA is a long way away."

"I'm not looking forward to it, but I'm resigned to it."

"And I don't feel comfortable about your old car. You'll be lucky if it makes it."

"Well, I trust 'Old Blue.' Waino went completely through it, checked everything, and even changed the oil. Oh, by the way, I talked to a friend in California and I can stay at her place until I find one of my own."

Orphan put the bone at Hank's feet and lay down looking up at Hank and Maggie. Maggie put her head back and looked at the ceiling. Hank sat in silence, his hands folded in front of him.

"Why don't you take off your coat and stay awhile. I'd offer you coffee, but the pot is packed up." Maggie leaned forward and wiped her eyes. "Have you thought about it any more Hank? The art school, I mean?"

"I haven't heard from them."

"Well, you can always come to California and wait to hear out there."

Silence filled the room and became suffocating. "I don't think I can leave right now." Hank said quietly, hoping that Maggie would not hear.

"I didn't think so." Maggie whispered back. She took a deep breath; put her head back on the sofa and exhaled slowly. "Is it Uncle Andre?"

"Yeah, that's part of it." *I don't know what the rest of it is,*

God, I hope she doesn't ask.

"What's the rest of it Hank?" Maggie said, looking directly at him.

"Maggie, I'm not sure. Maybe it's just that I'm not ready for California." Hank paused, looking at her. "And before you ask, I don't know when or if I will ever be ready for California."

"Yeah, I guess I knew that." Maggie stood, stretched, and went into the kitchen.

With one leap, Hemingway was on Hank's lap. "Maggie..." Hank sat with the large cat on his lap, not knowing what to say. He could feel the vibrations of the cat as the purring grew louder. "Maybe you could wait until after Christmas to leave?"

Maggie came back into the room with a bottle of red wine and a wineglass. "I thought about that, but I would like to be out there and settled by the first of the year so I could have my next assignment lined up." She poured herself a glass of wine and sat on the couch. "You could come out to California for Christmas."

"Maggie, I will see what happens. I mean with Uncle Andre and all. Maybe later, sometime after Christmas, maybe we can work something out; or maybe later next spring."

"Maybe." Maggie started her second glass of wine. Wiping her eyes with the back of her hand, "Maybe when hell freezes over."

"Do you need any help moving any stuff?"

"No, no thanks. I just need to get these boxes in the trailer. Orphan's things are in the kitchen. Maybe you could take everything tonight so they won't be in the way."

"You're sure you want to leave Orphan with me? I mean, I will take good care of him, but he's been with you so long and all."

Maggie motioned Hank over to the couch next to her and said, "I know you will Hank, and besides, I don't have a place out there yet, and I don't know if I can find any place that takes dogs."

Hank moved on the couch next to Maggie carrying Hemingway. Orphan moved over with his head on Maggie's feet.

Slowly, Hank's hand found Maggie's and their heads rested on each other. Maggie's hand moved up and cradled Hank's head.

Hank woke up still sitting with Hemingway on his lap and Maggie by his side sleeping. A quick check of his watch showed midnight. Quietly, he stood, kissed her softly on the cheek, and whispered, "I'll see you in the morning before you leave and help you with the rest of these boxes."

He stood in the doorway watching Maggie. There was a great desire to go back in and spend the night. "Come Orph, let's go." Hank picked up the dog supplies and quietly slipped out the door with Orphan.

Forty-Seven

Hank was up early, checked the weather on television, and had his cup of coffee. "Let's go dog." Hank picked up Orphan to cross the street towards Maggie's apartment and looked up just as the old blue Volvo pulling the U-Haul trailer turned the corner and headed out to Upper Skanee Road towards L'anse, Route 41, and California.

Hank felt his heart break. It broke into a thousand shards of anger, pain, fear and sadness that tore at him. His vision blurred as his eyes filled with tears. As he stood in the middle of Main Street in Fairhaven, Michigan holding the little white dog, the anger and fear subsided leaving only pain, and sadness and he realized he was wrong. Life does not go on as usual when someone you love leaves, it changes forever.

Maggie's leaving was followed by what seemed to be day after day of endless low gray cumulus clouds, uninterrupted snow flurries and bitter cold temperatures. Hank spent his evenings in front of the fire with Orphan going over blueprints and specifications for the mill complex. During the day, he buried himself in physical work trying to fill the emptiness left by the departures of the most important people in his world.

THE LAST DEER HUNT

The drab and dreary winter days were made gloomier by the daily trips to the hospital to spend time with Uncle Andre. The ride to L'anse afforded time to dwell on time spent with his uncle and the sadness of seeing his uncle slowly deteriorating. Some days, Uncle Andre was lucid, alert, and sometimes angry. Other days, his mind was poor and any conversation was difficult.

The hospital will have to release Uncle Andre soon when the insurance stops. Where to put him? The two nursing homes in the area, The Golden Autumn and The Twilight Years, did not have good recommendations and would have to be checked out. Any others were just so far away.

God, what if this goes on for a long time? Andre will slowly wither away. He will never improve. How long before he dies? No, don't even wish that; don't even think that!

"O.K. Orphan, it's been five days and we haven't heard anything from Maggie. Let's see check the mail. Maybe we can find some intelligent life out there, Toto."

"Arf."

"No mail for us. Nobody loves us Orph. Maybe if we write first, somebody will answer."

Hank wrote:

December 15h, 1983

Dear Maggie,

I am not sure if you are still on the road or if you are already in L.A., but I hope everything is going okay. I worry about you driving across the mid-west this time of the year.

I am really sorry that I missed you before you drove away. I got to your apartment just in time to see your Volvo go out of sight over the bridge. I was tempted to run all the way to California after you to tell you how much I would miss you, but you were gone.

I miss you tonight. I did not think I could ever miss anybody this much again in my life. I think Orphan is depressed, hell, we both are. There is so much going on around here and I try to bury myself in everything at once, and I still can't get you out of my mind.

Uncle Andre is doing okay, some days his mind is as clear as a bell, and other days, he can't seem to remember anything. He needs help in doing just about everything.

You know, I keep thinking about this Pettiford thing. Somebody once said, 'It ain't over till it's over,' and there is something still nagging at me. I can't put a finger on it. I can't seem to come to closure on it.

Everybody here says to say Hi to you.

Please write or call soon. I really would like to hear from you.

Much love,
Hank. Orphan says Arf.

Hank found the address of Maggie's friend in Los Angeles, addressed the envelope and put the letter in the mailbox.

Sitting in front of the fire, the warm memories of Maggie merged with the realization that she was gone and his heart filled with loneliness. Orphan jumped up on his lap and nestled his head under Hank's arm and they watched the flames dance until they were asleep.

The next day the sun finally broke through and helped to brighten his soul as Hank headed towards Baraga Memorial Hospital.

"Hello Uncle Andre." Hank sat in the plastic chair and watched his uncle, not sure if Uncle Andre was inside the frail body that sat on the bed in front of him or if was Mr. Grumpy or Mr. Angry.

"Hello Hank." The words were distinct and spoken with clarity. Today Uncle Andre was here in the present. "How's the weather out there?"

THE LAST DEER HUNT

"Cold and a lot of snow." Hank opened the newspaper he had brought, expecting to spend the time reading.

"Yeah, well this is the Upper Peninsula and it is winter here." Uncle Andre slipped off the bed, standing wobbly. "Damn, it's hell getting old," he said. "Can't seem to do anything for myself anymore. How's the house? Is it ready for me when I go home?"

"Uncle Andre, there is...." *How the hell do I tell him he can't go home again?* "Nothing to worry about, I checked it this morning." *When do I tell him?*

"That's good. I can't wait to get out of this place. Full of old sick people. How's your girl friend, what's her name?"

"Her name is Maggie. She went to Los Angeles, left a week ago."

"Smart woman Hank. Warm out there in California. You should high-tail it out there to be with her. Don't think you need to hang around here because of me. As soon as I get home, I'll be all right."

"It's okay Uncle Andre. I can't leave Fairhaven now; there is so much to do at the mill. By the way, Patti Culpepper wants to come over and talk to you. She needs to talk to some of you old-timers who might remember details about some of the old mill."

"Yeah," Uncle Andre said, brightening up, "That would be good. I would like to do that. Send the young lady over." Uncle's face turned up in a mischievous grin.

"Hey Andre, you behave yourself around the women, okay?" Hank smiled at his Uncle.

Uncle Andre gave Hank a smile back, no teeth, but a happy smile, happy that he would be able to do something other than just lie helplessly in bed.

Hank made a mental note to bring some historical materials with him the next visit to go over with Uncle Andre. After a big hug and good-byes, Hank left with a promise to be back soon.

"Henry, now you make sure you bring my things when you come next time. I gotta get out of here."

Hank stopped at the post office and mailed Maggie's Christmas package then headed home, hoping to hear from Maggie. Nothing on his answering machine, Hank checked the mail. A letter from Maggie that he quickly tore open.

December 19th, 1983

Dear Hank.

 Yea, I made it! It was a long tiring trip, but I am finally here in Los Angeles and staying with my friend Chris.
 I just got your letter, thanks. I am really and truly sorry I drove away so early and missed you. It really was a dumb thing to do. I hate long goodbyes and I guess I was upset with you because there was no way I could convince you to come with me. Now I wish I had waited for you, there is so much that I left unsaid and I miss you so much already. I hope you forgive me.
 I think I found a nice condo in Santa Monica. It's about two blocks from the beach and I can bike to Topanga State Park. We will know by the end of this week if we get it. I know Hemingway will be happy to settle down. He really does not like traveling.
 Hank, I have been thinking about Fairhaven and us. You know, I was only going to stay there for about a month to do that article and as soon as it was done, I would just pack up and leave. But then I met Sandy, and weeks turned into months, and months turned into years and everything changed. I never meant for us to become involved like we did, but it just happened and I am so very glad that it did. I am so happy to have met you.
 I hope Uncle Andre is doing well. What do you plan to do about him Hank? It is a shame that this happened to him, but you have a life too.
 I went out today and bought a little fake Christmas tree.

THE LAST DEER HUNT

It is the ugliest tree I have ever seen. I decorate it while Hemingway knocks all the ornaments off.

I guess I really do miss Fairhaven this time of the year. Christmas up there is something special. But I will miss being with you most of all. Please give my love to Orphan and say hi to everyone for me.

As soon as I get settled in I will get you my new number, but until then, you can reach me at Chris' place 213-555-3454 or keep writing. Please, please.

Love you and miss you,
Maggie and Hemingway

P.S. Let us talk on Christmas Eve
P.S.S. It is 79° here today

"Oh yeah, rub it in. It's 7 degrees above zero here!"
Maggie's comment about Uncle Andre bothered him. It made him feel that he had to choose between California and Fairhaven and between Uncle Andre and Maggie.

A second letter was from Vietnam, which Hank opened slowly.

December 10th, 1983

Hey Guy,
How are things back in good old downtown Fairhaven, Michigan? Hope everyone there is doing well.

It is so eerie being back here. But it is good that I can get the chance to confront my ghosts and demons.

We have eighty-five degree weather tonight and I'm sitting outside sipping on a beer. You know, I just realized that I'm looking at the same sky you guys can see up in Fairhaven. The Big Dipper is up there and Orion is out hunting, I can see his sword. Yeah, the same skies, but what a different world.

Just to let you know, I have found the perfect young lady! She's intelligent, beautiful and sassy...and eight years old! Of course, I say the same about all the kids in the orphanage. We have twelve children now, and twenty-two on a waiting list. We would like to move faster, but everything gets held up in the local bureaucracy. I don't know if I told you, but Gus has put up a very generous donation towards the orphanage. We really need to build a second wing.

Give everyone my best.

Missing you, Frenchy.

Hank felt better. At least Maggie and Frenchy were safe. Now to figure out what to do with Uncle Andre.

The next morning, Hank let Orphan out, but as soon as he was done, he just wanted to get back inside away from the cold. Hank headed down to the diner.

"Hi Lucy, how you doing?" Hank took off his coat, sat at the only open stool at the counter, and took the cup of coffee she offered.

"Pretty good Hank," Lucy replied, sweeping her arm over the diner. The booths were full, the regulars engaged in their usual conversation and a number of young professional people talking over piles of papers in front of them. Men in construction gear and hard hats filled the counter stools. "I've got an ad in the paper for a short order cook. I can't keep up with the business anymore."

Hank sipped his coffee. "I heard from Frenchy last week."

"Yeah, me too." Her face lit up at Frenchy's name. "Yep, said he was doing well..."

Hank smiled back at her as they shared the emptiness that Frenchy left behind.

Lucy wiped down the counter, but seemed to be staring

off into a different time. "You know Hank, there have been a lot of changes around here, but this will always be Frenchy's Diner."

Only two days until Christmas. Hank went to Marquette to finish his shopping and decided to stop at Northern Michigan University to see what they had for art courses. He had just finished lunch at the Sweetwater Café near the University when a familiar face came through the door of the restaurant. "Mary. Mary Walstrom! What a surprise. What are you doing in Marquette?"

"Same as you Hank, Christmas shopping. I live in Marquette now. Gosh, it's so good to see you. I haven't seen you since Sandy died. I've been following what's been going on with this Pettiford situation. Isn't that something eh? Who would have thought what went on out at his house. You just never know."

"That's for sure. But I think this is all behind us now."

"And gosh, wasn't that something what Fuzzy did to you and that photographer out in the swamp, eh? That man is unbelievable. You were right you know, what you told me back there in that bar."

"I'm not sure I remember..." Hank was desperately trying to pull back the memories of the many smoke and beer filled evenings in the tavern.

"Oh, sure you do, Hank. Don't you remember you told me that Fuzzy would never change and that I should stop trying to blame myself for what he did?"

"Yeah, I kind of remember." Little by little, slender threads of memory made their way back into his brain.

"Well, that night you told me if he ever hit me again, I should just take the boys and leave. Well, you know, he did...and I did. I moved in with my sister in Munising and went back to school to be a nurse. That's something, eh? Me a nurse. Oh, by the way, how is your Uncle Andre doing?"

"Sometimes he's okay, other times, he's totally out of it. I'm not sure what I can do when he has to leave the re-hab center."

"Well you know I work with the elderly now. If there is something I can do, you let me know. There is nothing I would like better than to move back to Fairhaven. Here, I'll give you my telephone number."

Hank went to a sporting goods store and bought a new pair of snow boots. While there, he quickly checked on a new telescopic fishing pole and reel to replace the ones that were broken in the river. A new creel would be nice also. *Heck, better wait till spring to see what I'll be doing or where I will be living.*

The windows of Tracy's Travel Agency were filled with pictures of warm and sunny California and Hawaii. *Three months till spring,* Hank thought as he looked at the clock and thermometer hanging over the bank. Twelve degrees above zero.

On the drive home from Marquette, Hank's thoughts were on Maggie. *She got a fake tree. That's funny. I guess in L.A. that's about all you can find. But what am I talking about; I don't have a tree yet! I'll have to go and get one first thing tomorrow.*

The mail yielded the usual seven or eight catalogues, bills, a few Christmas cards, a letter from the California Institute of Art, and a small letter from Diane. Her letter held a small picture of a grinning baby.

December 18, 1983

Dear Uncle Hank,

That's right little brother, you are now an uncle. Meet young Mr. Henry Duval-Towers. Yep, named after you as your Christmas present.

Suzan and I adopted him last week. Isn't he the most adorable little baby? And don't you think he looks a lot like me? Just kidding!

So now, my world is just about as complete as it can be.

THE LAST DEER HUNT

How about you? How's Uncle Andre? It's too bad that you have to be responsible for him when you have so much to do for yourself.

Thanks again for having me out there for Thanksgiving, I had a great time, and it was good to meet everybody again. Now it's your turn to visit us and with Little Hank here, you got another great reason to come.

Merry Christmas and lots of love,
Sis.

Hank put the picture of the baby on the refrigerator with a magnet. *All babies look the same.* The baby looked back at him, all smiles. *Nope, this one looks special. One more reason to go to California.*

"Over here boy," The tail started to wag, the ears perked up and the dog-smile came across Orph's face as he ran towards his friend and onto his lap. "What do you think dog? Re-runs of Bonanza?"

Orphan covered both of his ears with her paws and let out a low long moan.

The next morning Hank went out early to the large field across from the mill and the trees behind it. "It will be good to have Uncle Andre come home with us for Christmas." The dog ran in circles in front of Hank, leaping through the snow on its little legs. After two hours of snow shoeing between the balsams, firs and spruce, Hank and Orphan went back, picked out the first small balsam he had passed and quickly cut it off at the base. "It's too bad Uncle Andre won't be home to help decorate it." Hank said, dragging the tree back to the Ranger pickup.

Hank dialed Maggie's number on the phone slowly, filled with anticipation. This would be the first time they talked since Maggie moved to California. Three rings and Maggie's voice came over the phone.

"Hello?"

Hank felt his heart skip a beat. A deep breath, "Hi Maggie, Hank here." He let his breath out slowly.

"Hank! My God, is this really you? I don't believe it." Her voice quivered as she spoke. "It is so good to hear your voice. I was just going to call you. Honest, I really was."

"Maggie, it's good to hear you too. I called just to hear your voice. What's happening out there in California?"

"Oh Hank, you first, you tell me what's going on back home. How are Orphan and Uncle Andre?"

"Both are doing fine. Andre for the most part is happy. We are going to have him come over here for Christmas. I'll go and pick him up later. How is Hemingway?"

"I think he's settled down now. Found a window to hang out in and sleeps cuddled up with me."

Hank refilled his coffee. *Her voice is just the same*

"I really would like to come out there Maggie, but..."

"But what?" Maggie said, hanging on each word, the excitement quickly fading.

Hank hesitated, taking a breath and talking slowly. "I just don't know what I am going to do about Uncle Andre. After New Years, I am going to look at nursing homes in the area. I just don't think I can leave him right now."

"You are one really great guy, you know that Hank? I think it's great what you are doing for your uncle. I will not force you to choose between him and me. We need to do what we need to do. Perhaps, in the future..."

"Yeah, this won't last forever, and the school will still be there, if that's what I want." Hank waited for a response, and then added, "Could you possibly come out here, at least to visit?" Hank held the phone, listening to the silence.

Again, Maggie measured her words. "I don't think so Hank. I think I need some time right now. I have a couple of opportunities to go on assignment. I might look into one of them."

Again, the silence filled the phone.

"Hank, it's Christmas, let's look at the bright side."

Hank could feel the tone of her voice change, but the

sadness was still behind the words. "Yeah, you're right. I got your package yesterday, but haven't opened it. You must have bought out all the stores in California."

"And I got your package. Why don't we open them?"

Hank deliberately removed the craft paper from the large box and opened it, only to find it filled with a number of packages wrapped in Christmas gift paper. Holding the phone in the hollow of his shoulder, he could hear paper being rattled on the other end of the phone.

"Holy cow, look at this!" Hank unwrapped a long package. "It's beautiful. It's a telescopic fishing pole, just like the one I broke. Where the heck did you find this out there? I didn't think anybody in California would know what a telescopic pole was."

The rattle of paper could be heard on the other end of the phone. A giggle, then a loud laugh. "Hank, you shouldn't have! I will never be able to thank you enough for this."

Hank could hear Maggie trying to figure out what she unwrapped. In almost a whisper, Maggie said, "What the heck is this thing?"

"Give up?"

"Yes, I have no idea what this thing is."

"It's an ice-fishing rig. You put the bait on the line and put it in the hole in the ice. When a fish bites, the line releases the red flag, which pops up in the air. You just pull up your fish."

"Hank, you are crazy. Where am I going to find a hole in the ice out here? And what do I use as bait? And where is the six-pack of beer?"

"That sweetheart, you have to get yourself."

Hank held up the next present and shook it. "Doesn't rattle." He stripped the paper from the package. "Nice Maggie, this is a beautiful creel, this is all woven wicker. It's got to be the best I've ever seen. It is wonderful. Thank you Maggie. Thank you very much. Now your turn."

Maggie gave a soft whistle. "Oh Hank, this is so beautiful.

You made this wood inlay of the wolves, they are so beautiful. I love the way you wove the male and female adults together behind the two cubs, and then intertwined them all together. Where did you find all the different color woods?"

"I have a shop full of different woods. Might as well use them for something."

"Hank, this is truly beautiful. When are you ever going to believe that you really are that good? Is this the Marquetry technique you mentioned some time ago?

"Yes it is."

"Well, I am impressed. You know you can sell these. They would be worth a lot."

"I don't think I am ready for that yet. I don't think they are good enough yet."

"Oh Hank, of course they are good enough. When are you going to realize that you are good enough?"

"Okay Maggie, you made your point."

"Well, if you ever are ready, let me know, I can find a lot of customers for you."

"Yeah, I forgot, you are very good at marketing."

"Oh Hank, open another present will you?"

Hank opened his last small package. The newest most up-to-date reel He had ever seen. Looking at all the fishing gear around him, a thought moved quickly through his mind, *is this a hint that she thinks I'm going to stay up here?*

As if she read his mind over the phone, Maggie said, "You know Hank, there's great fishing out here too."

"Merry Christmas Maggie."

"Merry Christmas Hank. I love you."

"I love you too, Maggie." Hank sat listening to the dial tone. The words stayed on his tongue. Orphan lay on the floor looking up at Hank, one ear cocked up.

"I love you Maggie."

Forty-Eight

New Year's Eve 1983, and the Svenson and Haakila VFW Post # 5834 was packed and in a festive mood. People in little party hats carrying drinks and noisemakers were crowded around the bar and the tables were filled with champagne bottles and snacks. Roy Haakila and his band were blasting out a rousing polka and the dance floor was full.

Patti Culpepper motioned Hank to join her. "My new look. Like it?" Her hair was cut very short, the gray was gone, and her trademark horned rim glasses were missing. "Contacts," Patti said, anticipating Hank's question. "I've decided to not let this long cold winter get me down this year. Speaking of which, how is Maggie doing out in sunny and warm California?"

"She's doing fine, she found a nice Condo near the ocean. It sounds really nice."

"Then why don't you get off your butt and go out there and see her?"

"I'd like to, but I have so much going on around here and with Uncle Andre..."

"Oh hell Duval, take your uncle with you. All that warm weather and beautiful women in bikinis would either cure him or kill him – either way, he would die happy."

"It does sound nice out there doesn't it? But I need to really think about it."

"Well Hank, while you're thinking about it, there's more than enough work for you around here," Pattie paused, "and you could do very well for yourself."

"I'll think about it, Patti. I don't want any favoritism."

"Not to worry, there will be more than enough work to go around, everybody will make out just fine, including all those yokels down at the Bayside Tavern."

"Thanks Patti, you guys have done a great job. Speaking of which, where is Sarah tonight?"

"Oh haven't you heard? She and Ben Epstein are quite an item now. They're down in Ann Arbor at his parents' home for the holidays."

The crowd was loud and in a party mood but Hank was not into celebrating tonight. "Think I'll head over to the hospital and see how Uncle Andre is doing."

The evening air was clear and cold as Hank walked around the millpond. The lights of the town twinkling across the pond and in the clear cold night air, he looked up at the canopy of stars. *There's the Milky Way, and there's Orion moving further to the south. Wonder if Frenchy is seeing the same sky tonight? Hell, I don't even know if it's night there now. Hope his nightmares have gone away.*

Hank turned the television set in Andre's room to a channel showing New Years Eve being celebrated around the world. From the loud snoring coming from his uncle, he decided to let him sleep. After an hour, Uncle was still sleeping, Hank decided to head home. Maybe Orphan would keep him company.

Hank tried to call Maggie, but no one answered.

January 5th, Hank was up early and after the morning chores, He picked up the mail.

THE LAST DEER HUNT

Thursday, January 2, 1984

Dearest Hank,

    Happy New Year! I hope you and Orphan had a good New Years Eve. I ended up going out with some friends to a club. The music was too loud and we didn't get home until one in the morning. I would have given you a call, but it would have been four in the morning there.
    Great news! The February issue of the magazine will hit the stores next week. Check it out; your artwork really is great. I have received all kinds of compliments on the article from everybody who has seen it.
    Is there anything new on the Pettiford thing? I don't think the courts will ever do anything anymore.
    Everything is happening so fast out here. We just moved into our new place this week. We have just unpacked the essentials and I found out that I pulled a new assignment today. I plan to leave in about a week to go to Crater Lake National Park in Oregon for about a month to do a story about some mountain lions that have been reportedly causing problems with livestock.
    Hemingway was so happy to have a place to settle down and now I am going to have to leave him with Chris at her place. He's getting old and I wouldn't know what I would do with him in Oregon.
    Hank, as soon as this assignment is up, I'm going to find a way to get back up there and see you. I'll try to keep in touch with you.

Love you much,
Maggie and Hemingway

    Hank re-read the letter wanting it to say more, wanting it to say 'Come out to me, I need you so much,' or perhaps, 'Hank, I'm going to leave everything and come out there to be with you.'

Hank shrunk back as he followed Mrs. Tuttle on the tour of the Golden Autumn Nursing Home. Old people sitting in wheel chairs, leaning over, sleeping or rocking themselves, others using walkers and baby steps to take forever to travel the length of a hallway decorated in cheap austere blandness. Blank faces and pleading eyes followed Hank as he followed Mrs. Tuttle. Pleading for what? *I'd be afraid to ask*, Hank thought.

The next day, Hank followed Mrs. Morgan through the halls of The Twilight Years Nursing Home. The same blank faces, the same old broken and bent bodies, and the same awful smell permeated the overly warm air. An old friend of Uncle Andre's, Mr. Stuttgart lived in The Twilight Years, which made it the front runner of the two unacceptable choices.

Another stormy winter night. Another lonely night. Hank put another log on the fireplace and picked up the large pile of papers Patti Culpepper had dropped off. More materials for the mill restoration project. Hank went outside to bring in another load of wood. "Supposed to be down in the minus twenties tonight Orph."

Orphan went over to his bed and pulled his old blanket over his head.

Hank poured a cup of coffee, sat at the kitchen table and wrote.

January 6, 1984

Dearest Maggie,

Happy New Year to you too. I tried to call, but you were out. Yeah, I feel old too. I went over to the hospital to see Uncle Andre and to watch New Years Eve on television, but all he did was sleep. I came home and fell asleep by 10:00 P.M.

Uncle Andre is about the same. I am not sure he always

understands where he is, but if you keep him in the moment, he seems to be enjoying life.

I have been checking out some of the nursing homes around here for Uncle Andre, and they are quite bad. I'm not sure what I can do yet.

Sounds like an interesting assignment at Crater Lake. I hear it is very beautiful in Oregon and I hope everything goes well up there.

I will be looking for the magazine. I'll call one of the stores over in L'anse to see when it will be in. I don't know if Maude's Convenience Store even carries it.

It is not the courts I am concerned about with the Pettiford case. There just seems to be a lot of inconsistencies in what the guys say, nothing definite, but just a feeling that nothing adds up.

I think about us often.

Love, Hank and Orphan.

Thoughts ran through his mind as he tried to understand his own feelings and fears, but no answers came to him. He sat watching his uncle, how much older he looked, how quickly he seemed to go down hill. The nurse brought in breakfast and Hank helped his uncle with the oatmeal. Hank said, "Hey Uncle, what would you like to do today?'

"Hell Hank, why don't we hitch a ride out to California, you can hook up with that young girl friend of yours and I can chase the cute chicks in their bikinis down Santa Monica Boulevard."

"Uncle, what would you do with one of those cute chicks if you caught her?"

"That ain't a problem, I'd never catch one."

Hank laughed, and then taking hold of his Uncles hand, said, "Uncle Andre, today, we need to move you to a rehab center."

"Why don't I just go home?"

"Because you're not quite ready, and there is no one to take care of you at home."

"Why don't you?" Andre put his head down and said softly. "No, I can't ask you to do that. That wouldn't be fair to you." His body heaved with a sigh of resignation. "I guess I'm just a useless old man, ain't worth a plugged nickel."

"Uncle, as soon as I can, we will get you home. I promise. Now, why don't we just read paper? We could catch up on the news, sports, weather, and comics."

"I'd like that Hank, but you don't need to do the news, I don't give a damn about what's going on out there, but would you mind going through the obituaries? Seems like all my old friends are dying off."

"Anything you want Uncle." Hank said, opening the paper and reading. The obituaries done, he read the comics.

Uncle Andre shook his head. Don't know why folks call them funnies or comics, ain't nothing funny about them anymore."

Andre dozed off and Hank let him sleep until with heavy heart, he woke him up, and with the help of a nurse, moved him into the truck for the trip to the re-hab unit of the Twilight Nursing Home. On the ride over, Hank did his best to convince his uncle that this was only a short-term solution and that Andre would not be put in the nursing home. He was sure he was not successful; Uncle Andre sat in silence, his face drawn tight, and Hank could see tears on his uncles cheeks. At the re-hab center, Uncle Andre continued to be silent and followed instructions as if a robot. He sat staring off in space and refused to acknowledge Hank when Hank tried to say goodbye.

Back home, Hank read the letter he received from Pat Johnson. It was a summary of the arraignment and hearing. He found paper and pen, and wrote.

THE LAST DEER HUNT

Saturday, January 7, 1984

Hey Gang,

    Happy New Year and a belated Merry Christmas. Hope this message finds you in good health and enjoying life.
    Good news (I think), I heard from Pat Johnson and it looks like the county district attorneys office is not going to pursue the case, at least not in the foreseeable future. But I guess that unless some new information comes forward, it will just stay open.
    Everything here is doing okay, my uncle is doing about the same, Hope to hear from you guys soon.

Hank

P.S. the magazine with Maggie's article and my lousy drawings will be in the stores next week if anyone cares.

    Hank wrote four more copies for each of the other men and added them to the pile of outgoing mail. Then he got a cup of coffee, sat in front of the fire with Orphan and re-read the summary report. Half way through the report, he stopped. Something was creeping back into his mind, something that did not make sense. Slowly, he replayed all the events of the Pettiford case in his mind. Getting a piece of paper and a pencil, he started writing.
    August of 1965, the Pettiford incident; July 1967, headstones destroyed; September of 1968, Vic had gun at cemetery; and October of 1968, Vic shot dog. Hank went over the list again and again, adding incidents as he thought of them. At May of 1966, he added 'Joined gang and mill water tower graffiti.'
    "Wait a minute," Hank stared at the paper. "That's it, that's what has been bothering me. I remember returning Vic's lighter and his uncle said Vic was out of town in July of

1967. He let out a long slow whistle. "Vic couldn't have destroyed those headstones with that German Luger. Then who could have done that?"

Hank was not sure he wanted to know the answer.

But first, Uncle Andre needs to be moved to Re-hab. Hank had weighed all the facts, investigated all the angles, and plotted all the positives and negatives into any of the nursing homes. Then he asked John deer and the answer was that Uncle Andre would come home to live with Hank.

But first, with heavy heart, and with the help of a nurse, loaded Uncle Andre into the truck for the trip to the re-hab unit of the Twilight Nursing home.

The first days of January followed each other in shades of gray dreariness.

Then the weather broke and the January thaw started on the tenth of the month and lasted for five days with the temperatures reaching the high thirties. Melted snow and slush filled the streets, but the bright sun cheered up spirits and put smiles on the faces of those people who were out and about.

Hank drove slowly back from the re-hab center in L'anse with Uncle Andre and Orphan sitting between them. Uncle Andre watched the countryside pass by as they rounded Keweenaw Bay. When they turned onto Upper Skanee Road, he turned to Hank, "It's good to be going home."

"Yes it is Uncle Andre." It felt good that Andre was aware that he was coming back to Fairhaven, but as Hank watched his Uncle sitting quietly, looking out the window, he knew these flashes of recognition were becoming less and less. As they pulled into the driveway of Hank's house, Andre looked quickly around and Hank could not tell if it was a look of recognition or resignation.

Mary Walstrom was there to greet them. She had agreed, along with four other women to form a company that would provide home assistance to a number of elderly in the Fairhaven area.

As Mary fluffed the pillow behind Andre's head and the

two were engaged in some unheard conversation, it seemed that Mary and Andre would do well together.

Along with the usual mail, a large envelope with a return address of the Art Institute of California caught his eye. Looking down at Orphan, Hank waved the envelope. "I guess that means I should open this letter from the art school, right?" Slowly, Hank slid the contents from the envelope. A number of documents providing information on the school and a form letter. Slowly, he opened the letter and read.

Dear Mr. Duval.

We are happy to inform you that you have been accepted for enrollment into The Art Institute of California. We have enclosed a statement of your financial aid package and forms to fill out.

We hope you will be joining us for the spring semester...

Hank finished the letter and slowly put it back in the envelope. "Well dog, should I tell Maggie?" After six attempts at starting to write, Hank finally wrote;

January 9, 1984

Dearest Maggie,

Heard from the school today, it appears they liked what they saw. Scary. As Groucho Marx said, "I don't want to belong to any club that would admit me. Maggie, this scares the heck out of me. I'm just this kid from the sticks. How would I ever going to fit in with all of these talented sophisticated people. Well, anyway, I will think about it, and then I will confer with John Deer.

Oh yes, I also uncovered the fact that Vic Pollo could not have shot up those headstones in the cemetery. What that means is that some other person, or persons had that Luger. I'm not quite ready to jump to conclusions, but this means that Vic may not have been the one who killed Pettiford. Stay tuned.

Love always,
Hank

Hank buried himself in going over blueprints of the mill and caring for Uncle Andre. The routine was the same every day. Walk Orphan, feed him, take care of Uncle Andre, and wait for Mary to come in. Go to the shop and pick up paper work or tools and head downtown. In the evenings, he would relieve Mary, feed and bath Andre and spend the time reading to him. On those days when Mary could not work, Hank would work from home.

Every day, he checked the mailbox for mail, hoping for a letter from Maggie or Frenchy. Today, between the piles of junk mail, there was a letter from Eddie.

Saturday, January 13, 1984

Hi Hank,

A belated Merry Christmas and Happy New Year to you. Got your letter, thanks. Just a quick note to let you know that I'm not doing too badly now, but I struggled during the holidays. The worst seems to be over now. I'm going to AA meetings and do what they call the twelve-step program. I think it's more like the 144-step program for all the times a person has to re-start. I now have a mentor, a very pretty young woman named Willow. Can you believe it? This 19-year-old ex-druggie is helping me to dry out!

THE LAST DEER HUNT

Willow and I are going to Quebec next week to see her family. She calls me Van Gogh because I only have one ear.

One of the issues I am still trying to deal with was that I felt the guys had abandoned me that night at Pettiford's house. They told me that I had to keep Pettiford busy for about fifteen minutes and they promised me that they would watch out for me. But then Pettiford started to grab at me and nobody came back for me. It was a good thing Vic showed up when he did and blew Pettiford away. I've been working on this and I feel like I'm able to deal with it at last, but it would help if you guys would help me understand what happened.

Eddie.

Winter returned with a vengeance. The wind and clouds swung around from the east, filled up with snow over Lake Superior and headed south to dump it over Northern Michigan. Even in an area accustomed to heavy snows, everything was pushed to the limits and emergency services were stretched.

This would be a good time to clean out some of the stuff in the basement. Dusty box after dusty box was brought up and put on the card table in front of the woodstove. Old newspaper clippings, recipes, magazines, songbooks, old 33 RPM vinyl records, and pictures. So many pictures, mostly black and white, but many faded color pictures. At least six generations of cameras took an infinite assortment of pictures. Some pictures were as small as a 2-inch square and required a magnifying glass to see the tiny people and tiny objects. Minutes slipped into hours as piles of memories were sorted and re-sorted, some going directly into a large trash basket, others, into various piles. Cups of coffee later, Hank had marked each pile and put them into various shoeboxes and other containers. The piles of pictures were left on the table and these were shuffled into various smaller piles by dates guessed at, people guessed at and objects guessed at. While the storm howled and the snow continued to pile in up in six feet high drifts, Hank sat and studied each picture.

Pictures of Mom and Dad, picnics, sightseeing, family get-togethers, or just posing for pictures. Pictures of Mom with her ribbons from the state fair for baking. Pictures of Mom with Hank and Diane as babies, toddlers, youngsters, and teens.

Pictures of Dad with fish he caught, with birds and rabbits from hunting and with deer from many different hunting seasons hanging in the back yard. A picture of Hank standing over a deer with a knife. "Whoa Orph, this is interesting." Holding up the picture for the dog to see. Orphan responding enthusiastically to finally being paid attention to.

"This is one of the pictures Dad took of the buck he had shot back in 1963 before somebody stole the deer head." Another trip to the basement and Hank returned with the dirty old head of John Deer. A long examination of the picture and Hank sat back. "Yep, this is the same buck, but it has that stupid smile. Yeah, sure, this is the same head that Percy won the deer contest with in 1963 and hung in his barber shop for years before Frenchy picked it up and put it in the diner. Damn, so old Percy was the one who stole Dad's buck." Hank sat holding John Deer shaking his head. "I think I'll send the information about this buck to Boone and Crockett and see if this deer was a record."

After the fifth day, the storm broke and the sun came out. Uncle Andre was in good spirits and in a good state of mind. Hank picked up Patti Culpepper and the three of them went over to Marquette to have dinner at the Sweetwater Café. Patti had brought some books from the Arvon Township Historical Society and a tape recorder and after dinner, Patti and Uncle Andre spent over an hour in laughter and loud conversation as Andre filled her with his version of the history of Fairhaven. And unless someone had the memory to contradict what Andre said, this conversation would become part of the official history of Fairhaven, Michigan.

Finally, a letter from Maggie.

January 15, 1984

My Dearest,

Hank, do not give me that 'poor little hick from Fairhaven' routine. You are smarter than most of the people in Los Angeles and most of the artists in this area would sell their soul for your raw artistic talent. You belong in art school where you can take this talent and really do something with it.

Hank, you have grown so much since I met you. You just need to have a little more self confidence and you could be anything you wanted to be.

Please think about the school, and about me.

And yes, please keep me informed about this new development in the Pettiford case. Sounds like it just took a very interesting twist.

Love Maggie and Hemingway.

The weather continued warm and sunny. On the first of February, things were going well and Hank felt good. The warm sun on his face, he decided to walk over to Frenchy's Diner. Ten o'clock in the morning, something was wrong, the diner was closed. A small note on the door just said 'Closed until further notice.' Quickly Hank climbed up the stairs leading to the apartment above the diner where Lucy lived.

Lucy and Hank stood in silence, Hank not wanting to hear, and Lucy not being able to talk, her body shaking with her convulsive sobs.

"Lucy, what is it? Is it Frenchy?"

Slowly, she nodded and handed Hank a crumpled paper, then slumped back like a rag doll.

Hank slowly un-crumpled the small newspaper article. "Three Vietnam veterans were killed today in an orphanage in Plauku Vietnam while trying to evacuate orphans after an unexploded bomb was found. None of the orphans were injured and local authorities called the three veterans heroes..."

Hank felt his heart sink and the sadness flooded over him. Reaching out, he held Lucy tightly feeling her shudder from her crying. Reaching up he wiped the tears from her cheeks, and forced a smile. "Frenchy always wanted to be a hero. Now maybe he will find the peace he was looking for."

Lucy looked up at him and nodded. "I will be going to his funeral. I need to say goodbye. I need to find my own peace. He was the nicest person I ever knew."

"And he was my best friend, but I won't be able to make the funeral. I want you to say goodbye for me."

Lucy gave him a quick hug, her eyes filled with tears, those same eyes that Hank remembered as the sparkling eyes of the young orange haired Pixie that seemed so long ago. But now, her eyes filled with sadness.

Hank called Mary and asked if she could come in early. He was feeling closed in and needed to get out and get some fresh air. His heart was heavy, and again the sadness swept over him in waves, closing in on him. Taking the snowshoes out of the garage, Hank moved quickly over the snow, scaring up pure white snowshoe hares waited until the last minute to dart in front, their long back legs moving them to safety. Standing on millpond rock, the wind on his face helped clear his mind. Frenchy lived a good life, he was a good person, and he died doing what he wanted to. Hank would mourn his loss, but as he snow shoed back through the evening shadows, the intense sadness melted and the

THE LAST DEER HUNT

empty place in Hank became filled with the memories of what he and Frenchy had together.

Back home in the garage, as he was putting the snowshoes away, he noticed a small box. Puzzled, he turned the box over and around until he finally remembered. It was a box that he and Tom took out of the camp just before it caved in. Opening it, he found hand written papers, a copy of a news article and an old photo of his hunting friends. It was blurry, but he could make out Gino, Ollie, Tom, and Bob standing in the cemetery.

His coat off, Hank watched his frail old Uncle and Orphan playing catch. Andre would throw one of Hank's old slippers; Orphan would chase it, pick it up, and leap back into Andre's lap where he would drop it for another throw.

Hank shook his head. *Wonder what that old man thinks about? He never complains or says anything about how he feels.* Finally, the game of catch ended and Hank moved Andre in front of the fire and turned on the television for Andre to watch his favorite show, reruns of Bonanza. Uncle Andre was in conversation with Pa, Little Joe, Adam and Hoss back at the Ponderosa. He ignored Orphan sitting on the floor with the slipper ready to retrieve.

Uncle Andre took a turn for the worst on Valentine's Day. A series of micro-strokes further reduced his ability to remember or reason and increased his dependency on others for assistance.

Mary suggested that it might be time to re-examine the need for a nursing home. This time, Hank had to agree that he should revisit the local nursing homes and even the ones more distant. It didn't seem like Uncle Andre would mind very much anymore.

Maybe on Valentine's Day, there just might be a letter from Maggie.

Yes, Maggie finally sent mail.

February 11th 1984

Dearest Hank,

    The saddest news. Old man Hemingway died in my arms last night. I buried him in the little garden in the patio behind the condo and planted catnip on his grave. He was such a wonderful furry person and I will always remember how he kept me warm all those long cold winter nights up in Fairhaven.
    Chris called yesterday and told me Hemingway was very sick. I took the first flight back to L.A. Poor old guy, all he could do was lie in my arms. Damn, I feel so bad that I wasn't here for him. I should have taken him with me to Oregon. All I can do is cry. I would have called you, but I'm just a big blob of sobbing mush today.
    I need to get back to Oregon tomorrow. We're at a very important point in the whole story. Christ, I think those ranchers are ready to shoot us. You would think by listening to them, that we liberal creeps from California are the cause of all the problems. According to them, these four mountain lions have killed and hauled off 250 head of cattle in six months. When they were asked to produce one dead cow, they found some excuse why there were no carcasses.
    This whole thing with Hemingway makes me realize how much we need to be with people we love. I will call you very soon. I'm sorry that I haven't been in touch, but we are in the middle of nowhere up there. It's incredible, not a phone booth, an ATM, or a Starbucks coffee shop anywhere. How primitive!
    Missing you so very much

Love Maggie

P.S. Please give Orphan a very hug for me tonight.

THE LAST DEER HUNT

Hank did. The memories of Hemingway filled his thoughts. *Damn, I really liked that stupid cat.* Hank wandered around the house until three in the morning. He checked on Uncle Andre again, not hearing any snoring coming from the bedroom. A quick moment of panic went through him. *What if he's gone?* Once inside the room, his uncle was lying on his side facing away from the door. Hank could hear quiet sobs coming from inside the old man's chest.

"What's wrong Uncle?" Hank said so quietly that he wasn't sure if he had said it out loud.

"Hank, it's time for me to go. I'm nothing but a burden on you and I'm no damn good to myself or anybody else."

"Don't talk like that Andre. We still have a lot to do and we need your inputs on the town history." Hank tried to put a positive note to his voice, but was afraid it came out worried.

"You don't need anymore of the past young man, what you need is the future." Hank waited until the quiet sobs were replaced by hoarse snoring, and quietly left the room.

Forty-Nine

February slipped into March and no word from Maggie. St. Patrick's Day was only a week away followed three days later by the first day of spring. Uncle Andre was looking better and his mind was very clear. Hank looked up from the newspaper. "Hey Uncle, looks like we'll make it through another winter."

A hoarse laugh, "You might, young man, but I'm not going to be here." Uncle Andre sat back in his chair and smiled. It was the smile of a person who had figured out the answer to the question of the meaning of life and was happy with the answer.

"Yes you will, the Tigers start their spring training next Friday. Everybody thinks they have a good team this year."

"Hell, they ain't going to do nothing, they'll just find a new way to lose, just like they do every year."

The day was very cold and Orphan was quick with his task. Mary would be in today so Uncle needed to be dressed and have his bath before she arrived.

Hank knocked on the bedroom door. "Come on Uncle, let's go, it's daylight in the swamp."

No answer. No snoring. Hank opened the door and went into the bedroom. The pile of blankets on the bed lay

THE LAST DEER HUNT

still. Panic raced through Hank's mind. "Come on Uncle, get up," a shake of the blankets, no response. Hank pulled the blankets down, uncovering Andre's head. Uncle Andre was looking back with blank staring eyes and a smile. *Jesus, he's dead.*

The next three days were busy with funeral arrangements. Gustafson's funeral home took care of everything and the funeral was well attended. The priest gave a good eulogy and at the request of Uncle Andre, Patrick McDougall played Amazing Grace on his bagpipe and there was not a dry eye in the funeral home. Hank said his goodbyes and wiped his eyes. *How come I feel so guilty that Uncle Andre is gone? I never knew freedom could feel so wrong.*

"It's been too long Hank. We should never have been apart this long." Maggie's voice came over the telephone, spread gradually into Hank's soul, and took his breath away.

Hank reached down deep inside trying to find the right words. "It has been too long. I would do anything to be with you tonight. I should come out to California tomorrow. I don't have anything here to hold me back now. Or you could come out here; you could write and travel from here."

"No Hank, I don't think we should try to work this out right now over the phone. You just lost Uncle Andre and I am just finishing my assignment here. It will take me about three or four weeks to wrap up some things here, and I will come up there to visit. We can work it out then."

Hank sat back on the couch. Everything had moved so quickly over the last two weeks. He had let so much slide while he attended to Andre's funeral arrangements.

He looked at the large pile of papers on the table in front of him. "Might as well get to it, Orph." And picked up the first envelope.

"From the Boone and Crockett Society. It's about Pa's buck; you know, the one from Frenchy's Diner, John Deer, yeah, that one. Well you know what Orphan, that buck would have been good enough in those days to have won first place for the largest deer ever taken in the State of

Michigan." Hank poured another cup of coffee. "Isn't this something? Pa tried so hard for so long to find a trophy buck so he could be somebody important. Strange how he felt that if he had this set of antlers, people would respect him." Hank took a deep breath. "Didn't do any good for Percy Twill."

    With Orphan lying on a rug at his feet, Hank sat down in front of the fire with the small box he had found in the garage. The box contained a number of papers, a newspaper clipping and an old photo. The papers had been wet and were illegible. He carefully unfolded the old newspaper article and found it to be a clipping about the damage to the headstones in the cemetery back in 1967. Hank put the newspaper clipping down and picked up the photo. The photo was old and Hank had to squint to see the figures. A very young Ollie, Bob, Gino and Tom were standing close together in the cemetery holding a German Luger. "Looks like pictures from the cemetery when Vic showed us the gun."

    Getting his glasses, he studied the photograph. "Funny Orph, I don't remember anybody taking this picture at the cemetery that day. Wait, I'm not in this picture. And I don't remember Ollie and Tom at the cemetery that day. So how..." Flipping the photograph over, the writing was so faint and blurred that he could barely make it out; a date, June, 1966.

    Hank picked up the photograph of his buddies in the cemetery and studied it, slowly turning it over and over in his hand. He felt it rising, the anger, disappointment, and outrage. "Oh, yeah, I should have known, I should have figured it out a long time ago." Slowly and deliberately, he dialed Gus' number and left a message to meet him at Frenchy's Diner.

    The diner was quiet; most of the lunch crowd had already left. Hank held out his hand and motioned for Gus to join him in the booth. "Thanks for coming."

    "My pleasure Hank. It's good to see you again. I am

THE LAST DEER HUNT

sorry about Andre." Gus said, accepting the coffee brought by the young waitress.

"Yeah, Uncle Andre's only regret was that he never got to chase all the pretty girls in California." Hank smiled across the table, then turned serious.

Leaning across the table as far as he could, Hank said quietly, "I have a dilemma and would like your legal advice. It seems we, I mean I, may have made a mistake about who killed Pettiford. "I should have figured this out before. It all adds up. First, at Pettiford's house that night, Eddie said that Pettiford yelled out, "What do you kids think you're doing?" He said kids, plural, more than one. Then, my buddies said that on that night, Vic told them he had shot and killed Pettiford with the rifle after Pettiford caught him with the loot. That was wrong. Vic couldn't have shot Pettiford with the rifle for the same reason none of us could have killed Pettiford with the rifle. When the gun was dug up, all six slugs were accounted for.

"But," Gus shook his head. "What about Vic shooting up the cemetery?"

"Yeah, I almost believed that, but then I remembered that I had gone over to Vic's house to return his lighter in July, 1966. Vic was out of town at the time somebody shot up the cemetery. The only people who could have had the Luger at that time were...yep; my good old buddies and they got the Luger at Pettiford's when they shot him and killed him. Vic didn't have the Luger until 1968 when he showed it to us in the cemetery. "

Gus stroked his chin, thinking. "But why did those guys give it to Vic after all that time."

"My guess is that Vic figured out that the guys robbed and killed Pettiford and blackmailed them. They gave him the gun to shut him up."

Gus nodded. "I think I'm getting the picture."

"And if that's not enough, here is the icing on the cake." Hank took out the picture and placed it on the table in front of Gus. This picture was taken in the summer of 1966. A year after Pettiford was murdered and two years before Vic had the gun."

"That all seems to make sense, who do you think was involved?"

"I'm not sure. I don't think Eddie had anything to do with this, but I believe the rest of my so-called friends were in this together. My guess is that they set the whole thing up with the intention of robbing Pettiford's house. I believe they had already planned it for some time and then I showed up at the mill and made such a fuss, they decided to take me along although they didn't want to. I believe what happened is that when Pettiford suggested we play hide and seek in the house, the guys would rob the place. While that was going on, Eddie was supposed to distract Pettiford. But Eddie got more than he bargained for when Pettiford tried to molest him. One or more of the guys were running through the library with their loot, including the rifle and Luger from Pettiford's military collection. I'm not sure which guys, but Pettiford saw them, yelled, and went after them. Someone shot Pettiford with the Luger, but when they heard me coming, they dropped some stuff, including the rifle and ducked out of the room."

The young waitress came with coffee refills. Hank continued. "To cover their own butts, they tried to convince me I must have shot Pettiford, maybe to shut me up. I had completely blocked every thing out of my mind and everything was okay until they dug up the body. Then when I was able to remember everything that happened that night, and I was sure I could not have shot Pettiford, and with Vic conveniently dead, they decided to blame him.

"Did they try to shift the blame to the Sloan brothers by planting the rifle with them?"

"No, actually they didn't. Eddie had dug up the rifle, but couldn't get it to work so he hid it down by the river where the Sloan brothers found it."

Gus, fascinated by Hank's story, had not touched his coffee.

THE LAST DEER HUNT

"I've been struggling with this ever since I figured it out. I've come close to saying the hell with it, but when I realized they had lied about everything, I got so damned mad at them. At first, they kept saying I must have shot Pettiford, and I believed them. Then they convinced me that it was Vic who was guilty, and I believed them again. All that time, they were telling me that everything they were doing was to protect me. Yeah sure, was I ever gullible?"

Gus sat quietly, letting Hank try to sort through his feelings.

"Damn Gus, I can't get past the idea that our whole relationship was based on lies."

"So, what do you think you should do?"

"Well, I did what Frenchy and I would have done. I asked John Deer."

"You don't mean that old smiling deer head." Gus laughed.

"Yeah, like Frenchy always said, John Deer has all the answers."

"Okay Hank, what did this deer head say to do?"

"It said I have no choice, I want this to go to the state police, and they can deal with it. Can you handle this for me?"

"Are you sure this is what you want? These are your buddies."

"Buddies? You call these people buddies? With buddies like them, who needs enemies? Take this stuff to the police."

Gus nodded. "You have to do what you have to do Hank. You realize of course that the chances of this going anywhere are little or none. And the incident with the headstones in the cemetery has a ten year statute of limitations." Taking the box of papers from Hank, he started to stand.

"Oh Gus, one more thing." Hank reached down and opened the pink box containing his mother's poems and stories. "My mom would have wanted you to have these." Then putting the military medal on top of the box, said, "I believe this is yours. The distinguished flying cross, one of the top medals anyone can get for bravery in Canada."

Gus picked up the medal and put it aside, then picked up the top paper, unfolded it, read silently, slowly re-folded the paper, and sat back staring through time and space filled with memories. "Hank, if I have hurt anyone, I am truly sorry."

Hank put his hand on Gus' arm, "No Gus, there is no need to apologize, for a brief time, you made someone the happiest person in the world." Hank stood, waved goodbye and quickly walked out the door.

Fifty

Spring had finally come to the North Country of Michigan. The snow was gone, except for here and there where the sun could not break through. Large flocks of geese appeared overhead heading back to their summer homes in the far north of Canada. Chickadees hopped from branch to branch of the sugar maples pecking at breaks in the bark to get to the maple sap that comes out with the warm days and cold nights.

Warm temperatures and April showers pushed up skunk cabbage through the muddy bottoms of the bogs, fiddlehead ferns had just started to break out in the upland hardwoods, and if one looked hard enough, it was possible to find arbutus or an occasional Lady Slipper.

Maples and beeches had filled the woods with their delicate hues of new green leaves and the oaks were just starting to show new lighter shades of green. Birch, hickory, and other trees added their own hints of yellow-greens and the alders and brush along the river were in full leaf.

Maggie stayed with Hank for two weeks, spending her days getting caught up with her friends and her quiet evenings enjoying the time with Hank.

The next morning, Hank woke Maggie up before light. After a quick breakfast, Hank came into the bedroom with a pile of clothes. "Big day today, Maggie."

"Yes, it is," she said, looking at the airplane tickets back to California; lying on the dresser. She had taken a chance that perhaps Hank just might be ready to take the plunge. "Hank, we have got to talk about this, please?"

"Not now Maggie, we have something we have to do first."

Maggie looked through the clothes Hank had brought in, all of his old jeans and work shirts. "What the heck could that be?"

Hank laughed, "We are going to try out the new fishing gear I got for Christmas."

Maggie stood on the bank of the river and lifted the visor on her hat, feeling the warmth of the sun on her face Maggie was dressed in Hank's too big old jeans, his old flannel shirt with sleeves rolled up the elbows. She stood watching the fishing pole hanging out in the river in front of her, the line moving lazily in the current being held by a sinker located near the bait.

He waved to her as he came into view around the bend in the river. "Wow, are you making a serious fashion statement or what?"

She waved back. "Actually, I was thinking about starting a whole new line of fashion fishing wear. What every girl needs to catch a fish, or a man. What do you think?"

"Fish don't care." Hank laughed. He was in hip boots standing in the river, just above the deep hole; he worked the bait downstream along the banks and under the brush, moving the line into the dark deep pool, playing it expertly in and around the rocks where the big brown trout might be lurking.

Hank was abruptly interrupted by the sound of the drag on Maggie's reel and the fishing line from her pole going straight out across the hole, nearly tangling in his line. He reeled in as fast as he could while Maggie's pole arced over with its tip nearly in the water, the line screaming out as the

THE LAST DEER HUNT

reel drag protested.

Maggie's hat was flopping as she jumped up and down, her hands clapping as she squealed repeatedly. "Look, look, I got one, I got one." The tip of Maggie's rod was touching the water.

"Grab the darn pole," Hank yelled, standing near the bank, trying to reach Maggie's fishing line.

"Don't Hank; leave it alone, I got this one!" She grabbed her rod just as it was pulled into the river and she felt the line slowing down as it started to run upstream.

"Keep the line tight," Hank yelled as he pushed toward her. "Or you'll lose it."

"Hank; shut up and let me do this myself." Maggie yelled back, she pulled up on the rod, feeling the line so slack. "Where'd it go? Damn, did I lose it?" She said, reeling the line as fast as she could.

The rod bent over again and the line went taut, the fish racing upstream. Maggie stepped into the water and moved out until she felt the water reach nearly over her knees.

Hank had moved over to her with his landing net ready.

"Give me the net Hank, let me get this one."

The fish was tiring, but had changed course again. As it passed by, Maggie leaned over and made a swoop with the landing net and the fish was in.

Struggling to stand in the cold water, they watched the net with the large fish inside. Hank could only stand and look in amazement. "Isn't this something, it's a brook trout. The lunker is a brook trout and all this time I thought it had to be a German brown. Never heard of a Brookie this big. God, this thing must run twenty-six inches and must weigh over eight pounds! That has to be a record."

The fish was still fighting, trying to return to the river and life. Hank carefully reached in and unhooked the fish, holding it up by its gills. "Beginner's luck."

Maggie poked him in the side. "Nah, pure skill." She stood admiring the fish, "I heard brook trout are the best eating fish in the world. And you said it would probably be a record. Would it be worth keeping?"

"Nah!" they both said in unison as Hank knelt at the riverbank and carefully let the fish go. The large trout slowly disappeared into the dark waters of the deep pool.

They lay side by side on a blanket in the warm afternoon sun. Maggie watching the light playing off the constantly changing flow of the river. "Wow, this has been a fantastic two weeks. I'm so glad you and Orphan are looking so well."

"And you too, Maggie. You look wonderful."

Somewhere along the river, a blue heron grocked, announcing its return from somewhere down south.

"It's so wonderful about Sarah and Ben getting married, and running the new arts center. And Patti has been elected as the township supervisor," Maggie giggled, "Which must have really infuriated old Percy Twill."

"That's for sure and when I confronted him about the deer head, he tried to deny it, but everyone knows that he stole it from Pa. And did I tell you that Fuzzy Walstrom is serving three-to-five on about a half dozen charges."

"What about your buddies? How do you feel about all of that?"

"Well, as you know, it didn't turn out the way I would have hoped, but the bad dreams have gone away and I know I had nothing to do with it. I feel I can deal with it and finally move on."

Maggie watched the clouds as they formed over the lake, moving off to the southeast. "And Sandy got her bracelet."

"Yes, thanks for going with me to the cemetery. I finally was able to say goodbye to Ma, Pa, Uncle Andre...and Sandy."

Maggie looked at her watch, got up on one elbow and looked down at Hank.

"It's getting late and we have one more decision to make."

THE LAST DEER HUNT

"Maggie," Hank was in front of her, looking into her eyes. "I grew up here; this is where my roots are."

"Sounds like you've made your decision. Are you sure?"

"Yes, this is my world, this is where I belong."

"But Hank, what about the school? That's a once in a lifetime opportunity."

"I don't need anything other than what I have here."

"You might end up regretting this rest of your life."

"I don't believe so. But what about you Maggie? What is it you want?"

"I guess this is selfish of me, but I want the best of both worlds. I want to pursue my career and have you." Maggie took a deep breath, "It appears that I can't have both."

"You do have another choice Maggie. You to stay here with me."

"Hank, I...I'm sorry, I can't commit to that right now. Maybe down the road a bit, but not right now."

They sat facing each other on the bank of the river. Maggie leaned forward and held Hank's face in her hands. "Last chance Hank Duval, come with me to California. I got an extra ticket just in case." Her eyes pleaded with him, "I promise you will be happy."

Hank put his hands over hers, "Maggie, I'm happy here."

"Yes, Hank, you have everything you could ever want here...but not me."

"And out there, you have everything out there you're looking for...but not me."

"Touché, Hank." Maggie looked up at him and slowly moved her hands down the side of his face, cupping them in her lap.

Changed into new clothing, Hank drove the Ford Ranger along the river, going by the old Renaissance wood products mill now displaying its new sign, 'THE FUTURE HOME OF THE CORA ANDERSON CENTER FOR THE ARTS,' then across the Slate River Bridge. He drove down Main Street, past Frenchy's Diner with its Eiffel Tower flashing, and turned onto Upper Skanee Road and concentrated on his driving. Maggie watched out the window in silence as the countryside passed by on their way to the airport.

Printed in the United States
105817LV00004B/236/P